THE MANHUNTER

Gordon D. Shirreffs

"Written by the hand of a master!"
—*New York Times*

**Two classic Westerns in one low-cost volume!
Save $$$!**

BOWMAN'S KID

"You're in my way, mister," Lee warned.

Chisos calmly nodded.

"Is it a duel you want, Texas? Shall we stand back to back like little Southern gentlemen and count off ten paces to turn and fire?"

"Just make your play, mister, any time you're ready."

Lee looked sideways. "Looks like one of your rifleman friends is getting ready to beat you to the kill, mister."

Chisos turned his head. Lee's six-gun exploded....

RENEGADE'S TRAIL

Lee Kershaw looked toward the darkened canyon. A breeze sprang up. Metal clicked against rock high on the moonlighted slopes overlooking the labyrinth. Lee hit the ground a fraction of a second before the Sharps bellowed and sent an explosive bullet whispering right over where Lee had been standing. The bullet blew itself up against the rocks fifty yards beyond Lee. The breed sonofabitch was shooting by instinct. No living man could have seen Lee in those shadows—no living man by Queho, that is....

THE MANHUNTER

BOWMAN'S KID/ RENEGADE'S TRAIL

GORDON D. SHIRREFFS

LEISURE BOOKS NEW YORK CITY

A LEISURE BOOK®

October 1995

Published by

Dorchester Publishing Co., Inc.
276 Fifth Avenue
New York, NY 10001

BOWMAN'S KID

one

Someone or something was being stalked in the darkness of
the New Mexican night. There was an uneasy, unnamea-
ble feeling in the graveyard quiet. Lee Kershaw ground-
reined the tired dun. A ridge of broken rock sawtoothed
its low crest against the night sky. Lee replaced his boots
with his *n-deh b'keh,* the thigh-length, thick-soled, button-
toed desert footgear of the Apache. He folded down the
thigh parts and tied them in place just below his knees.
Nothing moved except the distant, flickering light of the
ice-ship stars against the dark sky.

It was Mescalero country, and the Mescaleros were ru-
mored to be restless and making war talk in their mountain eyrie just to the north; but they would not hunt for
man or game at night. The most favorable time to hunt the
white man was when the first pewter-hued traces of the
false dawn tinted the eastern sky. That was the time when
the white man's energy and spirits were at their lowest
ebb, and the White-Eye was soft for the killing. And if by
chance it was the Mescalero who was killed at dawn light,

his soul would not be doomed to wander in the Shadow Land during eternity.

The dun nudged Lee with his nose. The two big, blanket-covered canteens were empty—*dry* empty. The waterhole was over the ridge and deep hidden by the darkness. Lee withdrew his Winchester '73 from the saddle scabbard and levered a round of .44/40 into the chamber. He let the hammer down to half cock.

Lee had come north from Fort Davis in Texas, riding and walking at night to avoid the heat of the late summer and the threat of the predatory Lipans, who were raiding into West Texas. Lee had come north because a man had come to him in a Fort Davis saloon and asked him to meet a *vaquero,* one Vicente Galeras, at Tinaja del Muerto on the second Wednesday of the month. Now, whether or not he met Vicente Galeras at the *tinaja* over the ridge did not really matter, at least for the moment. It was the water that mattered, as it always did in that dry and broken land.

Lee catfooted up the slope with the warm and fitful night wind blowing against him. He shoved back his hat and let it hang between his shoulders by the chin strap. He went to ground just below the crest, then inched forward, using a ragged bunching of gramma grass on the crest for cover.

The *tinaja* was in a dark and haunted hollow at the base of a limestone rock formation that somehow managed to seep good clear water into the shallow rock pans, or *tinajas,* at the foot of the formation. It was not a good place. The water had saved lives, but it had also cost lives. The early Spanish explorers had learned that fact the hard way. The Mescaleros had used the spring for centuries as a death trap for both men and animals. The Spaniards, with their macabre skill in geographical nomenclature, had named the haunted place Tinaja del Muerto—the Jar of Death. The place had never failed to live up to its name and evil reputation.

Something down at the spring rustled drily, like a cricket testing its reedy night song.

The man had found Lee drinking alone in the Fort

Davis saloon. Lee had just finished a dirty and dangerous job along the Rio Grande, and his springs needed unwinding with the lubrication of much fiery brandy. "Duke Bowman needs you at the Broken Bow, Kershaw," the stranger had said. "But don't go straight there. A man by the name of Vicente Galeras, a *vaquero* of the Broken Bow, will meet you at Tinaja del Muerto on the second Wednesday of this month." He had placed a curious silver button in Lee's hand. "This button will identify you."

Lee had looked down at the button. "Who says I am going at all?"

"Only this," the man had replied, covering the silver button with ten crisp one hundred dollar bills. "I was told this is your usual first week's fee."

Lee watched with faint amusement. "And who are you?"

"My name does not matter. I am a lawyer who has done some services for Duke Bowman. I received the money and the button by registered mail in El Paso. I had already planned to move my practice to Fort Worth. It is just as well. If I returned to El Paso, I might be signing my own death warrant. They may not know for sure I contacted you for Duke Bowman, but I'm not taking any chances."

"Who are *they?*"

The legal eagle had looked quickly right and left, and then behind himself, and had lowered his voice. "The Dakins," he had said.

"There's something loco about this. The Dakins, brothers, cousins, and other shirttail kin, have been the heart of Bowman's Running MB *corrida* for at least twenty years."

"Times have changed. The old *corrida* is gone, at least the native New Mexicans are, leaving the Dakins, and they are trying to take over the Broken Bow."

Lee had carefully placed the silver button on the table and had covered it with the bills. "Take back his money and his goddamned trick silver button, mister. I'd rather work for the Devil himself than for Duke Bowman."

The stranger had nodded. "Bowman mentioned the possibility of this in his letter. But he also wrote: 'Let the money talk to Lee Kershaw. That's his kind of language.'" The stranger had stood up and emptied his glass. "If you do go, Kershaw, *watch your back*." When Lee had looked up from the tempting pile of money, the only indication that the stranger had been there was the batwing door still swinging from his hasty exit.

That same night Lee Kershaw had ridden north with a cool thousand dollars and a peculiar silver button in his shirt pocket. Perhaps it was more for curiosity's sake than for money that he headed out to Tinaja del Muerto—curiosity to meet a *vaquero* whom he had vaguely known long ago and to learn why Duke Bowman, the *muy hombre* of the Broken Bow, needed Lee Kershaw, manhunter.

A man coughed softly in the darkness near the *tinaja*.

The dried gramma grass on the ridge crest moved a little, and its shadow lightened.

Lee bellied on loose blow sand between boulders still warm from the heat of the day's sun, hoping to God he would not run into a night-hunting sidewinder, which bites quickly without the honest, strident warning of rattles.

The scent of a man came to Lee, compounded of stale sweat, tobacco smoke, dusty leather, and just a hint of fermented horseshit for piquancy—*Parfum de Vaquero*. He moved forward in silence.

The rifle muzzle touched the nape of the *vaquero's* neck. "Do not move," Lee's soft voice warned. "Open your left hand." A silver button was placed in the palm.

"*Gracias a Dios*," whispered the *vaquero*. "Señor Kershaw?"

"You have the button," replied Lee.

The wind sprang up quickly. The sere brush across the *tinaja* rustled drily like the mating song of crickets.

"Don't move suddenly," warned Lee.

A rifle muzzle across the *tinaja* flamed, and the crack of the explosion mingled with what seemed to be the sound of a stick being suddenly whipped into thick mud. The *vaquero* turned left and flung up his right arm. He was hard hit and made no sound when he went down. The shot's echo died away, and the smell of burnt powder drifted on the wind.

Lee felt the warm and sticky wetness on the man's chest. "What does Duke Bowman want of me?" whispered Lee.

His answer was a thick and liquid cough that sprayed his face with a warm froth. "Talk, damn you!" urged Lee. The man moved a little. "I was to guide you in to see him secretly." Lee bent close. "But why?" he asked. "They mustn't know why he sent for you," gasped Galeras. The *vaquero's* head dropped forever.

Lee pried open the clenched hand of the dead man and removed the button from it. There was the faintest of scraping sounds on the blow sand, and then it was deathly quiet again—the usual brooding quietness of Tinaja del Muerto. A man had died there that dark night. *Bueno!* The spring was sated—for a time.

The dun raised his head and slanted forward his ears. A lean shadow drifted noiselessly through the darkness. Lee unhooked the canteens from the saddle. Something moved on the ridge crest. Lee faded behind a boulder. Leather scraped against rock on the ridge. Lee reached out and rifle slapped the dun across his rump. The dun obediently trotted toward the west and away from the ridge.

A rifle exploded flame and smoke on the ridge. The shot echo slammed back and forth between the canyon walls. The dun galloped off into the darkness.

"Keep on going, Kershaw!" yelled a hoarse voice. "Don't come back, *manhunter!* Hawww! Hawww! Hawww!"

The boulder stood alone in the darkness.

The sound of the dun's hoofs rataplaning on the hard ground died away in the darkness to the west.

The sound of voices came from the *tinaja.* Water splashed.

"Let Galeras lie there for the buzzards and the coyotes," said a hoarse-voiced man. "Serves him right for thinkin' he could fool me, Chisos."

"He shoulda known better than that, Cass," a dry Texas voice said.

"If that really was Lee Kershaw," put in another voice,

tinged with the soft archaic Spanish accent of a native New Mexican, "he will come back."

"I scared the hell outa him," blustered Cass Dakin. "He won't come back, Nuno."

"Maybe," said Nuno doubtfully. "Would it not be better to make sure of him? Two dead men, in this case, are far better than one."

"He won't be back," insisted Cass. Hoofs rattled like pebbles in a gourd. In a little while, the sound of the hoofs died away to the east.

The *tinaja* sank back into its habitual brooding quietness.

two

The faint sound of bubbling, slobbering water came from the darkened Tinaja del Muerto and then died away.

Lee stoppered his canteens and dragged the body of Vicente Galeras back from the *tinaja* into a deep cleft in the rocks. He risked lighting a candle. He frisked the stiffening body and set aside a pint flask and a pack of Lobo Negro cigarettes. He snapped the dirty string that held a green-hued, imitation silver cross about the *vaquero*'s neck. He had recognized Galeras as one of the best of the Broken Bow *corrida,* or the worst, depending on whether you were a friend or an enemy of Duke Bowman. He had been one of the loyal ones, a man whose god was Duke Bowman. The imitation silver cross had likely been only lip service to that other god.

Lee took a flat velvet-covered case from the *vaquero*'s shirt pocket. He opened it to look at a beautiful, dark-haired young woman of perhaps eighteen years of age and a sober, big-eyed boy of perhaps three or four years of age standing beside her, brave in velvet trousers, high black stockings, and button shoes. He wore a neat little *charro-*

type jacket with six large silver buttons. As closely as Lee could tell, the buttons were exactly the same as the one he had in his shirt pocket.

The dun whinnied softly through the darkness.

Lee dragged the body deeper into the cleft and covered it with loose rock. He watered the dun and then led him through the limestone formation to a spot where the mountains to the east could be seen. He fed the dun and then threw a blanket on the ground. He fell asleep with his half-cocked Winchester on one side of him and his Colt in his left hand.

Lee awoke when the wind shifted. There was a faint grayish cast in the eastern sky beyond the looming mountains. He ate a little and then shaped and lit a cigarette. The dawn grew swiftly across the arid land as he smoked.

Thirty miles to the west of Tinaja del Muerto there were mountains, and beyond them the Rio Grande, the only water in all that distance.

Faint dust wreathed up close to the base of the notched pass in the eastern mountains. That pass led over the mountains to the Broken Bow country. There were two alternatives known to Lee by which he might reach that country without risking the pass. He could go south and round the end of the mountains on the Texas side of the Texas–New Mexico Territory border. He could go north for twenty miles through the dry and waterless country to a shallow pass that cut through the northern end of the range. On the far side of that pass, perhaps fifteen miles to the south, was Ribbon Creek; but there might not be water there, for it was a time of great drought.

The sun warmed the empty land. The limestone mountain range rose six thousand feet above the desert country, the upper two thousand feet forming an almost sheer escarpment. On the eastern side was the great *estancia* of Duke Bowman, the Running MB, better know as the Broken Bow, from the river which gave the range its name. It was the best ranch country on that side of the mountains. It was perpetually watered, heavily timbered, and rich with mineral deposits. The man Mark Bowman, better known as Duke, had seized that rich land thirty-five years past from the Mescaleros, whose natural heritage it had been. He had driven Indi-yi-yahn, the almost legendary Mescalero war chief, from that valley and in later years had killed him with his own hands.

Lee took out the silver button and studied it in the growing light. The embossed design was intricate and curious—a pair of script letters M & B, or in rangeland parlance, a Running MB. The letters passed through a stylized bow, broken in the arc by the interposing letters.

"What would Duke Bowman want of me?" mused Lee.

He looked again at the eastern mountains between him and the Broken Bow. They stretched north and south for seventy-five miles with the highest and most rugged part just over the Texas line dramatically culminating in a towering eight thousand-foot peak. The mass of the range, however, was in New Mexico Territory, extending northward in the shape of a gigantic ridge that was gashed with twisted canyons, sheer plunging slopes and drops, and towering cliff faces. The view from the west could easily deceive one into thinking that the eastern face was the same barren wilderness of limestone rock, but on the eastern side, the slopes gentled into deep, pine-forested canyons and clear, running streams.

"Go home," the mind voice warned.

Lee lit another cigarette.

"Duke Bowman breaks all men," added the voice. *"All men . . ."*

No one but a fool, or a madman, *or* Lee Kershaw would attempt a crossing of the burning, arid country to the north to reach the north pass of the range.

"There are the Dakins," warned the voice.

Marsh Dakin was a hard, dour man, Texas bred, who had ramrodded the notorious Broken Bow *corrida* for over twenty years, backed by his younger half-brothers Sid and Cass, and his much younger cousins, Ben and Charles, the latter nicknamed Reata. There were others—shirttail kin, Pecos River men. They had all the vices of a highland clan and none of the virtues, except loyalty to Duke Bowman, and that now seemed to be gone.

Lee led the dun down the slope to a long, low ridge

which would shield him from anyone looking west from the mountains.

By noon, the baking, rocky soil seemed to be lifting and wavering in the heat-shimmering atmosphere like a flapping blanket. The thin dust rose about man and horse. The sun reflected up from the ground to burn into Lee's eyes and into his very brain, seeking to strike him down.

three

Cass Dakin lowered his battered field glasses and looked back over his shoulder. "That's a dust devil," he said.

"How can you be sure?" asked Nuno Mercado. "The dust is always behind that ridge, and it keeps moving north."

A lean young man squatted teetering on his bootheels, rolling a quirly. His light blue eyes, seemingly as guileless as those of a baby, looked down the long, heat-shimmering pass toward the illusive thread of dust drifting upward on the lower ground. "The wind is blowing from the northwest," he said.

"I still say it's a dust devil, Chisos," insisted Cass.

Nuno Mercado eased his sweating crotch. "Mother of the Devil," he cursed. "This place is the hallway to hell!"

"Imagine how it is out there," said Chisos as he lit up.

"I run Kershaw off last night," said Cass.

"That so?" asked Chisos politely. "Then how come we ain't seen no dust devils to the west or the southwest?"

Cass eyed the young Texan. "I say he turned back."

Chisos didn't play the game. "Just as you say, Cass."

17

He stood up. "But if that dust out there *is* Kershaw, and he gets around these mountains to reach the Broken Bow, you'll have a helluva time explainin' it to Marsh, and what's worse, your sister Stella. Personally, I'd rather explain it to him than to her."

"They ain't tellin' me what to do!"

Chisos yawned a little and covered his mouth with his hand. "That so?" he softly asked.

No one but a fool, or a madman, *or* Lee Kershaw would cross that devil's furnace in the heat of the late summer at a time of great drought. The thought was that of Nuno Mercado. "There is no water down there," he said, almost as though to reassure himself that Lee Kershaw would not attempt the crossing.

Cass turned away from the cool and level stare of Chisos, glad of some excuse to break the contact. "See?" he said triumphantly. "He can't get to water for two days, and he can't live out there without water for even one day."

"Unless he tries for North Pass," put in Chisos.

"No," insisted Cass. "I outsmarted him. I figured he was headin' for Tinaja del Muerto, and I was right."

"Anyone could have figured that," argued Chisos. "*And*, he's still alive."

"But Galeras ain't! Whatever the old man told Galeras to tell Kershaw, he never had a chance to tell him, did he?"

"We can't be sure of that," said Nuno. "There *is* someone down there, moving to the northeast," he added firmly.

"It's Kershaw then," said Chisos with conviction. "He knows the old man wants to see him, and by Jesus, he's goin' to see him!"

"I still say he's gone west!" shouted Cass, all mouth and no reason.

Chisos mounted his horse. "Well, you're the *patrón*," he said.

"Where the hell do you think you're goin'?" snapped Cass.

"Back to the Broken Bow."

"I ain't said we should!"

"Well, in that case, just what the hell do you aim to gain by sittin' around here fryin' your ass?"

"Kershaw still might try to get through this pass."

"God give me strength," murmured Chisos.

"Well, what would you do?" demanded Cass.

"I thought you'd never ask! Kershaw is either holed up down at Tinaja del Muerto waitin' for darkness, or that's him raisin' that dust down there. I think that's him, headin' for North Pass. He's tryin' for Ribbon Creek. We'd better get back to the Broken Bow and have Marsh send some of the boys up that way to get him there. If Kershaw lives through today, you can bet your ass he'll head for Ribbon Creek."

Chisos was right, but Cass Dakin fancied himself a leader of hard men—like Duke Bowman had once been and like his older brothers, Marsh and Sid, were now, to say nothing of his older sister Stella. He was jealous of Chisos Martin. The young Texan had just turned twenty-one in the past month. Five years younger than Cass, he was already showing signs of leadership and had caught Marsh's eye more than once, to Cass's embarrassment. "Ain't no living man can get across that desert this time of year," he said.

"Want to bet ten bucks?" asked Chisos.

"Don't bet," said Nuno to Cass. "This man Kershaw is not human. He can do things no living man can do. Some of my people claim he is a *brujo*—a male witch. They say he can turn himself into anything he likes. It is also said, on good authority, by a priest I happen to know, that he can make himself invisible. . . ."

Chisos doubled up with laugher as he handed a ten to Nuno. "Put up or shut up, Cass," he invited.

Cass handed the ten to Nuno. "One of these days," he murmured.

Chisos eyed the big man. "How fast is Kershaw with the sixgun, Nuno?" he asked over his shoulder. "As fast as me?"

"He is still alive in the most dangerous business in the world, that of hunting dangerous and desperate men."

"You didn't answer my question."

Cass looked at the cocky young Texan. "There's always someone, somewhere, that's faster than fast guns like you, Chisos."

Chisos smiled. "I haven't met him yet."

"You will. You will," promised Cass.

Chisos laughed confidently as he rode up the pass. He had the supreme confidence of a man of twenty-one, from Texas; he had neatly filed five notches on the butt of his Colt in the past three years, and Chisos, with true Texas arrogance, *never* counted cholos or Indians.

four

The massive limestone house overlooked the Broken Bow where the river rushed in a great arc from the narrow canyon thrust into the looming mountain behind the ranch. The almost perfect arc of the river had long ago been broken by a gigantic collapse of the limestone cliffs that beetled across the river from the level ground where the ranch buildings were located. The rock fall had formed a natural dam, which had in time been circumvented by the river, thus giving the river, the valley, and, in time, the Running MB Ranch the name of Broken Bow.

The great limestone *casa* was ramparted like a medieval fortress, and on diagonally opposite corners of the flat roof, Duke Bowman had built squat towers, each of which provided covering fire along two sides of the house. Loopholes pierced the house and tower walls, and the few windows were fitted with heavy shutters.

Beyond the *casa* was a dark *bosque* of cottonwoods and willows, and on the fringe of the *bosque* were the older log buildings of the ranch. Only two lights shone through the darkness—one in the original low *casa*, and the other in the northeast tower of the great limestone house.

The valley had long ago been the hereditary home of the Mescaleros. Thirty-five years earlier, before the Civil War, Mark Bowman had driven the Mescaleros from their home. Twenty years later, the Mescaleros, led by their great warrior chief Indi-yi-yahn—the Killer of Enemies, had made the fatal mistake of trying to take back their ancestral home. Twenty-two blood stiffened scalps of thick, black, Mescalero hair had been hung on the barbed wire of the approaches to the Broken Bow. The legendary medicine shirt of the Mescaleros, worn that bloody day by Indi-yi-yahn to assure victory, had been stripped from his dead body by Duke Bowman, the man who had killed him in hand-to-hand combat, and hung on the wall of the tower room. The Mescaleros, in time, had put the twenty-two scalps in the backs of their memories; they had never forgotten the medicine shirt. Without it, the war power of the Mescaleros had been broken, and their good medicine gone forever.

Lee catfooted through the *bosque*. There was a haunting loneliness about the darkened *casa*. Faint light showed in the chinks of the northeast tower's shuttered windows, and a faint wraith of smoke drifted from its chimney.

Something moved in the shadows of the *bosque*.

Lee stopped.

The great dog growled deeply in his throat and charged.

Lee swung his Winchester barrel hard across the gaping fanged jaws of the beast. The dog raised its head upward and sideways. The razor-edged *cuchillo* sank into the left side of the dog's muscle-distended throat and ripped cleanly and easily across it. Lee leaped backward to avoid the spouting gush of dark blood. The dog fell heavily, thrashing powerfully with its hind legs among the thick layer of leaves. The butt of the Winchester dropped with killing force at the base of the dog's neck.

Lee stepped back. Nothing moved except the wind-disturbed leaves.

Lee dragged the heavy body to the river and dumped it in. It swirled out into the fast current in an easy curve toward the deep, dark waters that curled whitely at the base of the sheer limestone cliffs across the river. It sank at last, leaving a swirl of ghostly foam on the dark surface of the river.

five

Duke Bowman sat in a heavy, rawhide-covered chair, staring
into the flickering, shifting kaleidoscope of color hovering
over the thick bed of embers in the beehive fireplace. His
big, liver-spotted hands rested almost lifelessly on the
hardwood arms of the chair. An Argand lamp, turned low,
stood on a table beside the chair. The light from the top of
the lampshade shone on what seemed to be the headless
and legless trunk of a gaunt body that hung on the wall
above the fireplace, its outstretched arms in the shape of
crucifixion. It was the dusty, bloodstained medicine shirt
of Indi-yi-yahn, made from the well-tanned skins of two
strangled fawns and decorated with the mystic symbols of
sun, moon, rain, stars, water beetle, and spider, as well as
many others to pray to in time of need. The prayers of
Indi-yi-yahn had always been answered, that is, all but the
last time.

Slowly Duke Bowman raised his head. The lamplight
shone on the baldness of it; the freckled expanse of taut,
shiny, dry skin that had once been thatched with bluish,
iron-gray hair, the shade of the finest high-carbon steel.

Slowly the big man turned to face the slight draft that had suddenly blown into the room from an opened window.

The shadowy figure in the corner spoke softly: "What do you see in the color painting of the embers, Duke?"

"Who are you?" demanded Duke.

Lee held out his left hand so that the lamplight shone on the silver button he held.

"Where did you get this?" asked Duke.

"From an anonymous legal gentleman in Fort Davis who padded this button with a thousand dollars in cash."

Duke looked toward the closed door.

"The house is cold and empty," said Lee. "There is only a woman in the old log *casa*—Stella Dakin."

"The others are hunting for you, eh, Kershaw?"

"They're hunting in the wrong places."

"Vicente Galeras brought you here?"

"He's dead. They killed him at Tinaja del Muerto." Lee held out his other hand to show the silvered cross. "Proof," he said. He opened the velvet-covered photograph case. "And this," he added.

"Did the others see that photograph?"

"Not while I was around."

"How did you get in here?"

"Through North Pass."

"From Tinaja del Muerto at *this* time of the year?"

"I'm here," said Lee simply.

"No one saw you?"

"Only a dog outside. He's in the river now."

Lee came closer to the old man. "I haven't much time," he said. "The wolves may soon be gathering outside. What do you want of me?"

"To do something for me which I can no longer do myself. You see the change in me. You may know of the change in my old *corrida*. Vicente Galeras was the last of the loyal ones working for me."

"And lies in an unmarked grave because of it. Where are the others?"

"Driven one by one from the Broken Bow by the Dakins. Some of them are still in the valley, *beyond* the limit of my range. One by one, Kershaw, until I found myself alone here, a prisoner of the Dakins, while they wait for me to die."

"I'm all sorrow," said Lee drily.

"I want you to find the boy in that photograph. You have your first week's fee. I'll double your usual five hundred a week fee after that, until you bring the boy here."

"Who is this boy?" asked Lee curiously.

Bowman looked up at Lee. "If he's still alive, he's my only living relative. You saw the woman at the log *casa*. You know her?"

"Stella Dakin. She ran a 'house' in El Paso. They called her The Virgin Mary. Her common-law husband died under mysterious circumstances and left her his money. She was cleared of any charges of his death, but she had to leave El Paso. She served time in the Texas State Prison for blackmail, or extortion."

"When she was released she came here five years ago to act as my housekeeper," said Bowman quietly.

"You're joking!"

Bowman shook his head. "Now she claims she's my common-law wife, and so, will inherit the Broken Bow."

"Can she make the claim stick?"

"She is a fine-looking woman," replied Bowman. "It was lonely here in this big house. You understand?"

"You always were a lusty man, Bowman." Lee formed a mental picture of Stella Dakin. Broad of hip and thin of lip; powerful breasts divided from a heavy rump and strong legs by a too tiny waist that gave her body the appearance of a spider; mouth like a tight seam over tiny pearly teeth; great blue eyes that easily drew a man to her, until he realized it was not depth of character in those cerulean orbs but rather an emptiness of soul into which he was looking. "The Black Widow," added Lee. "What about the boy, Bowman?"

"He's my illegitimate son, Bart. A bastard, if you will."

"What about the lovely woman with him in the photograph? Was she his sister?"

"His mother rather. She was Rafaela Diaz. She was nineteen years old when that picture was taken with the son of whom she was very proud. She came here as my housekeeper when she was fifteen years old."

"That was a mistake on her part," said Lee drily.

"I talked her into my bed and bulled her the first night she was under my roof. But I had actually bought that girl, Kershaw. She was a *genizaro*—a mixed-blood."

"The Heirs of Sorrow. The Children of Many Bloods. From the *Valle de Lagrimas*—the Valley of Tears," softly added Lee.

"She had been captured by the Mescaleros and sold to the Comancheros, who, in turn, sold her to me. She was a virgin, surprisingly enough."

"Where is she now?"

"Dead for eighteen years. Murdered by the Mescaleros at the Massacre of Cinco Castillos."

"And the boy?"

"There were persistent rumors for years that there had been one survivor—a small boy of three or four years of age carried off by the Mescaleros. Some years later that button was sent to me by an old priest who lived in Santa Fe. He suggested that the boy might still be alive."

"Did you make an effort to find out?"

It was very quiet in the tower room. An ember snapped in the fireplace. There was a sudden rushing of wind through the *bosque*.

"It didn't matter in those days," said Bowman at last.

"And you base your claim that the boy might still be alive on that silver button sent to you by an old priest many years ago?"

"There are no other buttons like that in the world! His mother was clever with her hands. She had cast them herself. She had the photograph taken just before she left here to travel north to show her son to her relatives up north of Santa Fe, near Las Trampas I think it was. They stopped at Cinco Castillos, and she died there."

"You let them travel north when the Mescaleros were on the war path?"

"I thought they were safe enough. Marsh Dakin rode with them, with an escort of some of my best *vaqueros*.

They turned back just before the Mescaleros attacked Cinco Castillos."

"Very convenient," murmured Lee.

"Look, Kershaw—I must find my son! He'd be a man now, fit to stand beside his father to take over the Broken Bow."

Lee placed the photograph, the button, and the thousand dollars on the table. "I can't cross into the Land of Shadows to find a boy who vanished eighteen years ago."

"He may still be alive!"

"Forget it, old man. Keep your memories of a child-woman and of a sad-eyed little boy who never knew his own father." Lee turned away.

The crisp double-clicking of a pistol hammer being cocked stopped Lee in his tracks. "Turn around," ordered Bowman.

Lee turned with his hands raised to shoulder height. "Why?" he asked.

"The Dakins know I sent for you, but they don't know *why* I sent for you. I don't intend to have them find out."

"Your secret is safe with me."

Bowman shook his head. "Not if they catch you."

"They won't," said Lee.

"You can't get out of this valley alive unless I tell you how to do it."

"I'll risk it."

"You might, but *I* won't risk letting you try."

Lee eyed the grim old tyrant. "You really believe that boy is alive and grown into a man?"

"I *have* to believe it!"

"Would he even remember you?"

"Why not?"

"I have the feeling his mother took him from here and never intended for them to come back."

Lee's words seemed like a blow across the old man's face.

"Kershaw," he said, "will you try to find him?"

Lee shrugged. "Supposing I do? If I try to bring him back here, the Dakins will kill him, and maybe me, to keep him from getting in to see you. Why don't you turn to the law, Bowman?"

"Who would believe my word against the Dakins'? They've spread stories that I'm senile. If the law tried to find the boy and bring him back here to me, as I want you to do, the Dakins would stop at nothing to kill him."

"What makes you think I can do any better?"

"You're Lee Kershaw," replied Bowman. It was all he said, as though those three words had resolved the whole problem.

"I can hardly refuse after that," said Lee drily. He looked at the dusty medicine shirt hanging on the wall. "Who led the raid on Cinco Castillos?" he asked.

"Indi-yi-yahn."

"Did he know your woman and your son were there at the time?"

Bowman shrugged. "*¿Quien sabe?* Why?"

"It would have been sweet vengeance," said Lee.

"He would have killed the boy then, as well as the woman."

Lee shook his head. "His vengeance would have been greater to raise the son of Duke Bowman as a Mescalero, maybe with the idea that some day the son of Duke Bowman might become the instrument of his revenge on you."

"You talk like you read books!" scoffed Bowman.

Lee smiled. "I might have expected an answer like that." He reached up and took down the medicine shirt, which left a pale ghost of itself against the dusty wall.

"What do you intend to do with that?" asked Bowman.

Lee helped himself to two bottles of brandy from a liquor cabinet and a handful of Bowman's prime and clear Havanas. He rolled the shirt about the liquor bottles and cigars. "Diabolito is the present chief of the Mescaleros. He is the only son of Indi-yi-yahn. Rumor has it that his power is slowly being usurped by a rising young killer by the name of Baishan who has had a medicine shirt made for him that is supposed to make any other medicine shirt of the Mescaleros look like a cheap copy made in Kansas City for the tourist trade. Now, if Diabolito gets back the shirt of his father, he might very well talk business with me about what happened to your missing son."

"You're loco! They'll kill you on sight! What if they think the power of this shirt was lost when I killed Indi-yi-yahn? If that is so, mister, you'll look damned foolish standing there with a sickly grin on your face holding a dusty hunk of fawnskin painted with crazy symbols and stained with the dried blood of Indi-yi-yahn. It'll turn out to be your death warrant!"

"How do I get out of this death trap?"

"These mountains are pure limestone. The Mescaleros used to claim a man could walk underground through the caves for seventy-five miles from one end of the range to the other. Go up the canyon of the Broken Bow until you see a rockfall on the right hand side. There are three cave entrances there, but only one of them goes all the way through. You'll come out north of here, on the slopes this side of North Pass. For God's sake! Pick the right cave, Kershaw, or you'll never be seen again!"

"How will I know which is the right one?"

"The middle one," replied Bowman. He hesitated. "No, it must be the right-hand one as you face the rock wall."

"Great," murmured Lee.

"You'll have to walk out of the mountains," said Bowman. "You can't get a horse in there."

Lee shook his head. "I left my dun at Ribbon Creek, picketed back in a box canyon, and walked in here."

"You've got more luck than brains. The exit of the right cave will bring you out on the heights above the creek."

Lee studied the old man. "How do I know you're telling me the truth, Bowman? You might want to get rid of me after all."

"There was only one other person who knew about that cave. That was Vicente Galeras. That was how he got out of here under the noses of the Dakins and walked down to Tinaja del Muerto. There was no other way he could have gotten out of here."

Lee shrugged. "I'll have to buy it then." He walked to the window. He looked back at the old man. "When did you start to fail, Bowman?" he suddenly asked.

"About two or three years past. Why do you ask?"

"The change is remarkable. Who cooks your meals?"

Bowman was surprised. "Stella," he replied. 'Why?"

Lee thrust a leg through the window.

"Wait, damn you!" snapped Bowman with his old fire. "Don't start something you can't finish! Why did you ask me that?"

Lee looked back from the shadows into the pool of light from the fireplace and the lamp. The lamplight shone on the taut, dry skin of the balding head and the lifeless gray hair that fringed it. He looked into the dull eyes of the old man, aged too much for his time. He looked down at the limp hands on the arms of the chair.

"Tell me, Kershaw," the old man quietly asked.

"Do you know how Stella Dakin lost her first common-law husband?"

"You said mysterious circumstances, Kershaw." The old man looked quickly at the closed door. "Someone has opened the lower door," he said. He looked again at Lee. "Well?" he asked.

"Suspicion of slow arsenic poisoning," said Lee quietly.

The dull eyes looked steadily at Lee. "Yes," Bowman agreed. *"I see it now.* Kershaw, for God's sake, find my son and bring him back to me before I die!"

A footstep sounded on the tower stairway.

When Bowman peered into the shadows near the window, all he could see was the faded curtain moving in the night breeze that was creeping timorously into the musty room.

The door swung open. "Are you asleep, Duke?" asked Stella.

Duke shook his head.

"Vicente Galeras has left the Broken Bow," she said.

"It doesn't surprise me. He was the last one left of the old New Mexicans who once served me. He's left before. He'll come back."

"Not this time. He was ambushed and killed at Tinaja del Muerto."

"By Mescaleros?"

"No. By a man named Lee Kershaw. You knew him."

"Years ago."

"A paid killer. A bounty hunter."

Duke looked up into her hard face. "Who would pay to have old Vicente Galeras killed?"

"He had enemies."

"They were *my* enemies, not his."

She shrugged. She looked up at the ghostly light-colored area where once the shirt of Indi-yi-yahn had hung. "The boys are out hunting down Kershaw," he said. "Marsh told me to tell you not to worry—they'd find him."

Bowman laughed.

"What happened to that filthy shirt that used to hang up there?"

"I finally burned it. You've asked me enough times to do so."

She sniffed the musty air. She parted the drapes of the front window and looked down on the dark rushing river with its ghostly swirlings of foam riding the surface. "But why now?" she asked over her shoulder.

"Godalmighty, woman! Do I have to account to you for everything I do!"

"It's time for bed," she said resignedly.

"Mine or yours," he asked bitterly.

"You left *my* bed, Duke," she said.

"You never owned a bed in this damned house! You don't own a damned thing here! The clothes on your back are mine! The food you eat is mine!"

"Yes, Duke," she patiently agreed. She flicked her blue eyes about the room. Something else was missing. Something she had felt a few days before but had not been able to put a finger of thought on. There was a desk in one corner. She reached over to turn out the lamp, and as she did so, she tilted the shade a little. The lamplight touched the desk. Then she knew. The faded velvet-covered photograph case which had once stood there was now missing. She looked quickly at the bare place on the wall where the medicine shirt had once hung, and a piece of the jigsaw puzzle in her mind slipped easily into place. She turned off the lamp.

The door closed behind them. Their footsteps sounded on the stairs. The bottom door was opened and closed.

Lee Kershaw stepped back in through the window. He quickly searched the desk and found some fat-bodied candles and some packets of lucifers. He parted the drapes of the front window. Horsemen were on the river road riding toward the *estancia*. He catfooted across the room and out through the window. He crossed the flat roof and dropped lightly into the shrubbery at the base of the wall. He picked up his Winchester and passed noiselessly into the deep shadows of the *bosque* just as many hoofs clattered on the graveled road that led past the great limestone house to the older log buildings.

The sound of angry voices came to Lee from near the old log casa. Lee came up behind the barn and fattened a deep shadow just around the corner from the knot of Dakins standing beside the corral.

"I tell you he was here!" shrilled Stella.

"He ain't in the valley," argued Cass. "He went southwest from Tinaja del Muerto. Didn't he, Nuno?"

Nuno was careful. He was always careful on disagreeing with Cass Dakin. He had a healthy fear of the big man's fists. "It is possible," murmured Nuno.

"Why don't you ask *me*, Cass?" put in Chisos Martin. "I still say he made it to North Pass and crossed over to this side."

"We didn't see any signs of him at Ribbon Creek," said Sid Dakin.

"You won't find any signs of him anywhere," said Marsh Dakin. "Stell, what makes you so damned sure he was here?"

"I went up to get the old man to go to bed. That filthy old medicine shirt is missing from the wall. The photograph of that breed woman he used to sleep with and her bastard son is missing from his desk. He claims he burned the medicine shirt. Well, I've been after him for months to do that."

"So what the hell has this to do with Kershaw being here?" demanded Cass.

"Why *tonight?*" asked the woman.

"I don't get it yet," said Cass.

"You never will," said Marsh. "Go on, Stell."

"I think I know now why he sent for Kershaw, Marsh. It wasn't to help him against us. Kershaw doesn't get mixed up in this kind of business. He hunts men."

"So?" asked Sid.

It was very quiet for a moment. "Or boys that have grown up into men," added the woman.

"Such as?" asked Marsh.

"Don't you get it?" she demanded. "That loco old man sent for Kershaw to find his son—the kid that was taken by the Mescaleros eighteen years ago at Cinco Castillos."

"You been at the bottle again, Stell?" asked Sid.

"Shut up!" she snapped. "Put two and two together. Isn't it possible that he thinks his son is still alive?"

"He's dead," said Cass.

"A lot you know," put in Marsh. "By God! That just might be the old man's game."

"So what does the medicine shirt have to do with it?" asked Cass.

"If the Mescaleros took the kid with them, and he's still alive, living up in them damned mountains with them, Kershaw would have to have some means of getting in there to talk with the Mescaleros," said Marsh thoughtfully.

"He is mad!" cried Nuno.

"You should be so mad," said Chisos.

"The medicine shirt was missing tonight," added Stella. "The photograph was missing a couple of days ago. Odds are that Duke sent Vicente Galeras with the photograph to show to Kershaw at Tinaja del Muerto."

"I killed the cholo!" shouted Cass. "He never had a chance to talk with Kershaw!"

"Did you search Galeras' body after you killed him?" asked Stella.

It was quiet again. Feet scuffled on the hard ground.

"You didn't, did you?" demanded the woman.

"I can't think of everything," blurted Cass.

"You can't think of anything!" she shrilled. "Now you men get to hell out after Kershaw! All the time you're standing here he's moving and moving fast!"

"The man is not human," said Nuno Mercado gloomily. "He can do things no living man can do."

"Well, I'll admit he got into the valley somehow," said Marsh, "but he ain't going to get out of it so easy. Sid, you take Chisos, Cass, and Nuno north to Ribbon Creek. Take an extra horse apiece. If you see him, you may have to ride him down. Take extra canteens and food for a couple of days. Reata, you take some of the boys and head east down the valley toward the Pecos. Sid, if you don't see him, head north as fast as you can toward Cinco Castillos. That's the next waterhole north of Ribbon Creek, and that's where the kid vanished eighteen years ago."

"Loco," said Sid. "That's a trip into hell this time of year."

"*¡Vámonos!*" yelled the woman.

Horses were saddled. Booted men tramped back and forth. Hoofs rattled on the gravel.

"Two hundred dollars to the man who cuts him down!" yelled Marsh.

The hoofbeats died away in the distance. Lee turned to go.

"They'll have to kill him," the woman said suddenly.

Lee peered around the side of the barn in time to see Marsh light the cigarette in the woman's thin-lipped mouth. He saw the great blue eyes in the flare of the match like chips of glacier ice and with about the same amount of soul in them.

"Why didn't you go with them?" she asked Marsh.

"I'm going to take a look around here," he said as he lighted his own cigarette. The flare of the match showed the same color of eyes as Stella's, but smaller, though not any harder.

"Why?" she asked. "Are you afraid for me?"

Marsh laughed. "Not ever, Stell! You'd be a match for Kershaw any day. No. I'm going to take a look up the river canyon. Galeras somehow got out of this valley right under our noses. He didn't take a horse. He legged it to Tinaja del Muerto, but he didn't leg it through the pass or over the mountains on either side of the pass. There's a secret way out of here, Stell. I think the old man knows it and so did Galeras. The old man maybe told Kershaw."

"Maybe we can make the old man talk."

"No! We can't risk having him die on our hands. I don't want any investigation made around here."

"Wouldn't that settle the whole problem?"

"Not if Kershaw gets loose and finds Bowman's bastard son."

"Do you think the kid is dead, Marsh?"

"I don't know. But we can't risk that either. Kershaw isn't the kind of man who hunts for shadows."

"I agree. We'll have to keep after him until we kill him. If he does find Bowman's son, we'll have to kill the both of them to keep them from getting back here. We've got no other choice, Marsh. There's too much at stake."

Lee faded into the deep shadows behind the barn as Marsh levered a round into the chamber of his Winchester.

The river rushed along inches from Lee's moccasined feet as he felt his way along the rocky trail that seemed tacked to the side of the dark canyon. Beetling limestone cliffs hung over Lee's head. Lee looked back down the canyon. A tall man was picking his way over the great log that spanned the river.

Lee crossed the rock fall and scanned the dark wall of limestone. He turned his head and quickly stepped behind a huge tip-tilted slab of limestone that had fallen close to the cliff base. A tall man stood at the edge of the rockfall looking up the narrowing gut of the canyon. He scrambled down the loose slope and stood not five feet away from Lee. He rolled a cigarette and lit it, completely unaware of the man who stood almost within touching distance, with a hand resting on the hilt of his knife.

Marsh studied the dark canyon. The alternate flaring up and dying down of the cigarette tip lit his hard blue eyes and then let them drift into shadow. Finally Marsh flicked his cigarette butt into the foaming river and scrambled back up the rock fall.

Lee passed a hand behind himself into emptiness. He lit a candle and thrust it ahead of him into the cave entrance. He walked slowly forward. Something made him stop. He lowered the candle to see a yawning hole stretching perhaps thirty feet ahead of him into the inner darkness. The faint sound of swiftly rushing water came from the dark pit.

Lee left the cave. He tried another opening and got a hundred feet within it to light a mass of fallen rock that blocked the way. The third attempt found him in a twisting, smooth-floored passage that was cool and had an astringent odor to it. He walked into a large, domed cavern and held up the candle. The flickering light reflected from sparkling bunches of gypsum crystals on the ceiling and the walls and from iciclelike stalactites. The light shone on an emerald-hued pool of clearest water.

At the far side of the domed cavern, he picked up a stale cigarette butt. He sniffed it. "Lobo Negro," he said. Vicente Galeras had passed that way on his one-way trip to death at Tinaja del Muerto.

Lee lighted one of Duke Bowman's clear Havanas to celebrate the occasion. By the time the cigar had burned down to a butt, he felt a cool draft strong on his face. After a little while, he blew out the candle. There was a subtle difference in the darkness ahead of him. He felt his way along the passage, testing the way with the butt of his rifle. In a short time, he stepped out on the northeastern side of the great humped and rounded limestone ridge that extended northward to the shallow pass through which he had traveled on his way to Ribbon Creek.

He watered the dun in the darkness just before the false dawn.

The dun raised its head and slanted its ears toward the southeast. The dawn wind brought the sound of hoofbeats from the lower slopes. Two shadows—that of a tall, lean, moccasined man and that of a rawhide-booted dun—vanished into the thick brush and scrub trees to the north of Ribbon Creek on the way to Cinco Castillos.

seven

The five naked pinnacles of rock thrust themselves up from the flat desert floor like the outspread fingers of a warning hand held palm outward toward the traveler. The pre-moon darkness shielded the base of the pinnacles and the eroded ruins of Cinco Castillos. Beyond the pinnacles rose the towering wolf-fanged mountains—the citadel of the Mescaleros.

Lee Kershaw padded through the darkness with his Winchester at hip level, cocked and ready for rapid fire. The dun was ground-reined in the darkness behind him.

The low-mounded graves of the massacre victims were marked in the darkness by pale, sun-bleached crosses whose lettering had long ago been erased by wind-driven sand. There were thirteen of them.

"There were no survivors," the mind voice murmured.

A feeling of utter loneliness came over Lee.

Beyond the ruins and the graves was the base of the five pinnacles, as though five fat and dripping candles had let their wax run freely to congeal in thick masses about their bases. A man-made passage had been cut through the rock to allow access to the shallow rock pans, or *tinajas,* which somehow, miraculously, held water even through the great heat of the summer droughts.

Lee's soft footfalls echoed in the dark passage. He saw the faint glistening of the water. He knelt beside the first *tinaja* and cupped the water up with his free hand, keeping his eyes on the alert. The water stung his cracked lips and ran into his dry mouth and throat. Some of it ran down from his hand and dripped onto his sweat-soaked shirt and through it to his chest. Jesus, but it was good!

He stood up suddenly and whirled, thrusting forward his Winchester toward the mouth of the passageway. Nothing moved. There was an eerie, deathlike stillness about the haunted place.

He climbed a rocky pathway to stand between two of the pinnacles to look toward the south and east where the road from the Rio Penasco was first being lit by the rising moon. Nothing moved; no thread of dust stained the moonlight.

The moonlight touched the ruins. It lit up the eastern sides of the roofless, eroded buildings and cast their western sides into deep shadow against the light-colored caliche soil. It etched the shapes of the tilted crosses against the mounded soil of the graves.

Lee was alone at Cinco Castillos. He whistled sharply for the dun and walked down the rocky path to meet him. He unsaddled the dun as it drank. He rubbed him down and let him drift over to graze on a meager patch of dried grasses caught in a shallow pocket of drift soil. The dun had eaten the last of Lee's supply of oats the day before.

Lee kindled a fire. He opened out the three collapsible legs of his spider and placed it over the embers. He poured in the last of his bacon fat. When it sizzled, he placed the last of his hard *bizcocho* in the deep fat and then tastefully draped the last of his *carne seca* over the biscuits. He whistled the "Sago Lily" as he basted the hard, dried meat and biscuits.

The dun suddenly raised his head and slanted his ears toward the pa sageway. Lee turned, automatically reaching for his rifle. His hand was arrested in the motion.

A small figure stood in the mouth of the passageway.

Lee slowly stood up.

The figure was that of a boy of perhaps three or four years of age wearing a little gray *charro*-type jacket fastened with six large silver buttons.

It was very quiet except for the busy sizzling of the fat.

"I can't cross into the Land of Shadows to find a boy who vanished eighteen years ago," Lee had told Duke Bowman.

"I'm hungry, señor," the small boy said in Spanish.

"Forgive the little one, señor," a rusty-voiced old man said from within the mouth of the passageway. "Our burros strayed this afternoon and took our food with them."

"Come out into the moonlight," ordered Lee.

An old man came out into the moonlight. He held out his work-gnarled hands to show that he was unarmed. He took off his heavy sombrero and revealed a face wrinkled like a hide that has lain too long in the sun. "Candelario Melgosa, *servidor de usted,*" he said in the old-fashioned courteous manner. "The boy is my great-grandson, Basilio," he proudly added.

Lee nodded. "Your servant," he countered. He would not give his name.

The old man looked past Lee. "The food will soon burn," he politely suggested.

Lee took the spider from the fire. "There is plenty for all," he said. "Come and eat."

Lee was immediately struck by the resemblance of the boy to that of another small boy who had vanished from that very place eighteen years past. He served the food in equal portions. "How long have you been here?" he asked.

'Since before the dawn. We came from the north last night to avoid the heat of the day. While we slept, the burros strayed."

"They will come back for the water. What are you doing here?"

"We come from a village near Las Trampas, in the mountains to the north of Santa Fe. My wife, Filomena, was one of those who died here in the massacre eighteen years ago to this very day. Every year since then, I have come here on this date. This is the first year I have brought the boy. I am very old, you understand, and may not be able to come next year; so I brought the boy with me so that he might know where his great-grandmother lies."

"You came that great distance through the desert in the heat and at a time of drought with this little one?"

"On such a pilgrimage, senor, ones does not feel hardships."

"And the Mescaleros? One does not fear them?"

The old man shrugged. "God protected us."

Lee finished his food and fashioned two cigarettes. He placed one in the mouth of the old man and lit both cigarettes. "*¿Una copita?*" asked Lee, holding a thumb tip and first finger tip about two inches apart. "*Mil gracias,*" murmured the old man. "*Por nada,*" responded Lee as he poured the brandy.

Candelario sipped the fiery brandy. "You are traveling north?" he asked.

"I go to the mountains from here."

"But the Mescaleros, senor!"

"I have business there."

The old man looked quickly at the dozing boy.

Lee picked up the boy. "The boy is safe, *viejo*. I am not a Comanchero." He placed a blanket on a smooth patch of sand and put Basilio on it. He came back to the fire. "Your wife was traveling through here at the time of the massacre?"

Candelario shook his white head. "In those days, this place was a swing station for the stagecoach line that ran through here before the railway was built farther to the west. I was head hostler then, and my wife was the cook."

Lee lowered his cup from his mouth. "You were here at the time of the massacre?" he asked incredulously.

"I had gone to hunt stray mules. Just before the true dawn, I saw the gun flashes and heard the screaming of the people. I hid near the road and saw the last of the killing."

"So you really are a lone survivor."

"When the Mescaleros left, I buried the bodies."

"Thirteen?" asked Lee.

"Count the graves, señor. Of course, there was the little boy who was taken away by the Mescaleros."

Lee showed the photograph to Candelario. "Him?" he asked.

"I never saw the boy. He came here when I was gone."

"The woman? You recognize her? She died here."

Candelario looked at Lee. "What do you wish to know about her?" he quietly asked.

"I am hunting for the boy of this photograph."

"After eighteen years? Why?"

"I am paid to do such things. Tell me about the woman."

"She was hardly more than a girl. I found her wounded under a pile of the dead. I treated her wound and nursed her back to health."

"You are a *curandero?*"

"You know of the *Penitentes?*" asked Candelario.

"I know of the *Penitentes*," admitted Lee.

"I am the *Enfermero* of my *morada*. I care for the sick members."

"Go on," urged Lee.

"When she came out of the fever, she cursed the men who had left her and the boy to the hands of the Mescaleros."

"Who were they?"

"They had brought the woman and the boy here while I was gone, and then they had left to return to the Rio Penasco. Before God, señor! They must have heard the shooting and the screaming of the unfortunates here, but they would not return. Had they done so, they could have saved most of the lives of those who were slaughtered here."

"But you don't know who they were?"

"Only their brand. It was on the mules they drew the buggy in which the woman and the boy had been riding. The Mescaleros stole the horses from here, but they slaughtered the mules, for they love the sweet mule meat. I saw the hides of the mules. The brand was plain on their flanks, so . . ." Here Candelario traced a Running MB brand on the fine sand.

"And you never heard of the boy again?"

"Who knows? He may have been killed later. He may have been traded or sold to another tribe. He may have been ransomed. It is also possible that he was raised as a Mescalero and now lives in those mountains."

"And the woman? What happened to her?"

"She had me dig a grave for her and fill it with the bones of one of the mules, as a bitter gesture I think. I made a cross for it with her name on it—Rafaela Diaz, it was. I took her north with me when I returned to my village."

"Where is she now?"

Candelario shrugged. "She left the village shortly after we returned there. She went to Santa Fe. I never saw her again." Candelario studied Lee. "This lost boy, what does he mean to you?"

'A thousand dollars a week," murmured Lee.

"I do not understand."

Lee stood up. "Sometimes I don't either. I'll round up your burros. When the moon is down, take the boy from this haunted place. Travel during the night and hide out during the day until you are safe from the Mescaleros."

Lee rode past the mounded graves. The names of the crosses were long gone. Which one of them held only the bones of a mule?

The burros were not far from the ruins. Lee drove them toward Cinco Castillos. He looked to the south across the moonlit desert. Dust was rising thinly on the Rio Penasco Road. The fine field glasses picked out the shapes of three horsemen leading three other horses.

Lee drove the burros clattering into the passageway. He dismounted. "You'll have to leave right now, *viejo*," he said. "There are men coming here looking for me, and I don't want them to find me here, or you either, for they will make you talk. Get the boy out of here. Ride around behind the pinnacles, keeping them in between you and the men who are coming here. Do not raise any dust!" Lee thrust a pair of cigars into the old man's shirt pocket.

"Keep moving until it is dark again. Rest, and push on later before the coming of the dawn."

Candelario placed the dozing boy in his saddle and passed a rope about him to hold him there. He led the three burros through the passageway. Lee followed him, leading the dun. "Remember!" he called out. "No dust, *viejo!*"

Lee led the dun around the opposite side of the pinnacles and ran lightly, leading the trotting dun. He kept the pinnacles always between him and the Rio Penasco Road until he reached lower ground, out of sight of the ruins, where he mounted and rode steadily toward the distant moonlit mountains.

eight

Nuno Mercado kicked through a pile of fresh manure. "There was someone just here," he said over his shoulder.

"Mescaleros," said Cass.

"It was an oat-fed horse," said Nuno. "Mescaleros graze their horses. White men feed them oats."

Chisos pressed a hand down on the sand that covered the fire ashes. "Still warm," he said.

"From the sun," said Cass.

Chisos kicked at the sand and ashes. A smoking ember landed near Cass. "Some sun," said Chisos drily.

"Mescaleros," insisted Cass.

Nuno shook his head. "They never come here. Not for eighteen years. They fear the ghosts of the slaughtered."

"Superstitious bull," said Cass.

"Perhaps," agreed Nuno. "But *they* believe it." Nuno climbed the rocky path to stand between two of the pinnacles. "There is dust rising on the road to the north!" He plunged recklessly down to get his horse.

"Dust devil," said Cass.

Chisos led his horse at a run toward the passage. "There ain't no wind!" he yelled back.

Out on the road to the north, Candelario Melgosa looked back at the satisfactory cloud of dust he had raised by dragging a blanket behind his burro. He drew in on the rope and folded the blanket over his cantle as he heard the sound of many hoofbeats approaching from the south.

Chisos dismounted at a run. "Stay right there old man," he ordered.

Candelario politely raised his sombrero. "I was not planning to go on, señor," he said.

Nuno dismounted and looked incredulously at the old man, the little boy, and the three dusty, little, two-dollar burros. "Before God, *viejo,"* he said. "What do you do out here on the desert at night?"

"I avoid the heat of the day, señor."

"You were just at Cinco Castillos?"

Candelario nodded. "I cooked a meal there."

Cass rode up and dismounted heavily. He looked hard at the old man. "Your burros crap back there?" he asked.

Candelario smiled. "They have good bowel movements, señor."

"Don't get funny!" Cass looked triumphantly at Nuno. "See?"

"You think this old *paisano* has enough pesos to feed his burros oats?" asked Chisos.

"What were you doing at Cinco Castillos, *viejo?"* asked Nuno.

"I was visiting the grave of my wife, Filomena, who died there in the massacre eighteen years ago this very day."

"Was there anyone else there?" asked Chisos.

"I saw no one," lied Candelario.

Nuno looked at Chisos. "Maybe Kershaw went west instead of north from Ribbon Creek, eh?"

Chisos shook his head. "He had to come here for water." He reached over and plucked two cigars from the shirt pocket of Candelario. He sniffed at them and read the bands in the bright moonlight. "By God!" he said. "These are the Duke's private brand!" He gathered together the front of the old man's jacket and drew him close. "Now, you old bastard," he threatened, "you just tell us about the big gringo who was just back there at Cinco Castillos."

Candelario slanted his eyes to the west. A faint thread of dust showed rising in line with the mountains. "A tall man with reddish hair, short beard, and a big nose, and gray eyes that were cold, but showed warmth when he looked at my great-grandson. He rode a fine dun, a *tostado*—a beautiful horse, señores."

Cass ambled over to look down at the frail little man. "Where did he go?" he demanded.

"I don't know." Candelario slewed his eyes to look west. It was a fatal mistake. Cass turned and saw the thread of dust. He whirled. "You old bastard!" he yelled. "You were holding us here to give him time to get away!" He hit the old man once, a heavy solid blow like a butcher slamming his cleaver through a thick joint of meat. Candelario fell to the dust of the road and lay there with his neck bent at an awkward angle and with his eyes staring up at the man who had killed him.

Nuno crossed himself. He knelt beside the old man and went through his pockets. "Damn!" he said. "Not a centavo!"

Cass plucked one of the cigars from Chisos' hand. He lit it. "What the hell did you expect?" he asked around the cigar.

"He's heading for the mountains," said Chisos.

"And maybe the Mescaleros," added Nuno.

"Why?" asked Cass.

"He has the shirt of Indi-yi-yahn," said Chisos.

"Maybe they'll bury him in it," suggested Cass.

"There's more to it than that," mused Chisos. "He came here for information on the kid and the woman that were here eighteen years ago."

"He came here for water," said Cass.

Chisos nodded. "*And* information," he insisted.

"You think he's still hunting for the boy who was here eighteen years ago?" asked Nuno.

"That's what Stella thinks," said Chisos.

"Well," said Cass, "I, for one, ain't goin' up in them mountains after him, and to hell with Stella!"

Chisos shrugged. "If there is one man who can go up in them mountains and come out of them again, it's likely him."

"Bull!" snapped Cass. "I ain't goin' to sit around and wait for him."

"He might make it," suggested Nuno. "And if he does, he'll go on looking for the old man's son."

"Where's the next waterhole north, Nuno?" asked Chisos.

"Just to the northwest of the mountains. There are old ruins there, abandoned by the padres many years ago. If Kershaw comes down out of those mountains, that is where he'll have to go for water."

"He'll never make it," said Cass.

Chisos looked at him. "Ten bucks he does."

Cass rubbed his jaw. He grinned. "One week time limit?" he asked.

"Fair enough. If he doesn't come out of them mountains in a week, he'll never come out of them."

"What about the boy?" asked Nuno.

They all looked at the sober-faced little lad who sat in his saddle looking down at his great-grandfather. Cass dropped his hand to his Colt.

"No," said Chisos.

"You gettin' soft?" sneered Cass.

"That shot could be heard for miles! You want the Mescaleros to know we're out here?"

"I ain't that scared of the Mescaleros!"

"Well, maybe *I* am!"

Cass grinned.

"It is bad luck to kill a child," put in Nuno. "We can turn the burros loose and take the boy with us to the ruins. We can leave him with anyone who passes by."

"Like Kershaw?" jeered Cass.

Nuno looked quickly at the big man. "Why do you say that?" he asked.

"How the hell do I know! Why?"

Nuno crossed himself again. "I don't know," he said. He took the boy and mounted his horse. "What about the old man?" he asked.

"In a week the bones will be picked clean," said Chisos. "The buzzards by day and the coyotes by night."

Nuno watched the two Anglos ride back toward Cinco Castillos. The staring eyes of the old man had begun to unnerve him. He turned his head away and followed the others. A curious foreboding had begun to haunt him.

nine

The evening wind blew softly through the murmuring pines.
A stream chuckled as it raced between grassy banks. The
new moon was riding high overhead. A great fire crackled
and flared in a semicircular clearing against a backdrop of
a curved rock formation like the band shell in a public
park.

The Mescalero warriors seated on the packed dancing
ground formed a semicircle, a continuation of the curved
rock formation, the center of which was the great fire.
Smoke wreathed upward, and fat pine sparks soared
brightly through the smoke.

A faint whistling sound came from the dark shadows
within the woods behind the seated warriors. Something
moved within the woods. Suddenly and dramatically, as
though engendered from the earth itself or compounded
from drifting smoke and errant moonbeams, a grotesque
figure appeared at the edge of the woods, whirling over its
head a pierced and shaped piece of wood whose sound
was like that of a rush of rain-laden wind through the
great pines themselves. Faster and faster whirled the long

leather thong, and the sound of the bullroarer increased so that it carried to the depths of the dark woods. The strange and eerie figure of the *diyi* advanced slowly into the cleared area between the fire and the seated warriors. He wore the traditional medicine shirt of a Mescalero shaman, painted with the mystic symbols of water beetle, spider, sun, moon, stars, lightning, thunder, and rain. The shirt was old, well worn, and greasy to the sight and touch. Upon the *diyi's* head was a headdress made from a strangled fawn, from which protruded two polished buffalo horns. Under the edge of the headdress, his painted face looked like nothing human.

The *diyi* thrust out a hand toward the fire, and a great flare of reddish smoke swirled upward. He thrust out the hand again, and a glittering shower of *hoddentin,* sparkling mica crystals seemed to explode over the flames.

A warrior began to beat on a stiffened hide with a hooped stick. Here and there among the assembled warriors, some of the younger ones stood up and tied back their thick black hair. They drew the long flaps of their buckskin loincloths up through their belts to shorten them. They slung bandoleers of polished brass cartridges about their naked shoulders and chests. They picked up their weapons.

Four young warriors marching abreast, advanced to the fire and circled it four times. Two of them stopped on the north side of the fire, and two of them stopped on the south side. Singers gathered about the hide drummer. The four warriors danced in rhythm, moving toward each other to change sides and then to dance back the other way.

The dancers put cartridges between their strong white teeth and between their strong brown fingers. They swayed violently, dropping down upon one knee and then springing high into the air. Guns flashed and roared. An arrow was loosed through the fire and gun smoke, flashing in the moonlight. It seemed to disappear for a split second as it reached the zenith of its flight and then it turned over, reflecting the cold moonlight from the polished cane shaft and plunging downward to drive deep into the ground.

"Wah! Wah! Wah!" The dancers' hoarse grunting cries echoed through the shadowed woods.

One after another the younger warriors dashed onto the firelit dancing ground and swung into the stomping, pounding rhythm of the war dance. The older warriors did not move. They watched the dancers, and among them was Diabolito, the only son of Indi-yi-yahn, who did not want this war.

The *diyi* ran the show like a ringmaster. "You, Long Ear!" he cried out. "You, Long Ear! Many times you have talked bravely! Now, many brave people are calling to you!"

Long Ear obeyed the summons. He dashed in among the sweating dancers, thrusting his long double-barreled shotgun up and down in time with the heady rhythm.

"You, Yellow Bear!" shrieked the *diyi*. "You, Yellow Bear! There are brave people dancing here who would welcome you!"

Yellow Bear joined the dancers. He flourished his polished lance with all the skill of a drum major.

"Coyote, they say to you! You! You! You! They call you again and again!" cried the *diyi*.

Coyote dashed into the firelight. "Tudevia! Tudevia! Tudevia!" he called back. "You are a man! Now I am calling you! You, Mah-Ko! Mah-Ko! I call to you again and again!"

The scene became reminiscent of hell or the Celts dancing about the Beltane fires. Guns flashed and cracked. Warriors called persistently to those who still watched the dance. Sweat was flung glistening from taut, painted faces.

The drumming suddenly lowered in pitch. The dancers stopped calling.

"Baishan! Baishan! Baishan!" called the *diyi*. "They say to you! You! You! You! They call you again and again!"

A broad-shouldered warrior came trotting easily from the woods and leaped into the dancing circle. The firelight showed warm against his new medicine shirt. The yelling rose to a bloodcurdling pitch as Baishan dominated the dance. His entry had been perfectly timed, and now he was showing his stuff. It would be only a matter of time before he would dash from the firelit area through the woods to the waiting horses and carry the war party down the long mountain slopes to raid, kill, and pillage.

A tall, reddish-bearded man walked easily into the firelight carrying a dusty, folded-up, deerskin shirt of a dingy brownish color, stained with what looked like smears of black paint. A cigar was stuck jauntily in one corner of his mouth, and the bluish smoke wreathed about his lean, bronzed hawk's face with its piercing gray eyes.

The drumming stopped first. The singing died away. One by one the sweating dancers stopped still and stared at the White-Eye who had appeared among them as though summoned by their dancing, and wild chanting, as Baishan himself had been called forth.

The wind moaned a little through the tree tops. The moon was slanting down toward the west. The fire was crackling lower and lower over a thick bed of embers.

No one moved.

Lee walked easily to where Diabolito sat among the older warriors.

Baishan snatched the double-barreled shotgun from the hands of Long Ear. He swept back the hammers with a sharp cut of his left hand. He walked between Diabolito and Lee and pointed the ten-gauge muzzles at the face of the White-Eye. Lee looked into the eyes of Baishan over the barrels of the shotgun. "I came here to talk in peace with Diabolito," said Lee in passable Mescalero. He could not show a mote of fear in his own eyes; to do so would be to die at once with his face missing.

"Wait," said Diabolito to Baishan. "I am still the chief here. Let the White-Eye speak."

Lee slowly raised a hand and pushed the shotgun aside. "I came here, as a man, to talk with a man," he announced. He had put the issue squarely up to Diabolito and the older Mescalero warriors. Was Diabolito still the chief, and not in name only? There was no hereditary line of chieftainship among the Mescaleros. Diabolito had only succeeded his father Indi-yi-yahn because he had been the best warrior in the tribe, not because he was the son of

Indi-yi-yahn. Who was the best warrior now? Diabolito or the would-be usurper Baishan?

"I know you now," said Diabolito to Lee. "You came here years ago and fought against us. You are the one called Hunter of Men. The one who can kill so swiftly."

"Can he die as swiftly as he kills?" demanded Baishan. He did not want to lose face in front of this calm white man. The gods had been with him that night up until the very last moment when the White-Eye had appeared, seemingly from nowhere.

Lee walked around Baishan, expecting at any second to hear the double-crashing report of the scattergun and to feel the smashing impact of buck and ball in his back. He watched the eyes of the warriors who looked past him into the taut, painted face of Baishan, hoping he might get a split second warning if Baishan made his killing move.

At the last possible second, Lee suddenly unrolled the bloodstained medicine shirt of Indi-yi-yahn in front of Diabolito. He heard the gasping intake of breath from the older warriors.

"Where did you get this?" asked the chief.

"From the old man of the Broken Bow."

"The shirt means nothing now!" cried Baishan. "Did not your own father go to the Land of Shadows leaving that shirt in the bloody hands of that old devil of the Broken Bow? There is no power left in that shirt! Its medicine is lost!"

Lee slowly turned his head. "And how good is the medicine of your shirt?"

Baishan's face worked. He was no fool. He had always been able to think quicker than his fellows. "The power of that shirt went into that old devil of the Broken Bow. That is so, because we Mescaleros were never again able to challenge his power for that land which is ours."

Lee shrugged carelessly. "How can you prove that?"

"Through this shirt I now wear! It now has the power!"

"The White-Eye asked you how you can prove it. You did not answer him," said Diabolito.

"Let me fight him to the death. If I win, then my shirt

has the power. If he wins, then the power is still in the old shirt."

"You think fast for a Mescalero, sonny," said Lee quietly. Baishan had neatly caught Lee's tail in a crack.

Baishan stripped off his medicine shirt and wound it about his left forearm. He unsheathed his knife and drew it lightly across his left bicep to draw blood, which he sucked up and spat at Lee.

Lee felt his face skin tighten and his bowels loosen. "Sweet Jesus," he breathed.

Baishan stood there like a bronze image. Only the sweat moved on his broad chest and bulging muscles.

"You don't have to meet the challenge," suggested Diabolito.

"And if I don't?" asked Lee.

The answer was plain in the eyes of the old chief and on the faces of the warriors. The struggle for power in the tribe had now shifted from Diabolito into the hands of Lee, as the champion of the chief and the older warriors who had opposed the war talk of Baishan, who was backed by the younger hotbloods of the tribe.

Lee dropped his cigar and trod on it. "A thousand a week," he murmured. "I pay my own expenses."

"Do you pray to your god, Hunter of Men?" asked Diabolito.

Lee nodded. "In a sense," he agreed. He stripped off shirt and undershirt to reveal his lean, long-muscled body puckered with bullet holes and with the white cicatrices of old knife wounds scarring the hard flesh.

"I came unarmed," he said.

A knife was thrown at his feet. He picked it up and hefted it, testing the edge with a thumb. It was a cheap trade knife without heft or balance. Diabolito threw his own knife at Lee's feet. It was made in the Mexican fashion of the finest Oaxaca steel and seemed cunningly fitted to the strong hand of Lee Kershaw. He picked up the old medicine shirt and wound it tightly about his left forearm. He turned now to face the waiting Mescalero.

The moon was beyond the mountain now, and long

shadows filled the circle; few of the shadows were driven back by the light of the great bed of embers on the hard-packed dancing earth.

Lee drew the razor edge of the knife lightly across his left bicep. He sucked up the blood and spat it at Baishan. "Knife and awl," he flung at Baishan. The words had no meaning of their own. There were no true curse words in the Apache language; the implication of "knife and awl" had been lost in their history, but nothing worse could be said to an Apache.

Lee moved in on the attack. The coaching words of old Anselmo Campos, that master of knife fighting, came back to Lee, who had been born and bred a gunfighter: "Try to keep the light in his eyes. A knife fight does not last very long. It does not have the honor and tradition of the duel. An opponent dies slowly with many cuts but swiftly with one that is right. If you cannot kill him at once, weaken him with many small cuts until the chance for the death stroke comes. Above all! Keep calm!"

Lee stopped with his back to the light of the fire, weaving his body back and forth and sideways from the hips, knife partway extended, legs planted apart, balanced on the balls of the feet, and eyes always on the eyes of Baishan.

Baishan tested Lee's reactions. His blade came in high for the face and then dropped low, turning sideways for the swift and fatal disemboweling slash. Lee sucked in his lean gut and moved backward a little. He leaned forward from the hips, and his blade clashed against that of Baishan. The blades went slowly upward, locked together as each man tested the muscular power of the other. They stood there together, straining in the firelight, blade against blade and wrist against wrist in a grim tableau. The blades suddenly went down and sideways. Lee disengaged, and as he did so, he brought the point of his left elbow hard against the right jaw of the Mescalero in a little knife-fighting refinement of his own. Baishan was staggered. Before he could recover, Lee's blade had swept across Baishan's right bicep, drawing forth the blood, bright in the firelight.

Lee retreated. Baishan bulled in. His swift slash ripped into the deerskin shirt about Lee's left forearm. Lee made no effort to counter strike. Instead, he brought up his knee into Baishan's crotch in a smashing, sickening blow, out of sight of the watching Mescaleros. Lee grinned into Baishan's agonized face. "Cry 'Foul,' you sonofabitch," he said. His knife raked a red line across the Mescalero's broad chest.

Baishan retreated. Lee circled around to get the Mescalero's back to the great heat of the thick bed of embers. Baishan slipped sideways so that he stood in the area between the fire and the high rock formation behind the dancing area where the heat had reflected from the rocks.

They closed and fought with the shadow figures aping their every move on the rock face. They leaped in, retreated, swayed sideways and backwards, with the blades clicking and clashing and the sound of their moccasined feet beating a hard tattoo on the packed dancing ground. Again and again, Lee made his small stabbing cuts, followed always by the hard smashing impact of his elbow against the jaw of the Mescalero.

Lee forced Baishan back against the intense heat of the thick bed of embers. The heat seared against the backs of the Mescalero's legs. Lee bored in. Baishan's heels were in the embers. He could not stand the heat. He turned sideways to work his way from the fire. Lee's blade struck at the small of his back.

Baishan whirled. The *heshke* was on him now—the wild killing rage of the Apache, wherein he felt no exhaustion or pain, nothing but the overwhelming desire to kill.

"*Zastee! Zastee! Zastee! Kill! Kill! Kill!*" shrieked the *diyi*.

But Baishan did not meet in combat a modern, civilized, white man, trained to fight with fist, foot, and gun, but rather a transfiguration of a warrior who had gone back into his own Viking-Scots ancestry to match the *heshke* with the *berserker* rage.

They drove at each other like mad bulls; like ripping, tearing, clawing great cats; like leaping, fang-slashing *lobos*. Lee drove Baishan back toward the fire until his heels again rested in the embers. Lee struck at Baishan's face with the knife, and at the last possible instant, he turned his hand sideways so that the big knuckles, taut white in the grip about the hilt of the knife, smashed with stunning force against the sweat-dripping jaw of the Mescalero. Baishan staggered backward, ankle deep in glowing embers. Despite his Apache training, he shrieked in intense agony. He tried to get out of the embers, only to be met by a grinning devil of a white man who drove him back again. At last, he turned and plowed shrieking through the thick bed of embers toward the watching warriors, scattering the coals to either side, driving hard with the last of his will power to reach the far side.

Lee raced around the great bed of embers. Baishan staggered out of the fire. His moccasins were aflame. His feet were a seared, blistered mass of sheer agony. He could not go back. He charged like a true Mescalero, knowing he was to die, but trying to take his killer with him.

The knife flashed through the firelight and struck deep and hard in the chest of Baishan. He straightened up spasmodically. He swung once with his knife, inches past the sweating face of the white man, and then fell backward into the embers. His medicine shirt flared up, and in the eerie, flickering flamelight, his staring eyes seemed to come back to life.

Lee dragged the Mescalero from the embers. He turned to look at Diabolito. The chief sat there alone. Only drifting shadows in the deep woods revealed where the warriors had gone. "Will it be peace then?" asked Lee. Diabolito nodded.

Lee walked slowly to the chief. He unwound the medicine shirt of Indi-yi-yahn from his left forearm and gave it to the chief. Lee wiped the sweat from his body and pulled on his undershirt and shirt.

"Why did you really come here, Hunter of Men?" asked Diabolito.

Lee made up two cigarettes. One he placed between the lips of the chief, and the other he placed between his own lips. He thumb-snapped a lucifer into flame and lit the cigarette for Diabolito. "Were there any survivors of the massacre of Cinco Castillos?" he asked around his cigarette as he lit it.

"There was much blood there that day," the chief evasively replied.

"There is a rumor that a small boy was taken here from that place."

Diabolito nodded. "That is so."

"What happened to him?"

"I was not at the massacre of Cinco Castillos. I was in the south, stealing horses from the Nakai-Yes. It was my father who led the raid on Cinco Castillos."

"But the boy must have been here when you returned."

Diabolito was puzzled. "Which boy?" he asked.

Lee showed the photograph to Diabolito. "I am not sure," said the chief. "There were two boys of that age brought here at that time. One from Cinco Castillos. One from up north. He had been captured by the Jicarillas and traded to us for horses. Thus, there were *two* boys here, about the same age. After a time, I could not tell them apart. One of them was ransomed from us by a priest from Santa Fe, to give back to his mother. I was never sure that we let the priest have the right boy."

"And the other small boy?"

"He was raised as a Mescalero."

"Where is he now?"

Diabolito looked at the smoldering body of Baishan. *"There,"* he said quietly.

ten

It was a place of ancient ruins under the dreaming moon-
light. The roofless church dominated the other smaller
buildings. Beyond the ruins across bare flat ground was a
great *bosque* of cottonwoods and willows shielding the
spring from sight. Beyond the *bosque* was the great, ghastly white expanse of a salt *laguna* that stretched northward
for many miles.

Cass Dakin sat on the floor of the church nave playing
solitaire in the moonlight that came streaming through the
high windows. He looked up at Nuno Mercado perched in
the crumbling bell tower. "You see anything, Nuno?" he
called up.

"*Nada*," said Nuno.

"He ain't comin', Chisos," said Cass. "I win the bet."

Chisos shook his head. "There's four days to go."

"The Mescaleros got him."

"We should wait," advised Nuno.

"Jesus Christ!" snapped Cass. "You still think he ain't
human! Well, he can bleed like the rest of us, and he's
likely dead up in them mountains."

"Nothing is impossible for that man," insisted Nuno.

"I'd like to find out with a .44/40 slug," said Cass.

"He is very fast with the guns," warned Nuno.

"Faster than me?" challenged Chisos.

Cass turned over a card. "All right," he said. "We can wait. Go take a look at the horses and the kid, Chisos, and see if they're all right."

"I'll go when I'm ready," retorted Chisos.

The horses grazed in a large enclosure bounded by small cell-like rooms. A lean figure rolled over the wall and landed lightly on its feet. Lee Kershaw catfooted across the enclosure and looked in on little Basilio Melgosa, sound asleep on a horse blanket. Lee picked him up without awakening him. He carried him from the enclosure to a deep draw where the dun stood ground-reined. Lee returned to the enclosure and let the horses drift out onto the open ground where the grazing was thicker. He took his two big canteens and circled far around the ruins to come in toward the *bosque* on the shadowed side.

Chisos Martin looked into the enclosure. He looked into the cell where Basilio had been sleeping. He looked out across the open ground and saw the horses drifting half a mile away. He walked back into the church. "Throw down that pair of tens, Nuno!" he called up.

"The bet was that Kershaw wouldn't be here within the week," reminded Nuno.

Chisos smiled. "That's right," he agreed. "And the sonofabitch got here while we stood around in this damned ruin. He let the horses drift. He took the kid. He's likely in the *bosque* right now gettin' his water."

Nuno looked toward the *bosque*. "The moon is low," he said. "There are thick shadows in the *bosque*."

Cass stood up and reached for his rifle.

"Wait," said Chisos. "I'm aimin' to prove I'm a faster gun than Kershaw."

"That's loco," said Cass. "The three of us can make sure of him."

"Why bother?" asked Chisos. He drew his fine Colt and snapped open the loading gate. He twirled the cylinder to check the loads and then snapped shut the loading gate. He sheathed the sixgun.

"I can hit him from here with the long gun," said Cass.

"You can't even see him," said Chisos.

"We can sweep the *bosque* with slugs."

"Where's your sportin' blood?" jeered the Texan.

"This ain't sport! It's business! You listen to me, Chisos! You're good with the cutter, maybe one of the best, but there's always someone, somewhere, who's faster than you are."

"Marsh offered two hundred dollars for the man who cut down Kershaw. I'd cut my own brother down for that kind of money. Twenty bucks says I take him, Cass."

Cass seemed to have a flash of inspiration; rare indeed for him. He slowly nodded.

Chisos left the church as silently as a hunting cat.

Nuno looked down at Cass. "He shouldn't try Kershaw alone."

Cass grinned. "Why not? If Kershaw kills him, we kill Kershaw."

"And if Chisos kills Kershaw?"

"That Texas punk hasn't been nothing but trouble to me. Now, if he does kill Kershaw, he'll go crowin' back to Marsh to collect his two hundred bucks, which will make me look *very* bad, amigo. But, if I go back to Marsh and tell him it was me that killed Kershaw, I get the credit *and* the two hundred bucks, plus the twenty Chisos bet he could take Kershaw." The low cunning of the stupid showed on his broad face.

Nuno was puzzled. "But if Chisos does kill Kershaw, how can you claim you did it?" He saw the answer on the face of Cass. A cold feeling coursed through his body.

The only sound in the shadowed *bosque* was the metallic whirring of the locusts. Lee glanced toward the moonlit church. Nothing moved. He submerged his canteens in the water.

"Kershaw," the soft Texas voice said from behind Lee.

Lee turned his head. The man was nothing more than a lean shadow close beside the thick bole of a cottonwood. Lee slowly stood up. His rifle was beside his left foot.

"You are Kershaw, aren't you?" asked the Texan.

"You know I am." Lee slanted his eyes toward the church. Something moved in the bell tower. The shadow in a nave window was darker than it should be.

"You move fast. How did you get past the Mescaleros?"

"They like me," Lee drily replied.

"Why?"

"Personality," replied Lee.

"Maybe you're a breed of some kind?"

"We're all breeds of one kind or another—even Texans."

Chisos stepped away from the tree. "They say you're fast with a sixgun."

"I get by," said Lee modestly.

"My two compañeros back there think you might be as fast as me."

"Men of rare judgment," murmured Lee.

"So, I came out here to prove you are not."

"Backed by their rifles?"

"They'll keep out of it."

"As long as you kill me, is that it?"

"Is there a doubt in your mind?"

"How much am I worth in this killing business?"

"Two hundred cash in hand, and worth a helluva lot more in the long run to the Dakins."

"I thought I might be worth more than two hundred."

"Times are hard, Kershaw."

"I'll double that killing fee to let me pass."

Chisos laughed. "When I kill you, I get what's in your wallet, as well as the two hundred."

"And, if you don't kill me, you don't get a cent. But then, it won't make any difference if *you're* dead, will it?"

"You suggestin' that you can kill me?"

"You're getting the idea," admitted Lee.

The locusts had stopped their strident whirring. It was very quiet in the *bosque*—deathly quiet.

"You're in my way, mister," quietly warned Lee.

Chisos calmly nodded.

"Is it a duel you want, Texas? Shall we stand back to

back like little Southern gentlemen and pace off ten paces to turn and fire?"

"Just make your play, mister, any time you're ready."

Lee looked quickly sideways. "Looks like one of your rifleman friends is getting ready to beat you to the kill, mister."

Chisos turned his head. Lee's sixgun exploded. The .44/40 slug caught Chisos just below the heart. In the last instant before death, Chisos realized the stark truth—he'd never know whether or not he was faster than Lee Kershaw.

Lee dropped flat as the shot's echo racketed through the *bosque*. He snatched up his Winchester as he rolled over and over to get behind a tree. He rolled up onto his feet, firing as he arose, working lever and pulling trigger to slam out ten rapid rounds toward the church to keep down the heads of the riflemen. The last of the shots' echoes were rolling along the low hills as Lee ran through the smoke-rifted *bosque*. He plunged into the draw where he had left the dun and the boy. He tucked Basilio under one arm and mounted the dun. He raced toward the drifting horses and stampeded them, driving three of them north toward the glaring, moonlit expanse of the salt *laguna*.

Rifle fire sparkled from the church. One of the driven horses faltered in its stride. Lee was a mile from the ruins when he remembered the two canteens he had left submerged in the spring.

eleven

Cass Dakin hooked a boot toe under the body of Chisos and flipped him over onto his back. "Goddamned if I thought Kershaw was faster than Chisos," he said as he knelt beside the body and felt for the Texan's wallet.

"He wasn't," said Nuno quietly.

"He's dead, ain't he?"

"He did not die because Kershaw was faster with a gun. He died because Kershaw was faster with his wits. Did you not see Chisos look away from him a second before Kershaw fired?"

Cass nodded thoughtfully as he counted the bills in the wallet. "Chisos never cleared leather," he said. "Anyway, Kershaw ain't very good with the long gun. He didn't get near us with one of them shots of his."

"Mother of God! The horses!" Nuno legged it from the *bosque.* "They are all gone!" he yelled back a few minutes later.

"They'll come back to the water," said Cass.

Nuno walked back into the *bosque.* "Three of them are out in the open. He stampeded the other three."

67

"He must have known all along we were in the church. Yet he come right in here to the *bosque* to get water when the three of us could have gotten him easily with the long guns."

"He had to have the water. It was either that, or turn back, and *nothing* can make *him* turn back, *patrón*."

Cass grinned. "Oh, I don't know. Look there in the spring."

Nuno looked down at the two big blanket-covered canteens submerged in the water. "He will find a way," he prophesied.

"He'll die of thirst out there. Is the boy still here?"

"Kershaw must have taken him with him."

"Go round up them three horses. Kershaw won't get far ahead of us without water. If we keep pushin' him, we'll get him all right."

Nuno walked out of the *bosque*. Far out on the *laguna*, he saw a faint spark of light as Kershaw lighted a cigarette. Nuno crossed himself and went on to get the horses.

Later, in the predawn darkness, Cass Dakin and Nuno Mercado rode along the edge of the salt *laguna*, Nuno leading the spare horse. Cass laughed. "No water," he said. He laughed again.

"Wait, *patrón*," said Nuno. "Look there!" He pointed to a dark hole that showed against the ghostly white surface of the *laguna*. He dismounted and knelt beside the hole. He dipped a hand into the water and tasted it. "Brackish," he said, "but it will keep a man alive." He looked beyond the hole and then walked across the heavily hoof-trampled ground. He thumb-snapped a match into fire and looked down at a gutted horse. He walked back to the water.

"Well?" asked Cass as he shaped a cigarette.

"That man is the devil," avowed Nuno. "Look here! He drove the horses back and forth on the soft ground here at the edge of the laguna to raise the water to the surface. He dug his *pozito* just here because he saw the growths along the bank, indicating that there was water deep beneath the surface of the *laguna*. He watered the horses with it when it rose to the surface."

Cass lighted the cigarette. "So? He ain't got any canteens for him and the kid."

"Not so! See there! The dead horse? He gutted it and withdrew the large intestine. He filled it with the water—an Apache canteen! There is enough for him and the boy to make the next waterhole. He will ride the spare horses to death, if he has to, and then shift to the others. He is miles north by now!"

"No white man would drink out'a a thing like that," sneered Cass in disgust.

"Kershaw would, *patrón!* I think I will turn back now."

Cass rested an elbow on his saddlehorn and studied the dark face of the New Mexican. "Why?" he asked.

"I have the second sight, *patrón.* One of us will not return from the north. I was born with a caul on my face. I know these things, *patrón!* I have the gift of prophecy."

"You were born in a barnyard with cowshit on your face! Get on that horse!"

"At least we should send back for help!"

"We can telegraph back to the Broken Bow when we get north."

Nuno mounted his horse and reached down to pick up the reins of the spare. He waited until Cass rode on and then he swiftly crossed himself. In a little while, the *laguna* was quiet again, just before the coming of the dawn light. A coyote came trotting silently out of the mesquite. He drank daintily from the *pozito* and looked to the north. After a little while, he trotted to the dead horse and began to tear at the guts, left there courtesy of Lee Kershaw.

twelve

Lee Kershaw opened one of the ancient, warped double doors of the chapel. The warm spicy odor of burning candles flowed about his face. He looked back over his shoulder. He had lost a day's time in the ride north. A horse had gone lame, and the boy was wearing out. Lee led the boy into the narrow nave. The reredos behind the altar reflected the soft, glowing light of the many candles. The light brought out the lifelike flesh tones of the suffering Christ suspended on his dark cross against the whitewashed wall of the chapel and the bright droplets of blood from the piercing crown of thorns. The chapel seemed empty of life.

"Jesus," said Basilio.

Lee nodded. The faint sound of a mumbling voice came to him. He led the boy to the altar. The kneeling figure of a small-bodied padre was there, with the cowl thrown back from the pure white hair of his head.

"Padre Nicolás?" asked Lee.

The padre slowly turned his head. His dreamlike face

seemed made of old ivory that had the lines and wrinkles of ancient parchment on it. The old man got stiffly to his feet. "I am he," he said. "What can I do for you, my son?"

"I was told you would be here. You were once a missionary to the Mescaleros?"

The old man nodded. He looked down at the face of Basilio. "He has the face of a small angel," he said.

"Once you bartered with Indi-yi-yahn, the Mescalero chief, for the ransom of a small boy about the size of little Basilio here. You brought the boy back to his mother here in Santa Fe."

"There were a number of white children for whom I bartered. I was not always successful. One boy, I know, stayed with the Mescaleros and became a warrior. He was named Baishan."

Lee held out the photograph. The padre looked at it dimly. "That might be the boy," he said doubtfully. Lee held out the silver button. "Did he have a jacket with buttons like this?"

The padre eyed the button. "I am not sure."

"You sent this button to the boy's father some years past. To Mark Bowman of the Broken Bow."

"That might be, my son."

Lee was patient. "There were two small boys in the *ranchería* of the Mescaleros at the time you went there. One boy was captured at Cinco Castillos. The other was captured by the Jicarillas up north and traded to the Mescaleros. Which of those two boys did you ransom?"

"I can't remember."

"Where is the boy you ransomed?"

"I never saw him again."

"The woman who had the boy ransomed? Her name was Rafaela Diaz, was it not?"

"I knew her only as Senora Luz. Today she is known as Doña Luz."

"Where is she?"

The padre was surprised. "Surely you know who she is?"

"I would not have asked had I known," said Lee patiently. "Does she live in Santa Fe?"

"She has a great fine house on the Taos Road. She does not have a good reputation, my son."

"Why?"

"When she came here, she asked me to ransom her son. She had no money. She was very young and beautiful. She had no skills. It took many months for her to get the money to buy trade goods to ransom the boy. She had sold the only asset she had—her body. She became a whore, my son. In time, she became what you Anglos call a madam, with many girls working for her. Today she has an establishment for drinking, gambling, and prostitution. She is said to be very wealthy."

Lee shook his head. "Mother of God," he said quietly.

"If you seek her son, I warn you that she would do anything to protect him. She can be a very dangerous woman when crossed."

"Her son is still alive then?"

The padre shrugged. "So it is said. I do not know."

"Will you take care of this little one for me for a few hours? My horse is outside. I took the liberty of putting him in the stable behind the chapel."

The padre nodded. "The boy will be fed and given a place to sleep, my son."

"I won't be gone that long."

Lee walked toward the door. Once he looked back. The padre was again kneeling in prayer with little Basilio Melgosa kneeling beside him with bowed head, aping the old priest. Lee softly closed the door behind himself.

Lee walked into the establishment of Doña Luz. It was as the padre had said—for drinking, gambling, and prostitution. He stood at the long bar and drank good brandy. He watched a dark-haired beauty, perhaps in her middle thirties, walking between the tables. An exquisite tortoise-shell comb was in her raven hair. Her velvet dress was low on her naked shoulders, and the soft lamplight brought out the ivory tone of her skin.

Doña Luz came along behind the bar. She was truly beautiful, with the great, dark, and almost tragic eyes of

the *genizaro* and a complexion like the palest of ivory.
Diamond earrings flashed in the light of the many crystal
chandeliers. Rings sparkled on her lovely, tapered fingers
as she gestured, speaking to her many customers. When
she was still, she seemed like a painting done full length in
oils by one of the great masters.

It was half past eleven. Lee had found out that she always left the establishment at precisely midnight every
night in the week. Lee paid his tab and walked outside
into the narrow dark street. A carriage was waiting beside
the door of the establishment. Lee looked up at the driver.
"Are you for hire?" he asked a little drunkenly.

"No, señor," replied the driver. "I drive only for the
Doña Luz."

Lee nodded. He crossed the street and stood in a deep
doorway. Minutes ticked past. The driver got down from
the box and went inside the establishment.

The door was opened allowing a flood of soft light into
the dark street. It reflected from the dark, polished surfaces of the fine carriage. The carriage door was opened
and Doña Luz was helped inside. The door was closed.
The carriage moved as the driver climbed to his box. He
touched up the matched team of blacks with his whip and
drove toward the Taos Road.

The woman looked at the shadowy figure seated on the
front seat of the carriage. "If you are drunk, señor," she
said, "I will have the carriage stopped, and you may get
out. But do not let me see your face, for I will remember
it."

"I am not drunk," said Lee in Spanish. "I have come a
long way from the south to talk to your about your son."

A street lamp flicked its light into the carriage window
and against the lovely face of the woman. "I have no son,"
said Doña Luz.

A big hand was held over toward her. In it rested a
curiously embossed silver button. Another hand came out,
holding the opened photograph case. She glanced at the
contents of the hands and then looked toward the shadowed face. "Where did you get these?" she asked.

"Duke Bowman, señora," replied Lee.

"What do you want of my son?"

"His father wants to see him."

"I have no son," she said.

"His name was Bart. You took him from the Broken Bow eighteen years ago. He was taken by the Mescaleros at Cinco Castillos. You did not die in the massacre, señora. The grave once marked with the name of Rafaela Diaz holds only mule bones. A man by the name of Candelario Melgosa, a *Penitente,* took you north with him to his village near Las Trampas. You did not stay there long. You came here to raise money to buy trade goods to ransom your son. You sent a priest by the name of Padre Nicolás to deal with the Mescaleros. He brought back a small boy. He would be a man grown now. Where is he?"

"You know much," said the woman. "Perhaps you know *too* much."

"I was warned that you would do anything to protect your son and that you can be a dangerous woman when crossed."

She laughed. "All women are dangerous when crossed, señor."

The carriage was beyond the last of the houses of Santa Fe proper. Lee looked out of the carriage window. There was no sign of anyone else on the road.

"Are you afraid of being followed?" she asked.

"Not afraid, señora, just cautious."

"You may be one of the few living persons who knows my true name and origin," she said.

"Your secret is safe with me," responded Lee.

"As long as I do what you say. How much is Duke paying you to find my son?"

"A thousand a week," replied Lee.

The carriage rolled to a halt. The driver shouted. The wide *zaguán* doors of a high walled house were opened, and the carriage was driven within. The doors were slammed shut behind the carriage, and a heavy wooden bar was dropped into place. The woman smiled at Lee. "Safe at home," she said. Her dark eyes were enigmatic.

The driver opened the door, and his eyes went wide with astonishment when he saw Lee descend after Doña

Luz. He opened and then closed his mouth. He knew better than to question any of her activities, and strange men often came to the great house on the Taos Road. Lee looked beyond the driver. Two men stood just within the doorway watching him. He followed Doña Luz into her living room and closed the door behind himself.

Flickering firelight reflected from the highly polished surface of a grand piano. It shone dully on massive silver candlesticks in which slender candles burned. The candlelight shone on the full-length portrait in oils that hung over the fireplace. It was a twin in dress to the woman who now stood taking off her filmy *rebozo* while she looked into the fire.

"What do you see in the color painting of the embers, Doña Luz?" asked Lee. It was the same question he had asked Duke Bowman not so long past.

"I'll give you five thousand dollars in cash to walk out of here tonight and to forget that you ever saw me."

"I have been contracted to find Bart."

She raised her eyebrows a little. "You have a contract?"

"Verbally, señora."

"And you always hold to them?"

"I have built my reputation on that."

"And you always succeed?"

"I have never failed," he countered.

"I know that is not conceit."

"Professional pride, señora."

She sat down in a chair and looked up at him, studying the lean, bronzed face, the proud nose, the wide gray eyes, and the strong mouth and chin, graced with the short reddish beard. "There is brandy," she suggested.

He filled the glasses. He shaped a cigarette and placed it between her full lips. He lit the cigarette. "I'll double my offer," she said. "Ten thousand dollars."

"Evidently you don't understand," he said as he rolled a cigarette for himself. "I gave my word to Duke Bowman."

"You must think highly of him."

He shook his head. "On the contrary, but business is business."

"And you've risked your life walking in here for a thousand dollars a week?"

Lee shrugged as he lit up. "Professional hazard."

"There is more to it than that," she said wisely. "You are a man who must live on the very brink of danger. All else is dull and humdrum to you."

"My mother always said I wasn't too bright."

"Twenty thousand," she said. "That's my top offer."

"No alternatives?" he asked as he sat down.

"Only one." She looked at him steadily. "The only people that know you came here tonight are my servants."

"And they won't talk."

"You catch on very quickly."

A subtle transfiguration seemed to have taken place on her beautiful oval face as though it had come from deep within her. It was as though the compound of Spanish and Indian blood had split apart into its separate components, and now she seemed to be pure Indio looking at Lee through her great black eyes.

"Your son would gain much by going back to the Broken Bow with me," argued Lee.

"I can give him almost as much."

"It is his right."

"After eighteen years!" she cried with scorn. "Why now? For all those years, he never once concerned himself about his son or me. Why now?"

"His conscience may be bothering him."

"No," she said with conviction. "There is more to it than that. You may as well tell me the full truth."

There was someone close by, thought Lee. Probably behind any, or all, of the three doors that opened into the room. "You know the Dakins," he said.

"The faithful and devout," she sneered.

"No longer, señora. The old man is failing. Marsh Dakin installed his sister, Stella, as Bowman's housekeeper. I think you can guess the rest."

"The old ram couldn't resist getting into bed with her. So now she's probably claiming that she should inherit the Broken Bow because she is his common-law wife."

"She may be able to make it stick," said Lee.

"So now Duke is fighting back the only way he can—by trying to resurrect his long-lost bastard son to take his place. So help me God! Not because he loves the boy as his son, but because he cannot bear to see anyone take over the Broken Bow! Further, I am not such a fool as not to know that the Dakins would do anything to stop you from bringing Bart, *if* he still lives, back to the Broken Bow. I know those people! Marsh Dakin abandoned my son and me at Cinco Castillos."

Lee had no argument about that.

"They thought we both died there," continued Doña Luz. "That was where they made their great mistake. They should have made sure of me."

"But you never had any intention of returning to the Broken Bow," intimated Lee.

"I had learned to hate that old man."

"Because he would not marry you."

She looked into the fire. "I was thinking only of the boy."

Lee laughed. "You wanted that ring of legality on your finger—the circlet of respectability, and a name for your son. Why? Because you are a mixed blood. A *genizaro! And so was the boy.* No matter how much Anglo blood the old man had pumped into him, the boy still had the so-called taint of mixed blood, and he always will, and you can't do a damned thing about it!"

She turned her head slowly. There was pure black hate in her great eyes. "I know why you said that. To make my pride force me to tell you where my son is. You've failed."

"What difference can it possibly make now?" argued Lee. "The Broken Bow can be his. He can be a man in his own right, not waiting on his monthly payment from his mother. Money from a woman he possibly may not know, or what she is either."

"You have much insight," she admitted.

"He knows how you earned the money to pay for his ransom?"

"If you found him, would you tell him?"

"Not if you tell me where he is. I can find him if he is alive, with or without your help. If you don't tell me where he is, I can pay you off in dirty coin by telling him about you and your establishment."

"You wouldn't do that!"

"Try me, señora."

She stood up and reached for a tapestry bell pull.

"Wait," said Lee quietly.

She turned and looked down at the knife in his hand. "You'd never get out of this house alive," she warned.

"I can damned well try. Please walk ahead of me." He opened the door that led into the shadowed patio. A man moved in the shadows. "Tell him to stay where he is," ordered Lee. She held out a warning hand to the man. "Walk into the *sala*," said Lee. She walked to the *sala* door and opened it. A lamp guttered in the hall. The *zaguán* door showed with the great bar across it.

The woman whirled, thrusting her right hand inside the bosom of her dress. Lee thrust his left hand in after her hand and felt the soft, full warmth of her breasts and also the metal and wood of a derringer warmed by her flesh. "I should have known," he said. He pulled out the derringer and dropped it into a pocket. He looked down into her beautiful oval face and drew her close against his hard body, pressing his dry, sun-cracked lips against the soft, moist velvet of her lips.

He heard the soft step behind him. He shoved the woman aside and whirled to drive out a left jab that caught the man on the jaw and dropped him to the floor. His pistol clattered on the tiles. Two more men rushed into the *sala*. Lee thrust the woman between himself and the two men. She snatched up the dropped pistol. He flipped up the door bar and kicked open one of the doors. He ran out into the darkened road.

The rifle flashed from the shadowed brush across the road. Something slapped Lee alongside the head, and as he went down, he caught a second's glimpse of the woman firing across the road into the gunsmoke wreathing through the brush. His face struck the hard road, and he knew no more.

Boots thudded in the brush.

"Let him run," said the woman. She looked down at Lee. "Is he dead?"

One of the men knelt beside Lee. "He's alive," he reported. "He's just been creased. Half an inch more, and he would have been killed."

"Ramón, you and Jesus get him into the house. José, kick dust over that blood on the road and then come with me." She walked toward the far side of the road. A huddled figure lay in the brush. José lighted a match. They looked down into the dark face of Nuno Mercado. A blackened hole in the center of his forehead oozed blood and matter. José looked at her in admiration. "Bull's eye," he said.

She shrugged. "Get rid of this carrion tonight. Don't leave any traces." She walked back to the house.

Somewhere in the darkened hills a coyote howled.

thirteen

The aura was subtle, yet insistent—a skillful blend of ex-
pensive perfume, delicate odor of wax candles, fresh linen,
and the feminine scent, half compelling and half repelling.
The hard hand cupped itself under Lee's jaw and raised
his head, turning it a little to one side. "He'll live," the
man said in Spanish. "I've seen wild horses creased like
this for the capturing. They were all right later."

"Creasing will not tame this one," the woman said drily.

"Such men do not die easily," said the man.

Lee opened his eyes. He looked up into the lean, bearded face of the man named Ramón. "Looking at you, I'm
damned sure I'm not in Heaven," he said.

"I told you, Ramón," said the woman.

Lee looked at her. "You shoot fast," he remarked. "Did
you score, Doña Luz?"

She did not reply, but he could read the answer in her
face.

"Who died out there in the brush?" he asked.

"A New Mexican. Dark of skin. Pockmarked. Heavy

mustache. There was a scar on his forehead. The other man was nothing but a shadow in the darkness as he ran."

She jerked her head toward the door, and Ramón left the room. The opened door revealed that it was full daylight outside. She smoothed the coverlet with her graceful, tapered hands. "No one, outside of me and my people, *and* the man who ran off, know that you are here. Some of my people are in town now looking about for him."

"So, you are keeping me here to save my life?"

She filled a glass with brandy and held it out to him. "You could say that, although that is not the only reason."

He took the brandy glass and looked into her enigmatic eyes. "You could have gotten rid of me, and no one would have been the wiser."

"I still think I can convince you of the futility of looking for my son. My offer of twenty thousand dollars still stands."

Lee sipped the brandy. "I have a contract," he replied.

She walked to the door and looked back. "Your life is in my hands, señor. Think it over. You'd be a fool to try and escape, and even if you did, those who tried to kill you will certainly try again. They almost killed you last night. Think that over." She closed the door behind her.

Lee was out of the bed at once. He took two steps, was opened. Ramón and another man came in and lifted swayed sideways, clutched at the table, upset a silver candlestick, and crashed to the floor alongside it. The door Lee into the bed. Ramón pulled the coverlet up about Lee. There was a dark bruise on the side of the New Mexican's face, and Lee had an uncomfortable feeling that he was the man that Lee had dropped to the tiles.

"Is there anything you want?" asked Ramón.

Lee grinned. "My pants and a gun," he replied.

Ramón walked to the door. He looked back once as he followed the other man from the room. "The next time you try to get out of here we won't be so gentle." He closed the door behind himself. The lock clicked as the key was turned from the outside.

The boy Basilio was still with Padre Nicolás. If Doña

Luz found out about him, she might very well take the boy from the old priest and use him to pressure Lee into abandoning his hunt for her son.

"The boy means nothing to you," the mind voice said. "What is he after all? Just a pawn in this dangerous game."

Lee reached over and refilled his brandy glass.

"Take the twenty thousand *and* the woman," suggested the mind voice.

Lee sipped the powerful brandy. He closed his eyes. The beautiful oval face of Doña Luz, studying him thoughtfully, seemed to come through the mists of pain in his aching skull.

Once during that night, the door to the next room softly opened shortly after Lee had called out in pain. The woman came to the side of the bed. She wore a sheer negligee, and her long, dark hair was unbound about her bare shoulders. She placed a soft cool hand on Lee's fevered brow. At the time, he thought it was a dream.

fourteen

"*You should have made sure of him,*" *said Stella Dakin. She* still wore her traveling costume, an outmoded basque coat and a ridiculous hat that sat atop her head supporting a slightly dusty stuffed bird with staring glass eyes.

Cass sat on the hotel bed with his back against the brass headstead and his booted feet planted on the cover. "If it wasn't for that damned woman, we would have had him cold," he complained.

Reata lighted a cigar. He tilted his chair back against the wall. "Who is this woman?" he asked around the cigar.

"Doña Luz," replied Cass. "She runs a combination saloon, gambling hall, and whorehouse. We saw Kershaw riding in her carriage out to her big *casa* on the Taos Road. We waited in the brush across the road, like I said. Kershaw came bustin' through the door in one helluva hurry. I got in one shot and dropped him, but the woman fired and dropped Nuno. When I came back, I couldn't find Nuno's body. Kershaw's body was gone too."

"You should have stayed and shot it out!" snapped Stella.

"There was three men come outa that *casa!*" yelled back Cass. "You think I wanted to get shot to doll rags?"

"It would have been all right with me," she said coldly. "You've made a botch out of this, Cass. Both Chisos and Nuno are dead, and Kershaw is still loose."

"He's dead!" yelled Cass. "I don't miss with the long gun."

"You don't know for sure," said Reata.

"What happened to the cholo kid he brought here to Santa Fe?" asked Stella.

"While I was waitin' for you and Reata to get here, I poked about the town asking a few questions. When Kershaw reached here, he took the kid to a chapel out near the hills and left the kid with an old padre out there—name of Padre Nicolás. The kid is still there."

"Go get him," ordered Stella.

"Why?"

Stella took off her hat. "Because we might be able to use him to get to Kershaw, if Kershaw is still alive. Reata, you'd better go along so Cass can't botch this deal up, like he's done everything else."

Reata dropped his chair to the floor and stood up. "Should we bring the kid here?"

She nodded as she took off her coat. "I'm going to get some sleep. That damned train ride wore me out."

Reata closed the door behind himself. He looked at Cass. "Jesus, but she's riled. She's been that way ever since she got the telegram from you. She chewed out Sid for not going along with you like Marsh told him to."

"Sid is too goddamned lazy," said Cass.

"Maybe so, but he'd have never let Kershaw get this far."

They walked together to the stairs. "I still can't believe Kershaw beat Chisos to the draw," said Reata.

"He never done it! He tricked Chisos. He don't fight fair!"

Reata looked sideways at the stupid face of the big

man. "Why should he in this business? It's the results that count. So, Chisos is dead, and if Kershaw is dead like you claim he is, you didn't exactly give him a fair shake by drygulching him."

"That's different!" snapped Cass.

Reata shook his head as he walked down the stairs and into the lobby. "Cass," he said quietly, "sometimes I can't believe you."

They stopped outside the hotel while Cass rolled a cigarette. Cass lit the quirly. "Nuno claimed he knew one of us would not return from the north," he said quietly.

"So? It's him that's dead, ain't it?"

Cass nodded. He looked across the plaza as though seeking something in the shadows on the far side of it. "He always claimed Kershaw wasn't human. He said he could do things no other living man could do."

Reata grinned around his cigar.

It was as though Cass was talking to himself. "He crossed the waterless desert northeast from Tinaja del Muerto in the furnace heat to reach North Pass. He got into the Broken Bow without being seen by any of us, and he got out the same way. He reached Cinco Castillos and got away right under our noses. He went into them mountains full of Mescaleros and came out alive. He killed Chisos Martin, the fastest man with a cutter I've ever seen. He got drinkin' water out of a salt *laguna*—something I don't think Moses himself coulda done by striking the ground with his staff. He got north to Santa Fe without us catching him, and we rode two horses to death."

"Luck," said Reata.

Cass shook his head.

"What makes you think it ain't?"

"Reata, you know I'm as good a man with the long gun as you've ever seen. I couldn't have missed him the other night. It wasn't possible. I *know* I put a bullet into his *cabeza*."

"I believe you, Cass."

"Only one thing," said Cass slowly. "Supposin' he was taken into that woman's *casa* on the Taos Road? Supposin' he's still walkin' around?"

"Well he is, or he ain't." Reata looked quickly at Cass as he caught the full meaning of what the big man had said. "For Christ's sake!" he rapped out. "You're talkin' like a superstitious cholo now! He's either dead, or he ain't; and if he is, he ain't doin' any walkin' around! Not on this earth, he ain't! Now come on! I'll buy the liquor. We can get the kid later."

Jesus stepped out of a doorway beside the hotel as Reata and Cass walked toward a saloon. "It's him, Les," he said over his shoulder. "That's the big man who shot at Kershaw night before last. The other one is the man who came up from the train at Lamy on the stagecoach, along with the woman who wears the dead bird on her head."

"Who's the kid they were talking about?"

Jesus shrugged. "I know old Padre Nicolás," he said. "He takes care of a little chapel out near the hills. No one ever goes in there anymore. While they're drinking, you've just got time to get back to Doña Luz and ask her what we should do. I'll keep an eye on those two men. I need a drink or two myself." He grinned.

Les mounted his horse and rode off down a side street. Jesus fashioned a cigarette and walked into the hotel lobby. "I'm looking for a woman who registered here tonight," he said to the desk clerk.

"Only one woman registered here tonight," said the clerk. He turned the register. "See here? Stella Dakin, Running MB."

"That isn't her. Where is the Running MB?"

The clerk shrugged. "Broken Bow country, I think. Down south of the Rio Penasco and west of the Pecos."

Jesus walked outside and headed for the saloon.

Reata softly opened the chapel door. The warm candle-scented air blew about him and Cass. The slight bowed figure of the padre knelt before the altar. There was a much smaller figure beside the padre, aping his posture of bowed head and clasped hands. There was no one else in the chapel.

The two Anglos walked softly up the nave aisle. The

soft, flickering candlelight reflected from the great reredos behind the altar and from the flesh and blood tones of the agonized Christ on his cross.

Basilio slowly turned his head and looked up into the two hard faces shadowed under the wide hat brims. "This is the house of God, señores," he piped. "We are at prayer."

"Get up, kid," said Reata. "We're going to take you to your mother."

"I have no mother, señor."

Reata yanked the kid to his feet. He jerked his head toward the padre. "Start asking your questions, Cass," he said.

Cass reached out with a huge hand and touched the shoulder of Padre Nicolás. The old man fell slowly sideways and lay still. Cass knelt and looked into the waxlike face. "He's dead," he said over his shoulder.

The footsteps of Reata and Basilio echoed in the empty chapel. The door closed behind them.

Cass stood up and looked down at the dead priest. He could not take his eyes from the composed and peaceful face of the old man. It was deathly quiet in the chapel. The candle flames stood straight up in the draftless air. The light of the candles reflected from the staring eyes of the old priest, and they were looking directly up at Cass Dakin. The memory of another old man who had died under his fist came back to Cass. He too had stared up at Cass in the same accusing way. Cass looked quickly at the agonized face of the Christ. The carved eyes seemed to be staring at him too.

Suddenly there seemed to be a faint murmuring of accusing voices in the shadowed corners of the chapel and in the dark choir loft. Cass turned on a heel and ran from the chapel. He slammed the door behind him and fell over a body lying across the steps. He was half stunned. He sat up and wiped the blood from his face. He lighted a match and looked into the pale face of Reata. Reata's hat had fallen off and a large lump, tinged with blood showed on the side of his head. He was still alive.

Cass got to his feet and looked quickly about. "Kid?" he called out. There was no answer. The narrow street was deserted.

fifteen

Lee heard the zaguán *door slam shut, followed by the rattling* of hoofs and the grinding of wheels on the tiles. The door bar was dropped into place. He heard the faint murmuring of voices. Footsteps sounded outside, and the door was unlocked. Doña Luz walked in, removing her rebozo from over her fine tortoiseshell comb and dark hair.

Lee filled two wineglasses. "You're late tonight," he said.

She nodded. "There was some business to attend to." She sat down in the chair opposite to his. He made a cigarette and reached over to place it between her full lips. He lit it for her as she bent forward, and he had a hard time keeping his eyes on hers with the daring decolletage she affected. He leaned back and shaped a cigarette for himself. "Damned if I'm not beginning to like it here, Doña Luz," he said.

"There are some people who have come here from the south. A man and a woman. They met with the man who managed to escape the other night. She is Stella Dakin. He is known as Reata. I did not know either of them in my time at the Broken Bow."

"They are bringing in the first-line troops," he said.

"A woman?" she asked, arching her eyebrows.

"The deadly species," he said. "Do you suppose they know who you really are?"

She shrugged. "I doubt it." She smiled a little. "You are probably the only person here in Santa Fe who knows who I really am."

"You forget Padre Nicolás."

"He died this evening," she said.

"Suddenly I feel very alone."

"Your friends from the south are not sure that you are alive. In fact, the only people that *do* know you are alive are myself and my servants."

Lee inspected his cigarette as though he had never seen one before. "It's not a very comforting thought."

"Have you reconsidered my offer?"

"I have. The answer is the same."

"You could agree and take the twenty thousand and continue hunting for my son, could you not?"

"I don't do business that way." He refilled her wineglass. "You must think I am a fool."

She shook her head. "Obstinate, but not a fool. You haven't asked me about the small boy Basilio you left with Padre Nicolás."

Lee studied her. "What about him?" he asked.

She walked to the door and opened it. "Send in the boy!" she called out. The sober little face of Basilio Melgosa appeared in the doorway. She closed the door behind him and watched him run to Lee with outstretched arms. Lee gathered up the small figure.

"Very touching," she drily commented.

"Are you all right, *muchacho?*" he asked.

"I am fine," replied Basilio.

Lee looked over Basilio's dark head at the woman. "You play dirty," he said.

"Bart was about that age and size when we reached

Cinco Castillos," she said quietly. Her great eyes studied Lee. "Can you see now why I did what I had to do to get him back?"

"But you didn't really get him back at all."

There was sudden deep pain within her eyes. She looked quickly away from him. "At least he did not go back to his father," she said.

"So now neither one of you has him."

"It is enough for me that his father does not have him!" she cried.

"How did you find the boy?"

"Those people went to the chapel to get him. I was told they were going there. I didn't know who the boy was. My men took him away from them and brought him here."

"What happens now to the boy?"

She smiled confidently. *"That,* is up to *you.*"

"You seem to hold all the aces."

"I am a professional," she countered.

"Has it ever occurred to you that Duke Bowman is a dying man and that if Bart does not go there to take his rightful inheritance, it will likely pass into the hands of the Dakins?"

"The place means nothing to me! I hated it when I was there, and I hate it now!"

He studied her. "That's not true. How many years do you think you can get away with sending money to your son, wherever he is, without him trying to find out who you really are? He's a grown man now, not a boy. He can't go on through life like that. He has to make his own way. What better way than for him to take his place at the Broken Bow? In time, he could send for you, Doña Luz."

"Never!"

Lee shrugged. "I still intend to find him."

"Have you forgotten that I hold all the aces?"

He studied her. "If you intended to kill me, Doña Luz, you would never have allowed me to regain consciousness, nor stay here alive in this fine *casa* of yours."

She threw her cigarette into the fireplace. "Make me another," she said. She watched his skillful fingers mold the cigarette. "I've kept you alive because I think it might be interesting to tame you."

He placed the cigarette between her lips. "That can work both ways between a woman like yourself and a man like me." Take the twenty thousand, *and* the woman—the thought coursed through his mind.

"I could use a man like you in my business," she suggested.

"As a partner?"

"Hardly. Perhaps after a time."

"So you'd use me as a bartender, a stool pigeon, a shill, or a bouncer? Or perhaps as a pimp?"

She laughed delightedly. "No! But, we'd make a good team, Lee Kershaw. I don't like to admit it, but I need a *man.*"

"Santa Fe is full of men."

"None like you."

"I want to go home," said Basilio.

She looked down at him. He smiled winningly at her.

"And what about him?" asked Lee.

"We can send him home," Doña Luz suggested. "Where does he live?"

"A small village near Las Trampas. His people are *Penitentes.* His great-uncle is *Hermano Mayor* there."

Her eyes narrowed. "Sostenes Melgosa?"

Lee nodded. "You knew that village. Candelario Melgosa took you there after Cinco Castillos."

"I was only there a little while."

"There are *genizaros* there, Doña Luz."

"My people are from the *Valle de Lagrimas.*"

Lee shook his head. "Your people are of the north. Perhaps from the very village where Basilio lived."

She walked to the door. "Jesus!" she called out as she opened it. "Come and get the boy. Feed him and put him to bed. Do not let him get out of this house. You understand?"

She closed the door after Jesus came for the boy. She looked at Lee. "Do you always know too much about people?"

"It is my business."

"A dangerous business."

He shrugged. "I get paid well," he countered.

"You have until tomorrow to accept my final offer."

He looked up at her. "You're very tired," he suggested. "How long can you keep on in the role of Doña Luz, Rafaela Diaz?"

"Tomorrow is Sunday," she said quietly. "A day of rest for me and a day of decision for you. The wise man takes the bird in hand." She waved a hand toward the door. "Out there is death for you. Here there is security."

"And domination by a woman," added Lee drily.

He refilled her glass. "I thought I had a dream the other night," he said. "There was a fever in me, and I cried out in pain. A woman came to me in the darkness and cooled my fever with a healing hand." He looked into her dark eyes. "But it must have been a dream."

She drained her glass and walked to the door that opened into her room. "Good night, señor. Always remember that it is easy for me to hear you cry out in here." She closed the door behind herself. The key did not click in the lock.

Lee blew out the candles and sat in the chair for a long time looking into the shifting, weaving kaleidoscope of color in the embers of the fireplace.

The clock struck half past one. Lee emptied his wineglass and threw his cigarette butt into the embers. He walked to the bed and called out as though caught again in the fever. He lay down on the wide bed.

The door softly opened. She came quickly and silently across the room to place a cool hand on his forehead. Her long dark hair brushed his chest and face. He drew her down to him and pressed his mouth hard against hers. She did not struggle. "The fever seems to have left," she murmured as he withdrew his lips from hers.

"It's not the same one," he said. "Can you cure the other one?" She placed her cool hands on each side of his face.

"Remember that you are my prisoner," she reminded him, "and that I am responsible for your health."

She was a woman who had known many different men in her lifetime since the age of fifteen when Duke Bowman had bulled her, as he called it. Now Lee found out how she had been so successful in her earlier profession. She gave Lee the impression that he was the only one who had been able to satisfy her, and yet he wasn't even sure that was so. He'd never admit it to her, but he had never known a woman quite like Rafaela Diaz.

She lay quietly beside him, resting her head against his shoulder with the faint glowing of her cigarette tip alternately lighting and shadowing her oval face. The soft light glistened from the beads of perspiration on her full breasts. "You will take my offer then?" she asked.

He nodded. "Of course. But you can keep the twenty thousand."

She laughed. "How generous! But then, by staying with me, you'll stand to gain a great deal more than that cold money, my heart."

He passed a hand over her full body. "I've got the general idea," he admitted.

The clock struck half past two.

"Bart lives in the same small village where I sent him years ago," she said suddenly. "The one near Las Trampas, which Basilio calls his home."

"Why tell me now?"

She shrugged. "You'll find out soon enough. He lives with an uncle of mine, Gaspar Diaz. He is called Innocencio Diaz. He has been raised as a *Penitente*."

"Then thank God he does not know how his mother lives."

"He never will," she said.

He got up and refilled the wineglasses. He looked down at her. Candelario Melgosa had not mentioned Bart living in his village, but then maybe the old man had been sworn to secrecy by Rafaela Diaz. He held the glass to her full lips, and she drank greedily. He downed his wine and sat down on the edge of the bed, passing his strong hard hands up and down her body.

"So soon again, my heart?" she murmured.

"Look at me, my life," he said. She turned her lovely face toward him. His right cross caught her jaw at exactly the right angle. She lay still.

Lee stood up. He took a drink straight from the decanter and looked down at her body in the dimness. *"Madre mia,"* he breathed regretfully. He tied her ankles and wrists together with strips of her negligee and then gagged her.

He walked into the room in which she had slept while he had occupied her room. His clothing was in a wardrobe. His Colt was in a locked drawer which he had to pry open. He felt within his pockets and found the silver button and the photograph. Even his tobacco makings were in a pocket. He checked the Colt to find it loaded.

Lee rummaged through a desk. He found an address book which he slipped into a pocket. He could not find any letters. He eased open the outer door and looked into the dark patio. It seemed empty of life.

He found Basilio sound asleep in a small room. He placed a hand over the boy's mouth to awaken him. *"Muchacho,"* he whispered. "We play a game, eh? Do not make a sound."

The boy shook his head. "I don't like it here," he whispered.

"Neither do I," agreed Lee. He carried Basilio from the room.

A tiny spot of flame arced out into the center of the patio and exploded into a shower of sparks as the cigarette butt struck the tiles. Lee faded into the deep shadows. Footsteps sounded near the entrance to the *sala.*

Lee climbed to the flat roof and carried the boy across it. He hung by one arm from the parapeted roof and dropped lightly into the shrubbery.

Reata raised his head from the shelter of the brush across the road from the great casa of Doña Luz. Nothing moved. The night was graveyard still under the flickering stars.

The barrel of a Colt was laid hard and true—right across the side of Reata's head just between the top of the right ear and the brim of the hat. Reata went down silently. Boots grated softly on the hard ground in the shadowed brush.

The chapel was dark and still when Lee reached it. He saddled the dun within the stable and withdrew the Winchester from the saddle scabbard to check the loads. He led the dun from the stable. Swiftly he walked inside the dark and empty chapel. He lit a candle for the repose of the soul of Padre Nicolás and then closed the door behind himself. In a little while, hoofbeats sounded on the road that led north toward Las Trampas.

sixteen

The moonlight was bright on the piñon-dotted hills that sloped away on either side of the narrow road leading into a narrow gutted canyon. There was no wind to move the dark piñons and the thorned brush that encroached on the sides of the road. The only sign of life in the dreamlike landscape was a straight line of smoke, which rose from the chimney of the first of the houses that lined the road in the gut of the canyon.

Lee looked down at Basilio. "Is this your home, boy?"

"Yes—home," said Basilio happily.

Lee shrugged. Any place would be home to Basilio if it pleased Lee.

The country was isolated, remote, far from the better traveled roads north of Santa Fe and south from Taos. It was the home and refuge of *La Hermandad de Nuestro Padre Jesus* and had been so since the sixteenth and seventeenth centuries. The inhabitants were descendants of the first Spanish colonials and even now their daily life and customs were almost the same as those of the sixteenth century Spanish peasants. So was their religion and their brotherhood of *Penitentes,* preserved as though in a dusty museum case.

"He lives with an uncle of mine, Gaspar Diaz. He is called Innocencio Diaz. He has been raised as a *Penitente,*" Doña Luz had told Lee.

"I want to go home," said Basilio.

He too was of *Penitente* blood, the great-grandson of Candelario Melgosa, the *Enfermero* of the Brotherhood, and the great-nephew of Sostenes Melgosa, the *Hermano Mayor*—the highest elected official of the Brotherhood.

"*Largate! Largate!*" the mind voice warned Lee. "Go away."

The hoofs of the dun clattered on the sharp-edged stones, or *pedernales* of the road and awoke the sleeping echoes in the dreamlike hills. There was a windowless, coffin-shaped building on a knoll to the left, just before the first houses of the village. At the tip of the steeply pitched roof of the *morada,* the whitewashed cross shone in the moonlight as though fashioned of long-bleached bones. In front of the *morada,* there was another whitewashed cross with laths placed on either side from the tip of the upright to the tips of the arms, and with other laths placed from the tips of the arms down to the sides of the upright. It formed a square set on one point and quartered by the upright and crosspiece. Placed within the four equilateral triangles formed by the laths and the parts of the cross were other, smaller crosses, two to each triangle; and on the upper slanting parts of the diagonal laths, there were similar crosses. Lying on the barren ground in front of this ornate cross were other crosses, fashioned of immensely heavy beams; these were carried by penitent brothers during the Holy Week rites of the Brotherhood.

"*Largate!*" a harsh voice suddenly called out.

Lee reined in the dun. A man walked from the thick brush into the center of the road in front of Lee. He held a rifle in his brown hands. "*Largate!*" he repeated.

Something made Lee turn his head. The road was filled from side to side and five men deep with other villagers. Some of them reached down to pick up the murderous, razor-edged flint stones, the *pedernales*. These were the

stones used by the *Penitente Sangrador,* or *Picador,* the
Blood Letter or Pricker, to inflict the seal of the Brotherhood—three horizontal and three vertical gashes across
the naked backs of the novices of the *Hermanos de
Sangre,* or Brothers of Blood.

The first stone struck the back of Lee's left hand and instantly drew forth the bright blood. "Wait!" yelled Lee.
He held up the boy. "I have brought the boy Basilio Melgosa home to his great-uncle, the *Hermano Mayor* Sostenes Melgosa!" Before God, thought Lee, suppose, just
suppose now that this was *not* the village of the Melgosas.

"Wait here," ordered the sentry. He walked to the first
house on the right-hand side of the street. An old man
came to the door and then walked slowly up the center of
the road toward Lee.

Lee glanced back at the silent watching figures. They
could batter him to death in minutes if they wished. No
one in the outside world would be any the wiser if they did
so. His body would never be found. If anyone came looking for him, they would learn nothing. These people were
a world apart from nineteenth century New Mexico Territory; a closed society for over three hundred years.

The man was old. His hair under the sides of his ancient
felt sombrero was as white as the snow-capped tips of the
neighboring Sangre de Cristo Mountains in the winter
time. "Who asks for Sostenes Melgosa?" he asked.

"I do," replied Lee. "I have brought home Basilio Melgosa."

"Where is his great-grandfather, my brother, Candelario?"

"He is dead, senor," replied Lee. He held up the boy.
"See? Here is little Basilio."

The old man raised his head. The moonlight fell upon
his dried apple of a face; his eyes were like pools of milk.

"Christ's blood!" said Lee in a low voice. He slewed his
eyes sideways wondering how far he'd make it off the road
into the thorned brush before a murderous flight of *pedernales* brought him down.

"Send the boy to me, señor," said the blind old man.

Lee let the boy down onto the road. He ran with outstretched arms to the old man. The man spoke softly to the boy and then looked over Basilio's head toward Lee. "You are welcome here, señor," he said. "My house is your house."

Lee passed his bloody left hand across his eyes. *"Mil gracias,"* he said.

"You know of the Brotherhood, I think," said Sostenes.

Lee glanced back over his shoulder. The road was empty. "Some," admitted Lee.

"You happened to come here at a time when strangers are not welcome."

"It was not intentional, *Hermano Mayor*. I came here to bring back the boy, not to stare at your rites. Your beliefs are your own. I honor them as I know you would mine."

The old man bowed his head. "You do not have to leave tonight. There is room for you and the boy in my house this night. But it would be better if you left by daylight tomorrow."

Lee dismounted and led the tired dun toward the old man. Together he, Basilio, and Sostenes walked toward the house. "There is another reason you have come here?" questioned Sostenes.

"I am looking for a man. But I would have brought the boy back in any case. It is a coincidence that the man lives here in your village. His name is Innocencio Diaz."

"You are a man of the law?"

"No. I was hired to find him for his own good."

"Who hired you?"

"His father."

"That is very strange, for his father is long dead."

"That is not so," said Lee. "But, in any case, his mother said he lived here."

"His mother is also dead."

Lee opened and then closed his mouth. Perhaps Rafaela Diaz wanted it that way. "I'd like to see him," he said.

They stopped in front of the house. "Later I will tell you about him," said Sostenes. The milk-white eyes looked at Lee almost as though the old man could actually see him. "You do not lie to me when you tell me you are not from the law?"

"I am not from the law," repeated Lee.

"There is a corral behind this house. Put your horse there. There is food in the house to which you are welcome. There are *colchones* for your bed. Now, listen to me: Once you go into my house tonight, do not come out of it again. Do not look from the windows or the door, no matter what happens. If you do, I will not be responsible for what happens to you. Do you understand?"

"I understand."

Sostenes nodded. *"Bueno!* And now, good night, senor."

Lee watched the old man walk up the street where the canyon curved away out of sight.

Once again it seemed like a dream world. It was as though Lee Kershaw had been spirited back in time to sixteenth century New Mexico. There was no wind; there was no movement of any kind; there was no sound to break the deathlike quiet of the village and the surrounding hills. The coffin-shaped *morada* squatted in the moonlight. The crosses shone ghastly white like well-polished bones.

Lee unsaddled the tired dun. Now and again, he would look quickly over his shoulder as though he felt someone were watching him, but he never saw anyone. He knew they were out there nevertheless. He went into the little house and lit a lamp. Basilio was sound asleep on the *colchones,* or bed mattresses, spread on the hard-packed dirt floor.

Lee was not hungry. His skull ached where the bullet had creased it. He made a cigarette. Slowly he raised his head. A faint piping sound, almost indistinguishable, seemed to drift down the canyon, and then it died away.

He lit the cigarette. The sound came again, this time accompanied by a strident clacking sound. Lee threw the cigarette into the beehive fireplace. He blew out the lamp. He catfooted to one of the small front windows and eased open one of the shutters until it caught on the loose catch, leaving a gap of perhaps an inch. He peered up the moonlit street of the village toward the bend in the canyon where the shadows met the moonlight on the whitish road in a sharp line of demarcation, black-on-white.

The sound came closer; the thin, reedy piping and the crisp rattling sound of the *matraca*. Piping, in the villages of the Brotherhood, was never done for pleasure, but only during their rites. The sound now echoed from the narrow sides of the canyon.

Sostenes Melgosa appeared in the moonlight, walking in the center of the street and striking the ground at every second step with an iron-shod staff. Behind him came a man with bent head, reading prayers aloud from a copybook. The *Pitero,* or Piper, was next, accompanied by a man plying the *matraca* or clacker. The next man in the procession was bent over, walking deliberately on the razor-edged *pedernales* with his bare feet which left bloody footprints on the moonlit ground. His head was shrouded in a black hood, and he was naked from the waist up, wearing only short white trousers. In his strong brown hands, he held a *disciplina,* a whip of leather thongs embellished with tight knots, shards of glass, and bits of barbed wire. First the *disciplina* was swung over the right shoulder and then the left, in perfect cadence with the measured footsteps of the procession and the rhythm of the pipe and clacker. As the *disciplina* slashed home against the small of the man's naked back, bright droplets of blood flew out on both sides to speckle the ground. Behind the penitent was a man—a *Hermano de Luz,* a Brother of the Light, whose duty was to see that the penitent did not stint in the force of his blows.

"*Yo penitente pecador!*" cried out the penitent.

"I, a repentant sinner," translated Lee to himself.

Two more penitents appeared, accompanied by a *Hermano de Luz.* One of them swung a *disciplina* of barbed chain link, and the other one used one of the stripped fibers of the yucca plant. Each of them drew blood equally well. The glittering droplets of blood spattered in the moonlight. Now and again, one of the penitents would stagger in his stride from the savage force of the blows he was administering to himself. The eerie whistling of the pipe and the monotonous clacking of the *matraca* was in time with the crying of the penitents: *"Yo penitente pecador! Yo penitente pecador! Yo penitente pecador!"*

Six men appeared in the moonlight. A crudely made casket without a top was balanced on their shoulders. Lee could just make out the form within the casket. It was a man of slight build.

The strange and eerie funeral procession walked up the slope to the *morada* and into it. The door slammed shut, and the thick windowless walls cut off any sound from within.

The sudden silence was startling. It was as though there had been a dream procession. But the dark spots of blood flecking the light-colored road were proof enough that a *Penitente* procession had passed.

"Why at night?" said Lee aloud.

Lee smoked a cigarette, watching the *morada*, but no one appeared at the door. He lay down on the *colchones*. The memory of the cry *"Largate!"*, coupled with the recollection of the murderous *pedernales*, was enough to keep Lee within doors that moonlit night.

Lee opened his eyes. He got up and walked to the window. The dying moonlight slanted down into the canyon and touched the *morada*. The door gaped open. No sound came from within. There was no sign of life anywhere near it.

Lee left the house by the back door. He circled through the shadows and approached the *morada* from the rear. He walked on the shadowed side to the front of it. He flattened himself against the front wall and looked back over his shoulder into the dark interior. The waxy odor of candles and lamp oil came to him. He stepped inside quickly and closed the door behind himself. It was pitch black, and it seemed to him that the air within the *morada* was breathing slowly and heavily.

He lit a match. He looked into a miniature skull face, shrouded in a black shawl. It was Doña Sebastiana, the Angel of Death, seated on her heavy wooden cart whose wheels would not turn—the *Carreta de la Muerte*. The cart was usually dragged by several pairs of Brothers by means of horsehair ropes bound about their chests and sometimes around their throats. In her ugly, bony little hands, she held a tiny bow with an arrow nocked to the string, ready to shoot. The light of the match glittered from her deepset eye sockets, and it seemed to Lee that she had a speculative look in them.

He walked to the raised dais at the other end of the *morada* and risked lighting one of the candles. The altar cloth was black and decorated with finely embroidered skulls and crossbones. There were some crude, brightly painted *santos* on the altar, mingled in among several human skulls and a cross mounted on three steps. Lee surveyed the low-ceilinged room. The whitewashed walls were splattered with blood, some long dried, and some still fresh from that very night.

Lee searched about the altar. The Brotherhood kept records of their members, and Lee wanted to know when Innocencio Diaz had been born, and where; and when he had joined the Brotherhood as a *novio* to spend his five years as a penitent, or Brother of Blood, before he could be elevated to a Brother of Light. There were no records to be found within the *morada*.

Lee looked quickly over his shoulder. The candle dimly lit the altar area and the rear of the *morada*. Beyond the flickering pool of soft light were the shadows. Once he thought he saw someone, or *something,* moving stealthily along the blood-splattered wall, and his hand dropped to his Colt. He narrowed his eyes and raised the candle. There was no one there.

Lee blew out the candle and catfooted to the door, resisting an urge to rip open the door and get the hell out of there—*now!*

He eased the door open and slipped around to the shadowed side of the *morada*. He raised his head, thinking he had heard something beyond the ridge. He crossed the moonlit road, got his field glasses, and ghosted through the thorned brush and up the steep side of the ridge, going to ground just below the crest.

Lee focused the glasses on a group of men standing in a cleared area surrounded by the murderous thorned bush. A hole shaped like a grave was in the center of the clearing. The lidless coffin stood beside the grave with the shrouded figure of the dead person plainly visible in the moonlight. As Lee watched, the body was taken from the coffin and the shroud was stripped from it. The fine German lens picked out the emaciated face of a young man, perhaps twenty-five years old. The body was lowered into the grave without the coffin.

One man picked up a heavy rock and slammed it down with his full strength on top of the body. Other mourners did the same, and Lee could plainly hear the heavy thudding of the rocks against the gaunt body. Earth was shoveled back into the grave. Lee looked down the ridge behind himself. The village dreamed in the dying moonlight. There was not a sign of life anywhere within it.

Lee turned to look down at the grave. He narrowed his eyes. The clearing had vanished. The whole area was evenly covered with thorned brush. The Brothers were now walking rapidly toward the ridge. Lee wasted no time. He worked his way swiftly down the treacherous slope and through the ripping, tearing thorns. He looked back from the rear door of Sostenes Melgosa's house. A conical hat was just showing above the ridge. He closed the door behind himself and felt the hot sweat course down his body. He lay down on the *colchones*.

It was very quiet. There was no wind.

Sandals husked in the street. A man coughed. Then it was quiet again.

The front door was opened slowly. Footsteps grated on the dirt floor. A hand was gently placed against Lee's sweating forehead. The hand was lowered and placed over his thudding heart. The hand was withdrawn. Sandals husked on the floor. "He sleeps quietly, my brothers," announced Sostenes Melgosa. "He has not been out of this house. Good night to you all." The door was closed.

"How much did you see?" asked Sostenes from beside the bed.

Lee sat up. "Only a burial," he honestly replied.

"That was too much."

"I came here to find Innocencio Diaz. I haven't much time. I can't find him while lying here on your *colchones*."

"I told you I would tell you about him."

Lee rolled two cigarettes. He placed one between the old man's lips and lit it and his own. "Where is he, *viejo?*" he asked.

"If you saw the burial, you saw Innocencio."

"One of the mourners?"

Sostenes shook his head. "He sleeps," he said.

The thudding of the heavy rocks on the emaciated young body came back to haunt Lee. "He is dead?" asked Lee.

"He sleeps," repeated Sostenes.

"But why all the mystery? Why at night?"

"The Church recently prohibited cross carrying and flagellation in public. We have been condemned for our disregard of the proper authority of the Church. But that is no concern of yours. It merely explains why we conducted a burial this night."

"You explain the reason for performing your rites at night, but you have not explained the secret burial of Innocencio Diaz."

"I am coming to that. You know, of course, that we practice our rites during Holy Week. It is a great honor for one among the Brotherhood to be chosen as the Cristo, to be crucified on Good Friday. This year it was Innocencio Diaz who drew the paper pellet with the name Cristo written upon it. A lucky man," Sostenes's voice died away. "I have never been so fortunate," he added after a time.

"Innocencio bore the great cross well. It was a miracle. He was a small man and not very strong, but somehow he managed. He was crucified."

"With nails?" asked Lee incredulously.

"With wet rawhide," replied Sostenes.

Lee looked into the wrinkled face. There was no expression on it.

"The rawhide dries and constricts," continued Sostenes.

"The limbs of the Cristo turned blue. His head fell upon his chest. I, as *Hermano Mayor,* took a blade and made an incision in his side so that the blood gushed forth."

Lee threw his cigarette into the fireplace and quickly shaped another. He placed it between the lips of the old man and lit it. He made another for himself and lit it. "And he died upon the cross, eh, *viejo?*" he asked.

Sostenes shook his head. "Not then, senor. He lived."

"But that was last spring," said Lee.

"He was never the same," explained Sostenes. "If a Brother dies upon the cross enacting the Cristo, his soul is assured of salvation in Heaven. His grave is unmarked and remains secret for one year, and then his relatives are notified. But Innocencio Diaz lived. He could not speak and could hardly walk about. He lasted until yesterday."

"Just my luck," said Lee.

"What does that mean?"

Lee shook his head. *"Nada, nada, viejo.* Go on, please."

The old man shrugged. "We held his wake. The last rites were held in the *morada* tonight. He had requested burial *sin cajon,* without a coffin. We had promised that when he was selected as the Cristo."

Lee nodded. "Well, I hope for his sake, he does have eternal salvation."

"There is no question about that," said Sostenes firmly.

"You say his father and mother are dead?"

"There is no question about that."

"You knew them?"

"Of course. They lived here all their lives."

"He was truly the son of Gaspar Diaz?"

"It is so listed in the book of the Brotherhood."

"I wish I had found that book," said Lee without thinking.

It was very quiet. The milk-white eyes seemed to fix themselves on Lee's face. "There is a woman, one Rafaela Diaz," quickly put in Lee, "who claims that Innocencio was her son, the union of herself and an Anglo by the name of Mark Bowman, who lives in the south."

"I know that woman," said Sostenes. "Gaspar Diaz was her uncle, and Innocencio was her nephew."

"You are sure of this?"

"My wife was the midwife of this village. The mother of Innocencio had great trouble with his birth. I helped my wife in the delivery. The boy lived; the mother died."

"The lying *puta*," said Lee.

"She too had a son. I saw him once, years ago. She had him taken from this place, and we never saw him again. Have you looked for him in Santa Fe?"

"He's not there," replied Lee.

"One might look in Las Vegas," suggested Sostenes.

"What do you know of him?"

Sostenes shrugged. "Nothing."

Lee knew he would get no more out of the old man.

Sostenes looked steadily at Lee, although he could not see him. "My friend," he said quietly, "there are two reasons why you are still alive, and not dead and buried in an unmarked grave this night. First, you brought my great-nephew Basilio back to me. Second, because I lied to my Brothers by saying that you were asleep and that you had not been out of this house. I am not sure they believed me. Even now they may be talking about you. In any case, I must resign as *Hermano Mayor* and do severe penance because I did lie to them."

Lee had a vivid mind picture of a *disciplina* slashing away at the thin, scarred flesh of the old man's back.

"It would be wise for you to leave here tonight—*now*," warned Sostenes. He raised his head as though to listen. "They may be coming soon."

Lee pulled on his boots. He clapped his hat on his head. He buckled on his gunbelt. "One small favor, *viejo*," he said. "If anyone comes looking for me, you did not see me. You know nothing about me, eh?"

"I owe you that."

Lee looked down at the white head in the darkness. *"Mil gracias,"* he said.

"Por nada," murmured the old man. His thoughts seemed to be elsewhere. "Go with God, my friend."

The rear door softly closed. In a little while, the sharp

ears of the old man picked up the soft sound of rawhided
hoofs tapping on the earth beyond the stable. It was very
quiet again. Minutes ticked past. Then the knock Sostenes
expected came on the door. He could no longer hear the
sound of the hoofbeats. He opened the door.

seventeen

The early afternoon sun shone down into the narrow canyon.
Sheep drifted over a brown- and salmon-colored ridge,
which was dotted with dark piñons looking like cloves
stuck in a roasting ham. The faint sound of the *baaing*
drifted down the slopes. Bluish smoke wreathed up from
the chimneys of the adobes and the *jacals*. A burro brayed
harshly from a peeled-pole corral.

Reata reined in his claybank. He narrowed his eyes as
he saw the coffin-shaped *morada*, which squatted on the
knoll overlooking the one road that ran through the village. Reata turned in his saddle and held up a warning
hand to halt the buggy behind them.

Cass Dakin reined in the team. "What's up, Reata?" he
called.

Reata rode back to the buggy. "This is a *Penitente* village," he said in a low voice. "See the *morada?*"

"So?" asked Cass.

"They don't talk much to outsiders, especially Anglos."

Stella raised her head impatiently. The dusty bird on

her hat bobbed up and down. "You can always *buy* information."

"Not from these people, Stell," said Reata.

"Odds are that Kershaw never came this way, Stell," put in Cass.

"Ask somebody," said Stella.

"Like who?" asked Cass.

"That man in the doorway of that second house," replied Stella.

Cass drove the buggy up the road with his saddle horse trotting along behind it. "You there!" Stella called out peremptorily in cowpen Spanish. "We're looking for a man. Tall, broad in the shoulders, reddish hair and beard. Light gray eyes. A big nose. He had a small boy with him by the same of Basilio Melgosa. Have you seen him?"

The man did not move. His dark eyes studied the two big Anglo men with their hard and cold gringo eyes and their lowslung pistols. The strange woman with the dusty bird on her head seemed even harder and colder than the two men.

"I'm talking to you, mister!" shrilled Stella.

There was no answer from the man. He looked at the road behind the buggy.

Reata slowly turned his head. "Jesus," he said softly.

Cass turned to look. "Now you done it, Stella," he accused.

Stella looked back over her shoulder. A dozen sombreroed men stood in the sunlit road from shoulder to shoulder, so that no horseman or vehicle could pass unless they moved. They had no weapons in their hands. They did not need any. The road and its shoulders were littered with sharp *pedernales*.

Iron clicked on the hard road. An old bent man felt his way toward the buggy by striking the road with his ironshod staff. "What is you want?" he asked.

"Who are you?" suspiciously demanded Stella.

"Sostenes Melgosa, at your service," replied Sostenes.

"He has the same name and looks just like the old man you killed back at Cinco Castillos, Cass," said Reata out of the side of his mouth.

"For Christ's sake! Shut up!" snapped Cass. He wiped the cold sweat from his broad face.

"We are looking for a man and a small boy," said Stella.

"I heard you ask for them," said Sostenes.

It was very quiet in the sunlit road. The sheep had drifted over a ridge. Now and then a shadow raced along the road when one of the cloud puffs drifted overhead.

"We have seen no such man," said Sostenes.

Basilio Melgosa ran from his great uncle's house and came to stand beside Sostenes. He thrust a small hand into the gnarled hand of the old man.

"By Jesus," murmured Cass. "It's the kid, Stell."

Stella opened her mouth to speak. "Shut up," warned Reata. "Kershaw has been here all right, but for some reason they won't let on he was. For Christ's sake, don't let on you know that."

"Ask him if this road goes through the mountains," said Stella.

"It does," said Reata. "First to Penasco and then to Tres Ritos and Mora."

"What's beyond that?"

"Las Vegas."

"He couldn't have gotten past us on the road to get back to Santa Fe or to Taos. He's heading for Las Vegas. Drive on, Cass."

Cass picked up the reins. He did not move. The road behind Sostenes had slowly begun to fill with men.

"Is there another way through these mountains to Las Vegas?" asked Stella.

"Back about ten miles," replied Reata.

"We'll lose time going back. Drive on, Cass."

Cass got deliberately out of the buggy. He walked back to his horse. "I'll see you in Las Vegas, Stell," he said. "If you make it."

"What the hell is the matter with you two?" she demanded. "Two big men with guns afraid of a handful of greasers standing in the road without so much as a rock in their hands."

"That's what bothers me," said Reata. "The whole

damned road is covered with *pedernales*. You ever see a man get hit in the face with one of them?"

"It would be better to go back the way you came!" called out Sostenes.

"That's the warning, Stell," said Reata. "You drive up that road, and maybe you'll never be seen again. They're covering up for Kershaw."

"I'll go where I damn well please!" she snapped. "There are laws is this Territory!"

"That is so," agreed Sostenes. He looked toward the angry woman with his milk-white eyes. "But," he quietly added, "we do not see much of the law in this remote area."

How she hated to give in! The thin lines at the side of her lipless mouth drew down, and her curious blue eyes became fixed. "Turn the damned buggy, Cass!" she cried out through her fury.

Cass walked to the head of the team. He turned them around on the road and the shoulder with the hoofs and wheels grating on the *pedernales*. Cass got into the buggy and gathered the reins in his big hands. He slapped the reins on the dusty rumps of the team and drove toward the men who filled the road. They parted, making just enough room for the team and buggy, followed by the mounted man, to pass through them. Their brown faces were enigmatic. Reata whistled slightly off key as he passed them. He looked back from a bend in the road. The road was empty. The tightly shuttered houses seemed to look blindly at the road. The *morada* squatted on its knoll. There was no one in sight. It was like an abandoned village. Reata knew better. He did not look back again.

eighteen

There was something different and unusual about the wind-mill in the center of the Las Vegas Plaza. The night wind that swept through the plaza raised the dust and set something in motion alongside the windmill. Lee kneed the tired dun over toward the windmill. The plaza seemed deserted. Only the lights in the windows of the stores and other buildings surrounding the plaza gave any indication that there were people there.

Lee turned his head as he neared the windmill and found himself looking at a pair of booted feet swaying in the night wind. Lee looked up at the body, its neck and head bent at an awkward angle by the noose that had strangled the life out of it. A whitish rectangle showed on the breast. Lee stood up in the stirrups and snapped a match into flame, shielding it in a cupped hand to read the inscription on the card. "Cold-Deck Jim," Lee read aloud. "He was warned to stay out of Las Vegas. He came back. Our loss is Hell's gain. The Vigilantes." The wind blew out the match.

"Who are you?" the hard voice asked from behind Lee.

Lee turned in the saddle. A dozen men stood in the darkness. The lamplight from a nearby building shone dully on the barrels of rifles and shotguns. "Who are *you?*" asked Lee in return.

"Vigilantes," replied the big man closest to Lee.

"I'm passing through," said Lee.

"Maybe you are, and maybe you aren't."

The wind swayed the lynched body so that the boot toes tapped the small of Lee's back.

"Maybe you didn't read the placard we posted here the other day?" suggested the big man.

"Hardly," said Lee drily. "I just now got here."

The man handed Lee a placard. Lee lighted a match. "Notice to thieves, thugs, fakirs, and bunco-steerers among whom are J.J. Harlin, alias Off Wheeler, Saw Dust Charlie, Wm. Hedges, Billy the Kid, Billy Mullin, Little Jack the Cutter, Pock-marked Kid, Cold-Deck Jim Nelson and his partner The Las Vegas Kid, and about twenty others: if found within the limits of this city after ten o'clock P.M. this night, you will be invited to attend a grand necktie party, the expense of which will be borne by one hundred substantial citizens." He blew out the match. "This hardly refers to me," he said.

"We don't know about that. Who are you?"

"The name is Lee Kershaw."

"The manhunter?"

Lee nodded.

"He's lying, Sam," a bearded man said. "I used to know Lee Kershaw. He was killed down in Sonora last year."

The boot toes tapped insistently at Lee's back.

"Get down off that horse," ordered Sam.

Lee dismounted. A match was snapped into light and held close to Lee's face. "You sure, Kelly?" asked Sam.

"Positive! That ain't Kershaw!"

"Who's marshal here now?" asked Lee.

"Tom Bassett," said Sam.

"He knows me," said Lee.

"Come on then," said Sam.

Lee led the dun after the big man. The Vigilantes walked behind the dun. "I *know* he ain't Kershaw," insisted Kelly.

Lee tethered the dun outside of the marshal's office. Sam opened the door. He looked at Lee as Lee walked past him. "He'd better know you, mister," he warned. He closed the door behind Lee. Lee glanced back over his shoulder through the glass panel of the door. Several of the Vigilantes were lighting up, but their eyes were on the door.

"Marshal!" called out Sam.

Heavy footsteps sounded in the hall that led to the cells. A heavy set man looked at Sam. "What's up, Sam?" he asked.

Sam jerked a head at Lee. "You know this man?"

Bassett looked at Lee. "For the love of God!" he cried out. "Lee! Lee Kershaw! What the hell are you doing in Las Vegas."

Lee felt for the makings. "Passing through, Tom. Just passing through," he said quietly.

Sam grinned. "Sorry, Kershaw," he said.

Lee nodded. "What would have happened to me if Tom here hadn't known me?"

Sam shrugged. "You read the placard," he replied. He closed the outer door behind himself.

Lee sat down. "What's this all about?" he asked.

Tom took a bottle and glasses from a drawer. "The citizens got tired of the scum that poured in here with the coming of the Santa Fe Railroad. Las Vegas became a catchall for some of the worst rascals and cutthroats in the West. I couldn't keep up with them. The Vigilantes posted a notice; a warning to all that type to steer clear of Las Vegas. It worked."

"I saw some of the results," said Lee drily. "Cold-Deck Jim."

"He was one of the worst. He was here long before the Vigilantes gave him notice, and he figured he'd be big enough to stick it out. He was wrong."

Lee lighted up. "One of the Vigilantes claimed he knew of me. Said I was killed in Sonora last year."

Tom nodded. "The story was passing around. What are you doing up this way? You usually work along the border."

"Looking for a man," said Lee.

"Can I help?"

Lee took out the address book he had taken from the bedroom of Doña Luz. He thumbed across the pages to the only person listed with a Las Vegas address—James H. Nelson, c/o General Delivery, Las Vegas, New Mexico Territory. "James Nelson," said Lee. He looked at Tom. "You know him?"

Tom grinned. "Do I *know* him? You must be joshing!"

"I was never more serious in my life."

Tom shrugged. "You saw the body hanging from the windmill?"

"Cold-Deck Jim?" asked Lee.

"His full name was James Hitchcock Nelson, alias Cold-Deck Jim."

"My luck is running true to form," murmured Lee. "Do you know of a younger man around here whose last name is Diaz?"

"It's not an unusual name around here. What's his first name?"

"Possibly Bart," replied Lee.

"An odd combination of names, Anglo and New Mexican."

Lee nodded. "His father was Anglo. His mother was named Rafaela Diaz. She is a *genizaro* from the Las Trampas area."

Tom shook his head. "It doesn't ring a bell."

Lee emptied his glass. Tom refilled it. "Why is he wanted?" the marshal asked.

"It's not for any crime, Tom. It's a matter of inheritance. His father wants to find him. He hasn't seen his son for eighteen years."

"Sounds like a good story."

Lee nodded. "I haven't the time to tell you about it, Tom. This Cold-Deck Jim—what about him?"

"About fifty years of age. Came originally from Missouri. Served in the army here in New Mexico Territory.

Got his discharge and drifted into Las Vegas. Never seemed to have to work for a living. He was a gambler, pimp, and general all round bad apple."

"Where'd he get his money?" asked Lee.

"Every month a letter came for him from Santa Fe. That would be the occasion for a three day drunk. He usually ended up here in the *calabozo*. I usually let him go when he was sober—and dead broke."

"This partner of his—the Las Vegas Kid—what about him?"

Tom eyed Lee curiously. "He's about twenty-two or twenty-three years of age. Dark hair and light eyes. Some say he's actually the son of Cold-Deck. Others say the Kid drifted to him from somewhere and Cold-Deck raised him." Tom grinned. "Some upbringing."

Lee twisted another cigarette together. "Where was Nelson stationed in the Army?"

"Fort Marcy at Santa Fe, I think. Yes, that was it."

A little piece of the puzzle slipped into place. "Do you know where the Las Vegas Kid is now?" asked Lee.

Tom stood up. He took a cell key from a rack. "Come on," he offered. "I'll show him to you."

Lee stared at the marshal. "You mean he's here in jail?"

Tom nodded. "I had to lock him up for his own good. The Kid was never anything like his partner Cold-Deck, but he was heading for the same end. He came back into town with Cold-Deck, and Cold-Deck was strung up. I locked the Kid up. I figured I'd slip him out of town when things quietened down a little."

"You say Cold-Deck might have raised the Kid?"

"The Kid had been with Nelson as far back as I can remember."

Lee walked into the cell block after Bassett. All of the cells were empty with the exception of the last one.

Lee looked into the cell. A young man lay full length on a bunk with his interlaced fingers locked at the nape of his neck. His gray eyes flicked at Bassett. "You letting me out of here, Bassett?" he asked.

Bassett shrugged. "It depends on this man here, Kid."

The gray eyes studied Lee. "Who are you?" asked the Kid.

Lee studied the lean and handsome face of the Kid. There was a mingled resemblance there—the dark hair and complexion of the *genizaro* blood and the gray eyes and strong nose of Duke Bowman. "I can get you out of here, Kid," said Lee. "If you want to go."

"Where to?" asked the Kid suspiciously.

Lee looked at Tom. He winked at the marshal with the eye away from the Kid. "He answers to the description, Tom," he said.

"What the hell is this?" demanded the Kid.

"Open the door, Tom," said Lee. He walked into the cell after Tom opened the door. He looked at the marshal. "I'd like to talk with him alone," he suggested. The footfalls of the marshal sounded in the hall. The door closed behind Bassett.

The Kid sat up and rested his lean and graceful hands on each side of himself. Lee handed him the makings. The Kid expertly rolled a cigarette. Lee lit it for him.

"Gracias," murmured the Kid.

"Por nada," countered Lee. He sat in the one rickety chair in the cell.

The Kid blew a smoke ring. "Who are you?" he asked.

"U.S. Marshal," lied Lee. "Looking for a man like you on a federal charge."

"Lets me out," said the Kid. He grinned. "Now, if you had said a county charge, or a city charge, you might have the right man."

"I want to know something of your background," said Lee.

The Kid shrugged. "There isn't much."

"Was Jim Nelson your father?"

The Kid shook his head. "Sort of like a guardian, I'd say."

"Legally?"

"I never saw any papers, if that's what you mean."

"Where were you born?"

"In New Mexico. I don't know the exact place."

"What's your earliest memory?"

The Kid looked curiously at Lee. "You a doctor of some kind?" he asked. "Maybe a fortune teller? You want to read my palm?"

"You didn't answer my question."

The Kid looked at the tip of his cigarette. "I was sleeping. There was a lot of shooting. Dead people lying on the ground all bloody. Smoke rising from burning buildings. A lot of yelling. Indians gutting a mule and cooking the meat." His voice died away.

Lee shaped a cigarette. "Go on," he urged.

"The Indians took me up into the mountains. I don't remember much about that except that I liked it there. Then one day an old man came to get me."

"A priest?"

The Kid nodded.

"You remember who he was?"

"No. He took me to Santa Fe. He kept me there for a time and then took me somewhere else. A little village in the mountains. One day a soldier came and got me. He took me here."

"That was Jim Nelson?"

The Kid nodded. "After that I stayed with him. He always had money. We moved around a lot in the early days, but he always came back here."

"For what?"

The Kid shrugged. "Money. Someone was always sending him money. He told me it was his pension from the army."

"You have no recollection of your mother?"

The Kid shrugged. "I seem to remember a dark-haired woman. I don't know who she was. She always looked at me in a different way than anyone else."

"When was that?"

"I can't remember."

"Was it before you heard the shooting and saw the Indians?"

"I told you that was my first recollection."

"You saw her after that first recollection?"

"Once when I was with the old priest a young woman

came to the chapel to pray. The old priest would not let her in. She cried a lot. I never saw her again."

Lee opened the photograph case. He held it out to the Kid. The Kid stared at the photograph. "By God!" he cried. "I think it is her!"

Lee put a finger on the small boy. "And him?"

The Kid shrugged. "He means nothing to me."

Lee took the photograph. "I'm not so sure about that," he said. He held out the silver button. "What about this?"

The Kid looked at the button and then up at Lee. "Look," he said. He opened his coat. His lowcut velvet vest was fastened with three buttons exactly like the one in Lee's hand.

"Where did you get those?" asked Lee.

The Kid looked down at them. "I've had them all my life," he said. "Once there were six of them. Jim pawned three of them in Santa Fe one time. We had to eat. I kept the others. I've worn them all my life, one way or another. What do they mean to you?"

Lee stood up. "Just a job," he said. He walked to the door and opened it. He looked back. "Wait for me," he said with a grin as he clicked shut the lock.

Lee walked into the office. "He's my man, Tom," he said.

Tom refilled the glasses. "You can have him," he said. "Just don't let him come back here, Lee, or I won't be responsible for him. When will you leave?"

"Tonight. Now."

Tom looked thoughtfully toward the door. "The boys out there might not take too kindly to that."

"Is the Kid that guilty?"

"Mostly by association. Cold-Deck was a good teacher —of the wrong things. Gambling, a little pimping, and other odds and ends."

"I'll take him off your hands then. He won't be back, at least for a long time."

"Fair enough. How can I help you?"

"My horse is about worn out. I'll need two horses, one for me, one for the Kid. I'll lead the dun."

"Where are you heading?"

"The Broken Bow country."

"On horses? At this time of the year? Why don't you take the Santa Fe?"

Lee shook his head. "Can't risk it."

"Why? There's something queer about all this, Lee."

Lee lit a cigarette. "I'll come back someday and tell you the story. One thing more—there may be some people coming through here looking for me. You don't know anything about me, or the Kid. *¿Comprendes?*"

Tom nodded. "That story you're going to tell me some day better be a good one. I'll get your horses for you." He walked to the door and looked back. "One thing you'd better know, Lee. The Kid is one of the best men with a sixgun I've ever seen. Don't trust him too far. I know you can take care of yourself, but the Kid is as slick as a greased pig." He closed the door behind himself.

Lee refilled his glass. He took the cell key and walked to the Kid's cell. He opened the door. The Kid got up and came to the door. "I'm getting out?" he asked.

"With me," said Lee. "Is that your wallet lying there on the bunk?" When the Kid turned his head the Mattatuck irons were neatly snapped about his wrists.

"What the hell is this?" he demanded.

"Just a precaution," replied Lee. "I always promise safe delivery."

"You got a warrant for me?"

Lee opened his coat and touched the butt of his Colt. "Sure, Kid! I've got six of them in here, .44/40 and all fresh." He steered the Kid back into the marshal's office.

Tom Bassett came in the back way. "I got the horses, Lee," he said. "Led them and your dun around to the back. The Vigilantes are over on La Calle de la Amargura checking out the whorehouses on a tip from me. I said I had heard that Stuttering Tom and Benny the Poet had been seen over there."

Lee led the Kid to the back door. He looked up and down the alleyway. It was dark and empty.

Lee gave the Kid a hand up into the saddle of a chunky roan. "Where we heading?" asked the Kid.

"Kansas City," replied Lee. He thrust out his hand to

Tom. "I won't forget this, Tom," he said. Tom nodded. He held out a gunbelt heavy with a holstered Colt and full cartridge loops.

"This is the Kid's," he said. "I can't rightfully keep it." Lee hung the belt over his saddlehorn.

Lee mounted the bay and picked up the reins of the roan and the dun. He led them from the alleyway and alongside the plaza. The wind was whipping dust across the plaza. The body of Cold-Deck Jim swayed in the blast. Once, the Kid looked back before Lee led the two horses into a narrow side street that headed south.

nineteen

"*All I know,*" said Sam, "*is that a man who said he was* Kershaw came through here last night. Tom Bassett, the marshal, identified him."

"Tall man with reddish hair and beard? Gray eyes. Big nose. Riding a dun?" asked Reata.

"That was him," agreed Sam.

"Where'd he go?" asked Cass.

"He stayed with Tom after we left the marshal's office. We had some business on Church Street—the one called La Calle de la Amargura, the Road of Suffering and Bitterness. That's because all the whorehouses, saloons, and gambling halls are along there. I . . ."

"Where'd he go after he left the marshal's office?" interrupted Stella.

"Why, I ain't rightly sure. I found out later the marshal bought a couple of extra horses for Kershaw. He left the town about eleven o'clock last night."

"Which way did he go?" asked Reata.

"I don't know."

"Was he alone?" asked Stella.

"All I know is that Kershaw said he was passing through. He's a manhunter. There was only one prisoner in the *juzgado*. When Kershaw left, no one saw him go. But, the prisoner was gone too."

"Who was the prisoner?" asked Stella.

"His last name was Nelson, but everyone called him the Las Vegas Kid. I think Kershaw picked him up."

Reata looked at Stella. "What do you think?"

Stella nodded. "It's him all right. Or someone Kershaw may try to pass off as him."

"What are you talking about?" asked Sam.

Reata shook his head. "An old friend, mister. Thanks for the information."

Sam nodded. "Maybe the marshal can help you out!" he called after the three of them as they walked away.

"He'll be heading south," said Stella. "With about a twelve hour start. How far is it, Reata?"

"More than two hundred miles as the crow flies."

She narrowed her great blue eyes thoughtfully. "He'll have to travel slowly because of the heat. He'll have to go from waterhole to waterhole, and some of them will be dry at this time of the year. I'll get a telegram off to Marsh right away. He can have me met at Alamogordo. The next train is due here in about an hour. I might just make it down there ahead of him."

"What about us?" asked Cass.

She opened her purse. "Buy an extra pair of good horses for each of you. Keep pushing on after him. You might never catch up with him, but you can maybe run him into the net Marsh and I will have ready for him when he gets near the Broken Bow."

Reata shook his head. "We'll never catch up with him," he said.

"Not with Kershaw," said Stella. "But whoever that is with him, Nelson, or the Las Vegas Kid, or whoever the hell he is, might not be able to keep up with Kershaw. Kershaw will be limited to the Kid's endurance, not his own."

Reata nodded. "Yeah," he said slowly.

Cass looked uncertainly to the south. "Jesus, Stell," he said. "That's some ride you got cut out for us."

"You'll make it," she said.

"But you ain't never been out there at this time of the year, and in a drought year too!"

She shook her head. "No, and I don't intend to. Now get moving! *Vámonos!* I'll see you at the Broken Bow."

Reata shaped a cigarette as he watched her walking toward the railroad station. "Jesus God," he said quietly. "What a lawman she would have made. She thinks of everything."

Cass spat to one side. "Well, we don't have to do like she says."

Reata looked sideways at Cass as he lit up. "We will if we want to get our hands into a share of the Broken Bow."

Cass nodded. "Let's go get those horses," he said.

As they left the town heading south toward the Pecos, they heard the southbound train whistling for a crossing just outside of Las Vegas.

twenty

The key clicked in the lock of the Mattatuck irons. Lee re-
moved them from the Kid's wrists. The Kid rubbed his
wrists. "*Gracias,*" *he murmured,* "*mil gracias.*"

Lee looked back through the grayness of the dawn light.
He fashioned a cigarette and then handed the makings to
the Kid. He lit his cigarette. "*Por nada,*" he said.

The Kid lit up. "What's your real game, Kershaw?"

Lee looked at him. "Your father wants to see you,
Kid."

"I have no father. The only father I ever had is swinging from that windmill back in Las Vegas."

"Your real father is Duke Bowman, of the Running MB
in the Broken Bow country. You ever hear of him?"

"Who hasn't?"

"You can have the Broken Bow if you want it, and
what is more important—if you can *hold* it."

The Kid studied Lee. "This is loco."

"We'll water the horses two miles from here. That distance should give me just enough time to tell you the
whole story," said Lee.

The dawn light came over the open country as they watered the horses. The Kid looked sideways at Lee. "What about my mother?" he asked.

Lee made another cigarette. He lit it.

"You'll have to tell me," the Kid said. "I'll find out anyway when I talk with my father."

"He hasn't seen her for eighteen years," said Lee. "He thinks she's dead."

"But she isn't."

"She is Rafaela Diaz. A *genizaro*. She was supposed to have been killed at Cinco Castillos."

"She came to see me at the chapel in Santa Fe."

Lee nodded. "She's still alive, Kid. I think you know that. I also think you know who she is."

"Cold-Deck got drunk one night after he got my money from her in the mail. He wouldn't give it to me. I took it by force. He tried to cut me down by telling me all about her. He said he'd spread it all over Las Vegas if I took the money."

"But he didn't."

The Kid shook his head. "He would've been dead with a bullet in his rotten guts if he had tried to."

"She was doing it all for you, Kid."

"I would rather have had her dead."

"The damage is done now."

"And the old man? Duke Bowman? The sonofabitch who drove my mother into being a whore? What made him change his mind after all these years."

"Maybe you can guess, Kid."

"He doesn't really give a damn about me personally. All he's really interested in is keeping the Broken Bow away from the Dakins. That's it, isn't it?"

Lee shrugged. "Mine not to reason why. Maybe it's the way he *thinks* he's thinking, Kid. Maybe it's a lot deeper than that. When a man is dying and knows he's dying and still has his reason, a lot of things become clearer. He realizes, perhaps, the importance of other human beings, rather than the possession of material goods."

"You talk like a preacher!" scoffed the Kid.

Lee shook his head. "Read the Bible, Kid. It's all in there."

"And these Dakins? They'll kill to stop us, eh?"

"You've got the idea," admitted Lee.

"Then let me have my gun, Kershaw. I feel naked without it. I've worn it since I was sixteen."

Lee unhooked the belt from his saddlehorn and handed it to the Kid. "You may need it before long," he said.

The Kid settled the belt about his lean hips. "Well, now I feel better. We can take on half a dozen Dakins apiece, eh?"

Lee knelt to fill the canteens. "One apiece is enough," he said quietly.

"You think we're being followed?"

"I know we are."

"Why don't we backtrack and drygulch them?"

"That's not my game, Kid."

"I'll pay you when I take over the Broken Bow."

"Your father is paying me to bring you back there, not to kill your enemies."

"But that used to be your game, didn't it? Bounty hunting?"

Lee capped the first canteen. He would not answer that. The Kid was perceptive enough to know the answer anyway.

"How much do you get for a deal like this?" asked the Kid.

"Usually a thousand for the first week, five hundred a week thereafter. I pay my own expenses. Your father was in a hurry. He doubled the five hundred."

"Maybe you won't make more than a thousand or so."

Lee began to fill the second canteen. "Fill up on water," he suggested. "We've got a long dry ride ahead of us."

"Maybe you have—I haven't," the Kid said quietly.

Lee turned his head slowly and looked up into the handsome face of the Kid.

"I'm not too sure about this deal. It sounds fishy to me. Why are you really doing this?"

"I'm your fairy godfather," drily replied Lee.

"Well, maybe I'll just go down there alone. I don't need you."

Lee shook his head. "No. I'm being paid to deliver you to the old man."

"Maybe it's dead or alive?"

Lee stood up and studied the Kid. "You wouldn't do him any good dead, Kid."

"Maybe he just wants me out of the way."

"Then me coming up here after you doesn't make much sense, does it?"

The Kid shook his head. "You're a real pro, Kershaw. You could have killed me up in Las Vegas and maybe have gotten away with it, but you're too smart for that. No, you sprung me out of the *juzgado* and brought me out here where there isn't another soul for miles. Maybe you'll show up at the Broken Bow all alone and collect your blood money, and no one will ever know where I lie buried with a bullet in my back."

"For Christ's sake!" exploded Lee. "I told you to fill up with water! Talking is dry work! Now shut up and drink!"

The Kid slowly shook his head. "You go on alone, Kershaw."

"Drink and get on the roan," ordered Lee.

The Kid smiled, very thinly. "Make me," he suggested.

The sun was shining down on the dry and empty land. Lee looked to the north. There was no sign of dust, which didn't mean anything, for he had swung farther east than the usual waterhole route, which headed south in the straightest line, risking the fact that some of the lesser waterholes would surely be dry.

Lee whirled, drawing his Colt. He found himself looking into the muzzle of the Kid's sixgun. The Kid grinned. "Gotcha!" he crowed.

Lee smiled back. "I hope you don't think I gave you a loaded sixshooter," he suggested. The Kid flicked his eyes uncertainly down at his Colt. A spur jingled. The Colt was slapped hard to one side, spinning out of the Kid's hand, and the muzzle of another Colt was rammed deep into his lean belly just above the belt buckle. The Kid's Colt struck the hard ground and exploded. The soft .44/40 slug struck the roan right between the eyes, and he crashed to the ground.

Lee stepped back. "Get that saddle off the roan, and put it on the bay," he said. "Shift my saddle from the bay to the dun."

The Kid shifted Lee's saddle from the bay to the dun. He unsaddled the fallen roan with Lee's help and then placed the saddle on the bay. He put a foot into the stirrup.

"We walk," said Lee. "It's a long day's trip to the next water."

The sun was already burning up the empty land when the Kid led out the bay. He looked back once at the hard hawk's face behind him and then looked ahead. It was indeed a long day's trip to the next water—if there was any to be had.

twenty-one

The water had a look of stale chocolate about it. Lee raised
some of it in his hands and sniffed at it. He dropped the
water and wiped his hands on the sides of his trousers. His
lips were cracked, and his throat felt like a tube of corrod-
ed brass.

"The bay is done," croaked the Kid.

Lee looked at the bay. His legs were spraddled out and
gummy yellowish strings hung from his mouth.

"It was your brilliant idea to come this way," accused
the Kid. "What now, Kershaw?"

Lee shook the only canteen that had any water in it. He
looked across the empty desert country to the southwest.
"Cinco Castillos," he said, almost as though to himself.

"How far?" asked the Kid.

"Fifteen miles."

"We'll never make it."

Lee looked at the dying sun, a welter of rose and gold
over the distant mountains. "The sun will soon be gone,"
he said. "That should help a little."

"What about these mysterious people who are supposed to be following us? Maybe they went that way. They could be there now."

"We'll risk it," said Lee. "We have no other choice."

"We should have gone that way in the first place!"

Lee looked sideways at the Kid. "Sometimes," he said quietly, "you run off too much at the mouth."

Lee took off his hat. He poured the last of the water into it and held it out to the dun.

"What the hell are you doing!" exploded the Kid. He rushed at Lee, reaching for the hat. Lee rammed the hat up about the dun's nose, freeing his right hand. He caught the Kid with a backhander that sent him down on one knee. Lee's right heel caught the Kid on the point of the jaw and put him down for the long count.

Lee finished watering the dun. He put the cooled hat on his head and bent down to place the Mattatuck's on the Kid's wrists. He heaved the Kid over the saddle and led the dun toward the southwest and distant Cinco Castillos.

The sun was gone. The darkness was thick. The only sounds on the harsh earth were the scuffing of Lee's moccasins and the thudding of the dun's hoofs, hour after hour, without stop.

The moon came up after a time and touched a curious-looking rock formation placed on the desert like a sand castle built by a child on an empty beach.

"God damn it," husked the Kid. "I'll walk!"

Lee gripped the Kid by the belt and pulled him from the tired dun. He yanked the Kid up on his feet and shoved him in the general direction of Cinco Castillos.

Once, the Kid looked back as he stumbled along, into the hawk's face beneath the low pulled hat brim. There was no expression on Lee Kershaw's face.

A mile from Cinco Castillos Lee stumbled and fell. As he tried to get up, the Kid's bootheel caught him on the jaw and he fell back half-stunned. The Kid ripped Lee's Colt from its holster and held it on Lee. "Where's the key?" he demanded. Lee held out the key to him. "Unlock these cuffs," the Kid croaked.

Lee sat up, feeling his bruised jaw. "Try it yourself," said Lee. The Kid took the key and tried to fit it into the keyhole. "I'll hold the Colt for you," suggested Lee.

The moon was bright on the desert. The Kid looked toward Cinco Castillos. He looked down at Lee. "Unlock the cuffs, Kershaw," he said. "Or you don't get any water."

Lee stood up and looked toward the pinnacles. He shook his head.

"What's the matter?" demanded the Kid.

Lee looked at him. "I'm not sure," he said.

"Is there someone there?"

"*¿Quien sabe?*"

"You're bluffing, Kershaw!"

Lee shrugged.

"We can't bypass that water."

"No," admitted Lee. He reached over and unlocked the cuffs. "You'd better wait awhile, Kid," he advised.

"What's the sense of waiting?"

"There may be a reception committee there you won't like."

The Kid waved the Colt. "Lead the dun," he ordered.

Lee picked up the reins. He rubbed his bruised jaw. "You learn fast in some ways, Kid," he said.

Lee led on the tired dun. There could be no going back. They would never be able to reach the waterhole back north, beyond the one with the poisoned water. They could not bypass Cinco Castillos to try for Ribbon Creek. They were damned if they went to Cinco Castillos and damned if they didn't.

The Kid saw the ruins. He saw the mounded graves, lit by the moon. He saw the passageway that led in to the water. "Get moving!" he snapped. "*¡Vámonos!*"

Lee dropped the reins. He felt in his shirt pocket for the makings. "I don't like it," he said quietly.

The Kid snatched up the reins. He began to run awkwardly. "Stay there then and die of thirst!" he yelled. The echo flatted off from the pinnacles.

Lee lit the cigarette. The Kid vanished in through the passage. Lee stood there with the smoke doing his thirst no good. He threw the cigarette aside and walked toward the pinnacles. His footfalls sounded in the shadowed passageway. He stopped at the inner opening. A man squatted in the shadows beside the *tinaja* with a cigarette held cupped in his hand. The dun whinnied from the shadows beyond the *tinaja*.

"Maybe you were right after all, Kid," admitted Lee.

The shadowed figure nodded. Lee walked toward the water. The man stood up, drawing in on his cigarette. The flaring tip revealed the broad face and hard green eyes of Cass Dakin. A gun hammer clicked back into full cock. "Kershaw, you sonofabitch," said Cass. "What kept you so long?"

Lee whirled and dived back into the tunnel as Cass fired. The bullet slapped into the tunnel wall and ricocheted back and forth over Lee's head. He rolled over and over and jumped to his feet. He plunged out of the tunnel and hurdled the graves, heading for the ruins.

Hoofs thudded on the hard ground. Lee threw a glance back over his shoulder. A horseman was rounding the pinnacles and whirling a reata over his head. The loop settled neatly about Lee's chest, pinning his arms to his body. The horseman reined back his horse, and the reata tightened, snapping Lee back onto his lean butt; the shock traveled all the way up his back into his brain.

The horse was spurred forward and past Lee. Lee looked up into the grinning face of the rider and managed to get up onto his feet as the reata took up. He ran awkwardly after the horse with the grit and pebbles flung up from the rear hoofs stinging his face.

"Have a nice trip, Kershaw!" roared Cass from the rim between the bases of the pinnacles. "Go to it, Reata!"

Reata turned grinning. "Stay on your feet or die, Kershaw!" he yelled back. "How long do you think you'll last?"

They rounded the pinnacles out of sight of the howling Cass. Reata turned his horse toward the thick masses of thorned brush on the lower ground.

Lee drew his knife and sliced through the loop, but caught and twisted the reata in his left hand keeping up the drag on it. Lee timed his stride. He drew back the knife in his right hand and made a hard cast to save his life. The blade centered itself between Reata's shoulder blades. Lee let go of the reata. The horse took off through the thorned brush with Reata still bolt upright in the saddle. The moonlight glinted on the polished hilt of the knife.

Lee passed a hand across his burning eyes. He looked back at the pinnacles. Cass was not in sight. Lee slogged back toward the pinnacles. He found a place where he could use hand- and footholds to work his way up between two of the pinnacles. He rolled over the rim and lay flat looking down into the *tinaja* area.

"Your friend Kershaw won't be back," said Cass to the Kid.

"He's no friend of mine," said the Kid. "How about untying me?"

"Why?" asked Cass.

"I need a drink."

Cass shaped a cigarette. "You won't be needing it," he said.

Lee picked up a melon-sized rock.

"Kill him now," the mind voice said.

Cass lit his cigarette. "How do you want it? Back, belly, or head?" he asked the Kid.

"Why kill me?" asked the Kid.

"You're old Bowman's bastard, ain't you?"

The Kid shook his head.

"The hell you ain't!"

"What makes you think so?" asked the Kid.

"Because Kershaw wouldn't have brought you this far if he didn't know it, that's why!"

"He's wrong, mister. Bowman's kid was killed right here at Cinco Castillos by the Mescaleros."

"How do you know that?" asked Cass.

"It's common knowledge," replied the Kid.

"No, it ain't. Who the hell would care if the kid *was* killed here? That was eighteen years ago."

"How much do you want to let me go?"

"Make me an offer," suggested Cass.

"A thousand bucks?"

"Have you got it?"

"Not with me."

"Where is it?"

"In Las Vegas."

Cass blew a smoke ring. "Damn," he said. "You know how much the Broken Bow is worth?"

"I haven't any idea."

"Maybe a quarter of a million dollars," said Cass.

"How much of it do you think you'll get?" asked the Kid.

Cass thrust forward his head. "What the hell do you mean?"

"By the time your brother Marsh and your sister Stella get their hands into that property you won't get nothing, mister!"

Cass yawned. "I asked you before—how do you want it? Back, belly, or head?" He drew his Colt.

A strong arm encircled Cass's thick neck, and the rock came down with savage force against the side of his thick head. The big man clamped his chin down on Lee's arm and swung sideways. The Colt clattered on the hard ground. Lee's feet came up off the ground, and he was swung around. Cass raised his head and Lee fell heavily, knocking the Colt into the *tinaja*.

Cass rubbed the side of his head as he looked down at Lee. "Well, well," he said conversationally. "Where's my cousin Reata?"

"He took a long ride out into the desert," replied Lee. "He won't be back."

"And you come here for a drinka water, eh?"

"You've got the idea," said Lee. He stood up with his back to the pool. There were three horses in the shadows, two of them with sheathed Winchesters on the saddles.

"Looks like it's finally between me and you now, Kershaw," said Cass. "You killed Reata, eh?"

Lee nodded.

"You haven't got a gun, or you would have shot me

with it. You haven't got a knife, or it would have been between my shoulder blades. You killed Chisos and Reata by trickery. How are you in a fair fight?"

"Is there such a thing in this business?" asked Lee.

Cass looked down at his huge fists. "Well," he said slowly, "I am a sporting man, Kershaw. You lick me in a fistfight, and I'll let you pass."

"That's fair?" asked Lee.

"Man to man. Ain't *that* fair?"

"He'll kill you, Kershaw," said the Kid.

Lee glanced at him. "If he kills me, Kid, you're next." Lee bent down and scooped up a little water, keeping his eyes on Cass. "By the way, Cass?" he asked. "How did the old man Candelario Melgosa die?"

"I only hit him once," blurted Cass.

Lee stood up straight and tall. He unbuckled his gunbelt with its empty holster. He peeled off his sweat-damp shirt and undershirt to reveal his lean gut and long flat muscles.

Cass stripped to the waist. His muscles bulged, and his chest seemed hewed from solid oak. "Texas rules?" he asked casually.

Lee bowed his head. "Your choice," he said.

"He'll kill you, Kershaw," warned the Kid again.

Cass spat to one side. He closed his huge hands and thrust them out, turning the wrists outward so that his fists were presented one behind the other, in front of his block of a chin. He thrust forward a heavy left leg and placed his right foot in line behind it. "Time," he said seriously.

"I don't believe it," murmured the Kid.

"He means it," said Lee.

Lee began to move about just out of range of those dangerous blocks of fists. He threw a probing left and it met a hard forearm. He tried a right cross and hit another forearm. He circled about. "Stand still, you damned jumping jack," muttered Cass.

The right came in a straight jab that knocked Lee's blocking left out of the way and connected solidly with his jaw. He hit the ground and rolled out of the way of the descending boot. He came up on his feet. Cass hit him with a left and then a right, and he went down again. Blood leaked from his mouth. This time the boot caught him in the ribs with a jolt that knocked the wind out of him. He rolled over and Cass jumped, trying to land on his back with both huge feet.

Lee moved back, shaking his head. Cass threw a right. As he did so, he lowered his left. The fist fanned past Lee's jaw. Lee knew that if he went down again, he might not be able to get out of the way of those murderous feet. "Texas rules," Cass had said, and he had meant it.

Cass threw a right. It missed. Again he had lowered his left. He feinted with his left and rammed his right against Lee's belly. Lee's back slammed against the rock wall behind him. He drifted sideways and circled to get out into the open.

Cass shuffled forward throwing rights and lefts, but he didn't seem to be trying very hard to hit Lee, as though playing with him. He lowered his left as he threw a right, and at the same time, he looked toward the Kid. "Any minute now," he said. The hard left speared against his broad nose, and the vicious right came over the top of his lowered left arm and hit him square in the left eye. He grunted and bent forward. A left caught him in his meaty belly, and as he raised his head, the right smashed against his left eye again.

Lee backed away, breathing hard. His throat was dry and his tongue was swollen with thirst. Blood dripped from his abraded knuckles.

Cass pawed at his left eye with his right fist. He shuffled forward. He threw a right which fanned past Lee's jaw. Lee rammed out his left foot and caught the big man hard in the privates. As Cass bent forward in agony, a left smashed against his right eye, and a right almost completely closed his left eye for the evening.

"Time," said Cass.

Lee spat bloodily to one side. "Time, hell," he said. He moved in and hit Cass on his nose and slammed a left into the right eye.

"Goddamn you!" roared Cass. "Fight fair!"

The left just about closed Cass's right eye. A right caught him in the groin. He staggered back. A vicious one-two caught the left eye and then the right eye in turn.

Cass stood still, with his head held tilted back peering through his swollen eyes. Lee was just a lean shadowy figure moving about like a prowling cat, just out of fist range.

Cass lowered his head and thrust out his arms to charge against Lee, driving his hard skull into Lee's belly and throwing his arms about Lee's waist. They went down with Lee under the big man and the breath driven out of his body. He brought up a knee into Cass's groin, and as he felt the relaxation of the big man's grip, he broke free and staggered to his feet. He got in two good boots to the back of the head before Cass made it to his feet.

They circled each other—the tall, lean man with his fists out, weaving back and forth, and the huge-bodied Cass with his thick arms outspread, trying to see through the hairline slits between his swollen eyelids. Once again he charged. This time the cruel fists slammed into both eyes, and Lee was gone, backing toward the rock wall beside the *tinaja*. "You stink!" jeered Lee. "All you can hit are helpless old men!"

Cass charged, roaring like a mad bull, arms outspread and bull head lowered. Lee sidestepped at the last possible second. Cass rammed his bullet head full force against the rock wall and fell like a chopped tree.

Lee wiped the sweat and blood from his face. He knelt beside the water and scooped it up to his dry mouth. The drippings were like mercury in the bright moonlight.

"Is he still alive?" asked the Kid.

Lee sat down and thrust out his arms on each side of himself. He looked at the swollen face of the big man. The thick chest did not move. "Texas rules," he said quietly. "That was what he wanted."

"I'd like a drink," the Kid said.

Lee got to his feet. He untied the Kid and pulled him to his feet. "Help yourself," he said.

They sat there in the moonlight looking at each other.

"The next water south is Ribbon Creek," said Lee.

"How soon will you be able to leave?" asked the Kid.

Lee felt for the makings. "After we have a smoke," he replied.

twenty-two

The Kid stumbled and fell flat on his face. He did not try to get up; he did not even move.

"Keep moving," came the inexorable command.

The Kid got to his feet by a supreme effort of will. He thrust out a hand as though to balance himself, but he could not take another step.

"Stop posing," came the suggestion from behind the Kid. "Keep moving!"

The Kid turned and looked through the predawn darkness at the inhuman creature behind him.

"Keep moving, or you'll die here," said Lee.

"What keeps *you* moving?" he asked.

"Meanness," replied Lee. "Some people have determination; others have faith; me—Kershaw—I'm just *mean*. Keep moving!"

The Kid *moved*.

A faint grayish tint showed in the eastern sky.

"How much farther?" asked the Kid.

The dun whinnied sharply.

Lee gripped the Kid by a shoulder and dragged him backward.

They stood there in the darkness. Lee raised his head.

"What's the matter?" asked the Kid. A big dirty hand was clamped over his mouth.

The dawn light grew. The canyon wrens twittered sleepily, and then they stopped. There was no wind.

Lee looked up the slopes toward the great ridge that trended north, sawtoothed against the dark gray sky.

"Where's the water?" husked the Kid when Lee took his hand away.

The hand came right back again. Lee pulled his Winchester from its scabbard. He leaned close to the Kid. "Unsaddle the dun," he said. He vanished into the woods.

The Kid unsaddled the dun and drew his Colt.

A rifle exploded in the darkness. The echo was immediately chased by the echoes of half a dozen shots sounding like the sporadic ripping of heavy canvas. Smoke drifted through the graying darkness.

Lee came loping through the woods. He handed the smoking Winchester to the Kid. "Shoot that way!" he snapped, jerking his head. He ripped open a saddle bag and stuffed something inside his shirt. The Kid opened fire and ran the Winchester dry.

"Now!" said Lee. He dumped the saddle between some rocks and kicked brush over it. He ran lightly up the slope —not as though he had just walked for twelve hours straight across the dry country north of Ribbon Creek.

"Kershaw!" yelled a man. He stood up in the dimness and raised his rifle. Lee turned sideways, drawing as he did so, and fired from hip level. The man went down and rolled into cover, still firing. The slugs slapped through the woods cutting down twigs and striking into trunks.

Men yelled back and forth. Boots splashed in water. A horse whinnied in sudden panic.

The Kid slogged up the slope after Lee. His breathing was like that from the bellows of a forge. His legs quivered with the strain of working up the rugged slope. He fell over a log. He cracked a shin against a rock.

"Keep moving!" yelled Lee. He turned once and emptied his Colt right over the top of the Kid's head. He reached down and gripped the Kid by the gunbelt and half carried and half dragged him higher and higher.

Lee rolled over a slantways dike of rock and fell flat on his face with the Kid atop him. The fresh sweat broke out and brought alive the stale odor of the past several days' perspiration. Their lungs seemed to be on fire.

"Load the Winchester," ordered Lee. He shoved his hat back to let it hang from its strap and raised his head a little. He went down at once. A slug slapped the place where his head had showed.

Lee placed his back against a rock and felt for the makings. He grinned at the Kid. "Close, that," he observed.

"Broken Bow men?"

Lee nodded. He placed the cigarette between the Kid's lips and swiftly rolled another quirly for himself. He lit both cigarettes.

The faint sounds of shouting men came from the slopes below. They lay there resting and smoking. Minutes ticked past.

The sun shoved up its fat round face over the mountains far to the east. The heat seemed to come at once.

"Maybe they were just out hunting strays?" the Kid suggested.

Lee nodded. "Sure are—*us*." Lee pointed to a V between the rock dike and a huge boulder. "Take a look down that way, Kid," he said. "That might all be yours some day. Keep your head low."

The Kid bellied to the V and looked down the long tumbled slopes of barren rock to the lower timber-covered slopes. The sun glinted from the ripples of Ribbon Creek. To the right, southeasterly, he saw a great, dark curving line—the Broken Bow.

"The *estancia* is up the valley," explained Lee. "We can't see it from here."

"What happens now?"

"We go to see your father."

"From up here? There ain't no water above us. We

can't get over that damned mountain there to the valley.
We can't go down and get water. You let the dun go."

Lee scratched inside his shirt. "Have faith," he said
drily. "We can climb better and faster than the horse. Besides, I didn't want to risk having the dun break a leg. By
God! You ever see a horse like that dun? He outlasted
them all!"

The Kid crawled back under the cover of the dike.
"Helluva lot of good that'll do! They've got him now."

"They'll never keep him. I'll find him around Ribbon
Creek on my way out of the Broken Bow."

The Kid rested his sweating back against the dike. He
looked at the hawk's face across from him, with its hard
gray eyes, big nose, mahogany-hued skin, and reddish
beard. He saw the bruises from Lee's fight with Cass Dakin—Texas rules. He saw the mark where he had kicked
Lee. He watched the lean hands molding a cigarette with
swift and skillful precision. He heard the sounds of hunting men coming closer up the slopes below them. "Don't
you ever give up?" he asked.

Lee shook his head as he placed the cigarette between
the Kid's cracked lips. He lit it. "Nope," he said. "They'll
have to kill me first." It was not bravado with Lee Kershaw; just a simple statement of fact.

Lee lit his own cigarette. He leaned back against the
rock and closed his eyes.

"You think of everything," observed the Kid.

Lee shook his head. "Not everything," he corrected.

"Such as?"

"I have no way of foreseeing what will happen when I
get you to the *estancia* to see your daddy."

"But we *will* see him?"

Lee opened his eyes. "Why of course! What makes you
doubt it?"

The Kid had no comment on that question.

Lee snubbed out his cigarette. "Give me a hand," he
said.

Together they worked a boulder over just to the end of
the rock dike. Lee braced his back against another boulder

and his feet against the one they had moved. "You want to sight it?" he asked. The Kid stared at him. Lee shoved with all his force. The boulder rolled downward, and as it gained speed, it struck a downslanted sheet of rock and took off like a giant billiard ball into the bright morning sunlight.

Lee jumped to his feet. "Look out below!" he yelled through cupped hands.

They could hear yelling, cursing men below them on the slopes. "Goddamn you, Kershaw!" yelled Sid Dakin.

Lee grinned like a hunting lobo on a moonlit night when he sees his prey. "Lookit them run! Hey, Marsh! Raise your ass a little higher when you hurdle and put out your arms so!" Here Lee made an exaggerated pose with left arm outflung and right arm and leg straight behind him. A bullet slapped viciously into the rock dike.

Lee stepped behind the dike. "Time to move, Kid. It'll take them a while to catch their breaths. Their shooting will be wild and uphill. Now, you might not know, but when a man shoots uphill, he has a tendency to shoot too low, and when he shoots downhill, he has a tendency to overshoot." Lee kept on his impromptu lecture as he worked his way up a transverse cleft in the rock. The sound of the rolling, bounding boulder, accompanied by the clattering, rushing sound of loose rock and soil, died away. Dust wreathed up from far below, accompanied by the verbal smoke of the cursing Broken Bow men.

The sun beat on the eastward side of the huge ridge. The heat veils shimmered upward from the baking rock. There was no wind to move the heavy masses of inert air.

The Kid looked far down the shimmering slope and saw the glinting of the sun on the narrow ribbon of the creek. He looked toward the looping Broken Bow, flowing steadily down to meet the Pecos in the heat-hazed distance. He looked back over his shoulder at Lee taking a break in the hot shadow of a huge boulder. "We can't outlast them, Kershaw," he said.

Lee opened his eyes. "So, what solution do you have?"

"Go on down there and give ourselves up."

Lee took a shapeless mass of soft candle wax out of his

shirt front and rolled it in his hands to reshape it into a candle. "Evidently you haven't got the idea," he suggested. "That's Sid Dakin down there, *segundo* to his brother Marsh, who ramrods the Broken Bow. Now, Sid never got to be *segundo* just because he happened to be Marsh's half brother, Kid. Sid is lazy as hell, except when it comes to a gunfight or a shooting scrape—then he's all horns and rattles. Sid has his orders from Marsh and his sister Stella—the Black Widow. His orders are to kill the both of us. You, because you're the heir to the Broken Bow. Me, because I *know* you're the heir to the Broken Bow. Sonny, they don't ever intend for us to leave this mountain alive."

The Colt hammer clicked back. Lee looked up into the muzzle of the sixgun and stopped shaping the second candle. "Jesus," he said. "Are we back in that act again?"

The Kid looked down at Lee over the Colt. "I'm going down. I can reason with them. We can't live up here in this heat without any water. The farther we get away from Ribbon Creek, the quicker we die."

Lee placed the candles in the shade and felt for the makings. "I really ought to stop you now," he said.

"You think you can?"

The gray eyes looked steadily over the Colt. "Don't doubt it," replied Lee drily. "However, I'm tired of saving your ass from those buzzards down there. You go right ahead, sonny. You *reason* with them. Two things—leave the Winchester, please, and don't bother to let me know how you make out. I'll hear the shooting."

The Kid let down the hammer of the Colt. "What are you going to do with those candles?" he asked.

Lee shrugged. "I'll place one at your head and the other at your feet when they get through with you down there."

"That's not funny," said the Kid.

"It's not intended to be funny."

Lee lit his cigarette. He reached for the Winchester and levered a round into the chamber. He let the hammer down to half cock and looked slantways up at the Kid. "I'm ready when you are," he said.

The Kid let down the hammer of his Colt and sheathed it. He turned on a heel and threw a leg over a rock ledge.

He stepped over it into the full sunlight and began to walk stiff-legged down the slope, braking himself on the loose soil and rock.

It was very quiet on the mountainside. Lee slowly slid the Winchester barrel between two rocks, making sure the sun did not reflect from the metal. He eased back on the spur hammer, full cocking the rifle.

"Hey, Dakin!" yelled the Kid. "I'm coming down!"

There was no answer.

The Kid looked back up the slope. He saw nothing. The heat shimmered up sinuously, almost as though in an obscene dance from some Oriental bagnio.

"Hey, you!" Sid Dakin yelled. The echo fled down the mountainside and died away.

The Kid looked toward a huge tip-tilted slab of rock half buried in the talus slope just below him. A man stood there, out of sight of Lee Kershaw. He held a Winchester in his hands. The muzzle was pointed toward the Kid.

The Kid stopped walking. He turned slowly to face Dakin. There were other men hidden here and there on the slope, but they were not watching the Kid. Their half-slit eyes were looking over their gun barrels, through the buckhorn sights and over the knifeblade front sights, waiting for a clear shot at the wolf-man who was hidden high above them.

"Are you really Bowman's bastard?" asked Sid.

"He's not my father," said the Kid.

"Then why did Kershaw bring you back here?"

The Kid smiled a little. "You know Kershaw," he said.

Sid nodded. "I know Kershaw. That's why I think you must be Bowman's bastard."

Hot sweat worked down the Kid's sides. The rock burned up through his worn bootsoles as though he was standing on a griddle. The heat waves shimmered and swayed, and the hard face of Sid Dakin seemed to go into focus and out of it again. "Look, Dakin," said the Kid. "Let me pass. I'll get a drink down at the creek and keep on going. That's what it is all about, isn't it? I won't come back."

Dakin looked sideways at a man standing behind a

boulder watching upslope toward Kershaw. "You hear that, Cousin Ben?" he asked. "He won't come back. . . ."

"He's got that right, anyway," said Cousin Ben.

Dakin raised his rifle. "Get rid of that Colt," he ordered.

The Kid dropped his hand to his Colt. He jumped sideways and dropped. "Shoot, Kershaw!" he yelled.

Dakin jumped out into clear to get a shot at the Kid. The Winchester high on the slope cracked flatly. Dakin spun about, dropped the Winchester, and staggered back behind the slab of rock. The second shot's echo chased the first. Cousin Ben went down with a bullet in his left shoulder. Dakin gripped his right shoulder with a dirty left hand. Blood leaked between his fingers. "Get the bastard!" he yelled. "Get the bastard! Get the bastard!" echoed and reechoed the mountain.

A faint wraith of gunsmoke drifted high on the slope. There was no one in sight. Nothing moved except the shimmering heat veils.

The Kid lay belly-flat on the burning ground with about six inches of rock higher than his shoulders and butt and with his face pressed against the ground. He slanted his eyes sideways and looked up the slope. The place seemed as barren and deserted as a lunar landscape.

"Go get him!" yelled Sid crazily at his *vaqueros.*

No one went to get *him;* no one moved.

When darkness came over the burning land, Lee heard a faint scraping, rustling noise. He sat up and reached for the Winchester.

"It's me," croaked the Kid.

Lee dragged him over the rock dike. "Get on your feet," he ordered.

"I'm burned to a crisp," groaned the Kid.

Lee hooked a hand under the Kid's collar. He dragged him to his feet. "When the moon comes up, it'll be like daylight on these slopes. We've got tracks to make before then."

The Kid thrust his burned face close to the hawk's face, dim under the hat brim. "To where, Goddamn you! There ain't no water up there! There ain't nothing up there but death, you ornery bastard!"

"You want to go back down there again?" asked Lee.

The Kid turned and began to climb up through the darkness.

The moon tinted the eastern sky. The moonlight grew across the country east of the Pecos.

"Listen," hissed Lee.

The Kid stopped and looked down the slope. A rock was clattering somewhere in the dimness below them.

When the moonlight bathed the great barren slopes, there was no sign of Kershaw and the Kid.

A man gingerly peered over the sheer edge of the escarpment. "Jesus, Al," he said over his shoulder. "That's at least a two thousand foot drop down to the slopes."

Al grounded his Winchester and wiped the sweat from his burning face. "They ain't up here, Carl. That's all there is to it."

Carl looked back down the great eastern slopes, now bright in the moonlight. "We're the only ones got up to the top," he said. He looked sideways at Al. "What the hell we goin' to tell Sid when we get back down there?"

"Not a Goddamned thing," said Al. "Because, brother, I ain't going back down there. In fact, I ain't ever going back to the Broken Bow, and if you've got any God-damned sense at all, you won't either. Not while Kershaw is still around. I want no part of that devil."

They walked together back down the slope. In a little while, the sound of their voices and that of the clattering rock was faint in the distance.

Lee stepped out from behind a rock. "Come on, Kid," he said.

The Kid walked like an automaton behind the lean shape of Lee Kershaw.

"Here," said Lee. He pointed to a dark opening in the rock wall. He waved a dirty hand. "Open, Sesame!" he cried. He led the Kid by an arm into the cave. He lit one of his reshaped candles and held it up. "Aladdin's cave,

Kid. Beyond it are the riches of the universe for you." He led the way into the winding passage with the cool draft playing about their burning faces.

Lee stopped in the great, domed room and lit the second candle. He stuck each of them on a separate stalagmite and gestured toward the emerald pool. "The Waters of Nepenthe," he said.

The Kid fell flat on his belly, and his face went under the clear cold water. He raised his head when he had drunk. "There is a madness in you, Kershaw," he said.

Lee rolled the last of the tobacco into two cigarettes. He placed one in the mouth of the Kid and one in his own. He lit them with one of the candles. "We've got a few hours until the moon passes over the mountains to the west," he said. "Then I'll take you home, Kid."

twenty-three

Duke Bowman sat in his heavy rawhide-covered chair and stared into the flickering, shifting kaleidoscope of color hovering over the thick bed of embers in the beehive fireplace. His big liver-spotted hands rested almost lifelessly on the hardwood arms of the chair. Slowly he raised his head. He turned to face the slight draft that suddenly blew into the room from an opened window.

The shadowy figure in the corner spoke softly: "What do you see in the color painting of the embers, Duke?"

"Kershaw?" asked Duke.

"I've brought someone home, Duke," said Lee.

The Kid walked toward his father. The dull eyes of the old man looked up into the firelit face of the son he had never really known.

Lee dropped into a chair close to the draped front window and handy to the liquor cabinet and Duke Bowman's fine clear Havanas. He finger-parted the drapes so that he could see down toward the shadow-darkened river and the pale ribbon of graveled road that came up the valley from the east. He poured a drink of brandy and lit a cigar. He could hear the murmuring voices of the two men, father and son, but he wasn't interested in what they were saying.

"Kershaw," said the old man.

Lee looked up.

"Bart will need your help to take over the Broken Bow," said the old man.

Lee shook his head. "My job is done, Bowman. I'm a manhunter, not a paid gun."

"I didn't know you had any principles in that respect," sneered Bowman.

Lee blew out a smoke ring and watched it lift and waver in the draft. "The Kid can take care of himself," he said.

"Against those killers! He wouldn't have a chance!"

Lee looked between the drapes. "What killers?" he asked over his shoulder.

"Why, Marsh, Sid, Cass, Chisos, Reata, and some of the others, like Nuno Mercado!"

Lee turned. "Chisos is dead with a bullet in his heart. Nuno Mercado is buried in an unmarked grave near Santa Fe. Reata died with a knife between his shoulder blades. Cass butted out what little brains he had. Sid is up near Ribbon Creek with a bullet in his right shoulder. Cousin Ben has one in the left shoulder."

The old man blinked his eyes. "Who killed them?" he asked.

Lee refilled his glass. "It wasn't your son," he replied.

Bowman looked at the Kid. "It still leaves Marsh and some of his boys."

The Kid looked at Lee. "What about him?" he asked.

"I'm willing to bet his boys have left him. You'll have to face him down, Kid."

Bowman stared at Lee. "Are you loco! Marsh will kill him!"

Lee looked at the Kid. "He can take care of himself, Duke."

"I'll go instead!"

Lee shook his head. "No, Duke. He has to do it himself."

The Kid drew his Colt and checked the loads. He snapped shut the loading gate.

Hoofs sounded on the graveled road. Lee peered through the parting of the drapes. A lone horseman was riding toward the great limestone *casa*. He looked up at the tower.

Lee let the drapes fall together. "He's down there now, Kid," he said over his shoulder. He stood up and refilled his glass. He downed the good brandy and wiped his mouth. Putting some cigars into a shirt pocket, he walked toward the rear window.

"Where the hell are you going?" asked Duke.

Lee turned when he reached the window. "My job is done," he said. "It's up to the Kid now, Duke."

The old man opened and then closed his mouth. He looked quickly at the Kid. When he looked back toward the window, Lee had vanished.

"Let him go," said the Kid.

"Marsh and his boys will cut you down," warned Duke.

The Kid shook his head. "Marsh will be alone, Duke."

"What makes you think so?"

The Kid lit a cigarette. "Marsh is probably the only one of them who's not afraid of Kershaw."

Duke gripped the arms of his chair. "Good luck, son," he said. He did not look around as the door closed behind the Kid. He heard the soft husking of the bootsoles on the stone steps and then the quiet closing of the lower tower door.

twenty-four

Marsh Dakin turned suddenly in his stride as he walked to-
ward the lamplit log *casa.* "Who're you?" he demanded.

The Kid walked forward into the rectangle of light from
one of the windows. "The name is Bowman," he replied.
"Bart Bowman."

Marsh stared at him. "The bastard?"

The Kid nodded.

"How'd you get in here?"

"Kershaw," replied the Kid.

Marsh nodded. "I can't believe it."

"I'm here," said the Kid simply.

Marsh glanced up toward the tower. "You talked with
the old man?"

The Kid nodded.

Marsh smiled thinly. "And he sent you down here to
take over?"

"You're getting the idea," agreed the Kid.

Marsh slowly rubbed his jaw. "I've got half a dozen *va-*
queros within shouting distance," he said.

The Kid shook his head. "You're all alone, mister."

"So, then it's finally between me and you?"

"There's no one else here," replied the Kid.

"Where's Kershaw?"

"Gone like he came—unseen by anyone."

"And yellow as a canary!"

The Kid shook his head. "He did his job."

"Maybe you should have sent him to face me down."

The Kid smiled. "That wasn't necessary."

Marsh telegraphed his intent by moving his head a little. The Kid gripped the rim of his hat and sailed it towards Marsh's face. Marsh averted his face but drew and fired where the Kid had been standing. The Kid had jumped sideways and turned halfway in a crouch to fire from waist level. Marsh dropped his smoking Colt to grip his right forearm with his left hand. Shock was on his face. Blood dripped between his left fingers. The double echo of the shooting died away up the dark canyon of the Broken Bow.

The Kid picked up his hat. He picked up Marsh's Colt and thrust it under his gun belt. "Let me take a look at that arm," he suggested.

Marsh shook his head. "The bullet went clean through," he said. He took out his bandanna and tied it about the forearm, drawing the knot tight with his teeth. "You could have killed me," he said. "Why didn't you?"

"I've never killed a man," the Kid said simply, "and I didn't want to start now."

Marsh nodded. "Fair enough," he said. "I'll take my horse. He's my own, Bowman."

Marsh walked toward the log *casa*. He opened the door. The Kid followed him into the large living room. Stella Dakin sat in a chair beside the table. She wore her basque traveling coat and her ridiculous hat with the dusty bird atop it staring at the world with its glassy eyes.

"She's all ready to travel, Marsh," said Lee easily. He sat in a chair tilted back against the wall. A cigar was stuck in the side of his mouth, and his lean face was wreathed in thin smoke. He never took his eyes away from Stella.

Marsh looked at his sister. "It's all over, Stell," he said.

"You botched the deal," she said thinly.

The Kid studied her. He looked at Lee. Lee nodded. "She's the real enemy, Kid," he said.

"I've got something coming to me!" she shrilled.

"You sure have," said Lee drily. He relit his cigar. "The old man is slowly dying, Marsh," he said. He looked up at the foreman. "You know why?"

"I haven't any idea," said Marsh.

Lee let the chair tilt forward. He stood up. "Ask her," he suggested. He looked at the Kid. "Come on, Kid."

Marsh held up his left hand. "Wait," he said. "You've started something here, Kershaw. You'd better finish it."

"Did you know how her first husband died?" asked Lee.

Her eyes were fixed and set. The thin wirelike lines at the corners of her mouth drew down hard. "He's lying, Marsh," she said.

Marsh looked at her. "I wonder," he said.

"Duke Bowman has only a few months to live," put in Lee. "Remember how he used to be, Marsh? Up until five years ago, he could take on any man of his *corrida* with fist and boot. Now, look at him."

Marsh looked at his sister with horror. "I never believed that story about your first husband," he said slowly.

"He's lying!" she repeated.

Lee jerked his head at the Kid. They walked outside. They could hear the rising voices from within the log *casa*.

"What is it, Lee?" asked the Kid.

Lee looked up at the tower where Duke Bowman waited for slow death. "They called her the Black Widow once," he said. He looked at the Kid. "They breed with the male and then poison him so the young can live off his body." He looked toward the house. He shook his head. "I'll need a horse," he said.

"Take your pick," said the Kid.

"I'll go look for my dun."

"How much does the old man owe you?"

"About a thousand," replied Lee.

"I'll go get it."

Lee shook his head. He walked toward the corral. "You can mail it to me, Kid, when you get around to it."

Marsh banged open the door of the *casa* and stomped out on the log porch. There was a sick look of horror on his face. He mounted his horse and set spurs to it. The sound of the hoofs rattled on the hard gravel and died away on the river road beyond the great limestone house.

Lee led out a team hitched to a buggy. He led it to the front of the log house. He walked back to get his horse, which Marsh had led back to the corral.

The woman came slowly to the door. She looked at the team and the buggy and then at the Kid. "You'll be needing a housekeeper," she said.

There was no answer from the Kid. She got into the buggy and picked up the reins. She touched up the team with a whip. She did not look back as she drove through the dark shadowed *bosque*.

Lee walked the dun to where the Kid was standing in the road looking toward the *bosque*. The Kid turned. "I'll need a good ramrod here now, Lee," he said. "How about it?"

Lee shook his head. "It's not my line of business. Goodbye, Kid."

The Kid watched him ride toward the *bosque*. "Where do I mail you the money?" he called out.

Lee turned in the saddle and rested a hand on the cantle. "Why," he said, "to General Delivery, Santa Fe."

"You planning on working up there?"

Lee shrugged. "I had an interesting proposition up there, Kid. I'm due for a little rest. Thought I'd sort of scout out the lay of the land up there for future work."

"Vaya con Dios!" called out the Kid.

Lee did not look back. He raised his right hand and waggled it. In a little while, he was gone in the shadows, and the sound of the hoof beats was drowned out by the subdued roar of the Broken Bow.

RENEGADE'S TRAIL

AUTHOR'S NOTE

There was a halfbreed named Queho in the wild country where Arizona, California, and Nevada come together. In the early 1900s, he ran amok, but not wildly. He haunted the canyons and barrens, and unseen he picked off his victims with a rifle or perhaps with a knife. Legend has it that he killed twenty-three victims—sheepherders, travelers, prospectors, and lawmen. The number of victims included men, women, and children. Some say he killed no more than twelve people, but a dozen *or* twenty-three equally established him as a homicidal maniac. His first victim was murdered in 1910; his last known victim was a woman murdered in 1919. During the intervening years, some of the best manhunters and trackers in that area, white men and Indians both, found traces of Queho, but they never saw their quarry. Two prospectors were found murdered and mutilated after the death of the woman, but it has never been established that Queho was the murderer, although it is quite likely that he was. The posse that hunted Queho after this double murder did not find him, but they did find the skeletons of two unidentified men who had been murdered in that same area five years past. Three thousand dollars in rewards was offered for Queho's apprehension, but it was never collected.

Eleven years after the murder of the woman and the two prospectors, in the year 1930, Queho was seen in Las Vegas. He bought a can of peaches in a grocery store, paid for it, and departed from the store. He walked on Fremont

Street in broad daylight and then walked into oblivion and local history. He was never seen alive again, and if he committed any other murders after that, it has never been established that he did.

In 1940, two prospectors five miles upriver from El Dorado Canyon spotted a small cave near the base of a hundred-foot sheer cliff. The area is of volcanic origin, and caves are many. What drew the attention of the two prospectors was that the cave mouth was closed with a carefully laid rock wall. They broke down the wall and found the mummified body of Queho. Within the cave the prospectors found a Winchester rifle and a Hopkins and Allen shotgun, as well as a bow and arrows. There were empty and loaded cartridge cases, primers, powder and bullets, tobacco cans, various reloading tools and other tools, and a watchman's badge Number 896. The watchman had been murdered by Queho at the Gold Bug mill thirty years earlier.

The mummified remains of Queho were and may still be exhibited in the Las Vegas Elks Helldorado Village, along with his goods and chattels.

For my book *Renegade's Trail*, I borrowed only the name of Queho and the hideout cave in which he lived. The rest is fiction.

Gordon D. Shirreffs

ONE

IT WAS NEARING the Time of Little Eagles in Arizona Territory. A cold early spring wind swept fine gravel from the barren floor of the Hualapai Valley and bitter alkali dust from the dry Red Lake bed hard against the taut faces of the two men who stood at the heads of their tired horses looking to the north toward the distant and unseen Colorado River Canyon.

Lee Kershaw turned at last from the searching wind and stepped behind his dun horse to feel for the makings within his sheepskin jacket. "He's either headed for the Crossing or he's damned sure to be hiding out with the Hualapais," he suggested.

Queho turned to look at Lee. His strange, light-colored eyes, so startling in contrast with his dark face and thick, dark lips, studied the white man. "No risk the Crossing," he said quietly. "Hualapais all gone. You white men took them from home here, maybe eight years ago, to La Paz on Colorado. Many died there. Hualapais all gone, Kershaw. You knew that."

Lee lighted the cigarette within the sheltering cup of a big hand and then placed it between the thick lips of the breed tracker. He began to shape one for himself. He nodded. "I had forgotten," he said.

"I did not."

Lee nodded again. "I had nothing to do with it, Queho."

"But you're white," argued Queho.

Lee lighted the cigarette. "Don't start that all over

163

again," he quietly warned. "We came north to find Ahvote. Remember?"

Queho looked south. "Willow Grove Spring," he said.

"That's thirty miles southeast of here! Why the hell would he head south right back into the faces of the men following him?"

Queho took his cigarette from his mouth and looked at it as though he had never seen one quite like it before. "Maybe the woman be there now," he quietly suggested.

Kershaw looked quickly at him. "Mrs. Felding?"

Queho nodded. "Colonel Felding leave Prescott for Fort Mohave Reservation on inspection trip. Wife go along, eh?"

Lee nodded. He grinned. "He damned well wouldn't leave her back at Prescott with all the male wolves snuffling around her broad rump."

"He stay at Fort Mohave awhile, then take steamer to Yuma."

Lee looked thoughtfully to the southeast. He was tired, although he'd never admit it to the breed. When he moved in the saddle, the knife wound in his back, which had healed slowly because of infection, ached dully, and there was hardly any position he could take to ease the pain. He had been hurriedly drafted from a damned good poker game to start out after Ahvote, who had broken loose from the *juzgado* and killed a guard in the process. Ahvote was good at killing, a real professional by now.

"Ahvote want woman," added the breed.

"He's loco!" snapped Lee. "There'll be at least ten troopers with Felding and his wife."

"Ahvote want woman. Ahvote *get* woman."

Lee studied the scarred dark face of Queho. The man had an uncanny ability to forecast coming events.

"No sense to go on to river," said Queho.

"That's the way he went two months ago."

"Mean nothing."

Lee leaned against the dun. His shoulder was throbbing.

It wouldn't take much argument from the tracker at that to get Lee to turn back. Two things prevented him—to show weakness in front of Queho and to admit that Queho was right in that Ahvote *had* gone south, for Lee's pride would not let him admit that Queho was a better tracker than himself.

Queho knelt and passed a dark and powerful hand down the left rear leg of his sorrel. "Horse go a little lame soon," he said.

"Goddamn it! Anything else?" snapped Lee.

Queho stood up. "You know I'm right, Kershaw," he said quietly. "Besides, Queho responsible for you, Kershaw. You know that too."

"That's the Paiute in you talking now," sneered Kershaw.

Queho shook his head. "Mohave Apache," he corrected. "Ahvote Chemehuevis Paiute. *Not* Queho!"

Kershaw began to unstrap a saddlebag. "So, the Mohave Apache in you saved my life two months ago when Ahvote stuck a knife in my back and was ready to finish the job when you caught up with him."

He turned to look at the scarred face of the breed. Ahvote's knife had cut across Queho's broad nose and just under his left eye to score down to the bone clear to the point of the chin, missing the jugular only by inches. "What about the white man in *you?*" he added. "Are you your brother's keeper, Queho? God knows himself that you have nothing to owe to any white man."

Queho studied the lean, brown face of Lee Kershaw, thin from the loss of blood when Ahvote's knife-tip had sought his life source. "Maybe you forgot nigger blood too, eh, Kershaw?" he queried.

Lee took out the brandy bottle. He pulled the cork out with his teeth and drank deeply and again, until he felt the life-giving jolt of the brandy deep in his lean guts. He wiped his mouth with the back of a hand and held out the bottle to the breed. Queho shook his head. "Not now, Kershaw. One of us got to stay sober."

"Who's going to get drunk?" demanded Lee.

Queho shrugged. "Maybe you. You got three whole bottles to yourself. Go ahead. Kill the pain. Queho take care of you."

"Up your ass!" snapped Lee. He drank again. The breed was right. Lee would never make it to Willow Grove Spring without killing the pain.

TWO

THE CAMP AT Willow Grove Spring slept in the cold and windy darkness before the coming of the dawn. Now and again the wind would sweep an invisible paw across the wide, thick bed of ashes that covered the still smoldering fire. When it did so, the red eyes of the embers would light up fitfully, and in the dim, uncertain light could be seen the forms of the troopers huddled under their blankets, furred by ashes, with their feet toward the fire and their heads buried from sight under the blankets. The horses and mules stood with their rumps to the keen wind and with their heads hanging low, picketed in a line among the thin skein of willows that curved around the shallow pool of water seeping from the rock formation above and behind the camp. When the fire flared up, the dim light would reflect itself from the dusty windows of the lone dougherty wagon. All that moved about the camp were the wind-thrashed willows; the flapping sides of the single A-tent that stood like a geometrically shaped ghost beyond the campfire and the dougherty wagon, and the thin wraith of white smoke that drifted downwind from the periodically aroused fire.

Ahvote came through the cold and windy darkness as silently as the drifting smoke. He stood in the darkness beside a tip-tilted slab of rock that thrust itself up from a rise above the spring. Nothing moved about Ahvote except for the slow rise and fall of his deep chest and his restless eyes as he scanned the camp. Earlier, there had been only one sentry, but now he was not in sight. But now, as the fire

167

flared up higher in a strong gust of wind, the light reflected from something that protruded from the half-open door on the lee side of the dougherty wagon. It was a booted foot with a polished spur strapped to it—it was the spur that had caught the firelight. Even as Ahvote watched, the foot moved and then turned over, to be joined by the other foot as the sentry shifted to get into a more comfortable position out of the cold pre-dawn wind.

Ahvote vanished noiselessly into the darkness as the sentry suddenly sat up sleepily within the doorway of the wagon to glance toward the blanket-covered form of Sergeant Elias Bentinck, in charge of the agent's escort to Fort Mohave. The sentry yawned prodigiously, mentally debating whether or not he could get a little more shut-eye before dawn. He never heard the opening and closing of the door on the windward side of the vehicle. He threw back his head to yawn and stretch, just in time for the razor edge of the butcher knife to rip open his taut throat-muscles from ear to ear. The body was pulled back into the dougherty. The door was closed. The other door silently opened and then was closed. The camp seemed just as it had been before the killing. The only difference now was the soft sound of blood dripping through a crack in the floor of the dougherty.

The blood-wet knife sliced through the back of the tent, and Ahvote stepped inside. An Argand lamp with the wick turned down as low as possible stood on a camp table. A cot stood on each side of the tent. A man snored softly in one of them; a woman breathed heavily in the other. Ahvote gathered together some of the woman's clothing and gear. Silently he left the tent and as silently returned. He stood for a time looking down at the red face and fat throat of "Kentucky Colonel" Will Felding, special inspecting agent for the Indian Bureau. Ahvote's strong hand tightened spasmodically about the haft of his knife as he looked at the red face of the man who had been the cause of sending him to prison in Prescott. He looked toward the huddled form of the woman. It had really been her who had been the cause of it, on second thought. She who had lied and *lied* about Ahvote to the fat white man and anyone else who would listen to her! To kill the fat white man would be sweet indeed, but revenge would be better served by stealing the fat one's woman and then laughing at him, from many miles of distance between them of course, as he laid the white woman again and again until she would beg for mercy.

The familiar spoor of the woman rose to meet his flared nostrils—the definable combination scent of female sweat, face powder, and expensive perfume. He had known that scent at Prescott.

Once the fat man rolled over and let a thick arm drop a hamlike hand onto the canvas groundcloth of the tent, but he had turned toward the windbellied wall of the tent instead of toward the side of the tent where his wife should have been sleeping. Had he done so and opened his eyes he would have seen the twisted blankets that now trailed down to the tent floor, and the emptiness of the cot itself.

Once, as the first gray tint of the false dawn washed against the eastern sky, a mule snorted in warning at the Indian smell, but after that, the camp returned to its normal routine of thrashing willows, bellying tent-canvas, and wind-drifting smoke.

THREE

COLONEL FELDING DISMOUNTED awkwardly from his tired bay and reached for his cased field glasses hanging from the saddle. The insides of his fat thighs were chafed raw and wet from hours in the saddle, but he could show no agony on his face in front of the hard-assed escort troopers, who had dismounted from their worn-out mounts and stood down the slope watching him and Sergeant Elias Bentinck. It had been Bentinck who had called Felding's attention to the movement on the side of the mountain to the north. Felding's thick fingers fumbled clumsily with the focusing screw of the field glasses. His breathing was harsh and heavy. Will Felding was a man whose blood pressure was dangerously high. He peered through the powerful glasses. "By God, Bentinck," he said in a strangled tone. "It's them all right!" He handed the glasses to the soldier. "By God," he added brokenly, "we'll never catch up with them now!"

Bentinck focused the glasses. First the pale face of Mildred Felding came into view. Her long blond hair (peroxided secretly at regular intervals, so as not to show the dark roots) hung down alongside her rather round face and over her magnificent bosom (all of it real), held up by the very latest type of support imported from Kansas City. Her shoulders were slumped, and she sat her saddle with her hands resting on the pommel. Bentinck shifted the glasses and picked up the dark face of Ahvote. The man stood at the head of the mule he had been riding, looking down toward the pursuit party. He did not seem much concerned. Why should he feel concerned? The troopers' stubby .45/70 carbines could never reach him at that range, at least with any accuracy, and by the time the troopers reached the foot of the precipitous trail, it would be long dark and he would be long gone beyond the mountain.

"Well?" Felding asked Bentinck.

The trail was narrow and treacherous, hardly a yard wide, with a two-hundred-foot sheer wall above it and a two-hundred-foot sheer wall below it. The foot of the trail was at least two miles away from the pursuit party. The trail seemed to turn into the mountain itself two-hundred yards beyond where the Paiute stood looking down at them. There was about half an hour of daylight left.

"Damn you!" snapped Felding.

Bentinck lowered the glasses. "The only thing we can do, sir, is to keep pushing him."

"The horses are worn out!"

"So are the men, sir."

"That's my wife up there!"

"Listen to *him*," murmured Trooper Nolan to Trooper Cassidy.

"Well, he can't call her a whore in front of us," said Cassidy wisely.

"Shut up there!" snapped Corporal Frantz.

"Ye *know* we're right, Corporal darlin'," murmured Cassidy.

"It was she who led that poor bastard on up there whin she was back at Whipple Barracks," added Nolan. "Wigglin' that fat rump of hers in front av any would-be stud."

"Like you," suggested Trooper Schmidt. "The voman iss a bitch!"

Frantz opened and closed his mouth. They were right. Besides, Felding could not hear them, and Bentinck would have agreed with them if he was not wearing three stripes.

"What to do!" cried Felding in agony. "She's so lovely! So sweet! So young! So helpless!"

Cassidy rolled his eyes upward. "Like a she-wolf in heat," he said.

Felding reached for Bentinck's booted carbine. "I'll kill her myself rather than let him ravish her!"

"We can't reach up there with a carbine, sir," reminded Bentinck.

"There are two men coming up the trail, Sergeant Bentinck!" called out Frantz.

Bentinck turned and raised the glasses. The lead rider was a cigar-smoking white man, a lean lath of a man whose reddish beard fluttered in the cold wind. The second man was a breed. "It's Lee Kershaw, sir," said Bentinck over his shoulder, "and that stinkin' breed Queho."

"Thank God!" cried Felding. "Kershaw will know what to do!"

Bentinck lowered the glasses. "Shit," he said under his breath.

Lee Kershaw waved a casual hand at the troopers (almost *too* casual, thought Corporal Frantz) and reined in his tired dun beside Felding and Bentinck. Queho dismounted and took the reins of Kershaw's dun as Lee dismounted. Lee eased his crotch and shifted his cigar from one side of his mouth to the other. "What's up?" he asked. Bentinck wordlessly handed him the glasses and pointed toward the mountainside. Already the hollows were inked in with shadows as the cold-looking sun sank westward. It didn't take Bentinck long to clue Kershaw in about what had happened at Willow Grove Spring.

Lee lowered the glasses and whistled softly. He looked back at Queho. "You were right," he said.

Felding caught Lee's fruity breath. "You've been drinking on duty!" he accused.

Lee nodded. "Keeps off the chill of the day," he agreed.

"What can we do now, Kershaw?" asked Felding.

Kershaw shrugged. *"Nada,"* he said.

Felding glanced toward the Sharps rifle in the long, embossed saddle-scabbard on Lee's dun. "Maybe you can reach him with the Sharps, Kershaw? You know that rifle better than I ever did. Will you try?"

"He's been drinking," put in Bentinck. "I'll try, sir."

Lee shifted his cigar. "*Never* volunteer," he said quietly.

"Maybe five hundred yards," said Bentinck.

"Closer to six hundred and fifty," corrected Lee. "No soldier-trained shot can make a hit on Ahvote at that range in this light, and uphill at that."

"Seven hundred yards," said Queho. It was the first time he had spoken. No one paid any attention to him. No one but Lee, that is.

"Well?" asked Felding. "By the time you get around to it, Kershaw, the Paiute will be gone."

"It's a wonder he's not gone now," said Lee drily. He raised the glasses again. He picked up the pale, frightened face of the woman. *Bitch*, he thought.

"You know there's no other rifle like that in this Territory," reminded Felding. "I won every damned match I ever entered with it before you came along and beat me at poker for it."

"Only two cases primed and loaded, Kershaw," reminded Queho. "No time to load more now."

"You let him call you that?" asked Bentinck. "He doesn't call you mister?"

Lee shrugged. "He's my friend. He saved my life." He jerked a thumb at the breed. "Get the Sharps," he added. He spoke out of the side of his mouth: "At least I *think* he's my friend."

"He might very well be the only one you've got," said Bentinck.

Lee eyed the truculent noncom. "That gives me some grace," he murmured.

Felding stamped back and forth in his impatience. He was tired. Ever since he had married Mildred two years past and had taken her on his inspection trips throughout the Southwest, he had been trying to act the part of a man twenty-five years younger than he was. The act was wearing him out, although he'd be the last to admit it publicly.

"Better use the Vollmer," advised Lee.

Queho nodded. He swiftly removed the vernier-tang sight from its mount and then quickly fitted the fine ten-power scope to the top of the long rifle. The scope was precision-made of the finest German glass by Vollmer of Jena, who had no peer in the business. It had cost Felding a small fortune in Denver. Queho lowered the breechblock and used the bullet-starter to seat the paper-patched 370-grain bullet in the rifling just ahead of the chamber.

"He'll be gone by the time the breed gets it loaded!" said Bentinck.

"Shut up," said Lee. "There's still time."

Queho withdrew the bullet-starter and slid the long brass cartridge loaded with 70 grains of powder into the chamber. He closed the breech and full-cocked the eleven-pound rifle. He held it out toward Lee. Lee shook his head. "You're on, Queho," he said quietly. "I can't risk a shot with this brandy in me."

"You're loco!" said Bentinck. "That breed can't shoot!"

"Watch him," said Lee. He turned and let Queho rest the long barrel on his shoulder. He took the cigar from his mouth, so that the smoke would not blow across the end of the telescope.

"Drunk or sober, you're the best shot here!" cried Felding to Lee.

"By the time we get through arguing," said Lee out of the side of his mouth, "Ahvote will be out of sight. Shoot, Queho, and be damned to them!"

Queho drew back on the rear trigger. The front trigger clicked faintly as it was set. Queho placed the tip of his finger against the front trigger and drew in a deep breath as he sighted. He let out half of it. For a few seconds the breed was absolutely motionless; then his fingertip almost imperceptibly tightened.

"Don't hit him in the head," said Felding suddenly. "I want his skull for a tobacco jar!"

Lee felt Queho move at Felding's callous remark a fraction of a second before the Sharps crashed out flame and smoke and sent a bellowing echo racing along the ground. An acrid cloud of smoke blew back against Lee's face.

"Goddamn you, breed!" yelled Bentinck as he looked through the field glasses. "You damned near hit Mrs. Felding! The Paiute is moving along the trail! Give me that rifle!" He handed the glasses to Felding and ripped the rifle from the hands of the breed, backhanding Queho with his free hand as he did so. Queho reeled back against Lee, blood leaking from the side of his mouth. "I'll get him, sir!" cried Bentinck as he snapped down the breechblock. Lee caught the empty cartridge-case before it could damage itself on the hard ground. As he came upward again, his right hand closed about the cartridge to form a hard fist, which hit Bentinck on the point of the jaw to drive him hard-assed onto the ground, while with his left hand, Lee ripped the rifle from the soldier's hand. He swung and handed the rifle to Queho. "Reload!" He snatched the field glasses from Felding and focussed them on the mountain trail, while Queho swiftly loaded the smoking Sharps with a packed bullet and the last primed and loaded case.

Ahvote was leading his mule and the woman's horse along the trail. Queho handed the rifle to Lee. He turned to let Lee rest the Sharps on his broad shoulder. With no trace of the good brandy evident, Lee sighted on Ahvote. He set the front trigger and tightened his finger on it. For a few seconds he was as motionless as Queho had been; then the Sharps crashed.

The troopers cheered, not so much because the woman had been saved as for the fantastic skill of Lee Kershaw. The big slug had hit Ahvote almost at the instant of his turning off the trail and out of sight. The Paiute had fallen, arms and legs stiffly outthrust, to pinwheel down into the shadows at the foot of the two-hundred-foot drop below the trail.

The shot echo died; the smoke drifted off.

"Thank God," breathed Felding. "Bentinck, go up there and get my wife."

Bentinck slowly wiped the blood from the side of his mouth. His hard green eyes never left Lee Kershaw. He said nothing, but the warning was evident in his eyes. He would not forget.

"There just might be a killin' between those two some day," suggested Trooper Nolan as he watched Bentinck ride with two men toward the foot of the trail. "That is, if Kershaw hangs around long enough."

"Aye," agreed Cassidy. "Ten dollars on Bentinck," he added.

"Ye're on," agreed Nolan, "but I think I shud give ye odds, Tim."

Felding looked at Corporal Frantz. "Get an oat sack for the breed here, Frantz," he ordered. "Queho, you go and get Ahvote's head for me."

Queho did not move. His dark face was enigmatic, but his strange, light-colored eyes swiveled to look toward the shadowed base of the mountain.

Frantz brought the oat sack to the breed but Queho would not take it. The noncom looked at Felding and shrugged.

"Take the sack, Queho," ordered Felding.

Lee bit off the end of a fresh cigar and cupped a lighted match about the tip of it. "He won't go near the newly dead, Felding," he said around the cigar. "At least not one he was instrumental in killing."

"That's Indian superstition!" said Felding.

Lee nodded as he fanned out the match. "Yup," he agreed. "It surely is. Besides, it's real enough to him."

"But he's only a breed! What the hell difference would it make to him?"

Lee shrugged. "Sometimes he thinks like a white man and sometimes he thinks like an Indian."

"You forgot nigger," said Corporal Frantz.

The sun was gone, and the wind had turned colder.

Lee ejected the cartridge case from the fine Sharps. He placed a wet patch in the chamber and pushed it through with a wooden wiping stick.

"I can order him to go," said Felding at last.

Lee shook his head. "You've got no authority over him," he said.

"He's a government scout, isn't he?"

Lee shook his head again as he started a second patch through the rifling. "Only when they needed him and they paid him by the day. They never honored him by taking him on the payroll. He's done his job. He found Ahvote, after you did, of course, but he knew Ahvote had come back south, which is more than I did."

"How did he know?" suddenly asked Felding.

Lee slid the Sharps into its long saddle-scabbard. "Beats the hell out of me," he replied. He looked sideways at Felding. "Maybe it's the Mohave Apache in him," he slyly suggested.

Felding flushed. He thrust out a thick finger toward the face of the breed. "You get your ass over there and get that goddamned head, breed, or you'll never get another job from the government!"

"Caesar has spoken," drily commented Lee. He swung up into his saddle. "Come on, Queho. Let's find some water. I'm hungry."

Queho turned toward his sorrel.

"I'm warning you!" roared Felding.

"He's coming with me," said Lee.

"To Prescott?" asked Felding.

Lee shook his head. "I had a bellyful of Prescott. I'm heading out of this country."

"Where to?"

Lee shrugged. "Fort Mohave, then maybe down the river to Yuma. After that? *¿Quien sabe?* Maybe the sun of Sonora will help heal this damned shoulder of mine."

"And he's going with you?"

"If he wants to," replied Lee.

Queho mounted the sorrel. "I go," he said simply.

"Wait," said Felding. He came closer to Lee and looked up into the bearded face shadowed beneath the hatbrim. For a moment Lee almost thought the agent was going to thank him for killing Ahvote and saving Milly Felding's life. "I want that rifle back, Kershaw," said Felding. "You know, like a trophy. After all, it did save my wife's life. Of course, you did kill Ahvote, but you'd never have made it without my rifle. I want it back, Kershaw."

"Like another trophy? Like Ahvote's skull for a tobacco jar?" Lee drew in on the cigar, and the flaring of the tip lighted his hard, gray eyes as they studied the face of the agent.

Felding nodded eagerly without catching Lee's point. "A pair of great conversation pieces for a cosy corner in the fine house I'll build some day for Milly and myself, Kershaw. Now, I'm willing to pay you double of what you think it's worth."

Lee touched the dun with his heels and kneed the horse away from the agent. He rode off down the slope followed by the breed.

"God damn you, Kershaw!" roared Felding. "Who the hell do you think you are?"

Lee looked back over his shoulder. "Why, *I'm* Lee Kershaw, *Colonel*. Now, who the hell do you think *you* are?"

Lee and Queho disappeared into the shadows far down the slope. The last sound the men on the rim of the slope heard was the crashing of an empty brandy bottle on the rocky ground; then it was quiet again, except for the dry, cold voice of the wind.

FOUR

A COLD, SEARCHING April wind swept across the barren country beyond Fort Mohave. It drove grit and gravel like buckshot against the post buildings and pitted the dusty window-glass. It rattled the halyards of the tall, warped flagpole and shaped the snapping garrison flag into what seemed like a sheet of corrugated iron painted in red, white, and blue. The Colorado River at the western edge of the post was being driven in hard-looking white-topped waves against the California shore. The wind tugged at the steamer *Mohave,* which was moored to the post's sagging wharf. Chunk firewood cut and piled by reservation Mohave Apache and Chemehuevis at the foot of the wharf was being carried aboard the *Mohave* for her return run downriver the next day. Metal clanged against metal as the engineers repaired the slow-speed, cross-compound engine to ready it for the dawn departure-time for Ehrenburg, where it would pick up ore from the dying placer mines of La Paz and Ehrenburg, as well as passengers from Wickenburg who waited at Ehrenburg for the down steamer.

The sun was slanting down over the California mountains when Lee Kershaw and Queho boarded the *Mohave* with most of their gear, destination Yuma. While Queho stowed away the luggage in the tiny double-bunked cabin reserved for Lee, Lee went out on deck. He bit the end from a long nine and lighted it. He raised his gray eyes over the end of the cigar to look across the dusty parade ground to where Mildred Felding and her husband were walking toward the wharf, followed by half a dozen troopers carrying their luggage and whose eyes were fixed on that fascinating rump action of Milly Felding. They weren't alone in their observations. The eyes of every other man on the post were looking around corners, from within doorways, or through dusty, gravel-pitted windows at that rump.

"I get saddles and other gear now," said Queho from behind Lee. "Where I sleep?"

"There are two bunks in there," replied Lee.

"You know I no can stay in there."

"You can as far as I'm concerned."

"But not him," said Queho. He jerked his head toward Captain Jack Mellen, who was descending the ladder from the pilothouse. "No Indian, no breed, sleep in cabins."

"I paid first-class passage for two," said Lee.

"Kershaw know better."

The breed was right, thought Lee.

"Someday I get you trouble—much trouble," said Queho.

Mellen came toward Lee. "Glad to have you abroad, Lee. Poker tonight?"

"Glad to be aboard, Jack. I might try a hand or two. You don't really need me though. Will Felding will stay up all night with you if you mention a game."

Mellen nodded. "Some say his wife is better at the game than he is," he observed as he watched her approaching the end of the wharf.

"She's better at a *lot* of games than he is," added Lee.

"It's a wonder he isn't wise to it—everyone else seems to be."

"I said she was better at playing games than he was," reminded Lee.

Milly was being helped onto the gangplank, displaying a high-buttoned patent-leather shoe rather tightly fastened about a too plump calf. As she raised her head, she boldly looked up into the eyes of Lee Kershaw. Jack Mellen did not miss the look. "They'll be in the next cabin to yours all the way to Yuma, Lee," he said.

"I'll keep the door between us locked at all times," said Lee drily. "You've got a dirty mind, Jack."

Jack grinned. "Just interested in the interplay between a predatory female and a real stud like yourself, Lee."

"You honor me," murmured Lee.

"I go now," said Queho.

Lee nodded.

"Where I sleep, Kershaw?"

Lee jerked a thumb back toward the cabin. "In there."

Queho looked at Mellen.

Mellen shook his head. "No, Kershaw," he said firmly.

Lee flicked the ashes from the end of his cigar. His gray eyes took on the blue ones of Jack Mellen. "I paid first-class passage for two," he reminded the skipper.

"No, Kershaw," repeated Mellen. "Personally, I don't give a goddamn if you want the breed in there with you, but the company won't allow it, and you know that as well as I do."

"He'll freeze his ass off on the freight deck, Jack!"

"I'll refund your money," said Jack.

Lee turned to speak to the breed, but Queho was gone. He looked down to the wharf and saw the breed walking silently toward the shore. "Can you imagine how he must feel?" asked Lee.

"Dammit, Kershaw! I don't make the rules! Why must you flaunt your damned tolerance in everyone's faces?"

Lee shrugged. "*¿Quien sabe?* He works well with me. He saved my life. I can depend on him, which is perhaps the most important of all. I suppose he's the next thing to a true friend."

"What is he anyway? Half Paiute?"

Kershaw relighted his cigar. "They say his mother was the product of a drunken Mexican teamster and a half-witted Mohave Apache squaw, and some say she was half

181

Chemehuevis, which is about the next thing to a Southern Paiute, but don't ever say that to *him*. He's proud of the Mohave Apache blood."

"And his father?"

"His father was a trooper when Negro cavalry were stationed here for a short time. He was a mulatto, or a quadroon, or an octaroon, but to the Army he was a nigger, and so was enlisted into a black unit. How the hell they classify such mixed white and black blood is beyond me."

"So, in a sense, he's not really a *half*-breed then?"

Lee smiled faintly. "Classifying, eh, Jack?"

Milly Felding appeared at the top of the ladder, followed by her puffing husband and the gaggle of luggage-carrying troopers.

"They say he deliberately missed that shot at Ahvote," suggested Mellen.

Lee shook his head. "No one can ever know that. He had no love for Ahvote. Besides, it was almost an impossible shot. You could have seen that had you been there, Jack."

"But *you* hit Ahvote! The story of that shot has traveled all over the Territory. You're a legend in your own time, Kershaw!"

Lee waved a casual hand. "Dumb luck," he said quietly.

"Well, Kershaw!" cried Will Felding jovially. "We're to be neighbors, I see!"

"All the way to Yuma," said Lee drily. He tipped his hat to Milly Felding and her great blue eyes widened as she smiled. She was an artist with those guileless-looking eyes. "Mister Kershaw can entertain us with his tales of manhunting, I'm sure," she said.

"He never talks about them, ma'am," put in Mellen.

"But he must! He's famous now, Captain Mellen."

Lee almost gagged. He turned away and looked toward the shore. The sun was gone now. The lights of the post winked on through the gathering darkness, and the lights of the steamer twinkled on the wind-driven waves like watered silk ribbon. There would be no more passengers.

Will Felding closed the door behind himself and his wife. The troopers walked toward the ladder. "You see that ass of hers, Charley?" one of the troopers asked another one. "Who could miss it?" retorted Charley. The troopers were still laughing when they reached the freight deck.

"Have to check the repair work," said Jack. "We leave at first light of dawn." His feet thudded on the ladder.

Lee Kershaw stood alone on the windswept deck with the tip of his cigar alternately lighting his face as he drew in on the weed or plunging it again into shadow as the tip dimmed away. Queho was taking a hell of a long time to get the rest of the gear.

Lee went into his cabin. He could hear the voices of Will and Milly Felding from the next cabin through the thin connecting door. Milly's rather shrill, petulant voice was overriding the deeper tones of her husband. It seemed she wasn't too happy with the accommodations.

Lee lighted the gimbaled lamp and felt about in one of his bags for a brandy bottle. He drank deeply and then again to take his mind off his aching shoulder. There was a good army surgeon down at Fort Yuma; an expert on knife and gunshot wounds. He was the real reason Lee was going downriver.

He stripped to the waist and eyed in the mirror his lean upper body with the faint whitish lines of knife scars and a few puckered bullet holes. None of them had taken so long to heal as the one that bothered him now. He heard the faint ringing of the dinner gong as he changed undershirt and shirt. He shrugged a little painfully into his coat and selected a few long nines, which he placed in his coat pocket. He eyed himself in the mirror. A lean and saturnine-looking face stared back at him with hard gray eyes, a startling contrast to the brown mahogany of his face and the reddish brown beard and mustache. "*Bien parecido,*" said Kershaw to himself. He grinned as he blew out the lamp and left the cabin.

Queho stood at the after end of the hurricane deck and watched Lee enter the little dining salon behind the pilothouse. He hurriedly brought the saddles to the cabin and dumped them on the floor. He lighted a match and found a brandy bottle. He drank again and again, his throat working convulsively. He wiped his thick lips, grinned, and drank again and again.

FIVE

"YOU CAME WEST with the Army I believe, Kershaw?" asked Will Felding as he mounded the mashed potatoes on his plate and scooped out a hollow on the top. He reached for the gravy boat and neatly topped the hollow with the thick, brown fluid.

"No," replied Lee. "Born and bred in New Mexico Territory."

"But you did serve, eh?"

Lee nodded. "One hitch was enough, Colonel."

"They say you scouted for a time?"

"For a time," agreed Lee. He kept looking at Felding to avoid the rather intent stare in Mildred Felding's too large baby-blue eyes. "I didn't like hunting and killing Indians."

"I could have sworn you served longer than one hitch," continued Felding.

Jack Mellen shoved back his plate. "He did," he said drily. "But not in the United States Army."

Felding looked up quickly. "Eh? What does that mean?"

Lee smiled. "In Mexico," he said. "Sonora, Chihuahua, Coahuila, and a few other places."

"You mean—in the *Mexican* Army?" asked Mildred.

"Not exactly," replied Lee. "If you mean the *Federales*."

Jack grinned widely. "He means—*against* the Mexican Army."

Felding's jaw dropped. "A revolutionary?" he asked.

"A hired gun," replied Lee. "A gringo mercenary, if you will."

"Well, I'll be damned!" cried Felding. "You hear that, Milly?"

"Oh, Mister Kershaw has done *so* many romantic things!" she cooed.

"Not exactly," corrected Lee. "The pay was good, and in gold, when I got it. Seems like I never quite picked the right revolution."

Felding emptied his plate and refilled it. "But it's the man hunting in which you've made a name for yourself, eh, Kershaw?"

Lee nodded. He took out a long nine and looked at Milly. She nodded. "I love the smell of a good cigar," she said. Felding looked quickly at her, his filled fork halfway to his mouth. "You've never said that to me, Mildred," he accused.

Lee lighted the cigar over the top of the lamp. He was almost tempted to get off the steamer right then and there and wait for the next one, and if his shoulder hadn't been bothering him too much he would have done it.

"You're known from one end of the Southwest to the other as the best manhunter in the business, Kershaw," rumbled Felding.

Lee casually waved his cigar.

"He knows it too," said Jack drily.

Lee grinned. "Professional pride," he countered.

"How romantic!" cried Milly. "Man hunting man!"

"The most dangerous game in the world," said Lee quietly.

Felding waved a sceptre composed of his fork stabbed through a dripping piece of beef. "But you've never failed to bring in your man, eh, Kershaw?"

"Oh, Will," put in Milly. "It's sometimes dead or alive, isn't it, Mister Kershaw? I mean—you *don't* have to bring them in alive, do you?"

"I try," replied Lee. "I do not take on assignments where it is stated they want them dead or alive."

Felding shook his head. "It seems to me that it would be

much less expensive, plus the bother of bringing a man to trial after months of feeding him and quartering him, then the wages of the manhunter, the guards, the other personnel involved, sir! How much easier to put a bullet into your quarry and report that he resisted arrest, eh, Kershaw?"

It was very quiet in the little salon, except for the dry scrabbling of the night wind about the superstructure of the steamer and the steady, powerful masticating of Felding's teeth.

"Eh, Kershaw?" asked Felding at last as he swallowed his food.

"That would make me judge, jury, and executioner, sir," quietly replied Lee. "I *hunt* men. I do not judge them, *or* execute them."

Felding narrowed his eyes. "You're cheese-paring now, Kershaw."

"Do you still have my husband's rifle, Mister Kershaw?" asked Milly, to change the dangerous subject.

"It is *my* rifle, ma'am," replied Lee.

"I still want it as a trophy, sir," put in Felding. "I should never have put it up as a bet on that poker game."

No, you sonofabitch, thought Lee, because you never thought you'd lose it.

"I can offer you a good price," said Felding.

Lee shook his head. "By the way," he asked, "did you ever get your tobacco jar?"

Felding bobbed his head up and down as he cut into his meat. "Neatly cleaned by the post surgeon. The blacksmith cut off the top and hinged it. Mildred lined it with wine-treated deerskin." He smiled proudly at his young wife. "I have it in my cabin," he added. "Would you like to see it?"

"Not particularly," Lee said quietly.

Mildred Felding focused her great blue eyes on the enigmatic face of the man named Kershaw. Will was too slowwitted to understand Lee's reply, but *she* wasn't.

"A fine rifle that," said Felding. "By God! I've fired a few matches with it and never lost a one, but I've never seen a shot like that one you made that day, Kershaw."

"Keep it up, sweetheart," urged Mildred, "and he'll never part with that rifle you want so much."

Felding mopped up his plate with a piece of bread. "Perhaps it is only sentimentality, Kershaw, but because that rifle, and yourself of course, saved my sweet Milly's life that day, I'd like to have it."

"In that case," said Lee drily, "you'd have to have me along with it."

Felding quickly raised his head to stare at Lee, then caught the joke. He guffawed, and a big piece of gravy bread caught in his throat. He bent forward, choking and gasping, his fat face turning a purplish red. Lee was out of his chair like a cat. A powerful hand hit Felding in the middle of his fat back, and he spat out the bread onto his plate. He raised a tear-streaming face. "Thanks, Kershaw!" he gasped.

"*Por nada,*" replied Lee as he sat down. He saw the look of disgust on Mildred's face as she looked at her husband.

"The rifle," reminded Felding. "I'll double my offer."

"The money would mean nothing to me," said Lee.

"Every man has his price," reminded Mildred.

"No," corrected Lee. "There are still some men left who have no price."

"Like you?" she asked.

He stood up. "I didn't say so."

"Poker tonight?" asked Jack Mellen to change the subject.

"You're on," put in Felding.

"Lee?" asked Mellen.

"I have some reading to do," said Lee. "Good night." He turned and left the salon.

"That goddamned snob!" snapped Mildred in fury.

"Who? Kershaw?" asked Mellen in surprise.

"I wasn't talking to you," she said.

"Sorry," said Mellen. He stood up. "My chief engineer will join us for a game, Colonel." He left the salon cabin.

"That goddamned snob!" repeated Mildred.

"Who? Mellen?" asked Felding in surprise.

"No! That Kershaw! Him and his airs! Who the hell does he think he is?"

"I never thought of him like that," mused Felding as he reached for his dessert.

"You never think about him in any way! The man is two-faced!"

Felding looked at her. "How so?" he asked.

"Haven't you noticed how he looks at me?"

Felding slowly placed his fork on his plate. "What do you mean?" he slowly asked.

"Those that have eyes can see," she said archly.

"Mildred, if you have such accusations you had better be sure of them," he admonished her.

"Forget it!" she said. She stood up. "Are you going to sit there all night?"

"Poker," he reminded her.

"And you'll sit up all night drinking, leaving me alone in that damned tiny cabin?"

He stood up. "Why no! Not if you wish me to come with you."

She shook her head. "Enjoy yourself," she said. "You'd be no good to me or any other woman with all that whiskey you plan to drink."

"I only thought that we'd be awakened early by the sounds of the steamer leaving and that you might want your beauty sleep."

She leaned over and patted his fat face. "Of course, Will! Stupid of me not to think of that. You're a good man, Will, and a fine husband." She pecked a kiss at his fat face and left the cabin.

Will Felding sat down heavily and looked curiously at the door. He shook his head and attacked his dessert.

SIX

QUEHO SQUATTED WITH his back against the bulkhead, eating lower-deck fare from a tin plate resting on his muscular thighs. "Everything here, Kershaw," he said. He picked up his food with his hands and gnawed at it, but his curious eyes were on Lee.

Lee nodded. He sat down on his bunk and reached into his bag for a brandy bottle. The level was far lower than it had been when he had last drunk from it. "Where will you sleep?" he asked.

Queho shrugged. "*¿Quien sabe?*"

"Come up here in a couple of hours after everyone else is asleep. No one will know. The skipper and the colonel are in for an all-night poker session. They'll only leave the table long enough to piss over the railing."

"You sell rifle to fat man?"

Lee took a drink and shook his head. He was getting tired of talking about that damned rifle. It really didn't mean that much to him. He was basically a Winchester man.

"He still want rifle, eh?"

"I said I would not sell it."

Queho stood up and placed his plate on the table. He wiped his greasy hands on his thighs. "You pay me salary in cash, you say. How much, Kershaw?"

Lee shrugged. "Hundred dollars a month and food."

"*Enju!* How much you want for rifle?"

Lee studied the dark, scarred face of the breed. "Not you too?"

Queho nodded. "Look, Kershaw, you keep rifle for yourself and not pay me until rifle paid for, then you give to me."

"It would take months."

"No matter."

The face of the breed was broad, with the characteristic high cheekbones of his Indian blood, while his acquiline nose flared out curiously at the base into the flared nostrils of the Negro. The lips were negroid and his beard, a poor imitation of Lee's, was scraggly like an Indian's and kinky like a Negro's. It was the eyes that gave the man his curious look—the light eyes of the Caucasian.

"Well?" asked Queho.

"You know this type of rifle is not for you, Qucho," said Lee quietly.

"Why not!"

"It's not practical."

"I can shoot it good as you. Maybe better, goddamnit!"

Lee nodded. "That is possible," he agreed. "But you could have hit Ahvote with it that day, and yet you did not. You could have made a damned hero out of yourself that day, Queho. Why didn't you?"

"Because no one would make a hero out of a dirty breed, Kershaw. You know that."

Lee nodded. "Which brings us back to the rifle, Queho. How long do you think some white men would let you keep such a rifle? You ask for the truth. That's the truth! The rifle is not for you. Don't try to compete with white men in this country, Queho. Granted, you're as good a man as any of them, and maybe better than most, but you are not *white!*"

"I no anything! I no white! I no red! I no black! What the hell am I, Kershaw? You wise. Maybe *you* tell me?"

Lee drank a little. "You know I can't do that," he replied.

After a little while, the breed left the cabin and closed the door behind himself.

Lee shrugged. He stripped to his long-johns and raised the lampwick a little. He selected a thin, leather-clad book from his little library, placed the brandy bottle near at hand, lighted a fresh cigar, and settled himself in his bunk for some serious reading.

The cabin was pitch dark when Lee awoke to the sound of the inter-cabin doorhandle being gently tried. He raised his head. It swam a little from the brandy fumes. He could hear Queho breathing softly in the upper bunk. The doorhandle was turned again. Something clicked sharply in the lock. The door creaked gently as it opened. The full figure of Mildred Felding was silhouetted through the diaphanous negligee she wore by the soft lamplight behind her. The scent of her perfume came to Lee. She came softly toward him, holding out a hand. "Oh, Lee," she said tenderly. The mattress creaked in the upper bunk, and Queho turned to look over the side of the bunk full into the startled woman's face. She saw the dark, sweat-streaked skin, glistening in the lamplight, and the strange, light-colored eyes staring, as though a demon were peering at her with evil intentions through a smoky window of hell itself. "Oh, my God!" she screamed. Queho cursed. He had been as startled as she had been. He reached down and clamped a hand over her gaping mouth as she drew in full lungpower to scream again. She sank her sharp teeth into his hand and jerked her head backward. In an effort to free his hand he rolled over the side of the bunk and his free hand caught at the front of her negligee to save his falling. The thin, sweat-damp material ripped freely from shoulder to belly. Her great breasts, dewed with sweat, swung freely as she turned to flee.

Lee cursed softly as he thrust out his head from beneath the upper bunk. Queho was down on his knees, right in Lee's way. Lee shoved at him. Queho clawed out at the woman; his hands caught at the ruin of her negligee where it hung over her broad hips. Queho tore the material down about her plump legs and saw her wide, glistening white rump. "Jesus God!" he yelled in drunken fervor.

Milly ran toward her cabin, missed the door, hit the bulkhead, and seemed to rebound back into the room, striking her heavy rump against Queho's down-bent head as he tried to get up, driving him back against Lee. Lee pushed past the breed and stood up. Queho wrapped an arm about the woman's waist. Lee tore it loose, and Queho drove upward from the deck. His head caught Lee hard under the chin, and smashed him backward against the cabin door, which flew open. Lee landed flat on his back on the outer deck. The woman was screaming like one of the Furies, never seeming to run out of breath.

Feet thudded on the deck. Will Felding led the charge from the dining salon, followed by Jack Mellen and Jim Anderson, the big chief engineer. A heel caught Lee alongside the jaw as he tried to rise. He gripped the leg and upended Will Felding on the deck in front of Mellen and Anderson, and both men sprawled over the falling agent.

Lee jumped into the cabin and tried to separate Queho and the shrieking woman. Queho hit Lee, driving him back against Will Felding, who was just coming in through the doorway. Felding shoved Lee aside and snatched at Lee's loaded Colt lying on the table. He cocked it and whirled to fire into Queho's face. Lee knocked the Colt to one side and the six-gun exploded alongside his head, half deafening him and temporarily blinding him. A man coughed hard behind Lee. He whirled to see the engineer staggering backward from the short-range impact of the soft-lead, 200-grain bullet. He hit the rail and went over backward, to crash down into the shallow water between the side of the *Mohave* and the shore.

Will Felding smashed the smoking Colt across Lee's face and drove him back against the wall. The Colt exploded again, and the slug creased the side of Queho's head, driving him unconscious to the deck. Lee went down on his knees, covering his blood-streaming face with his hands. The Colt came down atop his head and drove him flat on his face on the deck. The last two things he remembered were someone shoving the Colt into his right hand and the incessant banshee-shrieking of the woman.

SEVEN

THE DISTANT MOUNTAINS seemed to smoke in the internal temperature. They appeared to move slowly and sinuously in the shifting, wavering veils of heated air, as though they had a primitive life-form of their own. They were leaden-hued and wrinkled, like the thick hides of huge prehistoric beasts half-buried in the harsh soil of the dessert that lapped at their bases and flanks. The desert itself was almost pool-table flat and almost naked of growth, except for a few metallic-looking plants that had somehow learned to survive in that land of hellfire. Shallow washes wove themselves in braided fashion across the heat-shimmering expanse of the desert.

In direct contrast to the erratic courses of the washes was the road at right angles to them. It was as straight as a bowstring and seemed to come from nowhere through the distant haze to vanish into nothing but more heat haze. The road itself was the only sign of man in that sun-cursed and empty land. There seemed to be no life on the desert or the mountains. It was the very core of the summer heat in the hottest summer known to the memory of the few men who had ever lived there. At that time of the year, the only movements usually seen were the shifting, writhing veils of disturbed air. There was, that one burning summer day, however, two other movements rare indeed in that land where heat and lack of water killed men. One of the movements was that of a thin wraith of saffron-hued dust rising from the road and moving so slowly it seemed hardly to move at all. The other movement was the slow rise and fall of the deep chest of the man who squatted in the very center of a wide wash that crossed the road. There was no shelter there from the full-burning stroke of the killer sun. A limp cigarette dangled from the man's thick lips. His curiously light-colored eyes were slitted against the reflected glare of the sun from the whitish caliche that paved the wash, and his sweat-greased hat was pulled low over his eyebrows. His elbows rested on his lean but powerful thighs, and his strong hands, dirty-nailed and corded, hung loosely between his bent knees. In the scant shade of his body there lay a well-worn Winchester '73 rifle polished with deer fat, and an almost empty bottle of rotgut whiskey. The temperature was hovering at 110 degrees in the shade.

Time seemed to stand still. The dust rose higher in the windless air, until at last the vehicle could be seen under it—an Abbott-Downing stagecoach drawn by four dusty, red-mouthed mules. The Concord coach swayed on its great leather thoroughbraces as the road dipped and sagged into the many dry washes, sometimes disappearing from sight, like a small vessel sinking into a deep wavetrough, only to emerge slowly into view again on the next rise before once again plunging down out of sight.

Soon the intermingled sounds of the approaching coach came to the waiting man in the wash, and his incredibly acute hearing picked out each individual sound, as a music-lover concentrates on picking out the part of each orchestral instrument in a complicated symphony. There was the steady thudding of sixteen hoofs; the slapping of the sweat-lathered harness; the strident jingling of the tracechains; the dull clucking of the sandboxes; the soft, greasy chuckling of the hubs; the hissing of the slim wheels on the hard sand of the road, and the occasional pistol-cracking report of the jehu's whip.

Slowly, the waiting man raised his faded bandanna to mask his dark, scarred face, leaving only a narrow slit for his curious-looking eyes.

196

The coach was close now. It dipped out of sight just beyond the wash. The man stood up with his Winchester hanging loosely in his hands athwart the upper part of his thighs. The lead mules showed up and plunged down into the wash, followed by the wheel mules and the swaying, lurching coach. The driver touched the brake to slow the descent of the vehicle. One of the lead mules caught the spoor of the masked man and snorted in warning, but too late.

The Winchester cracked flatly and the shot echo rolled evenly across the desert. Gunsmoke wreathed about the masked man, as the driver braked hard and drew in on the ribbons to halt the excited team. The brakes shrieked hoarsely and puffed out stinking friction smoke as the coach lurched to a crazy halt in the middle of the wash. The bitter yellow dust swirled on past the coach and mingled with the white gunsmoke drifing about the silent, masked man standing in front of the lead mules.

A woman screamed from within the coach. It was a familiar scream to the masked man. He had an excellent memory.

The driver quickly wrapped the ribbons about the brakehandle and raised his hands. He uneasily eyed the eerie-looking figure of the masked man, half-seen through the dust and gunsmoke as though he were a phantom figure not of this earth. There was a double-barreled, sawed-off ten-gauge shotgun lying at the driver's feet and a holstered six-gun at his side, but he was not stupid enough to make a move for either one of them.

It was very quiet except for the harsh breathing of the mules.

"There ain't no registered mail or bullion on this rig," volunteered the driver.

The curious looking light-colored eyes seemed to slide sideways to look at the coach.

"They's only three passengers—all wimmen; all for Prescott."

The masked man nodded. "I know," he said.

The driver was puzzled. He looked beyond the masked man. There was no sign of a horse. There was not even the faint comfort of a trail across the empty desert land.

"Tell them to get out," ordered the bandit.

The driver clambered down. As his feet struck the ground, he felt his six-gun being plucked from his holster, although he had not heard the sound of feet on the hard ground. He glanced down between his legs to see the toetips of dusty moccasins, and an uneasy feeling crawled up his sweating back. The driver opened the coach door. "Sorry, ladies," he said. "You'll have to get out."

Amy, an auburn-haired prostitute, was the first to get out of the coach. "Must be hot behind that mask, mister," she cracked. Her little joke fell flatly in the quietness. Mildred Felding clambered out next. She had put on some weight while summering in San Francisco. "You won't get away with this, mister," she said, as she tried to stare down the masked man.

"Seems like I am," the masked man said laconically.

"You know who I am?" she demanded.

He nodded. "Mrs. Felding," he replied. "Wife of *Colonel* Will Felding, special agent for Indian Bureau. You been in Frisco since about May, getting better from attack on *Mohave*." His voice was strangely muffled and distorted behind the damp bandanna that masked his face.

Mildred Felding narrowed her eyes. "You'll find yourself in deep trouble for this, mister!" she snapped.

"I'm *in* deep trouble," he countered.

Lucille, the slim, flat-chested, dark-haired favorite niece of the Governor of Arizona Territory, was the last one out of the coach. She had been called from her schooling in San Francisco to take over the Prescott household of her recently widowed uncle. Luckily, Mildred Felding had agreed to leave early for Prescott to chaperone Lucille during the long trip by sea, river, and coach to the Territorial capital. Maybe it hadn't been so lucky after all, thought the girl, and she hadn't learned to like Mrs. Felding one little bit during the long trip.

"Maybe all he wants are our purses, honey," soothed Amy.

"The Three Fates," drily commented the masked man.

"You've been reading books," accused Amy.

He shook his head. "Smart cellmate tell me about such things."

"The sun is hell on these ladies," reminded the driver.

"Sun is hell on whole goddamned country," corrected the bandit.

"Don't I know you?" asked Mildred.

"Dump luggage in road," ordered the bandit.

The three women stood together in the hot shade of the coach as the driver emptied out the boot.

"I *said* we should have had an escort, driver!" barked Mildred.

"Weren't none," said the driver. "Most of 'em was out chasin' someone." He slanted his eyes toward the masked man. "Seems like they were chasin' in the wrong direction."

"Well, where was our guard?"

The driver shrugged. "Got drunk last night. Got a knife between his shoulder blades. No one knows who done it. Couldn't find anyone else willin' to come along." He slid his eyes sideways again toward the bandit.

The masked man touched a small suitcase with a moccasined toe. "Each woman take one this size. Take only what you need. Long way to go."

They stood there looking uncomprehendingly at him. The prostitute looked out across the desert toward the distant mountains, which appeared to smoke in the intense heat. "Where?" she asked uneasily.

"Now!" ordered the masked man.

They obediently opened their luggage and threw out the unnecessary items. Mildred opened a light traveling trunk.

199

"These gowns came all the way from Paris," she said petulantly.

"Won't wear well in mountains," said the bandit. He reached inside the boot and brought out a long, polished wooden case made of the finest Philippine mahogany and fitted with German-silver hardware.

Mildred watched him out of the corners of her eyes as she began to pack a small suitcase. She was almost sure now who he was. Trouble was, she didn't *want* to be sure.

Lucille sobbed. She inelegantly wiped her nose with the back of a hand.

"Take it easy, kid," soothed Amy. "He's only a man."

"Fine advice," sneered Mildred, "but then, you've had a great deal of experience with such men, haven't you, *honey?*"

"And I got paid for it," drily admitted Amy. "What did *you* get out of it, *honey?*"

"Unhitch mules and hold them," ordered the bandit. "When you last water them? How much water left?"

The driver wiped the sweat from his face with a forearm. "They was a fresh team twenty miles back. They're about due for water now. I've got two big mule-canteens for them and two smaller ones inside for the ladies. That's it, mister."

The masked man swung up to the driver's seat. He reached under the seat and held up a small canteen filled with water. "Maybe you forgot this, eh?" he asked.

The driver shrugged. He was midway on his long and lonely desert run. It was twenty miles back to the swing station, but he had used about the last of the water there. The water wagon wasn't due in there until the next day. It was another fifteen miles to the end of the stage, and water. The next water south of the road was forty miles away. To the north of the road were the mountains, and if there was any water in there in the summertime only the Paiutes and the Hualapais knew where it was, and they never went in there during the summer. It was an evil place.

The three women finished packing and stood close together in the hot shade of the coach. "Each of you get up on a mule," ordered the masked man. They each clambered awkwardly up onto a mule, aided by the driver. Mildred's modish traveling skirt hiked way up, to reveal a plump calf encased in smooth silk. "It's been a long time since I've ridden like this," observed Amy. No one paid any attention to her.

The masked man stood looking down at the polished guncase at his feet. "Get shotgun," he ordered the driver over his shoulder.

The driver climbed up to the seat and placed his sweating, trembling hands on the Greener. It was loaded with Blue Whistlers holding 00 shot, and the wads had been split—enough power to take off the bandit's head at fifteen feet.

"Don't try it," warned the masked man without turning.

The Greener hit the ground. The bandit turned and bent to pick it up, and as he did so his dirty, sweat-slick bandanna slipped from his dark, scarred face.

"Jesus God," breathed the driver, and he was immediately sorry he had done so.

"Get down," ordered the bandit as he pulled up his mask. "You know me, eh?"

The driver shook his head. He had been afraid many times before in his life but with nothing like the fear that chilled him now.

The bandit cut lengths of the coach reins to fashion lead-ropes for the mules ridden by the women. He made a sling for the shotgun and hung it on the last mule. "Get the mules' canteens. Water the mules," he ordered the driver.

The driver hung the nose-buckets on the mules and filled the buckets from the big canteens, never taking his eyes from the bandit.

The bandit squatted in front of the polished wooden case and unsnapped the German-silver catches. He raised the lid to look down into the fitted interior. A heavy single-shot

Sharps M1874 rested in its velvet-covered receptacle. The sun seemed to make little trickles of bluish-tinted fire as it reflected from the new gold-and-silver-filled engraving about the breech of the fine rifle. It bounced bright rays from the polished silver plate fastened in the center of the inside of the lid. *"Enju,"* said the masked man.

"What does that mean?" asked Amy, low-voiced, of the driver.

The driver looked nervously up at her. "It means 'good'," he hoarsely replied.

"In what language?"

The driver looked at the bandit, whose full interest focused on the rifle and the fittings inside the wooden case.

"Well?" demanded Mildred impatiently.

"Apache," said the driver at last.

Mildred was not daunted. "That is my property, *you,*" she informed the bandit. "I had it specially engraved, and that case made for it in San Francisco. It is for my husband . . ." Her voice died away as the curious, light eyes of the bandit fixed themselves on her.

"Keep your mouth shut," hissed Amy out of the side of her mouth.

"I know him," informed the bandit. "I know how you got rifle. I know who it really belongs to. *You* know, woman?"

"Well, it was originally my husband's, and he lost it at poker to a man named Kershaw. Personally, I think Kershaw cheated at cards. I got it back for my husband."

"Kershaw?" asked Amy. "Lee Kershaw? I know him!"

"That doesn't surprise me," sneered Mildred, "knowing the both of you for what you are."

"How Kershaw lose this gun, woman?" demanded the masked man.

Mildred opened, then closed her usually ready mouth. "You tell me, eh?"

"Well, it was confiscated from his belongings when he

was sentenced to Yuma Pen. I managed to get it. *Repossess* it, I should say."

The man tapped the engraved breech of the rifle. "What it say here?"

"Ahvote. April, 1881," replied the woman.

"And here?" He tapped the plate inside the lid.

"Colonel Will Felding from his beloved wife Mildred, August, 1881."

"But it should say Lee Kershaw, eh, woman?"

There was no reply.

The masked man passed a dirty hand over the fittings in the case, the long Vollmer telescope, the vernier-tang sight, the globe-front sight, the brass-tipped wooden wiping rod, the capper, the bullet-starter, and the other accouterments and polished tools. He picked up and shook the brass powder-can. It was full. He opened the primer box to find it full. He opened the bullet-box to count at least fifty grooved and greased 370-grain paper-patched bullets. There was a roll of bank-note paper for further patching. He opened the long box of cartridge cases and stared down at the three two- and one-quarter-inch long brass cases. He looked up slowly at the woman. "Where are the other cartridge cases?" he demanded.

She was startled. "Well, they must all be there!"

"Only *three?*"

"I don't know about those things!" she cried.

He stood up, and his strong black-nailed hands opened and closed spasmodically. "Only three?" he yelled insanely. For a moment they all thought he was going to attack the woman; then he suddenly, almost too suddenly, calmed down. "All right," he said. "Maybe get more. Maybe three enough." He closed the lid of the box and snapped it shut. He fashioned a leather sling for the case and hung it on the mule opposite the shotgun.

The driver finished watering the mules. He took off the nose-buckets and walked to the coach with them and the two big canteens.

The masked man walked to the coach and opened a door. He reached inside and ripped up the worn upholstery with his powerful talon-like hands tipped by dirty, ragged fingernails. He thumb-snapped a match into flame and dropped it into one of the holes in the seat. A wisp of smoke quickly arose. In a little while, the fire was crackling merrily away as it ate swiftly into the horsehair stuffing and the worn leather. The smoke drifted from the windows and rose string-straight into the quiet air.

"That smoke can be seen for miles," warned Amy. "You'll give yourself away."

He looked at her. "Who's to see it?" he asked.

He had her there.

"Any water left in canteens?" asked the bandit.

The driver shook his head.

"Hang the other canteens on my mule."

"You sure no water in mule canteens?" asked the masked man again.

The driver turned from the mule and nodded.

"Enju! Start walking, mister."

The driver held out his hands, palms upward. "Where?" he asked piteously.

The masked man mounted his mule and sat it, looking down at the driver. "Take your choice," he carelessly replied. He looked toward the distant, heat-hazed mountains.

"I'll never make it to water! Takes three gallons a day for a man to walk in this damned heat! At least give me one canteen, mister!"

"Shit!" said the masked man. He led the three mules slowly up the wash.

"No living man can make it to water from here without a canteen!" yelled the driver.

"I can," said the bandit over his shoulder.

The driver stood amidst the gathering smoke. "I know who you are!" he yelled foolishly.

The Winchester '73 cracked four times, almost as fast as

the action could be described. The mule canteens jumped sideways and clattered to the ground, each of them neatly holed twice through by .44/40 slugs. The water ran from them into the thirsty ground before the driver could reach them to stop the flow. "God damn you to hell!" the driver shouted hoarsely.

There was no reply from the masked man.

In a little while, only a thread of saffron-hued dust moved across the heat-shimmering desert between the road and the infernal mountains.

EIGHT

AMY'S MULE STUMBLED and went down with the sound of a dry stick being snapped. Amy threw a long and shapely leg over the back of the mule and stepped clear of him as he went down. The mule struggled to get up, but his left frong leg was cleanly broken. Amy took her suitcase and sat down on it.

The masked man walked easily back to the downed mule. He gripped the halter and suddenly twisted the mule's head up and to one side. The razor edge of his knife sliced cleanly through the throat muscles, and he stepped quickly backward to avoid the sudden gushing of the dark blood. The women watched him in horrified fascination as he squatted beside the still quivering hulk of the mule and hacked out a square of the dusty hide. Darkness grew in the heat-soaked canyon as he worked. The only sounds were the blowing of the tired mules and the ripping of the knife through hide and flesh. Dripping chunks of the bloody meat were placed on the square of hide.

"Why?" asked Amy at last.

He looked sideways at her. "Good mule meat sweeter than pork," he replied.

"To a gut-eating Apache or a breed," sneered Mildred.

He looked at her over the upper edge of the bandanna. "You be eating some of this before too long and be damned thankful for it," he said.

"God forbid!" she cried.

"We'll see," he promised.

206

"Don't I know you?" she asked suspiciously.

"You should," he said over his shoulder.

"Some saloon or whorehouse?" sweetly asked Amy. The masked man shrugged.

Mildred took her courage in hand. She snatched at the bandanna and it fell free from the man's face. He did not turn. "I think I know you," she said quietly. He turned and looked up at her. *"Queho!"* she screamed.

"That, was a mistake," warned Amy. "The driver knew who he was. You saw what happened to him."

"The breed from Prescott and Fort Mohave," said Mildred.

Queho wiped the greasy sweat from his dark face. "What breed, woman?" he demanded. "Half-breed? Quarter-breed? Maybe *all*-breed, eh, woman?"

It was almost as though the woman was talking to herself as she mechanically replied: "Part Mohave Apache, part half-breed Mexican, and part white man."

He stood up and wiped his strong, bloody hands on the greasy thighs of his filthy trousers. "Maybe you forgot *nigger* too, eh, woman?"

"That too," she agreed.

He grinned, but there was no true mirth on his strange face. "So, what you call me now, eh, woman?"

"But you were sent to Yuma Pen with Kershaw for twenty years!"

He grinned. "Only few months. I no like it there. So I left."

"No man has ever escaped from Yuma Pen and lived to talk about it," said Amy wisely.

He wrapped the hide about the meat and fastened it with a long strip of the hide. "I did," he said matter of factly. "Get on mules," he ordered.

"There are only three left," said Amy.

He looked at Mildred. "You walk, woman."

"I won't be able to keep up!" she cried.

They all mounted except Mildred. "Follow the canyon

for three more miles," said Queho. "We'll stop for the night there." He kicked his mule in the ribs and led the other two mules up the dark canyon. Lucille's mule was badly lamed.

"I won't be able to keep up!" foolishly repeated Mildred.

"What about water?" asked practical Amy. "The canteens are empty."

He looked back at her. "Do you think even *me*, Queho, could live in here without water, woman?"

She had no answer for that question.

Mildred Felding stood there in the heat-soaked darkness with the hot, stinging sweat running down her tired body. Then she started up the canyon with a great swaying of her too broad hips. The heel snapped off from her left shoe. She went down on her too plump knees and abraded them. She looked up the dark slot of the canyon. She could no longer see them. Her damp and stringy yellowish hair hung over her sweating face. She could hear her heart thudding violently against her ribs. She did not dare look back down the canyon. There was nothing back there but the unknown, but it was that which really frightened her.

NINE

THE FIRST ARIZONA posse sent out to check the nonarrival of the stagecoach found the driver lying face downward at the side of the road where the coarse sand was smooth. His sunburned hands were dug clawlike into the sand, as though he had intended dragging himself on his belly toward the water that was five miles away in the opposite direction. Traced in the sand just in front of his hands was a wavering scrawl of one word—*Queho*.

The deputy sheriff shaped a quirly and lighted it, cupping brown hands about the flame of the match to shield it from the dawn wind sweeping across the dry and empty land. "He got confused during the night, poor bastard," he said around the cigarette, "and was crawling back the way he came. Sam, you and Ellis load him on that spare horse and you take him back, Sam. Ellis, you and that Pauite come with me."

They rode north on the rutted road as the sun came up in a vast, silent explosion that changed the color-texture of the land from soft and mysterious gray tones into the bright, clashing colors that would show distinctly in the clear morning light until the day's heat changed them into vague, murderous tintings that seemed to harbor a hint of insanity.

"The next water is thirty miles ahead, Dan," warned Ellis.

"We've got water," said the deputy.

"It's more than twenty-five miles west to the river."

"We've got water," repeated Dan.

The stagecoach had burned down into a blackened heap of ashes and heat-warped metal. The deputy poked about in it with a boot-toe. He kicked out some of the blackened metal fittings. There were metal buttons, hinges, strap metal, curious-looking odds and ends, and some hooks and eyes. He picked up a thin lath of steel. "Corset stay," he said.

Ellis looked at the empty whiskey bottle in the wash. "He likely headed into the mountains, Dan."

Dan glanced at the two big blanket-covered canteens hanging from the saddles of the horses.

"If it really was Queho, we'll never catch him now, Dan."

Dan pointed at the faint mule tracks in the wash, then jerked a thumb toward them, looking at the Paiute tracker. The Paiute trotted up the wash. Dan followed, leading his horse and the tracker's.

"We just ain't got enough water to get to them mountains and back to water again!" yelled Ellis.

Dan turned. "There was three women in that coach," he said. He turned and followed the Paiute.

The Paiute stopped at the foot of the mountains under the full blaze of the noon sun. Beyond him was a great surface of smooth rock. The mule tracks had stopped where he stood.

"Go beyond the rocks," ordered Dan. "Cast about."

The Paiute did not move.

"*Vamonos!*" snapped Dan.

The Paiute did not "*vamonos.*"

"He's scared stiff," said Ellis.

"No water," croaked the Paiute.

"You lie!" accused Dan. "There must be water in there."

"It ain't the water. It's Queho," put in Ellis.

Dan slowly shaped a cigarette, keeping his eyes on the flat rock and the rising slopes of naked soil up above them, shimmering in the blaze of the sun. They had enough water in their canteens to reach the water in the mountains—if there *was* water in there. Only God, the Paiute, and Queho would know where that was, and none of the three of them were talking.

Dan lighted his cigarette and drew his Colt. He cocked it and pointed it at the head of the Paiute. *"Git!"* he ordered.

The Paiute did not *git*.

"He's more ascared of Queho then he is of you," said Ellis.

Slowly the Paiute stepped up on the rock.

The heavy rifle cracked flatly, distantly, and the big slug slapped into the head of Dan's horse with the sound of a stick being whipped into soft mud. The horse went down without making a sound.

High on the sun-cursed slopes, a wisp of smoke drifted off. Then the smoke was gone. The slopes seemed as barren as a lunar landscape.

Ellis raised his head a little from the ground. "It's Queho all right," he said, quite unnecessarily.

"How do you know?" Dan already knew the answer. Only two men he had ever known could shoot like that—Stalker and Queho.

"We'll have to go back now."

"We'll wait until dark."

"We'll be broiled to death by then."

Dan raised his head. The rifle promptly cracked. Gravel was flung stinging against the side of his face. He dropped his head. *"Jeeesus!* That was too damned close," he murmured.

"He could have hit you. He's warning us off."

"Christ, but I hate to give up!"

"What else can we do?"

"Go back, I guess. I'll take the Paiute's horse. The sonofabitch can walk."

The Paiute had already "walked."

TEN

"*IT'S NO USE*, Jim," argued Dan. "You won't get the Paiutes to go in there."

Sheriff Jim Hathaway had spread the map in the hot shade of a rock pinnacle. He looked at the emptiness of the map, marked by a few dotted, straggling lines that were supposed to be trails, and by a few (all too few) markings for waterholes neatly labeled, "Dry in summer. Water usually unfit to drink."

The second Arizona posse to start after Queho squatted in the shade of their horses, dragging on limp cigarettes, feeling the hot and itching sweat run down their bodies, and thinking always of cold beer. The Paiutes squatted sleepily in the full sunlight. Now and then one of them would raise his head a little to look at the hazy mountains. It was an evil place. The man the fool white men were hunting was not a man at all, but the fool white men would not admit that to themselves. The Paiutes knew.

Dan passed a hand across his burning eyes. "He's on the loose in an area of damned near five hundred square miles, south and east on the Arizona side and north and east of the Colorado on the Nevada side. The only water we can be sure of is in the river, twenty-five miles north, and twenty-five miles west."

"That ain't too bad," said Hathaway. "We can go north to the water and then follow the river where it curves to the south."

"We've got them damned mountains between us and the river either way we go. We don't know the passes, Jim."

"The Paiutes do."

"You'll never get them to show you."

"He has to leave a trail."

"He never leaves a trail."

"The mules and the three women will leave a trail. He can't avoid that, Dan."

"It's been a week since he held up the stagecoach."

"The women will have slowed him down."

"If they're still with him," said Dan.

Hathaway had no rebuttal for that one.

One of Paiutes pointed upward. A hawk had dived out of sight into a canyon.

"There's something dead up there," said the sheriff. He rolled up the map. "Damned useless thing this. My old blind granny could have made a better one using a pointed stick in the sand."

They sent the reluctant Paiutes on ahead by foot. They moved through the difficult terrain like wisps of wind driven smoke and just as noiselessly. They knew Queho had the hearing and sight of a wild animal.

They found the swollen mule carcass in a slot of a canyon. The stench of the escaping body-gases hung in the windless air like a noisome plague. Three of the legs stuck up stiffly from the obscenely bloated carcass, while the fourth leg was thrust out at an awkward angle. Something moved in a rotting hole gouged into a haunch. "Maggots," said Dan. "Now where the hell do *they* come from?"

The carcass moved as though in answer, easing out a fearsome puff of gas. The possemen moved quickly away.

"He's got meat for a week from that carcass," said Dan. "No wonder the breed sonofabitch can live in here."

"No water," said a Paiute, pointing up ahead.

"Queho went that way," said Dan. "He'd have to have water for himself, the women, and the mules." He unrolled the map and stabbed a blunt fingertip down on it. "There! Three miles ahead!"

"No water! Map no good!" insisted the Paiute.

"Kick their skinny asses up the canyon like a good boy, Danny," urged the sheriff.

The posse rode up the canyon with the dull sound of the hooves clashing metallically on the loose stones.

One of the Paiutes picked up the heel of a woman's shoe.

"Might be from a Paiute squaw's moccasin," joked one of the men.

"That ain't funny," rebuked the sheriff.

The map proved the Paiute wrong, at least about the water not being there. There *was* water there, about two feet of it, covered with a floating layer of green algae, which also coated the swollen hairy flanks of a dead mule lying centered in the rock pan. The men moved back from the stench.

Hathaway clipped and lighted a cigar. He looked at the two pack-burros, laden with oval-shaped water kegs. "We've still got enough water to reach the river," he said thoughtfully.

"Useless," argued Dan.

Hathaway thumb-snapped a lucifer to light his cigar. "We've got to go on, Dan" he said, between puffs on the cigar. "You saw that heel back there."

"They're raped and dead by now, Jim."

"You know who two of those women are?"

"Colonel Felding's spouse and the Governor's favorite niece."

Hathaway nodded. "Exactly."

"And a prostitute," added Dan as a second thought.

The rifle exploded on the heights. The men broke for cover. The rifle cracked again, sending its echo tumbling and bounding after the first echo. The lead burro stampeded up the canyon. The second burro lay dead on one crushed water-keg, while water from the other keg, now bullet-punctured, ran down his dusty hide to the ground. No one ventured out of cover to plug the hole.

Hathaway cautiously raised his head. The end of his cigar was a ragged ruin.

"You see now what I mean, Jim?" asked Dan.

Hathaway carefully pruned the end of his cigar with a pearl-handled penknife. "What the hell would he want three women for anyway?" he asked in general.

"A *mañada*," suggested Dan. "You know—brood mares, like a wild stud stallion keeps. Somewhere north of here, Queho likely is setting up his own little Eden—right in the center of a hell on earth."

Nothing moved on the heat-shimmering heights. The lead burro had vanished with the loaded water-kegs.

"You might be right, Danny," agreed Hathaway. "But just supposin' them three women won't play beddy-bye with him?"

Dan drew a finger across his brown throat.

Hathaway relighted his shortened cigar. "We'll never catch him this way," he said. "Besides, there's a Nevada posse working on the other side of the Colorado. Maybe they'll get him. We'll have to turn back now."

You ever see a Paiute grin? *They* did.

ELEVEN

THE NEVADA POSSE had worked upriver on the
Nevada side until the narrow streak of shoreline had petered
out. Beyond where they stood, with the water lapping at the
sides of their boots, the river curved so that they could
clearly see both sides of the gorge called "The Gut" by the
rivermen. Here the river ran with a deceptive smoothness,
deep and strong, with an undercurrent that could suck a man
or horse down in a matter of seconds and hold them down,
tumbling broken-boned along the rock-studded bottom,
until the river let them up, perhaps five miles down the
canyon, drowned and smashed to jelly, hardly recognizable
as anything animal, vegetable, or mineral.

"You think he crossed the river, George?" a posseman
asked of the deputy sheriff.

"Here? Hardly," replied George.

"Maybe he's still on the other side."

"No," said George. He raised his field glasses and
focused them on a high point of the canyon wall on the
Nevada side.

"How can you tell?"

George handed him the field glasses. "Take a look," he
suggested. "That's him standing up there."

The four other possemen shrank back against the damp
side of the gorge. George grinned. "Hell," he said, "if he
had *wanted* to, he could have gotten all of us before we even
saw where he was shooting from."

"He ain't got a rifle in his hands," said the man with the

glasses. "It's him all right. How the hell did he get across the river?"

"How the hell does he do anything, Les?" countered George.

"What about the women?" asked one of the possemen.

There was no answer. No one wanted to answer.

It was George who broke the silence. "If he left them on the Arizona side, it's Arizona's problem."

"I wasn't thinking about that," said the posseman who had asked the question.

"What do we do now, George?" asked Les.

George felt for the makings. "Go back," he replied. "We'll have to try and get at him from inland."

"So, maybe he'll cross the river again."

George shrugged as he shaped a cigarette. He handed the makings to Les. "Then he'll be Arizona's problem again."

"How does he live up there?" asked a posseman.

"Nothing lives up there except maybe lizards and hawks," said Les.

George lighted up. He looked over the flare of the match at the lone figure standing motionless on the heights watching them. "He does," he said quietly.

They turned the horses, with their hooves clashing on the pebbles and splashing in the water, in full view and good rifle range of the man on the heights.

Just before the canyon curved again, George looked back. The heights were empty. Shadows filled the gorge. The river roared sullenly. It was as though no one had ever lived there and never would.

TWELVE

"YOU COOK, WOMAN," said Queho to Mildred Felding.

She raised her head from where she lay on the cave floor, trembling with fatigue. She raised a dirty, broken-nailed hand and pushed back her stringy, dirty blond hair from her badly sunburned face. The wave had long gone from her hair, and her curling irons lay blackened in the ashes of the stagecoach more than thirty miles away, along with her heat-shattered bottles of pomade, cleansing lotions, perfumes and perfumed soaps, and her unguents and colognes.

"You hear?" demanded the breed.

"I'm not a damned squaw," she hotly protested.

A moccasined toe caught her just below the left ribs. She got up on her hands and knees. The flat of a moccasined sole caught her on the broad rump and drove her face downward on the floor of the cave. She covered her head with her arms as she was kicked unmercifully to her feet. She stumbled toward the fireplace at the side of the cave.

"I only tell you *once* when I want something," he said.

"Bastard," she said.

He nodded. "Bastard, yes, and *man* too!"

She was wise enough this time to keep her mouth shut.

Queho broke the shotgun he had taken from the stagecoach. He ejected the brass cartridges and ran a swab through the twin barrels. He snapped shut the breech and placed the heavy scatter-gun on a set of pegs driven into the cave wall. He passed a dirty hand down the other weapons

218

that were racked from the floor to the low ceiling of the cave.

"You've got an arsenal there," commented Amy as she picked a bit of sharp rock from a bare heel. "You planning on a war?"

He turned slowly. "I collect," he said.

"Why so many?"

He scratched inside his filthy shirt and undershirt. "I am only one man," he replied, almost as though he was talking to himself. "Many men hunt me. Posses from Arizona, Nevada, California; Wells Fargo agents; Pinkerton men; Army. Many." He looked at the guns. He pointed to the top gun. "Winchester '73 in .44/40 caliber." He pointed to the others, each in turn. "Sharps Old Reliable in .50/70 Government; .45/70 issue Springfield; Winchester '76 in .45/75 caliber; Hopkins and Allen double-barreled twelve-gauge shotgun; Sharps .50/70 carbine." He opened an old ammunition box and held it out toward her. Half a dozen pistols were in it. "You know how I get all these fine guns?"

"I know how you got the last two," she quietly replied.

He grinned loosely. "All, I get like that."

The girl raised her head from where she lay exhausted on the floor. "You mean you *kill* men for them?" she asked.

"How else would I get them? But sometimes, like the driver, they have more than one gun."

"Thank God for small favors," said Amy drily.

"What does that mean?" he asked.

She looked quickly away from him. "Nothing."

He closed the box lid and picked up a cigar box. "Look," he said as he opened the lid.

"My God," said the girl. She covered her face with her hands.

There were at least six badges in the box, shining dully. "I collect these too," he said proudly.

"The same method?" asked Amy.

He nodded. "They come along with the guns," he said.

"Figures," said Amy. "Like marksmanship medals."

Queho nodded as he closed the box. He looked at the girl. "You, on the floor! You make beds!"

She sat up and looked at the haphazard pile of blankets and horseblankets, hides, and pelts lying at the side of the noisome cave. "There are no beds," she said.

"On floor! This ain't no hotel, missy!"

"How many beds?" she asked.

The other two women looked surreptitiously at the breed.

"How many you think we need?" he countered.

The army woman had lighted the fire. Smoke began to drift from the blackened, ash-choked fireplace. Queho leaped across the cave and kicked the smoldering wood out onto the cave floor. "Goddamn you, stupid woman!" he yelled. "You use dry wood! Squaw wood! You understand? Wood that not smoke! You want everyone within ten mile to see that goddamned smoke?"

She looked up at him, but did not answer. The answer was plain enough on her face.

He raised a fist, then lowered it. He laughed. "There ain't no one to see it out there anyway! Not today! Hotter than hell today! No water for anyone except river." He laughed a little wildly.

Amy watched the breed out of the corners of her eyes. There was something damned odd about his laugh. There wasn't any mirth in it. She had noticed it before, as she had noticed his changing moods. It was as though Queho drifted back and forth on the razor-edged line between sanity and insanity.

"How many beds?" quavered Lucille.

Queho was suddenly quiet. "Three," he replied.

"What about you?" she asked. She wasn't too bright.

He suddenly grinned. "Make mine twice as big as the others," he replied. "You maybe know why?"

No one answered him. In a little while he vanished around the bend in the cave just beyond the fireplace.

Lucille began to separate the bedding, now and again

220

turning her head away from the foul odors that emanated from the skins and pelts.

"Are you a virgin, Lucille?" suddenly asked Amy.

"I've been away to convent school," the girl replied primly.

"What does that have to do with it?" asked Mildred.

The girl was shocked. "Why, we *never* did things like *that!*"

"Your school was a lot different than mine then," said Mildred as she relighted the fire, this time with dry wood.

"Tell me the truth," persisted Amy.

The girl looked directly at Amy and shook her head. Maybe she wasn't lying after all.

Amy walked around the curve that led to the low mouth of the deep cave. Just below the overhanging roof of the cave mouth, Queho had dug down three feet to form a sort of wide trench. He had ramparted the outer side with natural-looking rocks, through which he had formed loopholes that were now plugged with bits of rock. Amy stepped down into the trench and up onto the firestep at the base of the rampart. She looked behind herself and upward. Here the towering cliff above the cave beetled out, so that one standing on the cliff rim could not possibly look down and see the rampart or the cave mouth. To the right and left of the cave mouth, the cliff again bulged out smoothly, so that the cave could not be seen from either side and could not be approached from either flank. The only possible approach to the cave was directly below the rampart. Here lay a great slanted talus slope that baked and shimmered in the brazen sunlight. A fly could not crawl up that slope without being seen from the cave. The approach was also noisy. As Amy had experienced the night before when Queho had driven the three exhausted women up the slope and over the rampart into the cave. Nothing, except perhaps a gecko lizard or a hunting wildcat could come up that slope at night without creating one hell of a clashing racket of sliding, falling rock.

Below the talus slope was the *malpais* land, a broken and rebroken area created and then destroyed centuries past by cataclysmic upheavals and subsidences; a never-never land seemingly frozen in a tangle of writhing labyrinthine passages of sun-soaked rock baking in the intense heat and full of blind passages and thick-bodied rattlesnakes. Far below the cave, and beyond the *malpais* land, was the river—a silver, glistening arc of perhaps a mile or two in length buried at the bottom of a sheer-walled gorge. Somewhere upriver from that trap of a gorge was the place where Queho had ferried the three women, one at a time, across the dark, rushing river. Amy had not seen where he had hidden the boat. They had climbed to the rimrock before then.

"It is farther than it looks," said Queho from behind her.

She had been surprised, so quietly did he move, but she did not show it. "How long have you lived here?" she asked.

"Maybe three months. Not sure."

"Alone?"

"Always. One time, long ago, I lived here too."

"Why did you take us from the coach?"

"Maybe I needed woman—a *squaw,* maybe."

"Yes, but *three* of us. . . ."

"I only knew of one woman on coach."

"The army woman."

"Yes."

She turned and looked up into his strange, brooding face. "How did you know she would be on that coach?"

He looked down the heat-shimmering talus slope and across the *malpais* land to the distant river. "It is enough for you that I *did* know," he replied after a time.

"You hate her."

His strong, dirty hands came together with force and worked one against the other, so that the veins stood out on their backs like writhing worms beneath the dark skin. His breathing came hard and fast.

"You could have killed her for your revenge, whatever it is."

"She had me sent to hell! I take her into a hell I choose now! She lie! She cheat! She bad all through! No good! No good."

Amy wisely shifted the subject. "The girl has not known a man," she said.

"How you know?"

"She told me."

Queho laughed. "Women fools. They believe only what they want to."

"And men do not?"

He searched her rather plain-looking face.

"Will you let her alone?" asked Amy.

"I boss here! You women do what Queho says you do!"

"That's not an answer," said Amy bravely.

"I won't take her tonight," he said. "If someone take her place," he added quickly, as an afterthought.

The smell of the breed almost sickened her. "I'll take her place," she volunteered.

He looked back at the cave. "The other one."

"She won't come to you, Queho."

He looked down at his powerful hands, greasy, dirty-tipped, with ragged broken nails. "She'll come. On her fat knees! Crawling to me! She'll come to me! You understand! Like *squaw!*"

"She never will."

His eyes held hers. She could not look into them, yet she could not turn away from them, and what she saw, or thought she saw, frightened her. He suddenly looked over her head, as though something else had crossed his confused mind. "I'll wait," he promised.

"I'll come to you tonight if you leave the girl alone."

He grinned suddenly. *"Enju!* But I won't be here tonight. Got to hunt. Three squaws eat too much. Need more food."

"What kind of game do you hunt in this country of hell?"

223

"My kind of game," he quietly replied. "You'll see." He walked into the cave.

Amy came into the cave a few minutes after Queho. He was gone and so was the Winchester '73. Queho was gone, but he had left his peculiar scent behind—a compound of stale sweat, urine, rancid grease, and foul clothing. It was not as unpleasant as it had been, thought Amy. Maybe she was getting used to it. "My God," she said at the thought.

Mildred looked up from her pallet. *"He's* not around here. What does that mean?"

"I think I'm getting used to his stink."

The three of them sat there as darkness filled the cave. After a time, Amy found a candle and lighted it. She walked toward the rear of the cave.

"Where are you going?" asked Mildred.

"Exploring. There must be another way out of here."

"It's dark, Amy," said Lucille fearfully. "He said we were not to make a light after dusk, for fear it would be seen from the outside."

"The light can't be seen from back here!" called Amy.

"Are you sure he's gone?"

Amy shrugged. "I'll risk it."

The seemingly solid rock of the heights was internally rotten, honeycombed with a bewildering lacework of labyrinthine passages pitted with deep holes that seemed bottomless. Three times Amy walked up blind passageways and once into a natural room that stank like an abattoir with a miasma of garbage, offal, and human waste left there by Queho. One of the passageways ended against a wall with a deep pit below it. Amy dropped stones into it and strained her ears, only to hear the stones strike deep, deep below in the stygian darkness. Once she thought she heard someone laughing in the darkness, but there was no one there—at least she *thought* no one was there.

Amy plodded back to the outer cave and found tobacco and papers. She expertly shaped a cigarette, lighted it from the candle, then blew out the candle.

"Well?" asked Mildred.

Amy drew on the cigarette, lighting her thoughtful face. "Forget it," she said. "Queho is the only person who knows the way out of there."

"Will he be back tonight?" asked Lucille anxiously.

"You'll be safe, honey," promised Amy.

"How do you know?"

"He told me."

"He seems to tell you a lot of things," slyly suggested Mildred. She shaped a cigarette in the darkness.

"Not being able to talk to men has never been one of my failings. I've found it too damned easy to talk with them "

"He's not a man! He's a rapist! A breed! A killer!"

"Have you ever wondered why?"

Mildred lighted up. "That's an excuse?"

"Born on the wrong side of the blanket. The catch-colt bastard son of a Mohave Apache squaw, who was herself a half-breed Mexican, and a man who was half black and half white, a mulatto, if you will, serving with black men."

"He was a nigger! A Buffalo Soldier!"

"I've heard they are damned good soldiers."

"Where did you hear that?"

Amy blew a smoke ring. "I've known a few army men in my time."

"Blacks?"

Amy looked at her through the darkness. "No," she denied quietly.

"You've sunk so low in your sex that some day even the nigger troopers won't want you!"

Amy smiled a little. "Come to think of it, Queho got into your lacy drawers down at Fort Mohave. How was it, sister?"

"Damn you! That was *rape!*"

Amy laughed. "You didn't answer my question."

"Well, anyway, if he does want a woman, he can have Lucy there."

"Maybe Amy will go with him," suggested Lucille.

225

"Maybe he won't want to risk a dose from her. You know what I mean, honey?" Mildred laughed. "It isn't so bad the first time a man takes you, honey. It hurts, but after a few more times, it's all right."

"But not here!"

"What are you saving it for?" Mildred grinned in the darkness. "I know! For your future husband! Is that it?"

"Of course I am! Didn't you?"

Mildred laughed. "It's not exactly the time for confession, honey."

Amy snubbed out her cigarette. "I'm beat," she said. "We might as well get some sleep tonight. Tomorrow night might be different."

They lay down on their pallets. Queho was gone in the flesh, but something of him lingered on in the cave. It was more than the animal odor he left—it was a brooding, haunting fear of the man himself.

THIRTEEN

THERE WAS A spring of cold, clear water that fed a wide and shallow pool that was set like a green jewel at the far end of a multi-colored canyon, wearing a fringe of willows and alders. The water was always cold and pure, even when the summer sun was blasting the empty desert beyond the down-sloping floor of the lower part of the high-walled canyon. During the day, there was the constant droning of insects mingled with the soft whispering of the dry wind gently swaying the leaves and allowing the sunlight to strike through the overhanging arch of the trees to glisten on the dappled water. Leaves that had dried and fallen into the pool would drift like small, curled canoes to form a golden, intermittently sunlighted mass floating at the upper end of the pool. When the sun shone fully on the mass, like a field of goldenrod, a man might dream of the gold he could not find in the mountains and desert beyond the magic of the canyon.

During the day, the canyon wrens twittered in the trees, and just before sunset, the cliff swallows would swoop down for flying insects. After sundown, in the shadowed dusk, the velvet winged bats would come from the openings in the cliff and fly in a mounting line like scraps of charred paper impelled by the night wind. In the soft darkness before the coming of the moonlight, there would be quiet splashings beside the pool, alternating with moments of utter silence as the shy nocturnal creatures drank and then listened to the night. Sometimes in the clear moonlight the deer would raise their dripping muzzles from the water to listen for the soft footed approach of the great old cougar who lived alone in the deeper reaches of the canyon.

It was a lonely place, yet a man was never alone there. The sun would shine though the gaps in the leaves to form a dappled, constantly moving rhythmic pattern on the surface of the pool that was almost like a silent kind of music—soul music.

Boot-soles scuffled on hard rock. Metal grated against metal. A heavy door was pushed gratingly open on long, unoiled hinges to bang back against a wall of solid living rock. Then it was quiet again, except for the heavy sound of breathing in the darkness. As the eyes became accustomed to it, there was the faint rectangle of the opened door, dark gray limned against the deep darkness of the natural rock cell.

Something scratched. A tiny bulb of flame spurted into fiery life at the tip of a match that was slowly raised to reveal a pair of eyes that glittered in the flame light. The eyes steadied on the dim figure of a man seated on the rock floor with his back against the wall and with his legs outthrust. A pair of iron cuffs ringed his bare, festering ankles, and between his ankles there was a heavy bar of stout strap-iron. From the iron bar there extended a heavy chain padlocked into a great rusted iron ring, whose hasp was sunk deeply into the rock floor.

"How are you, Kershaw?" asked the man with the match.

"I'll survive, warden," drily replied Lee Kershaw.

"I've often wondered how."

Lee closed his eyes. The dreamlike vision of the magic canyon and the charmed pool seemed to come back to him. "You wouldn't understand," he said. The warden closed the door and then lighted a candle. He placed it on the floor. "How long have you been in darkness?" he asked.

"One can't tell time in here."

"It was a week, Kershaw."

"If you knew, why did you ask? What do you want from me?"

"Maybe I came to see how you were."

Kershaw laughed. It was a rich and solid laugh; certainly not the cackling, dry-stick laughter of a man who had just spent a week as punishment for an infraction of the rules in total darkness in the notorious Snake Den of Yuma Pen during the very core of the summer heat.

"Few men can keep their sanity in here, Kershaw."

"Their name is not Kershaw."

The candle guttered a little, casting alternate patches of light on the thickly spider-webbed walls, only to shift them back into thick darkness again to seek another place to light.

"How much longer do you have to serve, Kershaw?"

"Nineteen years and a few months, I think."

"Nineteen and a half, to be exact. Understand that I want to impress that on your mind."

"It *has* been impressed on my mind, sir. I was judged by a jury of my peers, and sentenced by the toughest hanging judge in the Territory, influenced somewhat, no doubt, by the Governor of the Territory, who was, in turn, influenced by his esteemed friend Kentucky Colonel Will Felding, of the Indian Bureau."

"It could have been worse. Murder is a hanging offense."

"Hanging might have been the better choice over this place."

"Hell is tougher than Yuma Pen."

"If one has been to Yuma Pen, he *has* been to hell."

"You'll never last nineteen and a half years in here."

"I'll try."

The warden shook his head. He squatted on his heels and took out the makings. He shaped a cigarette and placed it between Lee's bearded lips. He thumb-snapped a match into flame and lighted the cigarette. *"Gracias,"* murmured Lee, always the gentleman. *"Por nada,"* responded the warden. He fashioned a cigarette for himself and lighted it. He

229

looked at Lee over the flare of the match. "Tell me, Kershaw, just between you and me—were you really innocent?"

"Every man between these walls will tell you that he is innocent. You didn't come here to ask me that. What difference can it possibly make now?"

"Because I can give you a chance to wipe out that nineteen and a half years you will not live to serve out. I'd like to know I helped an innocent man."

Lee Kershaw looked at his cigarette as though he had never seen one before. "Leave the makings," he suggested. "Close the door from the outside, please, and take the candle with you. I think better in the darkness."

The warden stood up with the candle in his hand. "You may be able to fool those stupid, illiterate cons out there in the yard, Kershaw, but you can't fool me. You're holding on to your reason with all the strength and willpower you have, which is considerable, I must admit, but it will not be enough, Kershaw! Right now you are gambling first with your reason and then you will gamble with your very life, and you will lose! Outside these walls, men like you are well-nigh invincible, but you crack like a rotten egg in here, as easily as those more stupid cons outside will do. The hell of it, Kershaw, is that you know I'm right!"

"You've been reading books again, warden."

"Once you are broken, there will be no going back."

"Hear, hear," Lee jibed softly.

The warden blew out the candle. "I'm going to walk to that door, Kershaw. I'm going to open it. Just call out to me before I close that door, Kershaw, because, before God, if you do not call out to me, you'll never again have a chance to leave Yuma Pen alive."

The Snake Den was as black as the anteroom to hell itself. Lee Kershaw heard the heavy breathing of the big man who stood there in the darkness looking down at him. The reek of the greasy candle hung in the stale, stifling air.

Sweat leaked from Lee Kershaw's body and ran itching down his sides. He closed his eyes.

Leather boots scuffed on rock. One step. . . . *The cliff swallows always darted swiftly about until dusk.* Two steps. . . . *When the sun was gone and the dusk came, the silent bats would come forth to relieve the guard of cliff swallows.* Three steps. . . . *It would be a little while yet before the velvet-footed coyotes came up from the desert to drink.* Four steps. . . . The doorhandle was turned, and a faint streak of grayish light showed between it and the wall. Before God! *What had happened to the spring?* There was nothing in the canyon now but utter darkness, like the darkness of the Snake Den, broken only by a faint and widening bar of gray light. The door hinges creaked. There was a moment's hesitation. The hinges creaked again, and the gap of gray began to narrow.

"*Wait!*" called out Lee.

The key soon clicked in the lock of the leg-irons.

FOURTEEN

THE WARDEN CLOSED the door behind himself and Lee Kershaw. "Here is your man, gentlemen," he said.

"Will he go?" asked a familiar voice.

Lee looked across the shaded living room of the warden's quarters into the face of Colonel Will Felding. Beside the agent sat a little wizened man wearing pince-nez glasses, who looked steadily at Lee like a bright-eyed little bird.

"Uriah Heep," observed Lee.

"I beg your pardon?" said the little birdlike man.

"This gentleman is Marcus Wrenn," explained the warden. "He is secretary to the governor."

"Uriah Heep," repeated Lee.

"Is he all right, warden?" asked Wrenn.

"He's all wrong," said the warden.

The merry tinkling of ice against the sides of a glass pitcher forecasted the arrival of Sarah, the warden's wife, bearing a tray with a pitcher of pink lemonade and three tall glasses. She served the three men.

"Make mine a beer, ma'am," suggested Lee from where he sat on the floor with his back against the wall.

"Of all the nerve!" cried Sarah.

"Get him a couple of bottles, Sarah," said the warden.

"Have you told him, Henry?" asked Felding of the warden.

"Only that he has a chance of wiping out his sentence."

"What about it, Mister Kershaw?" asked Wrenn.

Lee's gray eyes were on the two bottles of beer being

brought into the room by Sarah. They were tall and mistysided. Lee's throat went thoroughly dry and speechless. He gripped a bottle and twisted off the wire. The cap popped. The cold beer foamed and gurgled down Lee's throat. He lowered the bottle half-emptied. "Mother's own milk!" he gasped.

"I asked you a question," reminded Wrenn.

"You're representing the governor?" asked Lee.

Wrenn nodded.

Lee looked at Felding. "What's your part in the deal?"

"My wife, whom you will remember, Kershaw."

"You honor me," said Lee drily.

"Tell him, gentlemen," suggested the warden. "How's the beer, Kershaw?"

"Prime, warden," replied Lee as he raised the bottle.

"It's about Queho," stated Felding.

Lee looked slowly up at him. "He's alive?"

"That is correct."

"*Where?*" softly asked Lee. A powerful hand tightened about the neck of the beer bottle.

"Up north, somewhere along the Colorado River, perhaps in Arizona, Nevada, or even California. We don't know for sure."

"You're sure? I mean—that he's *alive?*"

"We're positive."

The bottle snapped in the crush of Lee's hand. Beer and blood intermingled and ran down to soak into his convict's striped trousers.

Sarah came bustling in to treat and bandage Lee's wound. She cleaned up the mess and brought Lee another beer. The warden tossed the makings to Lee.

"What is it you want from me?" asked Lee as he shaped a quirly.

"We want you to go in and get Queho," replied Felding.

"No man can do that," replied Lee.

"You can," said the warden.

"Only you," added Wrenn. "They say no man knows that country better than you do."

"That is not so," corrected Lee as he lighted up. "Queho does. What brought all this on?"

The three of them told him, each of them taking a part, as in the chorus in a Greek tragedy, until the bloody tale was finished.

Lee grinned wryly as he opened the beer bottle. "You've got to give him credit. Who else could have gotten away with it?"

"*You*, maybe," replied Felding.

Lee shook his head. "There would have been no incentive for me. I do not want your wife, Colonel. I never did. If I had escaped with Queho, instead of being quickly recaptured, I would have been in Mexico these past months, hiding out from the *Rurales*, of course, but safe from Arizona law." He shrugged. "But Queho thinks differently."

"Why?" asked Wrenn.

Lee looked up at him. "Because he is not a man of our society. The Indians never fully accepted him because he has the blood of black and white in him. The blacks will not accept him because he has the blood of Indian and white man in him. The Mexicans will not accept him because he has mixed gringo blood, and they are superstitious about the blacks. In short, gentlemen he is Ishmael. No! More! He is a pariah; a social leper!"

"Yet you seemed to have accepted him," suggested the warden.

Lee smiled crookedly. "I had no choice. He once saved my life. I could depend upon him. Later, we were cellmates for months. I killed time by trying to teach him. I thought I had grown to know him."

"I meant more than that, Kershaw. You went to prison partly because of him."

Lee looked into Felding's eyes and the agent turned away.

"No man can accept Queho'," murmured Lee. "*No man*. . . ."

"And yet, without you, he could not have escaped from Yuma Pen."

"We were supposed to have helped each other," said Lee drily.

"But, when the time came for Queho to make his choice, to keep on to freedom, or to turn back and help you, risking recapture, he abandoned you, the man who had helped him to escape, and he left you to the mercy of the Cocopah trackers."

Lee nodded. "They would have killed him, after torture, rather than bring him in alive, or perhaps *half* alive, as they did me, for their fifty dollars reward." The big, dirty hands closed tightly on the beer bottle. "I haven't forgotten that," he softly added.

"Some say," persisted the warden, "that the choice was yours—to escape yourself and leave Queho to the trackers, or to stay behind to lead the trackers astray so that he might escape, knowing all the time that you could not escape."

"Of such things are legends woven," said Lee quietly.

"Then you must bear no love for Queho," said Wrenn.

Lee smiled faintly. "Revenge is bitter fruit, gentlemen." His bearded face changed into an enigmatic mask. "Let's get down to business, gentlemen. Your deal? *Offer*, I should say."

Felding and the warden looked at Wrenn. He adjusted his pince-nez and cleared his scrawny throat. "If you will go in after Queho and rescue the two women he has kidnapped, the governor will grant you a full pardon."

"What's to prevent me from taking off for Mexico once I'm out from behind these walls?"

"Your word."

"You'll take that?"

"You are known to be a man of your word."

Lee slowly began to shape a cigarette. "A failing, in this

235

mercenary world. And what of Queho? Do you want him too?"

It was very quiet in the shade-darkened room.

"You know I will have to kill him to succeed," added Lee.

No one spoke.

Lee lighted up. "Or *he* will have to kill *me*. There can be no other way between us, gentlemen."

"We knew that," said Felding.

"The most dangerous game in the world," continued Lee, almost as though he was talking to himself. "Man hunting man."

"Who is better at that game than you are, Kershaw?" reminded the warden. "Or once *were*," he hastily corrected himself.

"Maybe Queho," quietly replied Lee, "although perhaps he doesn't know it himself yet. And, he will be playing on his own field, a distinct advantage at any time, with the odds being even if we are on more or less neutral ground."

"You talk like a professional," put in Wrenn.

"I *am* a professional."

"Well?" asked Wrenn. "What is your decision?"

Lee closed his eyes. The memory of the cool, shaded upper canyon with its spring would not come back to him. Instead, he saw nothing but the shifting, mind-cracking darkness of the Snake Den.

"Nineteen more years, Kershaw," reminded the warden.

"Nineteen and a half," corrected Lee. "When do I get the pardon?" He opened his eyes.

"Upon the delivery of the two women," said Felding.

"And the head of Queho in a sack? It will stink in the furnace heat."

"That will not be necessary," primly replied Wrenn.

Lee looked at the fat, sweating porcine face of Felding. "The Colonel, there, might want another tobacco jar," he murmured.

"I do not understand," said Wrenn.

"No matter, sir," said Lee.

"We will take your word on the death of Queho," promised Wrenn.

"Most kind,"murmured Lee.

"Will you go then?" asked Felding.

"All right," agreed Lee.

He stood up. "I'll need expense money. A bath, fresh clothing, guns, a horse, and passage upriver to Fort Mohave for myself and the horse. I place first priority on the bath."

Wrenn nodded. He placed five crisp hundred dollar bills on the marble-topped table. "Is that enough?" he asked.

"For starters. Do you want a receipt?"

Wrenn shook his head. "No records are to be kept of this transaction."

Felding stood up and took his hat. "I hope that you still do not harbor any ill will against my wife or myself for the charges placed against you by us at Fort Mohave."

"Little things like attempted rape, assault, and second-degree murder? No gentleman would hold such things against the character of a lady such as Mrs. Felding, sir, and yourself, of course, Colonel."

"You honor my wife and myself, sir!"

The warden looked searchingly at the bearded face of Lee Kershaw. He'd never be able to figure out the man.

"All I want to do," added Lee, "is to get my hairy old ass out of Yuma Pen, sir! I'd go into that country of hellfire to bring out Lucretia Borgia, if you had promised me a pardon for that."

"I do not care for that comparison, sir," protested Felding.

Lee shrugged. "I do not have to like your wife, sir, to try and save her life. I would do the same for any woman in such a situation."

"Good luck then," said Wrenn. He opened the door and let in a blast of heat and sunlight. Felding walked past him.

"One moment!" called out Lee.

They turned and looked quizzically at him.

"You mentioned that *three* women had been taken by Queho. Yet you have mentioned only two of them, referring to Mrs. Felding and Lucille Winston, the governor's niece. What about the third woman. Who is she?"

"She's nothing," replied Wrenn.

"Only a whore," added Felding.

"I see," said Lee quietly. "Only a whore. Nothing. . . ." They closed the door behind themselves.

FIFTEEN

THE COPA DE Oro Mine was situated high on the barren slopes overlooking the lower mountain spurs and the flat desert below them. Across the desert was the distant north-south road, and at right angles to that road was the branch road, a single, deeply rutted track that came straight as a bowstring across the desert toward the mountains until it reached the lower slopes, where it then vanished from the sight of anyone up at the mine by passing around behind a pinnacled rock formation, only to reappear at the eastern side of the formation to slant transversely up a treacherous road cut into the mountainside to ascend to the mine. It was a bad road to travel in full daylight, and at night it was virtually impossible to ascend.

A man watching the road from the mine could see all the way across the desert to the faintly distinguishable line of the north-south road until it turned behind the pinnacles. Thus, anything moving on either road could be seen because of the rising dust, at least during the daylight hours or on bright, moonlit nights. In the days of the Paiute troubles, a watchman was always kept on the heights above the mine to watch the roads. He wasn't up there to look for Paiutes, because they were never seen unless they wanted to be seen. He was there to watch for the rising dust that would forecast the coming of the vital freight-wagons delivering supplies to the mine. When dust arose on the branch road, it would then be time to send out an armed escort of mine employees to guard the freight wagons until they reached the mine. The ore wagons leaving the mine were never guarded, for a Paiute had little use for the white man's madness of gold. But the contents of the freight wagons were treasure indeed for the Paiutes.

For several years, since the Paiutes had been quiet and the Mohave Apaches had stayed, reservation bound, far to the south, it had not been necessary to keep a watchman on the heights. Now that Queho was haunting the empty land, coming and going in the infernal temperatures like a disembodied spirit, a watchman was again kept on the heights, softly cursing his fate. He sat under a square of worn and patched wagon canvas armed with a rifle and a pair of powerful field glasses, trying to keep awake.

This day, the dust moved along the north-south road until it reached the junction of the branch road in the late afternoon. Then the dust changed direction and moved slowly toward the east along the branch road. The sun was already slanting low to the west. The wagons were hours late. They would not be driven up the steep mountain road until daylight, therefore they would stop, by custom, beyond the pinnacles from dusk to dawn, out of sight of anyone up at the Copa de Oro.

The watchman this day picked up a melon-sized rock and dropped it. It struck the galvanized iron roof of the mine office far below and sent a dull resounding echo against the mountain flank. Melvin Lusk, the mine manager, came out of the office and looked up at the watchman.

"Dust on the road, Mister Lusk!" yelled the watchman. "It'll be the freight wagons!"

Lusk shaded his eyes and looked toward the dust. The wagons would not be driven up to the mine before daylight. He was shorthanded at the mine as it was. Even Queho would think twice before he jumped three tough teamsters armed and usually spoiling for a fight.

"Can I come down now?" called the watchman.

Lusk waved the man down. He went back into his office and closed the door.

The watchman reached the mine buildings just as the sun went down beyond the mountains.

The lead freight wagon ground to a dusty halt behind the pinnacles. The lead teamster clambered down to the ground and eased his crotch. He walked back to the other wagons. "We'll stay here tonight and go up at dawn," he said.

The three teamsters walked to the water barrel lashed onto the side of the first wagon. It was then that they saw the lean, moccasined man step silently out of the shadows of the pinnacles and slowly raise his cocked Winchester '73.

There was no moon that night. About midnight, three rapid-fire shots ripped out and echoed flatly against the pinnacles, rebounding to roll out across the darkened desert and then die away. No one heard the shooting up at the mine.

The sun came up behind the mountains and lighted the desert, warming the eastern face of the pinnacles. No dust arose from behind the pinnacles.

Manager Lusk shoved back his plate and drained his coffee cup. He lighted a cigar and stood up. "Joe," he said to the watchman, "go down and see what's holding up the wagons."

Joe rode slowly down the winding mountain road. The sun was already hot on his back. No smoke rose from a morning campfire beyond the pinnacles. Joe rounded the pinnacles. The three wagons stood in a line with their knife-slashed tilts flapping idly in the morning breeze. The twelve mules were nowhere in sight.

"Anybody here?" yelled Joe.

"Anybody here? Anybody here? Anybody here?" echoed the pinnacles.

There was no reply.

The roan shied and blew as Joe rode around the pinnacles. The three teamsters lay sprawled on the ground.

Early-rising flies were already swarming about the shattered messes soft-nosed 200-grain .44/40 bullets can make out of the backs of skulls when fired at short range.

The wagons had been carefully looted. A wide track of mule-hoofs showed on the harsh desert soil, vanishing into the northern distance.

SIXTEEN

"*IT CAN'T BE* more than a mile down to the river," insisted Amy.

"As the crow flies," argued Mildred. "Look! Those rocks down there are all up and down like teeth on a saw."

"There has to be a way! He must get his water from the river down there and I'll bet *he* doesn't climb over those rocks to get it. There must be a way through them."

"And what happens if we do get to the river?"

"We can follow it downstream until we find a mine or a ranch or something."

"I don't quite think we can walk along beside the river like we would on a pathway through a park."

"Maybe we can swim across."

Mildred laughed. "You'll end up miles downstream rolling along the bottom."

"He's been gone three days," said the girl. "Maybe he won't be back. Maybe he's dead or captured. There's no food left, and hardly any water."

Mildred eyed the girl. "You sound almost sorry that something might have happened to him."

Lucille looked up a little dreamily. "He hasn't been unkind to *me*. But I think he'll be back. They can't capture or kill *him*."

Amy eyed her curiously. "What's all this?" she asked.

"Hero worship," said Mildred drily. "He's probably the first man who's ever looked twice at her."

"He escaped from Yuma Pen," continued the girl,

almost as though she was talking to herself. She looked up brightly. "Have you ever heard of anyone doing *that?*"

Amy peered over the rampart. The heat waves rose from the baking talus slope and distorted the *malpais* land and the crescent of river beyond it. "There has to be a way through there!"

"It will be like a furnace down there," argued Mildred. "And the snakes! It will be alive with them!"

"They won't come out into the sun. It would kill them. We'll just have to watch where we step and where we put our hands."

Amy filled three canteens with the last of the water. "We can't stay here any longer, no matter how much you argue. If he doesn't come back by tomorrow, we'll die of thirst in here."

"Leave my water here," said Lucille. "I'm not going."

Amy handed her a canteen. "Get up," she ordered. "We haven't much time left to get down there before dark."

Lucille shook her head. "I'm staying."

Amy dragged her to her feet. "Come on," she ordered.

Mildred shook her head. "You won't get her to go that way, sister." She snatched Lucille's canteen away from her. "If you want to catch a rabbit like this one here, you've got to lure her with a carrot—in this case, the last of the water."

Amy took the Hopkins and Allen shotgun from the rack. She broke it to check the loads, then briskly snapped it shut.

"What do you intend doing with that?" asked the girl. "You wouldn't shoot him with it, would you?"

Amy clambered to the top of the rampart. "Try me," she cheerily replied. She dropped out of sight on the far side of the rampart.

Amy stopped at the foot of the talus slope. "Look," she said.

They looked up toward the cave. There was no indication whatsoever of the cave or of the rampart in front of it, so skillfully had Queho used natural materials to blend in his work with the surrounding features.

Amy walked into the labyrinth of the *malpais*.

An hour later, the three women staggered out of the natural baking oven, streaming with sweat and gasping for breath in the stifling, heated air. Their canteens were half empty.

"I'm going back," gasped Lucille.

"Where?" asked Amy.

Nowhere could they see the way they had come, or any feature that might identify the approach of the hidden cave.

"Come on," said Amy. She started back toward the *malpais*. Mildred followed her.

The girl stood there in the burning sunlight, staring up the slopes with burning eyes. She suddenly realized that Amy was right. She turned. "Wait!" she cried. The two women were out of sight. Lucille ran after them, right into the winding labyrinth from which they had just come.

The sun was low in the west. The two canteens were empty. "I knew we'd never make it! Damn you anyway!" snapped Mildred.

"I'm not licked yet!"

"The light is almost gone."

"We can wait until the dawn."

Queho found them sitting silently in the darkness. They were less than two hundred yards from the hidden way by which he reached the river for his water. He picked up the shotgun and jerked his head toward the heights, shadowed in darkness. He did not look back as he led the way. They stumbled and gasped behind him like two frightened little girls who had run away from home and had been overtaken by the hostile darkness.

Lucille was seated by the fireplace contentedly stirring a stew. She did not look up as the two women staggered into the cave. "Smells delicious," Amy observed drily. "What is it?"

"Stew! I made it myself!"

"Out of aged mule-meat?" asked Mildred.

Lucille shook her head. "Corned beef and dessicated vegetables."

"Where did you get it?" asked Amy.

Lucille pointed with her dripping spoon at a pile of boxes stacked against the wall. Blackly stamped on the yellow pinewood were the bold letters—COPA DE ORO MINE.

SEVENTEEN

"GODDAMNIT!" ROARED SHERIFF Jim Hathaway. He smashed a meaty fist down atop the map he had spread on a flat rock. "How in God's name Queho can vanish into thin air with twelve mules and about a wagonload of supplies is beyond me!"

No one spoke. The possemen quietly smoked, watching the red-faced sheriff out of the corners of their sunreddened eyes. The darkness of the desert persistently crept in about the wavering, shifting circle of firelight until someone threw more brush on the fire. A big coffeepot bubbled at the edge of the embers.

One of the men coughed, and the others looked accusingly at him. Then their eyes slanted outward into the soft darkness of the desert night. It was as though someone, or *something*, was watching them from the very edge of the firelight. The Paiute trackers were back in the shadows of the rocks, squatting on their heels, arms resting on their muscular thighs, lean and dirty hands hanging limply down. They could have told Hathaway that only Queho could hold up three freight wagons, kill three strong, armed men, and drive twelve mules off into the darkness laden with fine loot, only to vanish into thin air. The crazy white men still persisted in thinking they were dealing with a *man*.

"The Paiutes lost the trail three miles this side of the river, Jim," said the deputy sheriff.

"They'd lose their goddamned skinny asses if they didn't hold onto them with both hands!" roared the sheriff.

Dan looked toward the shadowed Paiutes. He could see the firelight reflecting moistly from their eyes. "It ain't that, Jim. They might have been able to track him right to the river but they didn't want to and nothing on God's earth can make them do that."

The fire died low. The thick bed of ashes peeped out a secretive ruby-red eye now and then, or a short-lived dancing sprout of flame. The flame would cast an eerie light on the tired faces of the possemen, only to die down and then reappear at another place in the wide bed of ashes.

Not even the Paiutes heard the lone man ghost silently through the darkness on moccasined feet. One minute he was not there, and the next minute he was there. His appearance was so unexpected that no one moved at first. Then the Paiutes, as one man, vanished back in among the rocks, to run silently through the darkness they feared almost as much as they feared Queho.

A Winchester action was quickly worked. The possemen stood up with their rifles in their hands.

"Who're you, mister?" demanded the sheriff.

"The name is Kershaw." Lee walked noiselessly to the fire. He filled a cup with the steaming, powerful brew. "You might as well turn back tomorrow morning," he suggested. "Queho will not be on this side of the river now. It's raining in the mountains to the east. The river is rising. You'll have the hell of a time getting across it, if you had that in mind."

"We did. You got here fast, Kershaw."

"Took the *Cocopah* upriver until it ran out of water. They're waiting for enough water to get upriver to Callville. I backtracked to find you here."

"How did you know where to find us?" asked the lawman stupidly.

Lee spat into the fire to raise a tiny spurt of steam. "A blind man could have seen your fire ten miles from here at dusk. I could hear you talking half a mile from here when the wind shifted."

The possemen surreptitiously studied the lean, bearded face of the man Lee Kershaw. Most of them knew him only by reputation. They knew he had been the man who had once traced down the Paiute murderer Ahvote and had brought him back to Prescott to await his execution. They knew, too, that if it had not been for Queho, Ahvote might have killed Kershaw. He was known as the best scout and manhunter in the Southwest and in Northern Mexico as well. That is, until he was put behind the bars at Yuma Pen. He was uncanny with a rifle (his seven-hundred-yard shot to hit and kill Ahvote was already legend); he was a lightning-fast draw with the six-gun; he was a man who could fight equally well under the Marquess of Queensberry rules, or with knife, fist, and boot. Strangest of all, he was self-educated and, incredibly, he even read books! His short service with Queho as his partner had established them as the best scouting-and-tracking pair in the business, with the odds being even as to which of the two of them was the better, and few takers on either one of them.

"Queho had a two day start this time," complained Hathaway. "The Paiutes lost his trail some miles on this side of the river."

"That figures." Lee smiled. "At least that's what they told you, Hathaway. They don't *want* to find him."

"And you can find him?"

"I'll take a look, Sheriff."

"You aim to hunt him alone?" asked Dan.

Lee nodded.

"I can send some of the boys with you," offered Hathaway.

The "boys" looked uneasily at each other.

"To help look for Queho or to keep an eye on me, Sheriff?" asked Lee. "The way you hunt for Queho, it's a wonder you get near him at all."

"You can do better?" asked Dan.

"I can," admitted Lee. He looked out into the soft desert darkness beyond the faint firelight. "He might very well be out there right now watching us."

"If he was," said Hathaway wisely, "you wouldn't be standing beside that fire like a clay pigeon."

Some months after Queho and Kershaw had been placed in Yuma Pen, they had made a well-planned break for freedom. Trouble was, they might have *planned* a double break, but *only* Queho had made it to freedom. Some said Queho had sacrificed Kershaw to make his escape; others said Kershaw had sacrificed himself to let Queho escape. Only two living men knew the answer to that one— Kershaw and Queho. Kershaw had never talked about it after his recapture, and Queho hadn't exactly stuck around publicly to give his version of the affair.

"Is there any help I can give you at all?" asked Hathaway.

"They told me you'd swear me in as a special deputy with a warrant for Queho. You know, like a hunting license." Lee grinned like a hungry lobo. "Besides, it will protect me from anyone who might mistakenly think I'm on the run from Yuma Pen."

"And what's to protect you from Queho?" drily asked Dan.

Lee shrugged. "In the game we will play, the first one of us who sees the other will likely win."

Hathaway took out a deputy badge and a warrant. "Hold up your right hand," he said. "Without the damned coffee cup in it!" He duly swore in Lee and gave him the warrant. "We've made a deal with California and Nevada. The badge and the warrant are as good in their territory as they are here in Arizona."

"They say Queho collects the guns and badges of the men who hunt him, Kershaw," needled Dan. "You know— like trophies."

"How many so far?"

"God alone really knows. Couple of deputies, a mine watchman, three teamsters. A Nevada deputy went missing two months ago. A Wells Fargo man went in after Queho and hasn't been seen since. Some say he has killed twelve men since he got out of Yuma. That would make you unlucky thirteen, Kershaw."

Lee looked at him. "Seems to me that *all* of them were unlucky, mister."

"Nevada is keeping a posse in the field at all times," hastily interposed Hathaway. "There are now two operating from Arizona and one from California. The Army is preparing to send in a strong patrol. There's little chance of him ever getting out of that hell's area where he's holed up."

Lee looked off into the darkness toward the unseen river. "He won't attempt a break," he quietly prophesied. "He'd condemned himself to a prison just the same as the one he broke out of, except that it's bigger, and a hell of a lot lonelier. Bigger, perhaps, but just as confining."

"You sound like you're almost sorry for him," accused Dan.

"There's no place for him in our society. The whites, blacks, Indians, and the breeds don't want him. No matter where he goes, he's already condemned. No matter where he tries to go, the law is hunting for him. Dead or alive, mister, with the emphasis on *dead*. He has literally condemned himself to life imprisonment in the barren mountains and lost canyons along the Colorado River."

Hathaway nodded. "With twelve mule-loads of supplies. He has an inexhaustible supply of water from the river. He has innumerable hideouts known only to himself, and has an armory of rifles, shotguns, and pistols, and plenty of ammunition for all of them."

"Coupled with the hunting-and-killing instincts of a predatory animal," added Lee. "He's king in those canyons, gentlemen, and don't you ever forget it."

It was very quiet again.

A horse whinnied out of the darkness.

Men grabbed for their rifles.

"Mine," said Lee.

When the fire had died down to a thick bed of ashes, Lee vanished into the darkness as quickly and as silently as he had appeared.

EIGHTEEN

THE DAWN LIGHT had crept into the river gorge an hour before and had slowly erased the deep shadows. The light grew. There was no wind. Nothing moved except the river, which now flowed swiftly and higher because of the rains in the mountains far to the east.

The faint mule-tracks had ended a mile from the river at the edge of an exposed rock-shield on the lower ground on the Arizona side of the river. Lee Kershaw squatted behind a rock outcropping that concealed him from anyone who might be watching the gorge from the almost sheer heights across the river. Behind Lee was a broken land; a mad helter-skelter of distorted and shattered rock virtually impossible for mules and horses to pass through; yet, somehow Queho must have gotten his loot-laden mules to the river and *across* the river. That was the puzzle.

Lee studied the upriver shore. There the rock shield slanted down under the surface, and just northeast of it there was a wide, gravelly beach.

Lee worked his way through the *malpais* land behind the rock shield. Here he found his first clue. It was a heavy stone, shaped like a great pear, whose heavier and darker side lay upward, indicating that some force had struck it and turned it over, and recently, for the sun had not yet had time to lighten the darker surface. A man's foot would surely break before it could upset such a stone, but a mule-hoof could easily kick it up and over.

Lee faded in among the boulders. He focused his field

glasses on the heights. There was no place a mule could gain those heights. There was a narrow declivity, just about wide enough for a man to struggle up it to the rim. It was like a three-sided chimney slanted at about fifteen degrees. It did not seem to quite reach the rim, but that might be an optical illusion.

Lower down the river gorge, the water washed against broken and tumbled detritus that had scaled from the heights. There was one place where a great sheet of rock had scaled off and fallen into the river athwart the current to form an abutment, behind which the silty water curled and eddied in a mass of yellowish foam. There some hardy water plant or tree had seemingly taken root to thrust up four ungainly looking stalks from what looked like a rounded gravel-bank circled by the yellow foam.

Lee focused the glasses on the plant. "Goddamn," he breathed. The four stalks were the upthrust legs of a dead horse or mule, extended from the gas-bloated belly like stick legs a child might have thrust into the belly of a toy clay animal. Beyond the dead beast there floated in the eddy a pale yellowish rectangle of some sort. The lenses picked out the bold black lettering on it—COPA DE ORO MINE.

Lee squatted in the hot shade, studying the river. He pictured twelve frightened mules driven into the rushing current to swim across at a transverse angle, heads held high, nostrils flaring redly, eyes wide with fright. Some of them must have made it across, but others had not. He looked upriver to where he had seen the overturned stone and estimated how much force the river had had against the laden mules to slant them across the river. Theoretically, if a mule swam strongly across the river, he would have reached the other side just about where the declivity reached the water's edge. Those that had not made it would have been swept downriver to be sucked under by quicksands or drowned. One of them had not gotten very far.

Beyond the heights was a never-never land that no Paiute in his right mind, and few white men, for that matter, would enter. To the Paiutes, it was a forbidden land—the haunt of evil tribal spirits of ferocious and murderous intent. To a white man, the principal deterrents were the heat, the almost utter lack of water, and the trackless barrens themselves. Men had been known to go in there and not to return. Some of them still lay in there, unburied and dried to mummies in faded clothing, staring up at the brilliant sun with eyeholes that could not see. Some of them had bullet holes in the backs of their skulls. Lee knew. . . . It was not a good place.

The hawk drifted high over the gut of the gorge, resting his wings on the updraft of air from the gorge. He floated over the heights on the other side of the river. Suddenly he tilted his wings and swept away from the heights to cross the river to the Arizona side. His slight shadow passed over the hidden man on the Arizona side but the hawk did not see him. Something up on the heights had frightened the hawk. There was only one thing that could put fright into a hawk in that country—*man*.

"Queho," said Lee softly.

Time ticked past in that place where time meant nothing. Nothing moved except the river and the heat-shimmering atmosphere, and the heat in the gorge grew and grew. Queho was up there watching the Arizona side of the river as Lee was watching the Nevada heights.

The long afternoon crept by. Lee sometimes dozed with his half-cocked Winchester across his thighs and his drawn Colt lying beside his right hand.

The long shadows came to ink in the river gorge and after a while they blotted it out altogether. Overhead, the sky was a long, narrow tapestry of mingled blue-gray stippled with twinkling diamond-chips of stars. The river rushed on, effectively drowning out the soft footfalls of Lee as he went to get his roan horse.

The box canyon brooded in a graveyard quiet. Lee stopped short. He faded into cover and made his catlike way up a slope to fatten the deep shadow of an upright boulder.

There was no sound from the picketed roan. Suddenly, he turned his head and looked toward the river, softly cursing the sound of it that overlay all other sounds.

Lee tested the brooding night with eyes, ears, and nose. A faint, rank odor drifted to him—*man*.

Lee catfooted into the darkness with his Winchester at hip-level, muzzle probing the way. The man-odor seemed to have passed from the box canyon.

He stumbled over the sprawled body of the roan. A questing hand went into the raw, hot, wet wound that had completely severed the throat. He was gone from that place of sudden death in seconds.

Minutes ticked past. There was no sound or movement other than the river.

Lee went back to the roan. The saddlebags had been taken. The two big blanket-covered canteens were missing. In a few seconds, Lee Kershaw was also missing.

He moved like wind-driven smoke through the darkness toward the river, his rifle at low port, fully cocked and ready for a snap-shot. He would only get one chance, for Queho would fire at the muzzle flash and he would not miss.

Lee went to ground, trying to skylight any movement against the blue-gray of the night sky. He saw nothing.

The night wind was now questing down the dark river gorge. It moaned a soft threnody over the more sullen murmuring of the Colorado.

Lee paused under a rock ledge whose upper edge overhung his head. He looked down toward the river. As his eyes became more accustomed to the darkness about him, he noticed something different on the light-colored ground in front of him. It had not been there when he had stopped under the ledge. It was a long shadow—the shadow of a tall man who was standing on the ledge *directly over Lee's head*.

The wind shifted. A faint odor came to Lee's questing nose—a mingled aura of sour grease, stale sweat, and an indefinable musky animal-like odor—*Queho*.

Lee slowly raised his rifle. The metal-shod butt clicked sharply against the rock behind him. Gravel pattered down about him as he leaped forward and swung for the killing shot. He saw only the faintest of silently moving shadow. The Winchester exploded stabbing flame and smoke toward the shadow. The smoke blew back into Lee's face. The shot echo slam-banged between the gorge walls and went racketing down the river.

Something splashed. Lee ran toward the river. It was like looking into a trough of India ink. He stood there with the water swirling about his calves, feeling his feet sinking a little too swiftly into the bottom. He sucked back a foot and threw himself toward the shore, just as he realized he had stepped into the edge of quicksand. He crawled up the slope and went to ground behind a ledge.

Minutes ticked past.

A coyote howl came from the heights across the river. Lee just about picked it up over the sounds of the river and the night wind, but he heard it and knew it for the voice of a man, no matter how well it was mimicked.

Lee let down the hammer of his rifle to half-cock. He went back to the broken rock formations and found a hideout in which to sleep until daylight. Queho would not be back across the river that night.

When the faintest gray pearl of dawn light crept into the gorge, Lee focused his field glasses on the opposite side of the river about where the declivity rose to the heights. As the light grew, he saw the shape of the little canvas-covered flatboat moored between rocks at the base of the declivity and partially hidden by brush, probably transplanted there by Queho, for there was no other brush anywhere along the base of the heights.

Lee slid his Winchester forward. He could just make out the thick rope that moored the boat to a stake driven into the gravel. His first shot split the stake. His second cut the rope. The boat floated out into the river, and before it swirled fifty yards ten more rounds of .44/40 slapped through the thin canvas-covered sideboards of the boat from side to side. As the last echoes of the fusillade died out and the gunsmoke drifted away, the boat filled with water and sank from view in a swirling eddy.

Lee crawled back into the rock formation. He cut a chew of Wedding Cake and stuffed it into his mouth. By the time he had the "sauce" worked up, he was paralleling the river behind the rock ledges as he headed downstream to keep close to the only supply of water for thirty miles.

NINETEEN

AMY QUICKLY RAISED her head from her pallet. "Listen!" she cried out in the darkness, but the faint and distant rifle shot echo had died away before the other women awoke.

"What was it?" asked Mildred.

"A shot!"

"Maybe you're hearing things."

"No! I heard it! I wasn't asleep!"

Amy got up and walked out of the cave to step up behind the rampart. The *malpais* land was dark and quiet. Only the night wind moved.

"It could have been Queho," suggested Lucille.

Amy shook her head. "He wouldn't give himself away this close to his hideout."

"Maybe he's hunting," Lucille brightly added.

"At night?" asked Amy.

"Maybe someone is hunting *him*," put in Mildred.

Amy nodded. "They can't get near him during daylight." She looked back at the two pale faces in the dimness. "Maybe we can go down there and find the men who are hunting him."

"You know what happened the last time we tried that," reminded Mildred.

"I won't go this time," said Lucille. "And you can't make me go either!"

Amy stepped down and looked at her. Mildred caught Amy's eye and shrugged as the girl went back into the darkness of the cave. Lately she had seemed strangely content, adapting herself very well to the confined life of the cave.

"Well," said Amy, "it's no use trying to get down there in the dark. Maybe we can wait until dawn."

"Unless Queho comes back before then," said Mildred.

"He'll be back," the girl said softly from the darkness. "They can't kill him."

The arched mouth of the cave was faintly limned in grayness when Queho came silently over the rampart and into the cave. A pair of saddlebags hung over his shoulder. He squatted at the bend of the cave and lighted a candle. He unbuckled the saddlebag straps and dumped out the contents of the bags. Bottles clinked on the hard floor. Queho picked up a bottle and pulled out the cork with his strong white teeth. He drank deeply.

"He's killed someone again," breathed Amy.

"I said they couldn't kill *him*," the girl whispered in fearful excitement.

In a little while he hurled the empty bottle into the rear of the cave. He lighted a cigar he took from the loot. The alternate flaring up and dying away of the tip of the cigar first glowed against his dark face, then cast it into shadow again.

The light grew from the mouth of the cave. A rataplan of gunfire echoed and re-echoed in the gorge. Queho jumped to his feet and snatched up his Winchester. He ran toward the mouth of the cave, stamping hard on Lucille's outflung right hand. She whimpered in pain. He jumped down behind the rampart, then up onto the step, thrusting the rifle forward and working the action.

The women lay silently. Lucille mouthed her trampled hand, fighting back the tears and sobs.

"He'll want a woman soon," prophesied Mildred.

"With all that liquor in him he won't be able to do any woman any good," said Amy, the professional.

"If he does want a woman," said Mildred, "you go, Amy. After all, it *is* your line of business, isn't it?"

"He doesn't pay," countered Amy.

"He's feeding you," argued Mildred.

"He's keeping all three of us alive," put in the girl.

Queho let the hammer of the rifle down to half-cock. He staggered a little as he came into the cave. He leaned the rifle against the wall and swept the guttering candle aside with one hand, plunging the rear of the cave into semidarkness. He slowly stripped off his filthy clothing. He stood there, naked and hairy, swaying back and forth on his bare feet. He opened the second bottle of booze and drank a third of it, his throat working convulsively.

"It won't be long now," whispered Mildred to the girl.

"He'll never make it," said Amy.

"A lot you know," jeered Mildred.

He turned and walked toward them. He ripped back the blanket that covered the girl and clawed away her thin nightdress. He stared down at her small, red-budded breasts. She lay there, staring almost hypnotized into his strange, dark face. He picked her up and carried her to his odorous pile of blankets and skins.

Amy sat up. "Take me," she offered. The bare heel caught her alongside the jaw and flung her back against the wall.

Queho pawed weakly at the girl. Then he slowly got to his feet and stood there swaying. Then he fell heavily across her thin body and lay still.

Amy wiped the blood from her mouth. "I told you," she said.

The girl lay motionless beneath Queho. The smelly, sweating hulk of the breed and the warm, wet flesh was close against her white nakedness.

Mildred picked up an ax. She walked deliberately toward the bed. Amy stepped in front of her. "This is our chance!" snapped Mildred. "You crazy bitch!" retorted Amy. "If you kill him we may never find our way out of here! There's only enough water left for today! He always makes damned sure of that!"

Mildred slowly lowered the ax. "Christ, but he stinks! Like an uncleaned cage in a zoo!"

"Get up, kid," said Amy to the girl. "It's all over."

Lucille did not move. There was almost a dreamlike look on her narrow face. The weight of the stinking male animal on her felt good. She had never been naked with a male before; she hadn't lied about that.

"Get up, damn you!" cried Mildred.

Amy rolled the breed over against the cave wall. "No use waiting, honey," she said quietly to the girl. "He can't do any woman any good today."

"I wonder if he ever could?" questioned Mildred.

Amy looked quickly at her. "What do you mean?"

Mildred dropped the ax. "Nothing," she hastily replied.

Lucille got slowly to her feet and passed her thin hands down her small, spare body. She walked to her pallet and began to dress.

"Aren't you going to wash the stink from you?" asked Mildred.

Amy watched the girl. "We haven't got enough water," she said. Lucille turned away from them and finished dressing.

Queho mumbled in his stupor.

"What's he saying?" asked Mildred.

Amy held her nose and bent close to Queho. He mumbled again and again. She stepped back. "One word," she said, "over and over—Kershaw, Kershaw, Kershaw." She looked at Mildred. "The only Kershaw I know of is Lee Kershaw, the manhunter."

"My God!" cried Mildred.

"What does it mean?" asked Lucille.

"Lee Kershaw was the man who was with that stinking breed at Fort Mohave when the two of them tried to rape me, anyway Queho did. Kershaw was too drunk to know much about anything, but he wasn't so drunk that he could

262

not kill the engineer of the *Mohave* who had bravely come to my rescue. Well, they put Kershaw and Queho away for twenty years in Yuma Pen. *That* took care of *them!*"

Amy shook her head. "Only Lee Kershaw," she corrected Mildred.

"They were friends?" asked Lucille.

Mildred shrugged. "I suppose so. Kershaw treated that breed as though he was human."

Amy nodded. "That sounds like Lee Kershaw all right."

Mildred looked quickly at Amy. "How well did you know him?"

Amy shrugged. "I worked in Tucson some years back. I knew him fairly well."

"A customer of yours, no doubt?" sneered Mildred.

Amy nodded. "I liked him," she said simply. She looked at Mildred. "You just said the two of them tried to rape you, at least Queho. I thought Queho had been sentenced *for* raping you."

Mildred looked quickly away. "I'll make the breakfast," she volunteered. It wasn't like her to volunteer for any work around the cave.

Amy looked through the items from the saddlebags. She held up a polished-steel mirror. Etched crudely on the back of it was one word—KERSHAW. "This is a prisoner's mirror," she said. "I've seen them before. These must be Kershaw's saddlebags."

"And Queho has killed him," said Mildred. "Maybe he escaped too."

"If he had, why would Queho kill him?"

Mildred wiped the sweat from her face. "How the hell should I know! I'm glad if he did, that's all!"

Amy shook her head. "He hasn't killed him," she said.

"How do you know?" asked Lucille.

Amy shrugged. "If he did kill Kershaw, who did that shooting after daylight down in the gorge?"

"Someone looking for us," said Mildred. "I wish to God Queho and Kershaw had killed each other."

Amy stood up with the mirror in her hand. "He did not kill Lee Kershaw," she said. "I think Kershaw is somewhere along the river looking for us."

Mildred laughed. "The heat is getting to you, sister!" For a moment she eyed Amy, then looked quickly away. "Kershaw is either in Yuma Pen, or he's dead."

Amy slowly polished the mirror against her dress as she walked to the mouth of the cave. She picked up Queho's powerful field glasses and uncased them as she stepped out into the bright morning sunlight beyond the mouth of the cave. She looked over the rampart and focused the glasses down toward the river gorge. "My God!" she cried back over her shoulder. "I can see a man walking on the other side of the river!"

"Let me see," said Mildred. She snatched the glasses away from Amy and refocused them. A lean, bearded man was walking easily downriver on the Arizona side. She could not see his face but the easy, catlike walk seemed familiar.

Amy turned the steel mirror toward the sun and began to flash it.

"What the hell are you doing?" demanded Mildred.

The flashes were shards of the purest silver and could be seen for miles.

Mildred walked back into the cave. A moment later she came out again. "Get down," she ordered.

"He'll be out of sight in a minute!"

Something double-clicked behind Amy. She looked down into the twin black muzzles of a shotgun and along the fat-polished barrels into a pair of glacial blue eyes. "Get down, damn you," repeated Mildred, "or I'll blow off your head!"

Amy lowered the mirror and stepped down. She walked into the cave. She looked back at Mildred. "Why?" she asked.

"It's really none of your business."

"It is when my life and future depend on it. That man

down there was Lee Kershaw. He might be the only hope we have of getting out of here alive."

"I'd get no more mercy from Kershaw than I would from that drunken animal lying there."

"Why? Because you railroaded the two of them into Yuma Pen?"

"I don't have to answer any of your damned questions!" Mildred walked toward the rear of the cave and out of sight.

"Why did you ask her that?" asked Lucille.

"Because she seems more afraid of Kershaw than she does of Queho."

"But why? I don't understand."

Amy shrugged. "I'd like to know the truth about what happened back there on the *Mohave* the night Kershaw and Queho were supposed to have gone on a drunken debauch and tried to rape *Mrs*. Felding. I'm wondering now if Queho raped her, or even *tried* to rape her."

"I don't think so," said Lucille quietly.

Amy studied her. "Why do you think he didn't?"

"Well, he hasn't touched any of us yet, has he?"

"You might have something there. However, he hasn't been around too much."

"Of course," coyly added Lucille. "he *did* try with *me*. I wonder why? With two experienced women of the world like you and Mildred, why would he want *me?*"

Amy looked curiously at the girl. "How would I know? There's something he wants from us. God knows what it is. It must be more than just a bed partner."

"I think I know," replied the girl. "He wants one of us to want him for *himself*."

Amy wiped the sweat from her face. "It's too deep for me, kid."

"He's too deep for anyone to understand, and yet that is what he wants. Perhaps that is what Kershaw tried to give him—understanding."

Amy nodded. "Lee Kershaw would be the one to do it,"

she agreed. "God knows Lee Kershaw is so deep himself he might just be the one person who ever understood Queho."

"Oh, I don't know!" cried Lucille.

Amy patted the girl's thin, plain face. "God help you," she murmured. She picked up the field glasses and walked outside into the brilliant, metallic-looking sunlight. She focused the glasses on the Arizona side of the river. The river had been turned into a flow of mercury by the bright sunlight. Nothing moved on the far side of the river. Amy walked back into the cave.

Lee Kershaw lay belly-flat behind a piece of forked driftwood driven into the gravelly shore. He had seen the brilliant flashing of reflected sunlight from the forbidding heights across the river. He placed a long branch into the fork of the stick, pointed approximately to where he had seen the flashing. He lay flat behind a ledge and hat-shaded his field glasses to keep them from reflecting the sunlight as he studied the heat-shimmering land across the river. He studied the terrain foot by foot but could not see any sign of man over there.

The sun was beginning to cook his back. Nothing moved across the river, but the heat-disturbed air wavering upward from the baking rock. Lee vanished into the broken rock terrain back from the shore. The river rushed on. The heat waves shimmered. Nothing else moved.

TWENTY

THE UPPERWORKS OF the steamer *Mohave* gleamed like a sepulcher in the soft light of the dusk. The river whispered along its sides. Long bars of gold were thrown on the dark surface of the river from the lighted windows of the steamer. A thread of smoke rose from the galley stack and drifted downstream. The *Mohave* was moored alongside a sandbank that was itself separated from the Arizona side of the river by a narrow and shallow channel.

"Ahoy, the steamer!" hailed Lee Kershaw from behind a boulder. He kept his head down. All steamers passing up or down the river, to Callville at the mouth of the Virgin River, the head of navigation, now kept armed guards on the alert when they were tied up for the night—because of Queho.

"Who is it?" called out a guard.

"Is Captain Mellen aboard?"

"Of course he is!"

"Tell him it's Lee Kershaw!"

"Show yourself, Kershaw!" called out Mellen from the deck in front of the pilothouse.

Lee thumb-snapped a match into flame and lighted his bearded face. He quickly blew out the match.

"Come on aboard!" invited Mellen.

Lee splashed through the shallow water to the sandbank. He gripped the railing of the steamer and easily swung himself up onto the freight deck. He walked up the ladders to the pilothouse. Mellen thrust out a strong hand. "I heard you had come up this way, Lee."

"When do you go upriver?"

"We're waiting for a rise. We passed the *Cocopah* yesterday on her way downriver. She had to turn back from about here because of low water." Mellen waved Lee to a chair on the deck in front of the pilothouse. He handed him a cigar and lighted it for him. "What the hell are you doing around here on foot?"

"Queho outsmarted me. Killed my horse and got away with my food and canteens. Took me almost two days to walk out of that damned furnace."

"You get a crack at him?"

"Only a snap-shot. He was like a shadow, Jack."

"You giving up the hunt?"

"To go back to Yuma Pen?" Lee looked up the shadowy river. "I either get Queho, or I go back to Yuma."

"Or he gets you." Mellen reached inside the pilothouse and brought out a bottle and two glasses. "Look, Lee," he quietly added. "Wait until we get our rise. I'll take you up river to Callville. You can get to Salt Lake City from there before anyone in Arizona Territory gets wise. Who's to know? I'll keep my mouth shut. You know damned well I never bought that story about you trying to rape Milly Felding and killing Jim Anderson."

"You found my Colt in my hand with one cartridge expended and your engineer dead in the water with a bullethole in his head," said Lee quietly. "Besides, I gave my word. When is the rise due?"

"We could see the storm over the mountains toward the northeast late this afternoon. I figure the rise should be here about two hours before the dawn."

"When will you reach the Gut?"

"About an hour after dawn."

Lee drained his glass. The whisky hit his guts like the blow of a mailed fist. "I want you to leave early, Jack. Can you drop me off on the Nevada side of the Gut?"

"Yes, but you'll need a horse, won't you?"

"No. I'll never get within shooting distance of Queho by riding a horse."

Mellen refilled the glasses. "You're a strange one, Lee. I don't think you harbor any hatred for Queho."

"When the time comes, Jack, I'll execute him as neatly as though he was dropped through the gallow's trap at Yuma Pen."

Mellen shrugged. He looked upriver. "Dangerous enough in full daylight and almost impossible in darkness."

"You can do it if anyone can."

"He'll hear us coming upriver."

"He knows this is the time of the year for the high water this far up the river. He'll be expecting to hear steamers now. If you don't stop, he'll never know the difference."

"You have a place to land? I can't put you ashore in there in a small boat, at least on the Nevada side of the river.

"I have a place," replied Lee.

Mellen nodded. "We'll try then."

Lee drained his glass and stood up. "I'll need some canvas and rope for slings, and food, tobacco, whiskey, and a canteen."

"Can do," Mellen said. "What's the canvas for?"

"A shroud for Queho."

"I knew I shouldn't have asked."

Later, as Lee was half-asleep in the same cabin where Milly Felding had made her late evening appearance to send Queho and Lee to Yuma Pen for twenty years, he thought he heard a rise in the pitch of the sucking and gurgling of the river along the side of the steamer.

The hand shook Lee awake. "Time," warned Mellen. "We're getting up steam."

"How's the river?"

"Rising steadily."

Lee slung his Winchester over a shoulder. He slung a canvas pack over the other shoulder and fastened a coil of rope to his belt in the middle of his back. He walked out onto the darkened deck and looked over the side. The sandbar he had crossed the night before was now under two feet of swiftly rushing water. He walked up the ladder to stand on the larboard side of the pilothouse.

The *Mohave* tugged at her moorings in the suck of the rising river. Mellen handed Lee a cigar and cupped a lighted match about the tip of it. "You'll have just about enough time to smoke that," he said. He lighted a cigar for himself and leaned from a side window. "Cast off aft there!" he ordered. He placed a negligent hand on the huge steering wheel that had the lower half of it sunken into the pilothouse deck. A fire door clanged from the main deck. The sound of hissing steam came from the exhaust valves. "Cast off forrrard!" commanded Mellen.

The inshore current got in between the starboard bow of the steamer and the nearby shore, and the *Mohave* began to swing slowly outward toward the center of the river. Mellen spoke into the voice tube. "Slow, ahead, Mac," he ordered.

The *Mohave* trembled like a hound dog evacuating peach stones as power was applied to the great Pitman beams that crank-turned the big stern wheel. The hissing of the slow-speed, cross-compound engine became louder and yet louder. The bows swung out toward midstream to meet the full rushing current of the rapidly rising Colorado.

Mellen judged the speed and power of the current. The river was almost holding the steamer in neutral. He whistled into the voice tube. "Half-speed ahead, Mac," he ordered. The stern wheel began to churn faster and faster, thrashing the dark water into creamy, frothing yellowish-white foam. The mutted *sssoooo-hhhaaaa, sssoooo-hhhaaaa, sssoooo-hhhaaaa* of the engine echoed louder from the higher land on the Nevada side of the river. The dark mouth of the first gorge loomed ahead of the slowly moving *Mohave*.

Mellen eyed the looming sides of the gorge. As the *Mohave* poked her blunt nose cautiously into the darkness, Mellen tugged hard on the whistle cord. The wet-sounding squawking of the whistle bounced an echo back and forth between the gorge walls. Mellen listened attentively.

"What the hell was that for?" snapped Lee. "You want the whole goddamned world to know we're coming?"

Mellen was not listening to Lee. He tugged twice at the whistle cord and listened again to the echoes. He shifted the big wheel and grinned sideways at Lee. "Nervous?" he asked. "Look." He pointed to starboard. A great rock-outcropping rose ten feet from the roiled surface of the river, rimmed with foam, like the foamy fang of a mad dog. "We'd have ripped out our bottom on that if I hadn't picked up the right-sounding echo from the other side of the river."

"Sorry," apologized Lee. Maybe he *was* nervous.

The *Mohave* slogged upriver at a steady pace with the whistle blasting hoarsely now and again. The fire doors clanged, and the chunk wood was hurled into the fires. The paddle wheels thrashed, and the racketing sound of the engine, working at full speed now, came echoing back from the gorge walls.

"How much further along, Lee?" asked Mellen. He pointed to the sky. The first flush of the dawn light was showing.

The *Mohave* entered the gorge. To larboard, or port, the rock walls rose sheer for nearly two hundred feet and to starboard the ground was broken away, eroded and tumbled into the river to form a loosely compacted steep-to bank. An uneasy feeling came over Lee. He had not figured in a rise in the river when he had planted his driftwood markers pointing to the approximate position of the place where he had seen the sun-reflected flashings.

"I hope, for my professional reputation," said Mellen, "that I'm not making this look too easy."

Lee shook his head. "That damned gorge ahead looks as though Charon himself would not attempt to ferry anyone across it."

"Charon?" asked Mellen. "The name is not familiar. What rives does he pilot on?"

"The Styx," drily replied Lee.

"Where's that?"

"Between here and hell."

Mellen nodded. "I know what you mean."

The dawn light was beginning to fill the gorge.

"Where's your landing?" asked Mellen.

Lee climbed over the railing and stood at the very edge of the hurricane deck, looking up the gorge with the faint wraith of smoke hanging about his face from the stub of cigar in his mouth. There should be a ledge of lighter-colored rock on the Nevada side that led to a V-shaped access to the rim of the heights.

"When?" asked Mellen.

Lee took the risk. He could not see his driftwood marker. Where he had placed the marker was now under five feet of swiftly rushing water. "There," he said, pointing ahead to the ledge.

"How will you get back out?" asked Mellen. He whistled into the speaking tube. "Stand by for Slow Ahead, Mac," he warned.

"When are you due downriver?"

"In two days."

"Can you time your passing through the Gut to about dusk?"

"I'll risk it for you, Lee."

"Look for me then, Jack. I may not be alone."

"Who'll be with you?"

"Three women—I hope."

"Slow Ahead!" shouted Jack into the voice tube, and at the same time he swung the wheel to steer the steamer close under the sheer wall. "Now!" he yelled at Lee. *"Vaya con Dios*, Lee!"

Lee leaped. He landed crouched and catfooted on the ledge. The edge crumbled. He caught hold with one hand as his feet went out from under him. His rifle sling slipped from his shoulder and the Winchester plunged into the river. He caught hold with his other hand as his holding hand slipped and the pack sling slipped from his shoulder. The pack followed the rifle into the depths. Lee hooked a moccasined heel over the ledge and swung his body upward. His Colt slipped from its holster and fell into the river.

The *Mohave* whistled as she passed beyond sight around the bend in the river. Lee worked his way onto the ledge and lay bellyflat. There was just enough room for his body. Rock crumbled from the edge as he moved a little. Inch by inch he reached back and loosened the coil of rope from his belt. He looped the rope about a projection and then about his body. He spat out the cigar stub and felt for the makings. He shaped a quirly and then lighted it. He looked sideways across the river toward the Arizona side. It did not look familiar. He looked behind his shoulder to see that the ledge petered out against the sheer rock-wall. He looked ahead. The ledge vanished twenty feet in front of him.

He closed his eyes and rested his head on his forearms. He had landed on the wrong ledge.

TWENTY-ONE

THE HOARSE SOUND of the steamer's whistling came faintly through the gorge. Queho raised his head from his bed. He stood up, naked except for a breechclout, and reached for a rifle. He snatched up his field glasses as he ran to the mouth of the cave. He focused the glasses on the gorge, but by this time the steamer had passed out of sight upriver.

"What was it?" whispered Mildred.

"Steamer," replied Amy.

"I didn't know they came up this far."

"Only when there is a rise in the river during the summer. That's why we haven't heard one since we've been here. The river must have risen."

"If that's so," said Mildred, "he must be used to it. Why is he out there now?"

"I wish I knew! Quiet! He's coming back!"

He came softly into the cave and quickly dressed. He took his rifle and a full canteen and vanished into the rear of the cave. Amy was out of bed in an instant. She snatched up a candle and some matches and catfooted toward the rear of the cave. She felt her way through the dimness. Now and again she would stop to listen but she heard nothing. The stench of the garbage and the latrine hole sickened her the deeper she got into the passageway.

She waited in the darkness, listening for any sound that would warn her of Queho's presence. Softly she walked into another passageway and tiptoed toward the deep pit at the end of it. She thrust her head over the edge. Far below her she saw a faint glow of light, and then it was gone. Something rattled against the side of the pit, and then it was quiet again. She risked lighting the candle. She felt along the edge of the pit and found a rope ladder runged with iron rods.

Amy ran back to the outer part of the cave and began to dress. "I think I know how he gets out of the cave back there," she said excitedly. "There's a pit with a ladder in it."

"So?" asked Mildred.

"I'm going to find out."

"You'll kill yourself if he doesn't do it."

Amy took a pistol from the ammunition box. She shook a lantern to see if the oil reservoir was full. She slung a full canteen over one shoulder.

"If he sees you he'll kill you," warned Lucille.

"So? It'll be better than sitting around here waiting until he does the job here or we die of thirst."

"He'll be back. He *always* comes back. They can't kill *him!*"

"Listen to her," jeered Mildred. "I'll swear she's got a schoolgirl crush on that stinking animal."

"He's not an animal! He's a human being like the rest of us!"

"Speak for yourself, honey," jeered Mildred.

"Who's coming with me?" asked Amy.

Neither one of them spoke.

Amy nodded. "All right. I'll go alone. If I make it, I'll bring someone back for you two."

"If you do," said Mildred gloomily, "he'll likely kill us and fight it out to the last. They'll never take him alive."

"They won't take him at all!" cried Lucille.

Amy picked up a coil of rope. She walked back into the cave and knelt beside the pit. She tied the rope to the lantern bail and then lighted the lantern and lowered it far down into the pit. "See? There's another passageway down there!"

"With him waiting in it," said Mildred.

Amy pulled up the lantern. "When I reach the bottom, lower the lantern to me." She thrust her long, shapely legs down into the pit to place them on the ladder. *"Adios!"* she said. She descended into the pit.

They sat there listening to her making her way down the ladder. "Send it down," she called up. Lucille reached for the lantern. A hand gripped her wrist. Mildred shook her head. Mildred leaned over the edge of the pit and felt for the ladder. She gripped it and began to haul it up as swiftly as she could.

There was no sound from Amy. She knew the game. She felt inside her dress for candle and matches. She lighted the candle and walked into the narrow passageway.

TWENTY-TWO

QUEHO MOVED NOISELESSLY through the *malpais.* The sun was slanting down on the river gorge. He passed through a natural passageway and turned hard right, then hard left. The sunlight streamed into the opening at the end of the passageway. He stopped there. The river rushed through the gorge twenty feet below where he stood. A rusted bucket and a length of rope lay in a niche above a large wooden keg he used for settling the silty river water.

Queho focused his field glass up the gorge. He turned and looked down the gorge. He squatted in the passageway and shaped a cigarette. He lighted it, all the time watching the river. There was someone out there. He could *feel* someone out there.

Fifteen feet above where Queho squatted and smoked, Lee Kershaw sat on his narrow ledge looking down on the river. He could not make his way to right, left, or up. His only possible means of escape was the river. Once in the powerful liquid grip of the river, he'd have to ride the flood down through the gorge until he found a place to land downstream. There were treacherous eddies whirling round and round, cone-shaped, perhaps a foot or two below the water level, and he knew damned well if he was sucked down into one of them he'd never come up again.

"No food, no water, and no way home," said Lee.

He looked upriver. The *Mohave* would not be coming down for two days.

The sun began to heat up the rock face behind Lee. A

man could not last half a day on that ledge in the full sunlight.

"Charon?" Jack Mellen had asked. "The name is not familiar. What river does he pilot on?"

"The Styx," Lee had replied.

"Where's that?" Mellen had asked.

"Between here and hell," Lee had said.

The temperature was already 100 degrees and rising steadily. The heat seemed to be really emanating from the rock behind Lee. It was as though the demons of hell far below the rock surface were stoking up the hellfires to roast Lee Kershaw from his perch.

Once his mind reeled; he was brought around by the rope cutting into his body. He opened his eyes to look directly down into the river, and as he did so, he could have sworn he saw a puff of smoke drift from the face of the rock fifteen feet below him. He eased back onto the ledge and fought with all his willpower to regain his senses.

He peered over the edge. A bucket sailed out and plunged down into the river, only to be hauled up again by its rope, brimfull and banging metallically against the rock face.

"At least I know where he gets his water," murmured Lee.

He wiped the sweat from his burning face. He'd have to risk the river.

Amy slogged through the overpowering heat. It was the same story as before—to enter the *malpais* labyrinth was to lose oneself. She sat down in the hot shade of a boulder and closed her eyes. Her canteen was long empty.

It was the smell that aroused her. She opened her eyes. Queho passed just beyond her, moving as silently as a gecko lizard through the *malpais*. Amy did not move, but she did close her eyes. Thirst clawed roughly in her throat.

Amy cautiously crawled over the baking rock. She worked her way toward the direction from which Queho had come. There was a sort of cave mouth there, hidden unless one was within twenty feet of it. She stood up and walked into it with her pistol in her hand.

She stopped short at the very brink of the river. She picked up the bucket and dropped it into the river.

Lee heard the clanking of the bucket. He leaned far over and saw the woman's arms and the back of her head as she drew up the full bucket.

Lee drew back. He loosened his rope from the rock projection and tied a sheepshank into it just below the loop. He replaced the loop about the projection, then severed one of the three short connecting sections of rope between the loops at each end of the hitch. He drew in hard on the rope, and the hitch held. He eased himself over the crumbling edge of the ledge. Slowly he let himself down hand over hand, then pushed his feet against the side of the rock face and bent his knees. He snapped his legs out straight, and swung out over the abyss to swing back in again, letting the rope run through his hands. He swung into the cave mouth and landed lightfooted right at the very brink of the opening where he had seen the arms of the woman and the water bucket.

Amy dropped the dripping bucket from her mouth and yanked the pistol from within the top of her dress. Lee slapped the pistol to one side and grinned at her. "Hello, Amy," he said cheerfully. "You're a long way from Tucson." She stared dumbfounded at him. "They didn't tell me you were one of the three women taken by Queho," he added. He cupped a big hand under her chin and gently tilted her head a little backward to look into her face. "They called you just a woman," he said. "You understand?" She nodded. She suddenly pressed the side of her face hard against his chest. "Oh God, Kershaw!" she murmured.

He raised her head again. "Where are the others?"

"Still up there, Lee," she replied.

"Can you show me the way?" he asked.

"I'm not sure. Oh, Lee! I just can't go back up there!"

Lee took the pistol. He half-cocked it and opened the

279

loading gate. He twirled the cylinder. The handgun was not loaded.

Lee took the dangling end of the rope and quickly snapped it upward to release the two loops and the unsevered connecting pieces. The rope fell down and he drew it in, minus about a yard from the other end that still hung from the projecting rock. He coiled the rope. "Is this where he gets all his water?" he asked. He looked into the settling keg. It was full of clear water, with a layer of silt at the bottom.

She sat down on the overturned bucket. "I don't know," she replied. "He only keeps so much up in the cave, maybe two or three days' supply."

Lee nodded. "Anyway, he's got a whole damned river here to get his water. How's his food supply?"

"Enough for months," she said.

"From the Copa de Oro Mine?"

She nodded.

"Weapons?" asked Lee.

She held up her two hands. "About ten. Shotguns, rifles, and pistols. Maybe more. He took a pistol, a shotgun, and a rifle from the stagecoach." She looked up at him. "Mrs. Felding was bringing the rifle back from San Francisco for her husband. Queho said it was yours."

Lee looked quickly at her. "A Sharps .40/70?"

She shrugged. "I don't know. She said it had belonged to her husband originally and he had lost it to you in a crooked poker game. The breech was engraved with the name of Ahvote and a date—I can't remember what it was."

"Maybe it was a date in April, 1881," he suggested.

"That was it, Lee." She wiped the sweat from her face. "I remember he was very angry because it had only three cartridge-cases with it. Mrs. Felding didn't know anything about it."

Lee nodded. "She wouldn't."

"Why was he angry?"

"Because he must reload those three cartridges before he

can fire them. Besides they only last so long after so many loadings, unless he can resize the cases."

"There were all kinds of tools and things in the box with the rifles."

"What about ammunition for the other guns."

"Boxes full," she replied.

"Sounds like he's got an arsenal," Lee commented drily.

She nodded. "And he knows how to use them, Lee."

He squatted and rested his back against the wall, looking at the empty Colt. "Great," he murmured.

"What can you do now?" she asked.

He took out the makings and shaped a cigarette. He placed it between her lips and lighted it. He fashioned another cigarette for himself. "Wait until dark," he finally replied.

"And then?"

"Just wait for Queho."

She paled. "You mean . . . ?"

He nodded. "He'll come looking for you once he knows you're gone. He doesn't know I am here. You're the cheese in the trap, Amy. He'll figure you'll need water. This is the only place where you can get it."

She passed a shaking hand across her sweat-streaked face. "He may think I've gone somewhere else."

"Where? You can't live a day in the barrens back from the river. You can't get down to water for ten miles upstream and another ten miles downstream. And even if you could, where would you go from there? He knows that."

She looked out across the sunlit river to its Arizona side. "I can swim, Lee," she said. "I'm good at it."

He pointed down toward the deceptive-looking cone-shaped eddies swirling around and around like a carousel, dimpling the swiftly rushing water. "Just swim into one of those," he suggested. "You'd never reach the surface again, Amy."

She looked at the lean, bearded face of Lee Kershaw. "What do we do now, Lee?"

"We've got plenty of water and tobacco. We're out of the killer sun. There's a bit of a breeze through here, hot as it is. It could be worse." He grinned. "We can kill the time by you telling me everything that happened to you and the others after Queho kidnapped you. I want to know about his cave, his movements—everything!"

Amy grinned back. "In the beginning . . . ," she started.

TWENTY-THREE

"WOMAN?" THE QUESTIONING tone came faintly into the darkened cave. There was no answer.

"Woman?" the soft call came again.

"Here, Queho," Amy called out faintly.

"Come out here," he ordered.

"I can't," she replied. "I sprained my ankle in the rocks."

It was very quiet. The subdued rushing song of the river sounded in the background.

Lee flattened his back against the side of the cave; the woman did the same, so that the breed could not silhouette them against the lighter area at the river-end of the cave. They could hear the breed's heavy breathing.

"You got gun?" asked Queho.

"No," she lied.

"You lie! Women tell me you got gun! Throw it out!"

She peered at Lee in the dimness. He nodded. She threw the gun clattering on the hard ground at the mouth of the cave.

It was very quiet again. They could no longer hear the breathing of Queho. Lee snapped his head around. The unmistakable odor of the breed had suddenly come to him but he could not see Queho.

"You crawl here, woman," said Queho.

He was only fifteen feet from Lee. Lee nodded. Amy sank down to her hands and knees and crawled toward the unseen breed. Lee could faintly make out Queho as he moved closer to the woman. "Let me see ankle," he said. Lee was startled when Queho thumb-snapped a match into light and bent over the woman. Lee closed in, knife in hand. At the last second, Queho must have been warned for he blew out the match and whirled to fire from the hip. The bullet did Lee no harm, but the blast of flame and smoke from the muzzle of the .44/40 Colt temporarily blinded him. Amy stood up and dragged at Queho's gunarm in the darkness, but he threw her off, as a rat is thrown by a terrior. Queho fired again, but Lee had gone down low and the flame seared across the back of his neck. His head caught Queho in his lean belly and drove the breed hard against the wall. The Colt clattered to the ground.

Queho caught Lee about the throat with his powerful hands and got a knee in the privates for his pains. As he doubled up in agony, a left uppercut snapped back his head and a driving right-cross hurled him toward the mouth of the cave. Lee made the mistake of charging in. A rock bounced from the top of his head, and he staggered back, half-stunned. His left foot went over the brink. He threw himself sideways to drop flat, but he went over the edge and caught hold with both hands.

Queho charged, but the Colt exploded almost in his face. He was not hit but was half-blinded by the flame and smoke, as Lee had been. He whirled and ran from the cave as Amy fired twice more.

It was quiet again except for the rushing of the river.

"Lee!" cried Amy. "Oh God! Where are you, Lee?"

"Here," he called back. "Give me a hand before he comes back!"

Amy made a loop in the rope and handed it to Lee. He caught hold as she passed the rope around a projection in the cave. He pulled himself to the floor of the cave, aided by Amy, and lay flat, breathing hard. "Give me the pistol," he said. She placed the Colt in his hand.

"Will he be back?" she asked.

"Not for a while," he replied. He sat up and half-cocked

the Colt. He snapped open the loading gate and turned the cylinder, feeling the ends of the cartridge cases. He felt only five of them. Queho, as Lee and others did, usually let his pistol hammer rest on an empty chamber. There wasn't a live round left in the cylinder.

"What now?" she asked.

He stood up. "We'll block the cave entrance," he replied.

"Then you're not going to try and find the cave?"

"Hardly," he said. "He knows someone is here now!"

"But does he know it is you?" she asked.

He looked at the pale oval of her face in the darkness. "I think so, Amy. You see, you called me by name. . . ."

They walked into the darkness, pausing now and then to listen, but no one came. Queho had Lee spotted now. He might be waiting out there in the darkness—waiting for his chance. The only retreat for Amy and Lee would be the return of the *Mohave*. If the river dropped suddenly, the steamer would be held upriver until the next rise came, which might not be for days.

"What if the river drops?" asked Amy suddenly.

Lee was startled. It was almost as though she had read his mind. "It won't drop," he replied. "Jack will come by about dusk tomorrow."

"And if he doesn't?"

Lee shrugged as he placed a rock on the barricade. "We'll try inland," he said.

"Not during the daylight. You know he'll be watching."

"Then we go by night."

"What happens the next day? I mean—is there any water inland? How far is it to water?"

Lee fashioned two cigarettes. He placed one in her mouth and lighted it, looking into her anxious eyes. "Jack will show up," he promised.

"You know we can't make it to water inland," accused Amy. "Not in this heat, anyway."

285

Lee sat down with his back against the wall. "You happen to have any food on you?" he asked.

She shook her head. "I forgot," she replied. "Do you?"

He smiled in the darkness. "In the river," he replied, "along with my rifle, pistol, and about everything else I needed to live in this country."

"Then there's really no hope, is there?"

"There's always hope," he quietly assured her.

After a while, they both slept.

TWENTY-FOUR

"IT'S ALMOST LIKE a ritual," whispered Mildred to Lucille. Queho squatted in the rear of the cave beside a lighted lantern. He had the rifle case open in front of him. The lamplight reflected from the polished breech of the rifle and from the accouterments and tools. He was selecting various items from the case.

Queho moved as he heard Mildred's voice. The lamplight shone on his dark sweating face. He reached up a hand and wiped his face. It was then the women realized that it was not sweat on his face, but blood. His shirt, too, was darkly stained about the left side. His breathing was harsh and irregular.

"You've been wounded!" cried Lucille. She got to her feet.

He waved her back. "It's nothing," he said.

"But it *is* something," she insisted. She walked to him and tilted back his head. His nose had been smashed, and blood ran freely from it. She placed a hand against his side, and he winced in pain. "Take off the shirt," she ordered. Silently he obeyed. The bullet had furrowed his left side just below the ribs and above the hip. She closed her eyes and turned away.

"Don't faint," sneered Mildred. "That is, if you plan to be an angel of mercy."

"Bring me clean cloth and some hot water," said Lucille. Mildred laughed. "Get it yourself," she said.

The young woman poked up the fire and heated water.

While she prepared to treat Queho, he went back to his "ritual," as Mildred had called it. He set primers into each of the three two-and-a-quarter-inch-long cartridge cases. He filled each of the cases with 70 grains of powder and pressed wads in on top of the powder. He took a dozen 370-grain .40/70 bullets and placed them one at a time in a small vise. Patiently he drilled into the tip of each of the bullets.

Lucille came to him and washed his face. She touched his split lips with a cloth dipped in antiseptic. His nose had stopped bleeding but was still misshapen. She bathed his flesh wound and wrapped a clean cloth bandage about his lean waist. She tied it neatly in place. He shrugged back into his bloody shirt without thanking her. She watched him from the shadows.

Queho opened a box of .22 caliber blank cartridges. He carefully pressed a blank base-down into each of the holes he had drilled into the .40/70 bullets. He lowered the breech of the rifle and inserted one of the bullets, seating it firmly home in the rifling just ahead of the chamber. He slid in a long cartridge case and raised the rifle breech to close it. He filled a canteen and slung it over a shoulder. He took a Colt revolver and loaded it. He placed it in a holster and buckled a gunbelt about his lean waist. He took his field glasses and slung them over a shoulder. He turned and blew out the lantern.

"Go easy on the water," his voice came out of the darkness. "It will take some time to get more."

They did not move. Minutes ticked past. Faintly they heard an iron rung clank against the side of the pit.

"She must be dead," said Lucille at last.

"Serves her right," said Mildred.

Lucille looked at her in the darkness. "I liked her, Mildred."

"She was a whore!"

Lucille did not answer. She lay down.

"I'm more interested in who he's after now," said Mildred.

"Maybe she's still alive."

"No. He's killed her. He wouldn't go to all that trouble with that damned rifle if it was only Amy."

"Maybe she's with the person Queho is after."

Mildred laughed. "Like who?"

"Lee Kershaw," replied Lucille.

There was no comment from Mildred.

The first shot broke the quiet just at the first light of dawn. The bullet passed over the top of the barricade and struck an angle in the cave wall. It exploded on impact, scattering wicked little shards of lead throughout the cave. Lee winced as a shard struck the back of his neck. The woman screamed in terror. Lee placed a hand over her mouth and looked into her widened eyes. "No use in screaming," said Lee quietly. She nodded. He withdrew his hand just as the second shot slapped into the outside of the barricade and exploded. "He knows I'm in here," said Lee as he shaped a cigarette. "He's probably made Express bullets out of his .40/70s. He isn't fooling with us, Amy. He means to mangle and kill." The third shot whipped clear through the cave and across the river. It hit and exploded against a boulder.

Lee sat between the woman and the barricade. It was very quiet. "Maybe he's gone," whispered Amy. Lee shook his head. "Maybe shifting to get a better place to shoot."

Minutes ticked past. Lee bellied toward the barricade. The bullet struck the arch of the cave-opening above the barricade and showered Lee with fragments. He rolled sideways and lay close against the side of the cave. The second shot hit the top of the barricade and exploded. Lee heard the distant booming echo of the rifle rolling away down the canyon. The third shot struck the wall of the cave and exploded. Amy cried out as a fragment bruised her left arm.

Then it was quiet again for a long, long time.

"I think I know," said Amy at last.

Lee looked at her. "Know what?" he asked.

"Why he shoots three times and stops."

"Go on," said Lee.

"When he found the rifle at the stagecoach he was very angry with Mildred because there were only three cartridge cases with it."

Lee nodded. "Figures. Well, he's got all day to do his reloading."

"Maybe he'll run out of bullets."

"He can always mold more."

"Maybe he'll run out of powder."

"He can always empty other cartridge cases."

Amy looked sideways at him. "It's pretty hopeless, isn't it? I mean, it's only a matter of time before he kills us, isn't it?"

Her answer was the distant booming discharge of the Sharps rifle, followed almost instantly by the smashing of the bullet somewhere within the cave or against the barricade.

Queho had not fired for hours. The long dusk shadows filled the gorge.

"Maybe he's gone?" suggested Amy.

Lee shook his head.

"Maybe he thinks we're dead. Why doesn't he come down here?"

Lee shrugged. "Why? Dead or alive he's got us cold."

She laughed.

He eyed her. "What's so funny?"

"He may have us," she replied, "but it sure as hell isn't cold." She wiped the sweat from her heat-reddened face.

The *Mohave* whistled twice upriver.

Lee leaned out from the river side of the cave and waved. He looked back at the woman. "Strip off your skirt," he ordered her. "You'll have to jump."

The paddle wheel of the steamer slowed down, then went into reverse to slow her speed. She swung in toward the heights. There was hardly a yard's clearance. "Jump!

Goddammit! Jump!" yelled Jack Mellen from the pilot-house.

Amy jumped cleanly. Jack whistled as he saw her white underdrawers fluttering as she crossed the gap and landed lightly on the deck. Lee jumped right after her. Jack Mellen swung the big wheel and whistled into the voice tube. "Half-speed ahead, Mac," he ordered. "We've picked up our cargo."

Lee looked into through a pilothouse window. "One down and two to go, Jack," he said. *"Gracias!"*

"Por nada," said Jack as he shifted his cigar. "Is Queho dead?"

"Not yet," replied Lee.

"Thanks, captain," said Amy.

Jack nodded. "My pleasure, ma'am," he said. It was a cinch that she was not the governor's niece *or* Mrs. Felding.

Amy read Jack's mind. "I'm the prostitute," she explained.

Jack tipped his hat. "Pleasure, I'm sure," he murmured. "You can have my cabin, ma'am," he invited.

She shook her head. "Lee and I will share his cabin. We're old friends. We've a lot to talk about on the run downriver."

Jack looked sideways at Lee. Lee was watching Amy walking regally aft toward the cabins with her long upper legs attired only in her underdrawers. She turned. "After all, I do owe you something Lee," she added.

He reluctantly shook his head. "You don't owe me anything, Amy."

"Then come for old time's sake," she offered.

Lee grinned. "I'll do just that," he agreed.

Jack Mellen leaned on the whistle cord and the hoarse, squawking echo carried through the river gorge like the crying of a lost soul.

TWENTY-FIVE

"YOU'RE PRESSING YOUR luck, Kershaw," said the Nevada deputy.

Lee leaned against his sorrel looking toward the east. The terrain was a kaleidescope of color under the late afternoon sun. Far to the east was a dark line of color against the sky. He began to build a cigarette as he watched the possemen leading the three horses up the steep trail. Three dead men lay across their saddles, bobbing stiffly with the motion of the tired horses.

"This is the second time in a week we went in there," continued the deputy. "The first time we never saw him, but we heard some shooting near the river. We couldn't even find the way to the river and ran out of water."

Lee lighted up, watching the dead men and their horses being led toward the road. The faces of the living possemen were taut, and their mouths were like tight seams against the brown of their faces.

"This time we got near the river. All we saw of him was the smoke from his rifle, and from three different places at that. Three times he fired at what I thought was an impossible range, and each time he hit a man. Then, for some crazy reason of his own, he stopped firing, and we managed to get our asses out of there. So help me Christ! Kershaw, if he had kept on shooting he might have gotten us all!"

Lee nodded. "Likely," he admitted.

The dark line was moving swiftly across the barrens.

"He might be watching us right now," added the deputy.

"Possible," said Lee.

"No one can get near him. *No* one! He knows every time someone comes anywhere near his hideout."

Lee nodded. "For sure," he agreed.

"Look, Kershaw: You got one woman out of his hands. Don't press your luck. The other two are likely dead by now anyway."

Lee shook his head. "I don't know that," he said quietly. He looked sideways at the deputy. "Besides, the one I got out of there was the one that was least important, at least to the people who made a deal with me to get the women out of there."

"I don't get it."

"Neither do I. But I made a deal. I either get the other two back or I go back to Yuma Pen to finish nineteen and a half years."

"You'll never get near him, I tell you! No man can live in that damned *malpais* country!"

"Queho can," reminded Lee.

"Well, he ain't exactly a *man*, is he?"

"He is—to me."

"You're a strange one, Kershaw."

The dark line was coming closer and moving more swiftly.

"I can't order any of my men to go with you."

"I'll make it alone," said Lee.

"You might get one or two of them to volunteer."

"They'll only get in my way."

"There's a hell of a storm brewing over the *malpais*, George!" called out one of the possemen to the deputy. "By Christ! Lookit them clouds!"

The storm was reaching the far side of the *malpais* country. A cool wind reached the posse and dried the sweat on their faces.

"When will you be back here?" asked Lee.

"Day after tomorrow," replied George.

"For sure?"

"For sure."

Lee nodded. "Look for me then, George." He mounted the sorrel and touched him with his moccasined heels. He rode down the steep trail to reach the grim edge of the *malpais*.

"You crazy!" yelled George. "In an hour the flash floods will sweep through those canyons taking everything with them. You can't live in there, Kershaw!"

Lee looked back. "It'll work for me," he called back. "He can't see me coming through that. It'll supply me with all the water I'll need and it'll drop this damned temperature."

"You'll get a hell of a lot more water than you'll ever be able to use!" shouted George.

"Five feet over his head," drily added a posseman.

Lee Kershaw did not look back. He entered the first canyon and was gone from sight just as the first great, fat raindrops plopped on the dry and thirsty land.

Torrential rains and roaring flash floods were usual in that country at that time of the year, but Lee had never experienced anything like the insane storm that smashed with howling sixty-mile-per-hour banshee winds and a hard-driven rain that struck like the lash of a lead-tipped whip.

The sorrel tried to turn and run with the storm, but Lee forced him on. The closer Lee could get to the river without being seen by Queho, the better his chances would be to get Queho.

Lee raised his head as he rose through a narrow canyon. It was the most dangerous route one could take during such a storm, but he could not get close to the river by any other way, and it would do no good to turn back now.

The roaring sound was subdued at first. Lee looked up at either side of the canyon. There wasn't any chance of getting the horse up out of the canyon that way, and Lee wasn't even sure he could make it to safety himself.

The roaring grew louder, filing the canyon with a

menacing sound. It was close, perhaps just around the next bend. Lee swung from the saddle and reached for his Winchester. He looked back over his shoulder and instantly forgot about the Winchester and everything else except getting his ass out of the way of the roaring wall of muddy water ten to twelve feet high that had swept around the bend in the canyon and was taking everything movable along with it in its mad rush down the canyon.

Lee leaped for the side of the canyon. His feet slipped. He dug clawed hands into the harsh earth and began to pull himself upward. Only once did he look back and that in time to see the sorrel being lifted to the yellowish foaming crest of the flood and then dropped behind and under the water to join the mixed cargo therein—brush, rocks, scrub trees, snakes, lizards and any other living creature that had happened to get in the way—but not Brother Kershaw.

Lee hung on with one hand, waist-deep in the icy churning water that tore at him to break loose his precarious hold. "Let go, you sonofabitch!" he yelled. He managed to pull himself higher as an uprooted tree bore down on him, menacing him with its Medusa-like head of thick outthrust roots.

Lee reached safety. He crawled under an overhanging ledge and yanked off his boots to pour the water from them. He watched the raging flood scouring away at the sides of the canyon. He leaned back and felt for the makings in his shirt pocket. He shaped and lighted a cigarette, sitting there like a fatalistic Paiute as the flood raced by hour after hour, accompanied by an eerie, grinding cacophony of sound and the savage drum-tapping of the rain.

It was dark by the time Lee slid and slopped down to the canyon bottom. The rain had stopped. The sky had cleared. Water was held in every cavity in the ground. It would remain there for two days at least until the forthcoming hundred-degree temperatures and broiling sun would literally suck them dry.

He walked on squelching through the darkness. There

would be a moon that night. More by instinct than any other reason, he climbed a ridge and looked toward where he thought the river should be, and in the first faint light of the moon he saw the river gorge about a mile away.

As the moon rose higher, the rays shone on the wet rock, giving it a cold, glittering appearance. It was very quiet. There was no wind.

Lee stopped behind a boulder. "Beats the hell out of me," he said softly. There was nothing he could recognize. He shoved back his wet hat and placed a chew of Wedding Cake in his mouth; as he did so, he saw a pile of loose, tumbled rock lying in a sort of V-shaped trough. He catfooted forward, stepped over the rocks and into the very cave where he and Amy had been besieged by Queho.

Lee left the cave and found a place to hide. As the moonlight grew against the face of the heights back from the river, he studied the area where he remembered seeing the bright flashings days past. Water was still running from the higher land and trickling over the rimrock to plunge far below to the talus slopes. The moon glittered from the falling water. "Lovely," breathed Lee. He shifted his chew and spat and then raised a hand to wipe his mouth but he arrested the action in midair. There was one place, about halfway down the cliff face where the water dropped but did not continue.

"It's a deep cave," Amy had told Lee. "The mouth of it opens out about midway of a sheer cliff, and part of the mouth is overhung by rock so that the cave itself can't be seen from up above. The cave mouth has a sort of level place that extends out beyond the rock overhang where earth had collected. Queho had dug down into the earth to form a sort of trench, and he had piled rocks just beyond the trench to form a barricade, through which he had made loopholes that he kept plugged with rocks. On each side of the cave mouth the cliff bulged out, so that no one might see into it from either side. Below the barricade was a steep slope of rock that had broken from the cliff face and fallen far below. That is the only way the outer mouth of the cave can be reached by anyone. It is very noisy when anyone walks on it."

"Sonofabitch," murmured Lee. He faded into the broken rock beyond the mouth of the water cave.

The moonlight was bright on the slope. A fly could hardly crawl across it without being seen. Little bright ribbons of water ran down the talus slope, braiding and interbraiding before they reached the bottom.

Somewhere to the left, around the bulging cliff, must be the secret entrance to the natural pit that reached upward to the rear part of the hideout cave. Lee squatted in the shelter of a rock ledge and shifted his chew. Either approach to the cave was dangerous. The slope was moonlighted and noisy. The rear entrance, so to speak, would be dark, and Lee would have to light his way, inviting a bullet out of the dark. It would be better to risk the slope after moonset, noisy as it was. A clattering sound caught his attention. Part of the talus slope had slid hissing down to the bottom of the slope, displaced by the running water. Nothing moved up at the cave mouth.

If he is up there, thought Lee, he would have checked on the noise coming from the talus slope. Or maybe, he added, he knew it was just a slide. Maybe it wasn't the right cave at all. Possibly if it was the right cave, they were all gone. Maybe the two women were dead.

"There's only one way to find out, Kershaw," the mind voice seemed to say to Lee. "Go up there."

The odds were high. But at least he had gotten out of Yuma Pen. He could walk across the barrens that night and the next day, well supplied with rain water in the hollows. It was about forty miles to the Utah line.

"You're a man of your word, Kershaw," reminded the voice.

The talus slide moved again, and some of it slid hissing and rattling down to the foot of it, not more than a hundred yards away from Lee. He looked up at the cave. Nothing moved up there. Damn the moonlight anyway!

Lee walked silently to the foot of the slope where it curved around the bulge of the cliff. He worked his way up the slope, temporarily out of sight of anyone up at the cave but a beautiful six-foot target for anyone behind and below him. Every step he made, as careful as he was, was noisy, and now and again he would start a small slide whereby he would make one step up the slope and slide back two.

He reached the bottom of the cliff and worked his way up toward the cave mouth. Nothing moved up there. Nothing moved on the talus slope.

He pressed close to the side of the cliff, softly cursing the cold, muddy water that dribbled down from high overhead and soaked through his clothing.

Fifty yards from the cave, he stopped to get his breath. He looked down the slope. A man had come out of the rock labyrinth. He wore no hat and walked as silently as a hunting cat, carrying a long rifle at the trail. The clear moonlight glittered on the breech and polished barrel of the rifle.

Lee froze in position. Queho was too far for Lee to risk a pistol shot at him. If he looked up. . . .

Detritus slid down the far side of the talus slope: Queho looked quickly back over his shoulder, but he did not look up toward the tall man who stood with his back against the cliff face looking down at him. Lee could feel the loose rock at his feet starting to move ever so slightly. Queho passed directly below Lee. The slide started the instant Queho had passed out of sight.

Lee worked his way up the slope covered by the rattling, clattering sound of the slide. He reached the rampart and swung up and over it to drop lightly behind it. One of the loopholes had not been plugged. Lee peered through it. Queho again stood at the bottom of the slope looking up toward the cave. Lee froze in position until the breed moved on out of sight.

Lee wiped the cold sweat from his face. The interior of the cave was dark. He felt for his matches and stepped into the dark interior, thumb-snapping a match into flame as he did so.

"Who is it?" cried Mildred Felding.

Lee turned toward her. "Lee Kershaw," he said quietly.

Her face set in sudden fear and her great, vacant blue eyes widened.

Lee looked past her. "Where is the governor's niece?"

Mildred would not answer: she *could* not answer this man. There was a greater fear of him in her than there ever had been of the breed Queho.

Lee turned, and the faint, flickering pool of light fell across the younger woman asleep in a bed that was much wider than the others Lee could see. The smell of the cave clung about Lee like an old familiar coat. "The stink in here makes my eyes smart," he said to no one in particular.

"He might come back," volunteered Mildred at last.

"How does he get into the rear of the cave?"

"There's a natural pit there. He has a rope ladder in it."

Lee nodded. "Amy told me that. Is there any other way?"

"She's still alive?"

"She is."

"Where is she?"

Lee shrugged. "Back in business in Prescott, as far as I know."

"The whore! She's safe enough! What about us?"

Lee looked at her. "I'm here now," he said simply.

"What can you do?" she sneered.

"Get you out of here," replied Lee.

"How much are you being paid?"

Lee slanted his eyes at her. "The highest price in the world," he replied.

"I knew it!" she crowed.

"My freedom," he said.

That shut her up.

Lee lighted a lantern. "Wake her up!" he ordered. "Get dressed. You get outside behind that rock barricade and watch that slope for Queho. Keep your head down!"

Lee looked at the arsenal Queho had proudly racked against the cave wall. He took down the Winchester '73 and filled the magazine with twelve .44/40 cartridges. He took a box of fresh .44/40's and put it into his pocket. He took a coil of light rope.

"Who is he?" cried the girl from behind Lee.

"Lee Kershaw, honey," said Mildred. "He'll get us out of here. Now get dressed."

"What has he done to Queho?" she demanded.

Lee turned slowly at the tone of the girl's voice. He looked at the girl's plain face and then questioningly across her dark head into the eyes of Mildred Felding. She nodded and then shrugged. "It's true," she murmured as she started to dress. "God knows it. . . ."

Lee walked into the rear of the cave. He knelt beside the deep, narrow pit and tied the rope to the lantern bail. He lowered the lantern as far as he could, past the dark mouth of the passageway where the ladder ended. He dropped the stones into the darkness below the feeble lightpool of the swinging lantern and only faintly heard them strike far, far below in the stygian darkness.

Lee pulled up the ladder. He took each gun in turn from Queho's arsenal. The rifles and the shotguns he smashed against the side of the cave bending the barrels. He threw them down into the pit. He removed the cylinders from the revolvers and bent the barrels, then dropped guns and cylinders down into the darkness. He heaved the boxes of stores from the Copa de Oro Mine down on top of the ruined guns and topped the heap by dumping a dozen cans of Kepauno Giant Blasting powder, also from the Copa de Oro Mine, into the pit. The sweat ran from his body.

"Why?" asked the girl.

Lee turned to look at her. "Simple strategy," he replied as he lighted a cigar he had found in a box among Queho's stores. "I'm destroying his arsenal and his base of supplies. I wish to God I could dry up the Colorado River so that he'd be out of water too."

She searched his lean, bearded face. "What will happen to him?"

Lee shrugged. "He won't be my problem when I get you women out of here."

She studied his face and looked into his eyes. "That's not true," she corrected him. "He *is* your problem. He's society's problem."

Lee shook his head. *"He's* a problem to society all right, but not the way you put it. Don't you understand? There never was a place for him in our society and he has made it impossible for himself to return there. He has tried to create his own little world here, and he has failed."

"Couldn't you have let him have it?"

Lee shrugged. "When he killed, as he has done, he left no place for himself, even *here*. He'll have to pay the penalty, ma'am."

"Are you his judge and jury?" she fiercely demanded.

Lee shook his head. "Not even his executioner. That is, not if I can help it." He walked past the girl toward the mouth of the cave. "Anything moving out there?" he asked Mildred.

"Nothing but dripping water," she replied.

"We'll wait until it is dark, then risk the slope. We'll have to move fast. He may hear our descent, but he won't be able to see us. We'll have to keep moving all night and hide out by day. He knows this area like the palms of his dirty hands."

She nodded. "The girl and I could stay here while you hunted him down, Kershaw."

Lee shook his head. "My job is to get the both of you out of here. I made no deal to kill Queho."

"But there must be a reward for him. Wouldn't that be worth your while?"

Lee relighted his cigar. "All I want is my freedom. After

I get that, I don't give a goddamn what they do about Queho. Let someone else track him down and kill him."

"You know there is no one but you who can do that."

"It's not for me."

She searched his face. "Are you afraid?" she sneered.

Lee fanned out the match. "Maybe," he admitted. "God knows, I never really expected to get you women out of here."

"We're not out of here yet!"

He nodded. He turned and walked into the cave. The girl was not in sight. He walked to the rear of the cave and past the pit until he found the noisome combination garbage and latrine room. The girl was not there. He looked up several blind passageways to find them empty. It wasn't until he found the ladder again hanging down into the deep pit that he knew where she had gone.

TWENTY-SIX

"GET DOWN THE slope," ordered Lee. *"Now!"*

The woman was badly frightened. "But it's like daylight! She will have told him by now that you're here!"

"All the more reason we've got to get out of here now! I don't plan to have him keep us holed up here until we run out of water, and he can damned well do it with that rifle of his."

"It's my *husband's* rifle!" she protested.

"Git!" he snapped.

Mildred got!

Lee picked up the last can of Kepauno Giant powder and a length of fuse. He sat astride the rampart and looked down the slope as the woman, softly cursing, made her way down the slope. There was no sign of life anywhere beyond the foot of the slope. It might take time for the girl to find Queho, and time for him to get back to the cave area, and in that time Mildred and Lee must be out of sight and under cover.

Mildred slipped and sat down on her broad rump. Like a child on a slide, she moved swiftly down the slope, accompanied by the clattering and hissing of the wet talus as it moved downward.

"Good going, Milly," thought Lee aloud. He grinned. "That broad rump of yours is good for something else after all."

Mildred reached the bottom of the slope and was smart enough to head at once for cover. Lee dropped to the slide and worked his way, part walking and part sliding, over toward the bulge in the cliff, with his eyes always on the lower ground. He reached the foot of the slide and melted into cover near Mildred. She lay face downward on the wet and muddy ground, and her breathing, more from fear than from exertion, was harsh and irregular.

"This way," said Lee.

"Damn you! Let me rest!"

"Move," he said implacably.

Mildred moved.

Lee scouted the entrance to the water cave. Nothing moved. He looked back at the woman. "Do you know how to shoot?" he asked.

She nodded. "Will taught me."

He gave her the Winchester. "It's at half-cock," he said.

"I know."

He jerked his head. "Get in among the rocks."

"There are rattlesnakes in there!"

He shrugged. "Get bit or get shot," he said. "Makes no difference to me."

She chose the danger of rattlesnakes.

Lee walked into the tunnel. He dumped the bucket and rope into the moonlit river. He shoved the settling keg in after the bucket and the rope. He placed the fused can of blasting powder within the entrance amidst the rubble of his improvised barricade and piled the rock atop the powder can. He fed the fuse out to where Mildred waited for him. He looked about. "Go that way," he said, pointing toward the west.

"Is that the way we get out of here? How far do we have to go?"

He nodded as he struck a match. "Through that canyon—maybe fifteen miles."

"Do we go tonight?"

He shook his head. "I've got to find Lucille," he replied.

"Forget about her! What about *me!* Are you willing to take the risk of losing *me* again just to save her?"

He looked at her. "I'll admit it's a hard decision to make," he drily replied, "but I made a deal with your husband *and* the governor. The deal was to get all three of you women out of here."

"You got two out! Isn't that enough?"

He applied the match to the fuse. "You're not out of here yet, lady," he replied. He grinned. "Better start running west, though, or maybe you won't get out of here at all."

She ran. Lee grinned at the familiar rump action of hers.

The explosion blew a cloud of dust and broke rock out of the cave entrance like a blast from a gigantic shotgun barrel. The thunderous echo bounced from the sheer cliffs on either side of Queho's cave and started a massive rushing of talus down the great slope. The echo slam-banged back and forth between the rock walls as it reluctantly died down the long canyon that led to the outer world. Then it was quiet again. The dust drifted in the now windless air and slowly dissipated.

Lee lay bellyflat between two boulders, with his elbows propped on the ground and his hands grasping Queho's powerful field glasses. The moonlight made the wet slopes and heights sharp and clear to the eye. Nothing moved. It was like a lunar landscape or the dream landscape of an artist mystic.

Lee focused the glasses on the cave high above the talus slope. There was no one there. Nothing moved.

"This is crazy," the woman whispered hoarsely from behind Lee. "The girl is lost! Gone! If he hasn't taken her with him he's killed her. Let's get out of here while we can!"

He shook his head. "I have to know," he said.

"You'll get your damned pardon! I'll see to that!"

He looked back at her. "I'll just *bet* you will, Milly." His hard, gray eyes forced her empty blue ones to turn away. "As long as I am the only one, outside of Queho, who knows the truth of what happened aboard the *Mohave*, you'll always be in fear of me, eh?"

"What the hell are you talking about?" she demanded.

"The truth, Milly, just the truth."

"You'll get your pardon!"

He nodded. "You're damned right I will, but maybe I want *more* than a pardon. Maybe I don't want to go through the rest of my life with false charges of assault, rape, and manslaughter hanging over my head. Maybe I don't want a pardon as much as I want exoneration."

She looked quickly away. "You've got to get me out of here to get even the pardon," she reminded him. "You can worry about the exoneration later."

"The only way I'll ever get that is for you to tell the truth."

"You can go to hell! You'll get your pardon. That's enough!"

He nodded. "I suppose so. I'll get *my* pardon. But will *you?*"

"Who'd believe you instead of me, Kershaw?" she sneered.

He shrugged. "A hell of a lot of people who really know you, Milly."

Lee turned to study the terrain. It was as before. It was as deserted as a lunar landscape. "It was a long time after Queho and I were cellmates that he told me the truth about you and Ahvote," he said casually over his shoulder. "How you led the poor bastard on and let him take you in your quarters when your husband was out in the field and you had been hitting the bottle in private."

"My God! He told you *that?*" she exclaimed.

Lee looked steadily back at her. He shook his head. "No," he replied, "but *you* just did."

She had been neatly trapped. Her great blue eyes slid sideways toward the Winchester rifle.

Lee grinned. "You kill me, Milly, and you'll never get out of this country alive."

"Look," she said quickly. "I'll make it up to you, Kershaw. Do you want money? I can get it for you! I'll go to

306

bed with you, if *that* is what you want. Ask me for *anything!* But for God's sake, don't say anything to Will about what you just said to me!"

He studied her for a little while. "God help you," he said quietly. "I don't believe anyone else can."

She had offered herself to this strange man and *he had turned her down!* Maybe he wouldn't talk about her when they got out of the *malpais* country, but for the rest of her life there would be the haunting fear that he *would* talk. She looked again at the rifle. The back of his head was only ten feet away from her—she could hardly miss at that range.

Lee heard the faint click of the rifle hammer as it was drawn back to full-cock. "The only person who can tell the truth about you, Milly, is yourself," he said without turning his head.

She let the hammer down to half-cock and stood up.

The heavy Sharps rifle flatted off and the inch-and-three-eights, 370-grain bullet explosively struck the breech of the Winchester. The woman screamed and involuntarily flung up her arms, letting go of the rifle. It arched out beyond the rocks with the moonlight shining on the fat-polished barrel to land on the steep, slick rock slope, and it slid and clattered down to come to rest fifty feet away from Lee, shining dully from the reflected moonlight.

Lee dragged the woman down into cover. A wisp of gunsmoke drifted off high on the slopes beyond the bulging cliff on the west side of the cave mouth above the talus slope. He looked back into the woman's drawn face. "Great," he said. "I ought to make you go down and get that rifle." She recoiled back from him. Lee turned away. "Milly," he politely suggested, "you ought to go back in the rocks and empty out your drawers. Keep your head down!"

The Sharps cracked again, and the exploding slug smashed the hammer from the Winchester. The breed must be using the Vollmer telescope. The third explosive slug smashed into the small of the stock and broke it.

Lee studied the slopes. The second and third shots had each come from a different position from the first shot. "Maybe four hundred yards," said Lee quietly. "The sonofabitch could thread a needle with that damned Sharps."

Lee shaped a cigarette. As long as it was moonlight and he had no rifle, there was no chance of getting at the breed. Maybe Mildred was right—maybe they should get out of there while they could, but even so, they'd have to wait for darkness, and then the breed would have a chance to move in. Lee could make it through the darkness as silently as wind-driven smoke, but the woman was heavy on her feet, and Queho could hear like a hunting wolf.

"You're pressing your luck, Kershaw," the Nevada deputy had said.

Lee crouched low and lighted the cigarette. As he raised his head, a puff of smoke swirled upward. The Sharps exploded, this time nor more than three hundred yards from where Lee lay hidden. The slug exploded against a rock twenty feet behind Lee and in front of where Mildred was busy. There was no sound from the woman. She had learned enough not to reveal her presence by sight or sound.

Lee ground out the cigarette and replaced it by a cut of Wedding Cake. He worked up the sauce. The moon was sailing westward. Before long, the shadows would fall across the *malpais* country and fill in the canyon that led to the outside world.

Lee crayfished backward, low on his lean belly, head turned sideways and close against the harsh earth.

The Sharps was fired. This time it was not more than two hundred yards away. The slug exploded right where Lee had been hiding. He crayfished with greater speed back into the shelter of the rocks where Mildred lay hidden. Shadows crept across the *malpais*. Lee worked his way back deeper into the labyrinth, hoping to God he wouldn't arouse an unhappy rattlesnake that might have been flushed from its hole by the flash flood.

Lee reached far over and placed his hat on a rock. The

bullet drove through it from one side to the other, going in small and coming out big enough for Lee to put his fist through as it landed in front of him.

The moonlight now shone only on the cliff faces of the northeast, while the canyon to the west of them and the rock labyrinth southwest were shrouded in shadow darkness. Lee worked his way farther and farther into the labyrinth. He wrinkled his nose. He had caught Milly's scent, that is, the scent she had left behind her. "Milly?" he softly called. There was no reply. Lee risked standing up, then catfooted deeper and deeper into the labyrinth. Maybe she had gone to ground nearer the river heights. Twenty minutes later, he knew she had left altogether. He looked toward the darkened canyon. "Good luck," he said quietly.

A breeze sprang up. Metal clicked against rock high on the moonlit slopes overlooking the labyrinth, and Lee hit the ground a fraction of a second before the Sharps bellowed and sent an explosive bullet whispering right over where Lee had been standing. The bullet blew itself up against the rocks fifty yards beyond Lee. The breed sonofabitch was shooting by instinct. No living man could have seen Lee in those shadows—no living man other than Queho, that is.

TWENTY-SEVEN

"HAVE YOU KILLED him?" Lucille asked Queho.

Queho squatted behind a rock ledge, still bright in the now waning moonlight, priming his three cartridge cases. "How did he get the other woman?" he asked.

"She saw him from the cave and went to him," lied Lucille.

"So he didn't get into the cave?"

She shook her head. "The other woman followed him toward the river," she lied again. "He never saw the cave."

He looked at her with the moonlight on his dark face and with his strange, light eyes that seemed to glitter like running water. "Why you not go with woman? Why you come to me, eh?" he asked.

She could not look at his eyes. "To warn you, Queho," she replied.

"That Kershaw come to kill me?" He laughed.

"He was sent to get us women. He has taken two of them now."

Queho shrugged. "Maybe he'll quit when he is ahead."

She shook her head. "You know him better than that, Queho."

He measured 70 grams of powder into a cartridge case. "Why you warn me that he come?" he asked.

"I didn't want to see you get killed."

He wadded the case. "Or maybe Kershaw either?"

She nodded. "I don't want to see *anyone* get killed, Queho."

310

He shook his head. "One of us will have to die."

"Can't you let him go?"

"He knows now where Queho's cave is! The woman will tell him!"

"So do I! So do Amy and Mildred!"

"No difference. Them women couldn't find this place again and wouldn't come back to show the way even if they could."

"I can," she said.

He filled another cartridge case. "You're still here," he reminded her. His strange eyes slid sideways to look at her pale face. "You stay with Queho, eh? Why?"

She shook her head. "Look," she said quickly. "Let me go and talk with Lee Kershaw. Maybe he'll take you back alive for trial. If you let me go, there may be amnesty for you."

He filled the last of the three cases with the last of his powder. "What *that* mean?"

"They'll go easy on you because of what you did."

He threw back his head and laughed. "Women!" he said. "They believe only what they want to believe." He looked at her. "You know what they do to Queho? Kill on sight! Like mad dog! They cut off head and take back in a sack to prove they got me! You think I am a fool!"

"But maybe Lee Kershaw can help you!"

He placed the wads into the mouths of the two cartridges and pressed them into place. "No," he said firmly. "Kershaw not help me." He placed one of his three remaining bullets into the chamber of the rifle and seated it firmly into the barrel with the bullet-starter. He slid in a long cartridge case and raised the rifle breech. He looked beyond the place where they were hidden. "I kill Kershaw," he insisted. "After that, stay here in the *malpais* with plenty food, water, guns, and tobacco." He slanted his eyes at her. "Maybe with woman too?"

She did not answer him. He placed the long-barreled rifle on a flat rock and peered through the scope. There were deep shadows where Lee had last been hiding. If he knew Lee Kershaw, the man would come through the darkness to find Queho. "How many guns Kershaw have?" he asked over his shoulder.

"Why, two I think. A rifle and a pistol."

"You sure about that?"

"Yes." Then she remembered how Lee Kershaw had destroyed Queho's supplies and arsenal. "Simple strategy," he had said. "I'm destroying his arsenal and his base of supplies. I wish to God I could dry up the Colorado River so that he'd be out of water too."

Queho laughed. "He's only got a pistol *now*." He patted the engraved breech of the Sharps rifle. "When daylight come, Kershaw dies. No chance for him. No chance at all."

"And the woman with him?"

He looked bact at her. "I have three rounds left," he replied.

"You don't want her anymore?"

"I never did," he replied. "Only wanted her to suffer and then die for what she did to me."

"And to Kershaw also?"

"I was thinking of myself," he said.

"And you want me?"

He did not look at her. The shadows were creeping up the long slope, erasing the bright moonlight.

"I asked you a question," she said.

"You want *me?*" he asked.

Lucille closed her eyes. "Only if you will give yourself up, Queho."

Long minutes ticked slowly past. "No deal," said Queho at last.

Stone clicked against stone in the deep quiet of the canyon. A shadow seemed to detach itself from a rock and move swiftly toward the next one. Queho fired at the movement. The smoke drifted down the slope, obscuring his vision. Mildred Felding lay flat behind the rock, breathing harshly, pressing her sweating face against the harsh earth. The gunshot echo died away down the canyon.

Queho snapped down the breech lever and the smoking cartridge case slid out. He seated the next to the last bullet and loaded the cartridge case in behind it. He closed the rifle breech and removed the Vollmer scope. He put the scope into its case and took the vernier tang sight from its little case. He fitted the sight into its mounts and screwed it home. "Scope no good at night," he said, almost as though to himself.

Queho looked at the girl. "You want to go?" he asked.

"You'll let me?"

"If you want," he replied. His eyes searched her face.

"I'll go only to talk with Kershaw."

"Waste of time," he said.

"If he won't agree to help you, I'll come back to you."

"Why?"

She hesitated. "Maybe because I want to."

"You know future? I'll tell you—heat, poor food, lousy water, loneliness. . . . Loneliness the worst. Man goes loco from that. Kill slowly. Maybe better to die by posse bullet than go like that. Maybe a year; maybe five years; maybe twenty. ¿Quien sabe?"

"But, if I were with you, it would not be so."

He laughed. "You loco already from being here too long." His dark face changed. "You go now. Call out to Kershaw. Tell him you coming. If you want to come back, you come at dawn, so I can see you. No tricks, eh?"

She shook her head.

"Go now," he repeated. "Before I change mind."

"Kershaw!" she called clearly. "Lee Kershaw!"

"Kershaw . . . Lee Kershaw . . . ," echoed the canyon.

There was no reply.

Queho grinned. "Maybe he think I shoot by sound. Maybe he right." He laughed.

"Lee Kershaw!" called the girl. "I'm coming down!"

313

"Don't shoot, goddamn you, Kershaw!" yelled Queho. "You shoot girl and you shoot pardon all to hell!" He roared with laughter.

"Come on down!" called Lee. He moved as soon as he yelled.

Queho looked at the girl. She stood up and hesitated. The breed said nothing. Maybe that is what she had expected. She climbed over the rocks and vanished from sight.

Queho listened. He could hear her progress down the long slope into the deep shadows of the canyon. Then it was quiet again. The moon sank lower, and the shadows came up the slope and covered Queho and his rifle, but he was still there, listening, listening.

TWENTY-EIGHT

"YOU'LL HAVE TO get that rifle of his," insisted Lee.

She sat wearily in the darkness. She could hear Lee chewing the tough and stringy meat he had taken from the cave. "I can't do that," she repeated for the third time.

"I don't trust him," repeated Lee for the third time.

"He doesn't trust you!"

He shrugged. "You see? It's hopeless. I'm taking you out of here before dawn comes and lights up this canyon like a Fourth of July fireworks display. I've done what I came to do. I never agreed to do anything about Queho."

"I promised him I'd come back to him if you wouldn't agree to help him."

He shook his head. "No go. Let him sit up there without his arsenal and his food. He'll get smart when he needs water."

"What will happen to him?"

He shrugged again. *"¿Quien sabe?* He's wanted by Nevada, California, and Arizona." He looked sideways at her. "You know how much combined reward money has been offered for him? *Five thousand dollars!* I could use that money!"

"But you said you didn't want him!"

He nodded. "That's right. I can't risk trying to take him when I have to deliver you and Milly back to get my pardon."

"But will you help him?"

"He's beyond help."

She covered her eyes with her hands. "I'll have to go back to him then."

Lee stowed a wad of Wedding Cake into his mouth and worked up the rich sauce. After a while, he spat to one side. "Tell you what," he suggested. "You go back up there and get that damned rifle of his away from him, and I'll talk business with him. Personally, I think you're wasting your time."

The girl didn't rise to the bait right off.

Lee rested his back against a boulder. He did not look directly at the girl, as though what she agreed to do was really of no concern to him. She wasn't too bright.

"He won't give it up," she said.

"Possible," he agreed. He spat to one side.

"What if he does?" she asked.

Lee wiped his mouth with the back of a hand. "I'll feel a hell of a lot safer talking to him."

"You're not lying to me?"

Lee acted shocked. "Me? Lee Kershaw! I'm known far and wide as a man of my word."

"Can I believe that?"

He leaned forward. "Listen," he said tensely. "I gave my word to your uncle's secretary and to Colonel Felding that I would not try to escape, but that I would try to get you women back to safety. By this time I could have been safely in Mexico or Canada. Did I go? No! Doesn't that prove I keep my word?"

"And you'll give me your word that no harm will come to him if I get his rifle for you?"

Lee leaned back again. "I give you my word that no harm will come to him from me, if you get his rifle from him," he promised.

She sat there for a long time. Lee was dying for a smoke but he knew if he lighted a cigarette that damned breed might put a bullet through his head.

"All right," she agreed at last.

"Call out to him then that you'll come up the slope at first light of dawn."

"And I can tell him that you'll help him?"

Lee nodded. "But don't tell him about the rifle."

"He won't let me get near it."

"You'll have to figure that one out."

"He won't leave it."

"Then goddammit, you've got to make him leave it!"

"But how?"

"Promise him the damned moon. Promise him anything!"

She nodded. "All right," she agreed. "If it will save his life, I'll promise him anything."

Lee shifted his chew and spat. He wiped his mouth. "You stay here then."

"Alone? Why?"

He grinned in the darkness. "Because if that damned breed comes through the darkness looking for me, he'll locate me by finding you, and *I* don't aim to be around in case he does come."

He was gone into the darkness.

TWENTY-NINE

THE FIRST PALE, pearl-gray light of the dawn flushed against the eastern sky. A cool wind swept through the canyon, ruffling the surfaces of the pooled rainwater.

"Queho!" called the girl.

"Queho . . . Queho . . . Queho . . . !" dutifully echoed the canyon.

There was no reply.

Lee lay well back watching the opposite slopes through Queho's powerful field glasses. Nothing moved.

"Queho!" called the girl.

"Queho . . . Queho . . . Queho . . . !" repeated the canyon.

Silence again.

Lucille glanced back over her shoulder. There was no sign of Lee Kershaw. Maybe he had left during the night.

Lucille walked across the floor of the canyon and paused at the foot of the slope. There was no sign of life. She looked back toward where she thought Kershaw must be hidden. There was no sign of life.

She started up the slope. Loose rock clattered and slid down the steep slope, awakening the canyon echoes.

Lee refocused the glasses. "Sonofabitch," he breathed. He could pick out the dark rodlike shape of the rifle barrel between two boulders. The barrel moved even as he looked, and he instinctively ducked his head. Slowly he raised his head. The rifle barrel was gone and the girl stood just this side of the boulders behind which Queho was hidden.

"I'm here, Queho!" she called out.

"Come on," he invited. He did not show himself.

She clambered over the boulders and sat down near him, breathing hard from her exertions.

"Well?" asked the breed.

"He's gone," she replied.

He narrowed his eyes. "You sure?"

She shrugged. "I couldn't find him."

"He's down there somewhere!"

"Maybe, but I didn't see him," she lied.

He nodded. "All right. We go back into cave. Get food. I need powder and bullets for cartridges."

She was desperate. Once he took her back into that cave, Lee Kershaw would have no chance of dealing with him. "It's no use," she said. "There's nothing in there anymore."

"What the hell you mean?" he demanded.

She shrank back from his fierce gaze.

"It was Kershaw," she explained. She told him what Kershaw had done in his cave.

"You mean everything gone?" he demanded. "Food, guns, powder, *everything?* Goddamn you! You lied to me! You say he not get to cave!"

She nodded. "I was afraid of what you might do if you knew about it!"

He looked back up the slope toward the hidden entrance to his hideout. "Jesus God!" he yelled. "I got to get bullets and powder!"

"It's all gone," she insisted.

Lee could hear the echoing voices but could not distinguish any words. He wished to God he had a rifle as he saw Queho's head pop up from behind the boulders. Then he saw the breed run up the steep slope toward the cliff face, *and he did not have his rifle with him.*

Lucille watched Queho vanish in among the rocks where the cave entrance was concealed.

"Now!" yelled Lee.

"Now . . . now . . . now . . . !" yelled the canyon.

She looked down at the long rifle and then up the slope. If he came back while she was taking the rifle to Lee. . . .

"Now! Goddammit!" shouted Lee. He jumped over a boulder and started to run down the slope.

She picked up the rifle.

"Get the cartridges and the gear!" yelled Lee.

She should have gotten wise then, but she did not. Dutifully she picked up the tools and parts and the two cartridge cases, one empty and the other loaded with the last of Queho's powder.

Lee sprinted across the canyon bottom, a clay pigeon if Queho changed his mind and returned from the cave.

The girl hesitated.

"You may save his life by bringing that rifle here!" yelled Lee.

She scrambled over the boulders. She ran down the slope. She tripped and fell and the rifle dropped to the ground. It spat flame and smoke and the slug whipped through the air a foot over Lee's head. He ran up the slope and grabbed the smoking rifle. He gripped the girl by an arm. "Hang onto the gear," he ordered her. He hustled her and the rifle down the slope and across the bottom of the canyon, expecting at any second to hear a gun report behind him and to feel the impact of one of Queho's pistol bullets.

He pushed her over the boulders. He let the rifle down beside her and looked back over his shoulder. The far slope was empty of life. He rolled over the boulders and landed on his hands and knees with his chest heaving and trembling and with the fresh sweat dripping from his bearded face. For a minute, he thought he was going to get sick.

The girl wiped the sweat from her face. She placed the tools and other items beside the rifle and looked down at them. "Why do you need those?" she slowly asked.

Lee opened the breech of the rifle and saw the spent cartridge case kick out from the impact of the strong ejector.

He caught the case and placed it on the ground. He opened the brass can of bullets and pushed the last one of them into the rifling ahead of the chamber by means of the bullet-starter. "Have you more bullets?" he asked.

"All you wanted was the rifle so that he couldn't use it against you," she said. "He's gone to his cave to get bullets and powder."

Lee took the last of the loaded cartridge-cases and slipped it into the chamber. He raised the breechblock by means of the lever. He shook the brass powder-box. It was empty. "One goddamned round," he softly cursed.

"That's why he went back to his cave," she repeated.

"And he trusted you with his beloved rifle, eh?" Lee grinned like a hunting lobo.

She stared at him. "What do you mean?" she asked suspiciously.

He raised the vernier tang sight and sighted through it toward the far side of the canyon. "Maybe eight hundred yards," he said thoughtfully to himself. "Better use the Vollmer scope."

"Kershaw!" she cried. "You gave me a promise!"

He removed the vernier tang sight and replaced it with the slim tube of the Vollmer scope, which was almost as long as the barrel itself. The sun was already beginning to strike the canyon and its slopes. The air was still sharp and clear. There was no heat haze and no shimmering of the atmosphere as yet. That would come with the greater heat of the day.

She reached out a trembling hand toward him. "Kershaw!" she pleaded.

He looked at her. "Shut up!" he ordered. "And keep your head down!"

He shaped and lighted a cigarette. He rested the long rifle on the flat-topped ledge directly in front of him and with his dirty right hand gripping the small of the stock. The cigarette smoke wreathed about his lean, bearded face in the shade of his low-pulled hatbrim. Patiently he waited.

"Kershaw," she said after a time.

He did not look back at her. "Yes?" he asked.

"You'll go to hell for this," she promised him.

He shook his head. He did not take his eyes off the sunlit slope far across the wide canyon. "I've already been there," he told her. "Remember, I was in Yuma Pen in the summer."

She was silent after that.

Patiently he waited.

THIRTY

QUEHO PADDED INTO the cave entrance. He turned a corner and lighted a match. There was a lantern in a wall niche. He lighted it and catfooted along the tunnel until he reached the end of it overlooking the deep natural pit. He hooked the lantern bail over his left arm and went quickly up the rope ladder. He reached the top and held out the lantern to survey his hideout. He cursed softly as he hurled the bedding to one side.to hunt for anything Kershaw might have overlooked. It was no use.

He looked at his empty weapons-rack. He ripped open the ammunition box where he had kept his extra six-guns, only to find it empty. The extra rounds for the big Sharps .40/70 were all gone. His breathing was harsh and heavy. He padded to the rear of the cave and slipped his hand under a ledge to retrieve a bottle of forty rod. He drank deeply, his throat working convulsively.

He unsheathed his Colt and half-cocked it. He opened the loading gate and twirled the cylinder. He slipped a round into the one empty chamber and snapped shut the loading gate. He replaced the Colt in the holster. He drank again.

He walked to the mouth of the cave and looked down the long talus slope. He could see the entrance to the water tunnel, now completely blocked by the collapsing of the roof. The nearest secret access to the river was some miles upstream, and Kershaw might have someone watching it from the Arizona side of the river. Queho might reach water ten miles downstream, but it was too close to the outer world, and Nevada kept a posse working in that area. The collected rainwater in the *malpais* would be gone by the next day under the broiling heat of the summer sun.

Queho squatted in the cave, drinking steadily. The girl had told him that Kershaw had dumped all the disabled weapons, the food, ammunition, powder, and other gear down into the pit. *Enju!* He, Queho, would go down into the pit and see what he could salvage.

He drank again and thrust the half-empty bottle inside his shirt. He hooked the lantern bail over his left arm and reached down with his left hand to grip the ladder. The lantern slipped from his arm and dropped into the pit. He heard it crash far below. The glass cylinder shattered and the oil reservoir split itself against a rifle breech. The oil leaked out and was caught up by the hungry flames. An eerie dancing light showed far below.

Queho got onto the ladder and hung there looking down into the depths. He could just make out the disabled weapons and some of the boxes of food. He let himself slowly down the ladder and reached the tunnel. He leaned out and began to ripple-shake the ladder until the hooks at the top released themselves from the upper end of the heavy pegs he had driven into the rim of the pit. The upper end of the ladder fell down and past Queho to strike its heavy iron rungs against a can of Kepauno Giant blasting powder, splitting the can wide open, so that the loose powder poured over the leaping flames. The other powder cans at the bottom of the pit exploded like an erupting volcano, and the narrow shaft funneled the flames, smoke, gas, and debris up the shaft as though it was a gigantic shotgun barrel. The blast struck Queho on the face and upper body and hurled him backward into the tunnel, where he lay half stunned with the searing agony of the burned flesh still to come through the sudden numbness of great shock.

THIRTY-ONE

IT WAS THE rumbling roar from what seemed like a solid rock cliff face that aroused Lee. Smoke poured out from the hidden entrance to the cave and drifted slowly upward in the windless air. It was thick, so thick that it masked the cliff face, so that when Queho did appear, his appearance startled Lee as though the devil himself had been conjured up from the depths of hell.

Queho walked slowly downslope through the smoke and made no effort to conceal himself.

Lee picked up the powerful glasses and focused them on the breed. "For the love of God," he breathed. At that distance the breed seemed to have been painted black from the waist up.

"What is it?" asked Lucille.

Lee lowered the glasses. "He must have been hit by the explosion. Look for yourself."

She raised the glasses and focused them. She turned her head away, sickened at the sight. "I'll go to him," she said bravely.

Lee shook his head. "No. You can do him no good."

"I can take care of him," she insisted.

He looked back at her. "No," he repeated. "I'm taking you out of here."

"You're only thinking of yourself!" she cried. "You won't get your pardon and the reward money unless you kill him and bring me out! Is that it?"

"Partly," he agreed. He looked across the sunlit canyon

toward the breed who stood there, seemingly staring across the canyon with eyes that could not see and would never see again. "Look at him," he suggested to the girl. "He's all alone. No supplies. No weapon other than a six-gun. Those are third-degree burns or I miss my guess. He'll be in terrible agony within a short time. Even a doctor can't do much good for him now."

It was very quiet in the canyon. Queho did not move.

"What will you do?" she asked. "The decision is yours, Kershaw."

Lee passed a hand across his eyes. The words of Will Felding aboard the *Mohave* came back to him: "It seems to me that it would be much less expensive, plus the bother of bringing a man to trial after months of feeding and quartering him, then the wages of the manhunter, the guards, the other personnel involved, sir! How much easier to put a bullet into your quarry and report that he resisted arrest, eh, Kershaw?" Then Lee had made his brave reply: "That would make me judge, jury, and executioner, sir. I *hunt* men. I do not judge them, or *execute* them."

It was a long shot and there was but one bullet. If Lee missed, he might never get near enough to use the six-gun on the breed.

"It's like judging an animal with a broken leg," said the girl. "Let him go, Kershaw."

Lee shook his head.

"He can destroy himself if he must," she added.

He shook his head. "And wander in limbo forever, shunned by the other spirits of his people?"

"You speak of him now as though he was a full-blooded Mohave Apache," she said.

He looked at the breed and then back at the girl. "Now," he said quietly, "he *is* acting like a full-blooded Mohave Apache."

"Then there is no hope for him?"

"None," replied Lee.

She waited a little while as the sun warmed the canyon.

Lee did not look at her again. "Start walking down the canyon," he said. "You can't get lost. There is only the one way. I'll catch up with you in a little while. We will find Milly further along, most likely. She can't have gotten very far."

She was quiet for a while as she looked across the canyon at Queho. Then she turned on a heel and walked down the slope toward the bottom of the canyon. Soon, the sound of her footsteps vanished. A light morning breeze began to blow up the canyon.

Lee shaped and lighted a cigarette. He drew in on it several times, then threw it over the rocks to land on the slope. The slight wind drifted the thin spiral of smoke toward the south. Lee full-cocked the Sharps rifle and squeezed the rear trigger. The front trigger set with a tiny click. Lee placed the tip of his trigger finger flat on the front trigger. He drew in a deep breath as he sighted, allowing for the slight crosswind, across the sunny canyon toward the distant figure standing motionless on the sunlighted slope. He let out half of his breath, steadied his aim, and squeezed off the shot.

The girl heard the slamming sound of the big rifle as it was fired. The echo flatted back and forth between the canyon walls and died away. It was very quiet again. The girl did not look back.

ENJOY THESE EXCITING WESTERNS BY WAYNE D. OVERHOLSER—TWICE WINNER OF THE SPUR AWARD!

Steel to the South. Clay Bond returns to Oregon determined to avenge his father's death. But he soon stumbles into a war between a cattle baron and local farmers fighting to win their railroad the right of way through the territory. Soon, Bond must choose between the end of the free range—or the spread his father died defending.

Fabulous Gunman. Every man, woman, and child in the West wants gunslinger Bill Womack to do their dirty work. But Womack is ready to hang up his six-shooters for good. Womack is determined to lead the rest of his life as a peaceful man—no matter how many men he has to kill first.

_3700-9 **(two Westerns in one volume)** $4.99

The Lone Deputy. Cole Weston owns all the land around Saddle Rock, Colorado, and he figures his money makes him the law of the land. The only man brave enough to stand up to Weston's brand of frontier justice is Deputy Price Regan. Regan will fight for what he knows is right—even if it means gunning down every last one of Weston's hired guns.

Desperate Man. As treacherous as a rattlesnake, rancher Cameron Runyon uses his wealth to get whatever he wants. But when his hired killers shoot down Dave Munro's father, Runyon learns that all his money can't pay off the price on his head.

_3782-3 **(two Westerns in one volume)** $4.99 US/$5.99 CAN

LEWIS B. PATTEN

Double the action! Double the value!
Two classic Westerns in one big volume!

Lewis B. Patten writes "gripping action novels of the Old West." — *Tulsa World*

Lynching at Broken Butte. For some strange reason, U.S. Marshall August Cragg makes the people of Broken Butte downright uncomfortable. When he's almost killed his first night in town, Cragg figures he'd better dig up the town's secret before the good citizens are digging him a grave. *And in the same action-packed volume...*

Sunblade. Land baron John Sunblade needs to be stopped before he destroys the whole territory. Everyone's gunning for him, but the S.O.B.s don't figure on having to fight the man who hates Sunblade most of all—his own son.

_3792-0(**two Westerns in one volume**)$4.99 US/$5.99 CAN

The Ruthless Range. Hoping to lay his reputation as a gunman to rest, Jason Mellor takes an alias and a job as ranch hand. But soon every cowpoke knows he's alive—and he'll have to kill a passel of backshooters to stay that way. *And in the same exciting volume...*

Death Rides A Black Horse. If anything happens to young Frank Halliday, foreman Rafe Joslin will inherit his ranch. With Joslin bent on making that anything happen, a showdown is the only way Halliday can hope to see another sunset.

_3741-6(**two Westerns in one volume**)$4.99 US/$5.99 CAN

Dorchester Publishing Co., Inc.
65 Commerce Road
Stamford, CT 06902

Please add $1.75 for shipping and handling for the first book and $.50 for each book thereafter. NY, NYC, PA and CT residents, please add appropriate sales tax. No cash, stamps, or C.O.D.s. All orders shipped within 6 weeks via postal service book rate. Canadian orders require $2.00 extra postage and must be paid in U.S. dollars through a U.S. banking facility.

Name _____

Address _____

City _____ State _____ Zip _____

I have enclosed $_____ in payment for the checked book(s).
Payment <u>must</u> accompany all orders. ☐ Please send a free catalog.